THE AUXILIARY CHILD

THE
AUXILIARY
CHILD

KARLI AMBER SMITH

Published by Karli Amber Smith
theauxiliarychild.com

First published 2025

Copyright © Karli Amber Smith, 2025

The moral right of the author has been asserted.

A catalogue record for this book is available from the National Library of Australia

ISBN: 9781764057202 (pbk)
ISBN: 9781764057219 (ebk)

Cover designed by Katy Donoghue, Giddyup Graphics
Typeset by Helen Christie, Blue Wren Books
Printed by Ingram Spark

*"There is no sacrifice that I would not make
for the real benefit of Russia and for her salvation."*

TSAR NICHOLAS II
1917

Part 1

THE THEN

Prologue

ST PETERSBURG, RUSSIA, 1901

You will cease to be.

As the thought crept into his mind, every possible scenario fought for supremacy, creating a cacophony not unlike cicadas on the brink of dusk. The endgame was clear, but the path to it remained deeply opaque. He glanced at the one he adored. Blessedly, his immediate future would be shaped by his and Alexandra's choices, and with this realisation, the noise was abruptly silenced.

It was but a momentary reprieve.

Nicholas willed his mind to settle as the church bells tolled, swiftly ushering his beloved into the private chambers at the rear of the chapel. Here they would have a fleeting moment of privacy under the guise of seeking a blessing from the Patriarch for their newborn child. The music danced beautifully throughout the stone chamber, yet it did little to calm his consort. Her fingernails dug into his hand, the leather gloves he wore the only barrier preventing her grip from piercing his skin.

"It's time," he said, placing his hand on her shoulder as they reached where his brother Michael stood in the shadows awaiting them. As his Empress paused to lift their newborn daughter from the carrier, her face was etched with the sorrow of a mother being asked to part with her child, and it pierced his very soul. A longstanding knowledge was today turning into a harsh reality.

"We will always love her, Alexandra, as will Michael," he said, watching her hold their daughter close to her chest in a heartbreaking final embrace. "You've known that this moment would come from the time of our betrothal, albeit we thought then for a second-born son. I know …" He paused to swallow his emotions. "I know this is hard. I love you. I love you and our daughter so very much, but we must do this. She is our divine legacy. Please. Please hand her to Michael."

"I need more time. I just need … more time," his wife sobbed, collapsing onto a church pew while still holding their baby. "Please, Nikky. More time," she begged, tears cascading down her face.

Nicholas gestured for his brother to follow him further towards the rear of the chapel, allowing them seclusion as well as his wife an extended goodbye with their daughter.

Michael followed and stood behind him, placing his hand on Nicholas' shoulder in a touching sign of brotherly solidarity. "How bears the one that stands in my name?"

There was no resentment in his question. Michael had spent many years understanding and accepting his lot in life. A lot by birthright, that saw him a Romanov. A lot by secret imperial decree, that had made him a non-aristocratic son of the United Kingdom. The first Auxiliary Child.

"He does well, although his penchant for already betrothed women needs to cease," Nicholas replied, placing his hand over his brother's before turning to face him. "How do you fare, Michael? Or would you prefer I call you by your Auxiliary name?"

"I fare well, and I answer to whatever name my Tsar chooses to bestow upon me," Michael said, lowering his head in a slight bow. "I can confirm there are no married women of interest to me," he continued whilst raising his head, "but I do look forward to more seriously courting once settled with Her Imperial Highness.

The woman who chooses to accept my story as a widowed father and take on a child not her own will truly be sent by God himself." He sighed deeply despite his stated resolve.

"It seems that perhaps something doesn't fare well, brother?" Nicholas asked.

Michael lowered his head once more. "It's a little difficult at times to think that any great love of mine will never really know me."

"I understand. We all wear masks of some kind, Michael, but yes, yours is more difficult to remove than most. Remember that anyone you choose to love would be at risk should you ever tell them the truth of your heritage or the story of the child in your care."

Michael nodded. "How's Mother?" he continued, looking up again as he changed the subject. "I'd hoped to have seen her but understand we can't take any risks with the handover. I can still hear her words when you and I first met: *My children, you are once again as one.*"

Nicholas could sense Michael's disappointment but was proud of him for his strength.

"She sends her love to her fourth-born son who has given up so much to ensure the bloodline of the Romanov dynasty."

Michael nodded absently, now seemingly lost in thought while watching Alexandra saying goodbye to her daughter. "Do you think she wept for me the way Alexandra weeps for the new Auxiliary Child?" he asked in a whisper. No sooner had the words escaped his mouth than Michael smiled and recomposed himself, putting out his hand towards Alexandra. "It seems your Tsarina beckons our return."

Turning, Michael retraced their path and carefully picked up an infant who was asleep in the arms of the Auxiliary agent who had accompanied him from London. The agent had been standing silently, but ever watchful, over the poignant family reunion.

"She's of Polish German descent. Born eight weeks before the Grand Duchess. A twin," Michael explained. "We pray she grows to share the same attributes as her two older sisters, both of whom are not dissimilar in appearance to the Tsarina when she was their age."

"And the rest of the family?" Nicholas asked as he carefully took hold of the baby his brother passed him. She was wrapped in blankets, sleeping peacefully and unaware of the important role in history she was about to assume.

"Having lost her first two children, both boys, in infancy and already raising two young daughters, the mother was deeply committed to nurturing her newborn son. The unexpected arrival of twins posed a dilemma, leading her to contemplate the difficult decision of abandoning the baby girl. She feared that another mouth to feed would be too much for her family to manage," Michael said solemnly.

"Importantly, Your Imperial Majesty, rather than wait for that decision to be finalised, we took measures to ensure the mother believed the girl had died," the agent added. "This guarantees that we will never face a mother's change of heart. No one will search for this child."

"Records?" Nicholas asked.

"There will be no registration of the girl's birth or death, as per the mother's request," the agent explained. "She wished for her family to know only of the boy's birth. As a result, history will bear no evidence of the girl. She will exist solely as a memory for the mother and her midwife, who, as one of us, we know will never reveal the truth."

"Thank you, Adri," Nicholas said, nodding gravely towards the agent before carefully carrying the infant to his wife.

"Alexandra, we need to leave her," he said softly but urgently as he wrapped his one free arm protectively around both his wife and their daughter. Even more softly he whispered, "Whether the prophecy is accurate or not, the security measure maintained by the Auxiliary is the one absolute way to keep the dynasty alive."

The weight of their sacrifice, crushing and all-encompassing, settled upon them. He held her as she wept, her body wracked with convulsive sobs. The cost of protecting their family's legacy was immeasurable.

"It's time."

"I know, but it's … it's …"

"So hard, my love – yes, it's devastatingly hard, but I'll ask you to please hand her to Michael now."

Alexandra slowly and gently handed their newborn child to her brother-in-law, and then Nikky placed the substitute infant in her arms. She held the baby gently, but her tears wouldn't stop. They fell, wetting the child's face, forever christening her a Romanov.

Leaning down, he kissed the Substitute's forehead. "We will love you as much as if you were our own. Whilst our blood does not run through your veins, you will be cherished, adored, and we will be forever in your debt for allowing our daughter to live on in the event of our demise."

Standing upright, he turned to Michael. "My brother, you have now ended your time as the Auxiliary Child and are officially appointed the Keeper. From here on, our daughter, born Grand Duchess Anastasia Nikolaevna of Russia, will be in your trusted care and will be known simply as Victoria Burton-Hall."

Michael handed his niece to Adri and then kneeled in front of the Tsar. "I promise you that I will love her as I would my own," he said, "Always and forever, brother."

Nicholas motioned for his brother to stand. "And our love for you is always and forever, Michael." Turning to acknowledge the agent with a nod, the Tsar took one last look at their beautiful baby girl before ushering his Tsarina from the room with an infant not their own.

As they walked, Nicholas glanced at his Empress, her eyes still glistening with tears.

"Please stem your sorrow, Alexandra. I'm proud of you, as will Mother be," he said. "Whilst you tolerate each other on my behalf, you are more alike than you believe. Both of you have endured great pains to protect the Romanov dynasty."

"But your mother has no idea the additional burden we carry, Nikky!" Alexandra whispered with force. "What we achieved today is nothing at all like what she went through with Michael, and you know it. I wish, no, I beg you to tell her!" she said, stopping to wipe her tears from the face of the child.

He shook his head with a look of steely resolve. "I wish I could tell her, but it would break her heart, and I refuse to be responsible for that."

"But you were happy to break mine," Alexandra retorted, instantly lowering her head to avoid any scrutiny.

"You know too well that as Tsar, I need you, my Tsarina, informed by my side!" he exclaimed, hearing the soft fury in his voice and willing himself to remain calm. "We need to support each other, plan and live every minute of every day … while we still have days to do so. My birthright aside, I also told you out of love, as without you, I am nothing."

His wife stayed silent and the infant lay peacefully in her arms, unaware of their angst. At this early age, children were so very impressionable. This child would have to be even more so.

"I know that the burden is all-encompassing," he continued, his voice softening. "Knowledge of the family's Auxiliary Measure is one thing – knowledge of the downfall of the Imperial Dynasty and Christianity is something else altogether. I need you to please just love me while you can and not let the secret of the prophecies tear us apart."

"I know. I'm so sorry, Nikky. I'm not myself today," she whispered, looking up again. "Please. Please promise me that you will make sure the child we have forgone will have everything she needs in order to be reinstated," she continued. "If you truly believe that we must be sacrificed in order to save Russia, then she is our only hope."

"My darling, you know well that I believe the prophecies to be true. My family has been targeted by the activity of hateful revolutionaries for generations. My grandfather was murdered by a revolutionary fanatic, my father had attempts made on his life, and I too, my darling, haven't been immune. The Auxiliary Measure was born from these very threats. The prophecies of Monks Terakuto and Abel sealed my fate. Our fate. We will fall holding the hand of Christianity, but it will be nothing compared to what His Holiness suffered for us," he said softly.

"And whatever great sorrows and upheavals that await us and Mother Russia will dim the gems of our earthly crowns," she recited. "I would call death comparable, my Tsar."

Nicholas watched despondently as she began to walk ahead of him. "But my Tsarina neglects to finish the words as they were scribed," he called after her in a defiant whisper. *"It will dim our earthly crowns, but because of this the glittering of our heavenly crowns will last forever."*

Alexandra kept walking.

"Please, Alexandra! I ask you to live each day like it's your last," he said as he hastened to walk beside her once again. "Love our girls, love the beautiful, unsuspecting infant you hold in your arms, love me, and love your life. For it is not *just* love that will conquer evil but *only* love. I and the Auxiliary will ensure Anastasia has the proof she needs to find her way home. Do not make that your concern. Promise me that you will focus only on our children. Give them the best lives they could possibly have for however long that may be. Promise me."

The Empress stopped and he paused beside her. After taking a deep breath, she again walked away, gently shaking her head. With a final sob, her shoulders slumped, and without turning back to look at him, she promised.

Chapter 1

TSARSKOYE SELO, RUSSIA, 1916

He ran his finger gently over the beautiful face in the photograph. It may have been black and white, but in his eyes, she shone in vibrant colour.

His Anastasia.

She was so much like her three older sisters and, somewhat disturbingly, so very like her substitute. His eldest girls would never know any different, and that was probably Nicholas' greatest regret. The Substitute had been doted on and adored by her siblings, blessed with their love, which his true Anastasia had never known.

He placed the photo securely back in a hidden compartment at the rear of his writing desk, unable to divert his eyes from the envelope that shared the space, addressed *To the Tsar in whose reign I shall be glorified.*

He, Nicholas, was that Tsar. In 1903, he was the one who insisted upon the glorification of Seraphim of Sarov against much opposition, having to assert his autocratic rule to ensure the canonisation took place. And in return …

He closed his eyes and calmed his breathing.

In return for anointing the holy man Seraphim, he'd been provided the most detailed insight into the future of his Mother Country, and it had involved sinful desecration and utter devastation. Death. Betrayal. Sorrow … and blood. So much dark and menacing blood seeping through the streets of Russia, its viscous red staining them as well as the hands and minds of his country's people.

Even with the envelope sealed and hidden away it resonated sadness, bringing tears to his eyes and pain to his heart. He would never forget what the words inside foretold: that the Russian people would lose their way and lose their faith, and that he would lose control of the people – not entirely due to faults of his own, but his actions would play a significant part. Seeing the anarchy as a sign of weakness, the non-faithful would enlist earthly demons to their cause and Satan would encroach upon the country, finally having his way after a brewing time of unrest. The unrest would boil over and the people of God would be persecuted. The Russian Empire would fall and Russian imperialism would be handed a cup of suffering, which he, as the ruling Tsar, and his family, would have no choice but to drink. With its consumption, the Imperial Family would offer themselves up as a sacrifice for their people. It was a monumental ask. The sacrifice would mean their deaths.

They would die in 1918, of that he was sure.

"If I am to be at fault for the fall of the Russian Empire then let me alone drink a cup of suffering, Lord!" He prayed feverishly and raised his head dramatically to the sky, hoping for divine intervention.

After a moment of thought, he slowly lowered his gaze. He knew his prayer wouldn't be answered for God had already intervened. Through holy men Terakuto, Abel and now Seraphim, God had relayed a message about the future, and his intention was clear. Imperialism and Christianity were to be no more.

But there was hope – not for himself as Tsar or those he most adored on Russian soil but for the child he'd given up at birth. Unlike earlier prophecies, Seraphim's words had also provided a reason for the desecration of the strongholds of Holy Russia. God wasn't abandoning them with no reason – he was persecuting them as a means to an end. He wanted then to live in a world without godliness in order to reignite their faith! The Lord's plan would take time, but a chosen one would rise when the Russian people were most ready to repent and be led to salvation. The chosen one would be his Anastasia.

"Four symbols of life, one every four years, will provide a lifeline," he whispered, feeling his resolve return. His focus needed to not be on his shortcomings as Tsar but on building a path to guide his daughter home, a concept he'd started working on shortly after her birth and which had evolved since, guided by Seraphim's words. That the saint had known of his idea so many years before it had been thought of was only possible by the hand of God. The Lord did indeed have a plan.

"As the path end is set, tell the child so noted within to seek the one who bears her name," he spoke more loudly, recalling the writing on the back of the prophecy's envelope. He smiled. Seraphim had given him a lot to go on, but whether his fourth-born daughter would need to seek an Anastasia or a Victoria he had no idea. No idea at all.

His attention hastily turned to the present as his wife entered his chambers. She moved at pace, having been summoned by him, her head lowered, but not enough to hide her boiling fury. Without adhering to imperial protocol of curtseying to her Tsar, Alexandra burst into a tirade.

"Must you summon me to talk of such filthy innuendo, my Tsar? You're only home from the front for a few days. Please, let's focus as we always promised we would on living every day. Allowing Alexei to wallow in the pain that his haemophilia brings upon him is not, in my eyes, keeping our promise made. I have nothing to answer for. Not to anyone."

Nicholas pointed at the folder on his desk that had been delivered to him from the Duma earlier that day.

"I know that, Alexandra, but I can't hold the members at bay much longer. The fact we have so many secrets, including Alexei's illness – for which we rely on the monk's healing – has fuelled lewd rumours, criticisms and anti-tsarist propaganda. Purishkevich even made a speech at the assembly stating that my ministers have been …" he paused to riffle through the folder and pull out the pertinent page:

> *… turned into marionettes, marionettes whose threads have been taken firmly in hand by Rasputin and the Empress Alexandra Feodorovna – the evil genius of Russia and the Tsarina – who has remained a German on the Russian throne and alien to the country and its people.*

He screwed up the page and threw it onto his desk in frustration.

"Ni—" she tried unsuccessfully to interject.

"Oh, there's more," he continued. "I've had word from another Duma member, Guchkov, that there is new support to charge your favourite monk with being a member of an illegal religious sect, the Khlysts. But my favourite by far is this one in today's press:

> *… any accountability for the growing corruption within the government has simply disappeared as our country heads towards utter chaos and ruin. It seems nothing can stop Rasputin and his harem of sexually promiscuous imperial women.*

"My God, Nicholas!" Alexandra snapped. "You know that is nonsense and that my relationship with Rasputin is only about our Alexei, our son! Our only son … and if the prophecies are ever revealed untrue, then he will also be our legacy. Rasputin is the only one who heals him."

He stared at her in disbelief and then slammed his fist onto his desk. "Do not take that tone with me. You know too well that the prophecies have predicted everything. All they stipulated would happen by now has happened, and rest assured, we will die. Alexei, too, will die. It is not our son who is going to save our bloodline and the future of our country, it is our daughter! To ensure her safety, we need the Duma and everything it represents aligned with us. Dear God woman, she resides in England, and I need the Duma to keep Cousin George on our side!"

"But you still have final say on everything, Nicholas!" she said, not backing down. "You only created the parliament and unshackled the press to save face after the revolution, but even still, you haven't given up your autocratic power. And perhaps you should have, because then we wouldn't need this cursed Auxiliary Measure anymore, and our beautiful daughter wouldn't be living a fake existence somewhere in the outer regions of England! To hell with King George. Use your power, Nikky! Tell them to stop. Make them stop these personal slights and attacks against me and our family."

Nicholas paused to make certain of his tone. They'd been through these ups and downs about the prophecies over the years, but this outburst was the most passionate he'd seen from her in a long time. *Was the monk actually asserting some kind of influence over her?*

Speaking more calmly, he said, "I know you feel a burning desire to ebb Alexei's episodes because you think it's your fault that he suffers due to the lineage of the bleeding disease. But, my love, I am begging you – no, I am telling you – it's time to address the problem that is Rasputin."

As he watched his wife's face and resolve crumble, Nicholas cursed the hell they'd found themselves in. She had married him for love, and he had given her in return a guaranteed death. The few days he'd been able to remove himself from the war were meant to be like bubbles of bliss floating within a surrounding uproar. Instead, they were drowning in the Devil's threats.

Alexandra breathed in and out deeply, trying to compose herself. "All I've been doing is what you asked of me. I've been protecting Alexei at all costs to ensure his life is as full as it can be before certain death," she sobbed. "I need you to help me, Nikky. Help me restore my reputation and that of our daughters. Please. Please stop the press calling us sexual servants of the monk."

"The only way to do that is to take care of Rasputin, and as Tsar, that's my final decision."

She looked at him defiantly as she managed to curb her tears. "Fine, my Tsar, but how exactly do you propose to take care of Rasputin when you've made it abundantly clear that it's essential our people maintain faith in us? We've supported him for so long, putting aside his horrifically wayward ways. Not even our families, including your beloved mother, know of Alexei's illness. So how do we now deal with things and not make the monarchy appear weak? How do we stop it from looking like I am at fault, and you're punishing Rasputin for things to do with me, as it's so lewdly claimed in the press? And how, exactly, do you propose to ensure the supremacy of the monarchy for when our daughter returns to rule in the name of Romanov by suddenly changing tack on Rasputin and bringing with it all these problems?"

"Is my Empress finished?" he asked calmly.

She cast her eyes to the floor.

"I want you to leave all that to me. And I also need you to leave right now. Rasputin has been summoned and will be here shortly."

Alexandra bowed her head and moved to leave. As she reached the door, she turned back to him solemnly. "Rasputin has never had any hold over me."

"I trust you, Alexandra, but I don't fully trust him."

"Then if you trust me, let me stay. Let us face him together."

He could allow her that much.

†

"Your most holy Tsar, you are a fish," Nicholas heard the monk say as he entered the chambers, "and I, well, I am the fisherman."

Rasputin closed the door and came to a stop in front of him, bowing dramatically before noticing they were not alone.

"Ah, Tsarina." The monk continued his theatrical display. "It's a pleasure, as always, and today the pleasure will absolutely be all mine."

Nicholas refused to take the verbal bait and willed his Empress to do the same as he summoned Rasputin to sit. The holy man declined and instead stood just inside the door, ominous in his dark robes, which looked dishevelled and unwashed. It felt as though the air was slowly being sucked from the room.

"Can you not already feel the hook piercing your skin and the blood dripping into your mouth, slowly choking you, my Tsar? I am suitably surprised if not, sir, being I have you hook, line and sinker."

Nicholas held the monk's gaze, and Alexandra sat rigidly in anticipation.

"Your silence is apt as what I have to say warrants your full attention, Tsar."

A coldness enveloped the room and Nicholas tried hard not to shiver. He placed his hand on top of Alexandra's momentarily to provide them both comfort.

"With all due respect, Grigori, I called you here today as I have some things to discuss with you—"

"I'm not having an affair with your wife, Nicholas, but I have most definitely and deliciously screwed her."

Alexandra gasped in astonishment and Nicholas jumped to his feet, but before either of them could speak, the monk released a deep, guttural laugh then continued his vitriol.

"Shall I hypnotise you now, Tsarina, and have you put on a show for your master? I am of course talking of myself, not the Tsar, although as a fellow man I'm sure he'd enjoy watching your talents." He grinned. "She's easy to manipulate, Nicholas. It's amazing what one will turn a blind eye to – or should I say a hypnotised eye to – for the love of a child."

"Enough!" Nicholas ordered. "You are here to answer questions regarding the material reported about you by the press and by my Duma. Perversion, slander and even Khlyst ties, Grigori! These are serious allegations, some of which you have already seemingly admitted to as evidenced by your conduct here today."

Rasputin stood quietly for a moment then offered an ugly smile.

"I may or may not be Khlyst. Does it really matter what a man tells the world, Nicholas? No, it doesn't. All that matters is the intentions of the man saying what he does, isn't that right? Even the Devil's own actions may be born from good intent. Do we therefore celebrate the notion, punish the result or both? Have not you, Tsar of all Russia, lied to your fellow countrymen and family with positive intent?"

Nicholas could feel his skin crawling. The monk was reeling in his fish. *What had his wife said to, or done for, this disgusting excuse for a man?*

"Alexei's illness is just one of your lies that I have dutifully kept secret, but let's not dwell on that," Rasputin continued. "All that matters as I stand before you today is that I know of the child, a Romanov child in waiting – or *in hiding* would be the correct description. One Grand Duchess Anastasia Nikolaevna of Russia in the care of one Grand Duke Michael Alexandrovich of Russia. The idea really is quite genius of the Dowager Empress, albeit heartbreaking for all involved … But you see, a lie underpinned by positive intent!"

Involuntarily, Nicholas turned to look at his wife. No words came to him as myriad thoughts exploded frantically in his head.

"My love … I … I don't understand what he speaks of. You must believe me," Alexandra beseeched. As still no words came to Nicholas, Alexandra turned her attention back to Rasputin. "You're despicable," she whispered.

The monk laughed heartily. "I do have my moments, Tsarina, yes. I may be reviled by many of the Russian people – the scar that binds my gut to my body is evidence that any number of them want me dead – but do not disregard that many of my fellow peasants support my success with the imperial court. Those people, my followers, should have such imperial deceit brought to their attention. A tsar who lies is a leader who cannot be trusted."

Nicholas' voice came back to him. "What do you want, Grigori?"

The monk winked at Alexandra before continuing. "My original desire was to obtain greater political power and have sympathetic members placed in the Duma. They would then guide the country's strategies and outcomes regarding non-orthodox religions such as Khlysty. Oh, apologies. I didn't confirm the Khlyst allegation earlier, did I? No, I was too busy making a point. Yes, I am Khlyst. In fact, I'm their almighty leader. Their Christ. It's really not as shocking as your reactions make it out to be."

Words once again eluded the Tsar allowing Rasputin to continue uninterrupted.

"Tsarina, you'd shared nothing of note before revealing the Auxiliary Measure, such is your mundane and trite existence, so I was suitably surprised. But now I'm able to stand before both of you and demand acknowledgement and power for my religion or my followers will kill both the Grand Duke and Duchess."

Nicholas needed to buy himself time. He needed to buy Michael time. Anastasia would not be harmed; he believed the prophecies. But his brother? He had no understanding of what dangers may befall Michael. Enough Romanov blood would be spilled in the next two years, including his own. He didn't want to lose any more.

"There is no child, Rasputin," he said calmly, trying his best to hide his inner turmoil and anger.

The monk smiled knowingly. "No child? I see. I thought it likely you'd deny my claims, and believe it or not, I do feel for your predicament. So, I am willing to give you time to think about what has been discussed here today. You have two weeks and I have two requests. If you do as I ask, your daughter and brother will not be harmed."

"There is no child!" added Alexandra, the fear and fragility in her voice apparent.

"First, as a sign of good faith for me allowing you time, you will remove Duma Member Purishkevich by the end of week one," Rasputin said, ignoring the Tsarina. "His cursed Duma speech was so … accurate. Second, you will publicly acknowledge Khlysty no later than the end of week two. Is that clear?"

It felt as if every breath of air had finally been sucked out of the room. The Tsar truly was a fish out of water.

"I will take your silence as agreement," said Rasputin, who made another dramatic bow to signal his leaving.

Neither Nicholas nor Alexandra spoke.

Rasputin bent down and placed an envelope on the floor at the Tsar's feet. "I bid you both farewell and leave you a copy of a letter I prepared before coming today – the original is in safekeeping should it be needed. It is entitled *If I Die*. And if I do die at the hands of nobility, so too will your loved ones. My faithful will see to it."

Chapter 2

TSARSKOYE SELO AND
ST PETERSBURG, RUSSIA, 1916

"I thought Germans were meant to be punctual?" the Dowager Empress exclaimed with irritation as Alexandra entered the waiting hall that had once been Maria's domain. Portraits of their ancestors lined the walls, their impressive imperial stories perfectly preserved in exquisite paintings enclosed in ornate carved frames.

The two women curtseyed to each other simultaneously, defying tradition. This act signified submission on Alexandra's part, as the reigning monarch was traditionally expected to receive a curtsey before offering one. Alexandra then went even further by approaching the Dowager Empress, taking her hand and placing a soft kiss upon it.

"Your request for an audience is timely, Maria, for I must beg your forgiveness. I have unknowingly sinned," she whispered.

Swiftly pulling back her hand, Maria spoke in a volume far from a whisper. "Alexandra, I, along with many of the monarchy's most devoted supporters, have nearly lost all confidence in your ability to govern the empire. I say *nearly*, as I like to trust that my son may see

19

or know something that I don't, but now … now you stand in front of me and confirm the rumours of your filthy illicit relationship that spits in the very face of your betrothal to my son? May Hell come down on you! Letting an imbecilic monk degrade you and defile our country?! Have you not noticed whilst satisfying the passion of your loins that Russia's military woes are immense, and our army has turned into a disorganised embarrassment? Russia is adrift, Alexandra, all because of you, and believe me, I will now do everything in my power to set *you* loose."

The Dowager Empress turned and made to storm from the room, but Alexandra reached out desperately and grabbed her by the arm.

"No. Stop! Please! Please, Maria, let me explain," she begged. "I hear your wrath, and to some degree I understand it based on Nicholas and I being so very private regarding our lives. But I implore you, I beg you, please let me set the record straight. A relationship with Grigori Rasputin is not the sin I refer to!"

Turning angrily, the Dowager Empress stared at her daughter-in-law intently. "Then what, pray tell, is your sin, Alexandra?"

The Tsarina took a brief moment to compose herself before continuing. "I want to start by expressing how truly sorry I am for not always sharing important information with you, things you should have known about and deserved to know. By confiding in you today, I am breaking Nikky's trust, but I believe you will support my decision. I need you to listen carefully. I require your help, and I need it immediately."

Without losing eye contact, Maria sat on the day lounge, seemingly stunned mute by what she'd heard. Alexandra waited for a response, and when none was forthcoming, she began.

"Rasputin's deception was masked to both me and to Nikky, but especially me," she explained, positioning herself on an adjoining lounge. If not for the tension between them, a painting capturing the coming together of two empresses of Russia would have made a beautiful addition to the palace wall. "I know the Duma despises me, and at times you border on hating my very existence," Alexandra continued. "You all see the war's demise as my fault – whether you whisper 'folly' or 'treason', it's not quietly enough. I have heard the ugly comments, and I'll confess that I initially retaliated. But now, I am ashamed to admit that you were right to question the monk's motives. I was wrong, and I've been deceived, blinded by my love for my son – your grandson, Maria. I trusted Rasputin, and his deceit was partly obscured by my instinct to protect Alexei and partly due to the monk's demonic hypnotic influence. His lies and treachery have now been fully exposed, and I urgently need your help to render him positively and absolutely dead."

"Dead?!" the Dowager Empress exclaimed in astonishment. "With pleasure, I assure you, but placing the dramatics aside for just a moment, what do you mean 'protect Alexei'? What on earth could a young boy seek from that despicable, lecherous peasant that he cannot get elsewhere? He is the heir apparent to all of Russia. He has no reason to want for anything, except perhaps a younger brother as his spare."

Alexandra sighed silently at the barb. She would not bite.

"I stand before you, overwhelmed with profound guilt and remorse. It should not come as a complete surprise, however, that I tell you Alexei is afflicted with the bleeding disease. It was always a possibility that a child of mine may suffer from it, carried via my womb. It's been the case for many granddaughters of Queen Victoria. His illness is my fault, so I have done everything in my power to heal him. The monk heals him, Maria."

A look of shock followed by sorrow and then realisation crossed her mother-in-law's face. Her only grandson had haemophilia, which undoubtedly meant he would never be fit to serve as monarch, even if by some miracle he lived long enough.

"Please say something, Maria," Alexandra whispered. "I know you never wanted me as a Romanov, but again, I beg you, I implore you, one mother to another, to please help me."

Slowly a new look crossed the Dowager Empress' face. Resolve.

"I think it would be wise for you to give me all the details so I can help you make informed decisions, Alexandra."

Alexandra nodded quickly and began to explain the hypnosis and the threats to Michael and Anastasia, sharing only the bare minimum necessary to gain support for getting rid of Rasputin while minimising her betrayal of her husband.

As she finished the tale, Maria also nodded, but in a much slower and deliberate way.

"I apologise for my reference earlier about dramatics, Alexandra. That was premature. I will ensure the monk takes his last breath within the week."

At the Dowager Empress' response, the Tsarina began to weep. Her gamble had paid off. The woman who had set up the Auxiliary Measure wasn't going to let it befall a murderous threat.

The anger that had been swelling inside Alexandra since Rasputin made his overpowering of her apparent, was released with her tears. Whilst Nikky had sent word to his brother Michael about the threat and fired the Duma member Rasputin had demanded, she'd thought of ways to have Rasputin exterminated. She was a woman most definitely scorned and she wanted revenge, even if that meant she had to fall at the feet of her mother-in-law, portraying herself as an inadequate tsarina.

She could breathe again. The Dowager Empress would take control and the prophecies regarding the downfall of imperialism remained secret between herself and Nikky, as did the content of the monk's letter and his claim to be the almighty Khlyst Christ. She had betrayed her husband only slightly.

"Alexandra. Did you hear me? Did I make myself clear?"

"Thank you, Maria. Yes. I understand what you're saying." She reached out and took the Dowager Empress' hands in hers. "Please know also that I'll do everything I can to find Alexei alternate care."

"Of that I have no doubt, Alexandra. Mothers will do anything to protect their children."

Alexandra realised that for the very first time, she and her mother-in-law were seeing eye to eye and silently bemoaned that it was under such horrific circumstances. As a wave of unease washed over her, her stomach started to tighten, stifling her earlier relief. The Dowager Empress would never have agreed to this course of action had she also known of Rasputin's threat of his supporters hunting down and ending the lives of all their family should he be killed at the hands of nobility.

"There is one more thing."

"Another sin I need to be aware of? I'm not sure I have it in me today, Alexandra."

"No. Simply a request," she said. "Please don't tell Nikky we spoke. Even though it would silence those in parliament and abroad who have questioned our desire to have Rasputin so intimately involved in our lives, Nikky would never agree to an imperial-sanctioned death warrant. It could instigate another peasant uprising, and we're still trying to strengthen our relationship with the people. He must focus on the war efforts … I can't have him distracted."

Maria stared at her wryly before her gaze softened. "What you really mean is that you cannot have him know you betrayed him by telling me your secret," she said. "Regardless, I do unequivocally agree with you. I will never speak to my son of this, and I will deal with Rasputin quickly and efficiently. I have allegiances who can help and who will keep their silence. The very same allegiances who secure our Auxiliary Measure."

Alexandra nodded. "I cannot stress how essential it is that no one ever suspect that nobility was involved in Rasputin's removal, Maria."

"I've already noted your desire to win back the people without angering the peasant folk, Alexandra. I always look after my own, and keeping our family's hands clean is a fundamental part of that. The monk has many enemies that can be held responsible for the spilling of his blood."

Alexandra could feel the knot in her stomach start to loosen. She'd kept the secret but warned Maria all the same. Michael and all their extended family would be kept out of harm's way.

"I don't know how to thank you."

Maria stood and curtseyed. As she turned to leave the room she added, "Whilst it pains me to say it, you must start thinking about preparing an imperial funeral. You need to save face with your people, and anything less than that will spark questions about Rasputin's death. That I do not need."

Now alone, Alexandra solemnly pondered the outcome of the meeting. *The monk had signed his own death warrant. She would not mourn for him.* Catching her reflection in a mirror, she flinched at how her face had aged. Her beauty was waning. Each line etched on her face carried the stories of her life: happy stories, sad stories and secret stories. Ultimately, it would be her corpse that bore the narrative of her death.

She slumped back onto the lounge and tears continued to run down her face, settling into the collar of her dress. The dampness left a dark mark that mirrored her mood. There were so many secrets bearing down on her, and whilst she felt solace, albeit guilt-laden, at confiding in the Dowager Empress about Alexei's illness and the monk's evil ways, she had a new secret to live with. She now carried the knowledge that the Dowager Empress would be responsible for orchestrating the murder of Rasputin.

†

Not even her many layers of clothing could stem the cold that was enveloping her body. It seemed to seep through every stitch of fabric and settle onto her skin as droplets of icy fear as she quietly waited alone in the small boat moored in front of the Moika Palace.

Every exhale formed a small cloud in front of Yelena's face. She hoped fervently that it somewhat covered her novice anxiety. All going well, her first mission would also be her first blood. The blood of the monk Rasputin. Her faith had taught her 'thou shalt not kill', but since a serious threat had become apparent to the Imperial Family, her new mantra was 'thou shalt not kill – except for the enemies of God'. And as God's representative on earth, any enemies of the Tsar were considered sanctioned.

"They're in the basement eating cake," Adri whispered as he returned and held out his hand. "Rasputin and Yusupov. Although I know Pavlovich and Purishkevich are also in the palace somewhere. Come. Let's walk to keep warm."

Thankful, Yelena let her superior guide her onto the river foreshore where they kept to the shadows as best they could. The fact it was more than two hours past midnight, with the moon covered by ominous-looking clouds, helped them immensely.

"Who eats cake in the middle of the night?" she asked, genuinely intrigued.

"Such is noble life," Adri offered her with a small smile. "They also have wine."

It was a very different existence to what she'd known at the orphanage, that was for sure.

"Where's Luka?"

"He's inside keeping watch."

"Inside?!"

"Well, yes. He and I went in. That's how I know about the cake and wine," Adri said, giving her arm a reassuring squeeze. "It's going to be okay. You've trained for this. You both have. They'll finish up soon, and when the monk leaves, we'll follow him and do what we need to do. I couldn't be prouder of—"

Yelena saw that Adri's attention had been diverted to a dark shadow quickly approaching them. His grip on her arm tightened before loosening again as Luka came into view.

Her partner's face was lined with worry. "We have a problem" he said. "They shot Rasputin."

"What?" Adri exclaimed in an urgent whisper. "Who? Where?"

"Surely they didn't think Rasputin's influence over the Tsarina enough to condone murder! These are educated people!" Yelena exclaimed. "A cousin and nephew-in law of the Tsar plus a member of the Duma!"

"Ex-member of the Duma. The Tsar had Purishkevich fired after that derogatory marionette speech," Luka reminded her. "And to answer your question, Adri, it was Yusupov."

Adri frowned. "This is not good."

"He left the basement for a short time and returned with a revolver. He told Rasputin that he'd better look at the crucifix on the wall and say a prayer … and then Yusupov shot him point-blank in the chest. One shot was all it took to down him, but all three of them were needed to take his coat and hat," Luka explained.

"What?" Yelena questioned, her eyes widening in disbelief.

"After Rasputin went down, Pavlovich and Purishkevich joined Yusupov, and after a quick consultation, Purishkevich put on Rasputin's coat and hat, and they all left together in a car."

"Okay." Adri breathed in deeply. "My guess is it's an attempt to make it look as if Rasputin left the palace very much alive. Most likely they'll be heading to his apartment. This is a good thing. I can only assume it means they have no intention of getting caught nor want to take responsibility."

"And to confirm, the body is still in the basement?" Yelena asked Luka.

"Correct. Lying where it landed on the basement floor amongst cake crumbs and spilled wine. And, whilst barely, still with a pulse."

"Luka! You could have led with that piece of information!" Adri exclaimed. "Come, both of you. We need to get him out of the palace and take care of things ourselves as planned. Quickly. We must dispose of Rasputin so there's no chance of those three so-called nobles being caught for attempted murder."

"Or for actual murder," Yelena whispered whilst frantically pointing out a car pulling into the palace grounds.

"That's the same car. They're back," Luka confirmed. "Let's go."

Yelena's heart thumped as she hastily followed Adri and Luka to a dark fenced palace courtyard that bordered the basement where the altercation with the monk had taken place. They huddled in the snow behind a pair of large fence pillars that provided them a makeshift hiding place.

"The quickest way in is there," said Luka, pointing to a nondescript door, bare of any lintel or decoration. "About six steps take you directly down to the basement door. It's the way I came out into the courtyard to fetch you. But there'll be no place to hide once we're in. It's risky."

"That's a risk—" Adri hastily swallowed his words as the door they had been discussing flew open, and a figure dashed into the courtyard. Unsteady on their feet, they misjudged the stone step and fell heavily to the ground as someone followed them outside. As they raised their head to the sky, as if seeking divine mercy, Yelena made out two things: first, it was a man bleeding profusely, staining the ground beneath him, and second, it was Grigori Rasputin.

"Yelena, now!" Adri whispered.

She hadn't needed the prompt; her breathing had slowed, and her focus had dismissed everything else the moment she recognised her mark. As the monk managed to get to his feet and began making his way slowly through the courtyard, she didn't feel herself position her gun between the fence palings, nor her finger on the trigger. She only felt a euphoric satisfaction as Rasputin's head jerked so violently that it seemed possible it may have been ripped from his shoulders.

Simultaneously, her rapture evaporated as she felt herself thrown backwards onto the ground. A sharp pain pierced her arm, and someone pressed down tightly on her mouth, preventing her screams. Her vision swam, but she could make out Adri leaning over her.

"You're okay, Yelena," Adri whispered into her ear. "A small wound. Just stay down."

"Bullseye. May Mother Russia be returned to greatness!" she heard a voice exclaim in hushed tones.

"Just as well, Purishkevich. He attacked me, for Christ's sake," another hushed but exasperated voice retorted.

"Well, you should have shot him properly the first time, Felix."

"Really, Vlad? It took you two shots."

"He must have seriously beaten you around, my friend. You're hearing things. I only fired once and was right on target. The evidence is lying sprawled out in front of you."

Adri leaned in close again. "Purishkevich and Yusupov … and now … Pavlovich."

"Keep your voices down," she heard another voice say, followed by a soft popping sound that she knew all too well, a bullet muffled by a silencer just like the one she'd used only moments before.

"If he wasn't dead before, he certainly is now," the voice she assumed was Pavlovich continued. "One in the back from me for good measure. May his spirit return to the hell from which he came forth and our Tsar seize the chance we have delivered him to restore the reputation and prestige of our great monarchy. Now, help me carry this filth back inside."

When the courtyard finally fell silent again and the basement access door was secured shut, Yelena let Luka and Adri help her to her feet. She felt faint, but overall the realisation of what she had achieved took prominence, giving her strength underpinned by adrenalin.

"All we can do now is make sure they don't get caught lest we do too," Adri said as he took his scarf and wrapped it tightly around her wounded arm. "Luka, follow them to make sure they dispose of the body properly. We know from the earlier theatrics with the monk's clothes that they don't want to be caught. Help them keep it that way."

Luka nodded and moved in close to gently kiss Yelena's forehead before disappearing into the night.

"Are you okay to walk?" Adri asked her.

"I'll have to be." She smiled weakly.

"Good work, Yelena. It was your bullet that took Rasputin's life, a bullet condoned by those in a position to endorse such decisions. Purishkevich's shot was off by a long way, and unfortunately you were in the firing line. You both fired at almost the same moment."

She nodded and swallowed a groan as he readjusted the scarf on her wound and pulled the knot tighter.

"And as for Pavlovich, he shot a bullet into a corpse so as not to be left out. Some very un-noble behaviour displayed by all of them tonight, but God should look on them favourably being it was you who completed what was asked of us."

"I want to help Luka. The pain is bearable," she said through gritted teeth.

"No. You've done enough. I need to get you home to rest and fervently pray that none of those three are stupid enough to ever speak of this night to anyone else and find themselves in Siberia for murder."

"Attempted murder," she replied, her smile widening as Adri's did. Her initiation was complete.

"Welcome to the Auxiliary, Yelena."

Chapter 3

KENT COUNTY, UK, 1917–1918

To my daughter.

A debilitating wave of remorse flowed through him, causing his gut to wrench. His hand instinctively settled on it, applying pressure to ebb the spasm. How would his daughter – correction, his niece – accept what she needed to? That she was not his child but that of a man neither of them had ever known as family?

"Why have you been sent?" Michael asked the empty room, addressing the envelope he held in his trembling hands. The envelope was sealed with wax, imprinted with the double-headed imperial eagle. His gut continued to churn. Something must be desperately wrong. It was against the will of the Auxiliary that anything be put in writing.

"But it is troubled times," he mused out loud. He himself had been born of such times, and it was because of them that he'd never gone by his true name. Never lived his true life.

He sat down in an armchair and let the sunlight filtering through the large drawing-room window warm his face. It did nothing to stem the trembling that had overcome him nor settle the fluids that threatened to escape his stomach.

On the lawn outside, he observed Victoria and Kathryn deeply engrossed in conversation with his wife, Hannah As she looked towards the house and spotted him, he waved. His heart still fluttered for her. They'd shared so many precious moments, but their entire relationship was based on half-truths. In all the time she'd known him, she had no idea who he really was.

Still, he thanked the Lord every day for allowing him to love the wonderfully strong, intelligent and inspirational woman that Hannah was. The fact that his birth country's laws didn't allow women equal footing to their male counterparts confounded him. If Victoria ever had to take the throne as a ruling Romanov, laws would need to be amended.

"Well, as they say, rules are made to be broken," he remarked. "Just like you," he continued, addressing the letter in his hand. "And you," he added, shifting his gaze to the second letter he had received. Also sealed with the imperial crest, this one was addressed to him. "You must be desperate, Nicholas," he whispered as he broke the wax seal and removed the letter, feeling cold fear intensify.

The letter was dated almost a month earlier. It had taken the Auxiliary agents some time to make their way from Russia, the journey fraught by challenges due to the ongoing war. One of the agents he'd known – Adri, the agent who had helped him with the sourcing and handover of the substitute child all those years ago. The other two were new. Additional security sent by the Tsar.

Three agents? Whilst the thought was reassuring, it also made his skin prickle. *What was going on?* He undid his topmost shirt button to give himself some air and began to read.

Michael,

I trust that my knowledge of English, though non-native, will sufficiently convey what I need to express as time is of the essence. The time comes to prepare for the future of the family. I've had word from the Lord's representatives what fate He has in store. I have no doubt from what has been foretold that my veins will bleed dry, but what has not been made clear is if yours are bound for the same fate. Do not question my belief as I have waited many years to ensure that the words prophesied would prove consistent with reality. This has been the case in every single instance.

Do not inform anyone else. I mean no one, not even the one to whom we both owe our lives. She does not need to fear more than she does already every day. I trust in you alone as you must without question trust in me. It is the one named for resurrection, our Anastasia, who shall live and be victorious, but only after the blood of those close to her is shed.

Of additional concern is that other threats to the Auxiliary Measure have become apparent. I implore you to be diligent, keep one eye open and take not a single risk. As the Keeper, you are the closest to Anastasia and all she has known as a father. Your Victoria. She needs you to prepare for the blood that will be extracted from my body, exhausting my life, but also for the likelihood that you may suffer the same misfortune. I need you to keep the letter I include for Anastasia safe for she will need it within the next two years. My words will guide her home even if you are unable to chaperone her.

I leave you with the knowledge that God has bestowed upon me the number four that has and will continue to intertwine with my life and those of my loved ones. You are the fourth-born male, Michael, and Anastasia is the fourth-born female. The words of God's disciples stipulate that trials and tribulations will follow until the fourth-born will again bring our kind to power, and her lifeline will be provided by four exquisite symbols of life.

Trust me.

Trust His Holiness above.

Trust that one day the people of the world will rejoice in the sacrifices you have made. Your undying quest to ensure the protection of hope, faith, love and luck will be your legacy.

Our legacy.

N

Michael sat far too long for a man who had to move quickly, debilitated by the quagmire of both fatalistic and hopeful words that his brother had delivered him.

Hope, faith, love and luck. He knew implicitly what those words referred to.

The egg.

A symbol of creation and new life, it was breathtakingly exquisite. A celebration of the birth of Grand Duchess Anastasia. Michael's was a perfect match for the original imperial Clover Egg and one of the few tangible things he was in possession of that tied him to his lineage. Others thought it a magnificent replica, but how misinformed they were.

The warmth that accompanied thoughts of the egg was quickly extinguished as an overwhelming foreboding returned. He didn't understand what the other threats against the Auxiliary Measure were. Did someone who shouldn't know where he and Victoria were? Or, more importantly, *who* they were?

Riddled with anxiety, he stood and desperately paced the room as his brother's words swirled in his mind. *Do not inform anyone else. I mean no one …*

He was conflicted. If anything was to happen to him, Hannah would need to protect the children and assist Victoria with her coming of age into her dynastical destiny. Every part of him wanted desperately to call his wife inside and confess to her his heritage and role as the Keeper, but he couldn't. He was bound to silence by the very heritage that no one knew was his. Or was he? The Auxiliary rule book had already been severely broken as evidenced by his brother's letter.

"I'm sorry, Nicholas," he said as he pulled some paper and a fountain pen from a drawer and started to write. All he could do was trust that Hannah loved him enough to do as he asked if danger was forthcoming and forgive him his secrets once they subsequently became known.

*... I cannot tell you everything I want to, my love, but I can allude
to what you need to know as well as tell you how much I love you ...*

By the time he'd penned his confession, the collar and most of the
back of his shirt was wet through. Carefully he folded the pages
and placed them in an envelope before sealing it closed with wax,
adorned with his family crest. "Burton-Hall," he whispered. It had
been his name for so long, but it still had an alien ring to it as it rolled
off his tongue.

He was broken out of his tortured reverie by the taste of blood.
He'd chewed a fingernail so forcefully that he'd broken the skin,
causing him to swear. *By God! Were they still safe here, and if they weren't,
where could they go that was safer?* He shook his head in frustration.
Despite the war raging against their country, perhaps it would be
safer for his family to blend into the hustle and bustle of London life
rather than remain at their beautiful, secluded country estate.

"Hannah! Victoria! Kathryn!" he called to his family through the
window. "Time to come inside. I've something to discuss with you.
We need to plan for a trip. A vacation of sorts."

Yet another half-truth.

He sighed. A lie by any other name was still deceitful, even if
deemed the will of God.

✝

Twirling in the last rays of the spring sunshine, her arms outstretched,
Victoria was giddy with excitement, much to the dismay of her
younger sister.

"You're going to meet a man, fall madly in love and leave me all
alone," said Kathryn ruefully.

"It's not the thought of a romantic beau sweeping me off my
feet, Kathryn, it's simply that we finally get to experience somewhere
new!"

"Victoria, you've been so many places!" their mother exclaimed
from her chair under the rotunda.

"I beg to differ, Mother. We've lived in the countryside all our lives, and trips to see our grandparents in another part of the countryside don't count. I love them dearly, but we've never been to London! I feel it's calling me. I can't wait to get lost walking around all those streets and see the beautiful fashions!"

"And start courting men, choose one, get married and forget all about us," Kathryn frowned.

"Well, you can both relax a little. We're not going anywhere until the war is over. No new house, no courting and certainly no marriages! I've made that abundantly clear to your father on multiple occasions. The streets of London are not safe right now," their mother stipulated forcefully.

"But Father says we'll be going soon, even if just for a visit!" Victoria exclaimed.

"As soon as the Germans stop bombing our capital, Victoria. Believe me, I pray every day that will be soon, but until that time comes, we're all staying right here," her mother said, tapping the arm of her chair. Her tone implied that the conversation was now over. "Come, it's almost dark. Let's head inside and prepare for dinner."

Victoria sighed. She recognised the tone; her mother had used it often with her father when discussing his wish to move to his inherited home on the outskirts of London. While he argued that being nestled among the city's masses, with access to quality bomb shelters and medical care, would be safer, her mother didn't waver. A city subjected to random bombings for over three years was hardly safer. So instead of going to London, Victoria's father had built them a shelter under the stairs in the basement, and she had to be content to escape to the city within the pages of books and magazines.

"Father and I will convince you both one day," she scoffed.

"Wishful thinking, my child," laughed her mother, who swatted Victoria's arm with a scarf. "I promise you, when the war is over I will personally take you to London, but if you don't get yourself inside and ready for dinner right now, I will personally—"

Victoria looked at her mother expectantly. *Why had she stopped mid-sentence?*

"Personally what?" she asked.

"Edward?"

Confused, Victoria turned to see her father running towards them from the house. As he reached them, she thought it looked as though he'd been crying, *but that was ridiculous – her father never cried.*

"What's all over your shirt?" Kathryn asked him, which drew Victoria's attention from her father's face to the vibrant red stains on the front and sleeves.

"Oh my God, Edward! Are you hurt?" their mother gasped.

He shook his head and tried to catch his breath. "I told you it wasn't safe here. I should have insisted! Adri has bought us some time …"

"Adri?" her mother asked, fear now readily apparent in her voice.

"I'll explain later, I promise. Just please, quickly, all of you inside and into the basement shelter I showed you. Go. Now!

"But—"

"No buts, Kathryn. For the love of God, just get inside. Now!"

This time it was her father's tone that told them the conversation was over. Quickly they ran inside the house in a state of utter confusion.

"But what's going on? Is it an air raid?" Kathryn questioned as their father lifted the false floor under the stairs. Victoria had never actually seen inside the space, nor had she wanted to. It represented danger.

"Kathryn, enough. Please just do as I say."

"But what about Jasper?"

"Forget about the dog," their father yelled, but then softened his tone as his youngest child bordered on tears. "I'll look after Jasper. I'll find him and make sure he's alright, but right now I need all three of you to carefully get down inside the shelter. Once you're in safely,

I need you to be still and quiet. The quietest you've ever been. Come on, Victoria, you first," her father encouraged.

Carefully Victoria stepped down into the small space. It only came up to her knees. She'd thought it would have been bigger.

"You'll need to lie down for me to secure you inside," said her father noting her surprise. "Okay, you next, Hannah, and then Kathryn."

Her sister had other ideas.

As their mother stepped down into the shelter, they all turned in fright at the sound of footsteps. Kathryn was running back up the stairs.

"Oh my God, where's she going?" exclaimed her mother. "Kathryn!"

"She'll be going to get Jasper. She loves that dog more than life itself," Victoria said.

"Edward! We must go and get her," her mother grimaced, starting to climb back out of the shelter. "I don't know what danger you think we're in, but if that is blood on your shirt then I can only assume it's extreme."

"Stay here, Hannah. Don't you dare move from this room. You're right. We're all in extreme danger. I promise I will explain, but right now I need you to stay here with Victoria, and most of all, I need you to trust me." He paused. "And know I love you."

"Edward, what in the name of God is going on?"

"Please, Hannah. I need you to trust me. Just lie down. Please, both of you, lie down so I can secure the hatch. It will be dark and that might be scary, but it's the safest place you can be right now. Come on. Quickly. I need to bring Kathryn back."

"Edward, we can all go. Now, together. We'll go to London if you want. I'm so sorry I resisted you," her mother said covering her face with both hands to capture her tears.

"Hannah. Hannah, look at me, please. It's not safe to move now. What I need from you right now, and you too, Victoria, is a promise. I need you to promise me that if for any reason I don't come back, you will leave here and go far away. Change your names and falsify your birth details. Most importantly, trust no one, unless you are approached by a couple named Luka and Yelena. They you can trust."

Her mother's sobs only increased.

"There is a box down near your feet, right in the back corner," her father continued. "You must take this with you when you leave. I cannot stress how important it is that you take it with you. And Hannah … Hannah … Alright, good, look at me. You too, Victoria. There is also something in the rotunda, secured underneath the centre clover tile. You must also take that with you. It's extremely important. Promise me you understand. Hannah?"

"I promise, and she promises too," Victoria offered quietly on behalf of them both.

"Thank you, Victoria," her father said as he leaned in to quickly hug each of them.

All her mother could muster was a nod in acknowledgement as she tried to compose herself.

"Now lie down," he said, and with a less than reassuring smile he secured them in their hiding place.

Her father had been right. Being hidden under the floor was dark and it was scary. Lying still came easily, but it was the size of their hiding place, the damp smell, the itch of dust and the sheer terror of an unknown threat that made her want to convulse and scream at the same time. Lying side by side with her mother, she was losing track of time. Was it five minutes or twenty since her father had left to fetch Kathryn?

"Should one of us go and help?" she whispered urgently to her mother.

"Be quiet, Victoria. Your father will—"

For the second time that day, her mother stopped mid-sentence.

A door slammed and multiple footsteps ran somewhere across the ground floor of the house. *Finally, he's found Kathryn,* Victoria thought. But her jubilance was interrupted by the sound of breaking glass. The footsteps stopped simultaneously. More glass shattered before additional footsteps could be heard and a loud voice spoke.

"Michael … or is it, Edward?"

She felt her mother tense and let out the tiniest of whimpers.

"Michael, son of Alexander, and … who do we have here? Ah, the child. Well, praise the Lord!"

Victoria had no idea who the unknown man was speaking of. Who was Michael and who was Alexander? If it was her father in the room with these strangers, he didn't speak, but she thought she could make out the sound of someone crying. *Kathryn?* The crying got louder momentarily but was then drowned out by some form of chanting.

As the first guttural bloodcurdling scream pierced Victoria's senses, reaching to the bottom of her very soul, she realised with an unequivocal truth what the chanting was.

It was the sound of death.

Chapter 4

YEKATERINBURG, RUSSIA, 1918

"Please, just stop."

Maybe-if scenarios didn't matter, but they persisted on badgering her consciousness.

Frustrated, the former Tsarina checked her daughters' handiwork. The weight of the precious gems slightly weighed down the hems of their petticoats, but once they were sewn into their hiding places the entire way around the bottom of the skirting, it didn't look too untoward. God willing, the guards would not be anywhere near the hems of her daughters' undergarments, even though the girls did flirt to obtain certain advantages.

"Go away," Alexandra demanded of the thought that had once again found its way to the forefront of her mind. She neither wanted nor needed to question her husband's actions, yet once again, her psyche demanded her attention on the matter.

"If my husband had refused to abdicate, it wouldn't have prevented our foretold deaths. Nothing could."

But it may very well have kept your family in the life they were accustomed to, not to mention free in their final days, retorted her consciousness.

"But it would have sparked a devastating civil war, leaving our country vulnerable and ripe for invasion by the relentless German forces," she fumed, seething at her own relentless doubts.

It was painful to think of Germany, Alexandra's birthplace, which her adopted country, Russia, saw as an enemy. Families were at war and had been for some time. Kinships were frayed and broken between the cousins of Europe.

Will you therefore be able to rely on them in a time of need? Another thought begged her answer.

"Go away. Just go away, go away!"

"My love?"

She turned to see her husband smiling at her. He seemed relaxed. She wished she could mirror his calmness, but this was not a well-planned, post-tsarist-life retirement to the Crimea. No. The time to flee had come and gone, and instead of living the rest of their days to the fullest, they were imprisoned, under house arrest, while the new government worked out exactly what to do with them. Would it be the one to send her family for receipt of their heavenly crowns?

"The children will be ready for us shortly. I'm really not sure what it is they have in store for us. All I know is that today's performance is a short play written by Tatiana, starring all four girls, and directed by Alexei," Nicholas explained.

Alexandra could feel spite rising in her and begged it to stop, but it was too powerful for her. "Well, I'm aghast that there's something about our lives that we don't already know. What an absolute joy," she spat, and the sarcasm instantly left a nasty taste in her mouth.

The pent-up frustration was such that the words brought on an instant guttural sobbing. Nicholas said nothing; instead he wrapped his arms around her until her crying subsided.

"I'm sorry, Nikky. I'm so sorry."

"I understand, Alexandra. It's alright."

"No, that was unfair," she said as she wiped her eyes and stood back from him, noticing that he too had glistening eyes. "It's just the waiting, Nikky. No, it's the knowing and waiting, as death creeps closer. It's over a year now since your bro— your stand-in brother's signature ended over three hundred years of Romanov rule and still we're no closer to anything except civil war! And we can do nothing whilst incarcerated. Being banished to Tsarskoye Selo, then sent to Siberia for our 'safety', and now, with Lenin and his Bolsheviks imprisoning us here ..."

"At least we are together," her husband offered. "The children are in relatively good spirits under the circumstances."

She shook her head vigorously in frustration. "Whilst the children are supremely confident that sympathisers secretly plot our rescue, Nikky, you and I both know that even should that romanticised White Army theory come to fruition, the prophecies state that we have less than six months to live. It's just getting harder and harder to keep up appearances. The wooden walls the Soviets have constructed around the house to hold us in are like a coffin; a daily reminder of what's to come. I'm not even afraid of death, Nikky; in fact, I ask for it to come forth. I'm ready. Anything would be better than this ongoing purgatory."

"We are not sinners, Alexandra."

"Our sympathisers are being executed and murdered, Nikky, so perhaps we are exactly that."

"Be patient, my love," her husband urged. "Imminent danger is not readily apparent. God will remain always with us, guiding our family to what destiny he's decided to bestow. And Rasputin's threat to obliterate the Auxiliary Measure has not been realised, even with my cousin and nephew-in-law's timely, yet altogether untimely, decision to be rid of Grigori. So let us at least be happy about that. Come. The children will be waiting."

"His letter said within two years of his death, Nikky. There is still time for Grigori Rasputin to eradicate the Romanov legacy from the grave."

Alexandra knew exactly how much time. There were six more months until the monk's two-year window of threat expired. She'd thought about it every single day since Rasputin's body had been pulled, wrapped in cloth, from the freezing waters of the Neva River. Alexandra prayed for Michael and their extended family every day, asking for their forgiveness in anticipation of the monk's threat ever coming to fruition.

Their nephew-in-law had claimed responsibility for Rasputin's death, driven by the desire to showcase himself as a patriot and man of action. A man determined to protect the throne from evil influence after having heard Purishkevich's impassioned Duma speech. She knew all too well that Felix hadn't been responsible for the final bullet that rid the world of the monk; that honour belonged to the Auxiliary. But the world, including the Khlysts, thought Rasputin had died at the hands of one very noble Prince Felix Yusupov.

"Alexandra. You know I believe only love will conquer evil. Worrying will do no good. The children love you and we them, so let's use that as our strength to be rid of any mental anguish. Please come and enjoy what time we have," Nicholas encouraged again.

She had nothing left to say. It broke her heart to question her husband, and as she'd told herself many times before, who was she to question the will of the Lord. She took Nicholas' hand and let him lead her to watch whatever creative entertainment their children had come up with to pass their time imprisoned. Whilst the touch of his hand calmed her somewhat, she could not help but feel a sense of intense dread.

†

"Please wake up!" a voice called to her. "Your Imperial Majesty, we need to get the children dressed. There is impending chaos threatening Yekaterinburg. We are all being moved to safety," said the voice, who she confirmed as their doctor when she pried open her eyes.

"Get up! Now! On. Your. Feet!"

That voice was not one of her family or servants and it sprang her consciousness to attention. Guards had barged into their quarters, the frigid night air seeping through the open doors prickling her skin.

"Botkin, I told you to get everyone ready to go. I suggest you failed the task," the head guard addressed the doctor.

Dr Botkin stayed silent, his head lowered.

Nicholas reached out and placed his hand on the doctor's shoulder and stared defiantly at the guard. "There is no need for criticism, Yurovsky. We're all moving as fast as we can having only just been woken by the kind doctor."

Yurovsky grimaced but didn't retort, and Alexandra feared that his response to her husband's words would be taken out on each of them in some other way, and no doubt soon.

She hastily pulled a robe over her nightgown and rushed to Alexei, who was still weak from his most recent episode. Carefully she helped him pull on some warm clothes and did her best to maintain a smile when a bayonet dug into her kidneys from behind.

"We said get dressed, German," another of the guards whispered into her ear as he lowered the bayonet and slid up close behind her. "I'd suggest you wash first but nothing can rid you of the filth that runs under your skin, in your traitor blood."

Her German blood was boiling. She wanted to feel her husband's reassuring touch but she had been separated from him. All she could do was swallow her anger and continue to help Alexei.

"No need to be self-conscious, sweetheart," a guard sneered towards Olga, who was hesitant to get dressed while strange men were in their rooms. "Christ, if it bothers you we're here, just cover your nightgown and that pretty flesh with a coat. Or on second thoughts, perhaps leave just a little bit of flesh on show for us boys. Come on, hurry up. We need to get on the move."

Alexandra silently thanked Nicholas for moving between the guard and their daughters as they each hastily changed into daywear and fastened their coats. Having also now changed into a basic dress herself, Alexandra secured her coat as requested.

"Where are you taking us?" she heard Nicholas ask.

"To safety," offered one of the guards.

"Why? And what of our belongings?" she added as she wrapped Alexei's shoulders in a blanket and followed the guards outside into the courtyard, leaving their personal items behind.

"Can't you hear it?" another guard asked as distant artillery fire shattered the stillness of the otherwise chilled night. "As for your things, there's no time. Call your mutts if you must but the rest of your things will need to follow in due course. You are not safe here anymore."

"Maybe it is you who is not safe," Olga retorted quietly.

"Yes. Maybe people who love us come to save us," added Maria in an impassioned tone as she picked up one of their three dogs and handed it to her younger sister.

The guards sneered and looked knowingly at each other as they continued to hustle the family through the courtyard then made them double back, all whilst the children called out desperately for their other two dogs, who seemingly didn't want to be found.

As they re-entered the house, Nicholas reached out his hand to Alexandra and she to him, enabling them the briefest of touches before the family were led down to a cellar underneath their quarters.

"Wait here. We'll go and prepare what's needed," one of the guards barked before turning to leave the family alone in a state of confusion.

"We're going to go home finally, I just know it," said Tatiana as the doors closed behind the last of the guards. "Father, your loyalists come! The White Army approaches! Why else would the Soviets be so scared? Though I'm not leaving without Ortipo."

"Or me without Joy," added Alexei defiantly.

"They've no doubt gotten themselves out through the gate and into a rubbish heap somewhere," their doctor offered.

"Yes," Nicholas nodded gravely. "They'll be back before morning, and we can have them sent on to us ... wherever it is that we're heading after this cellar."

"I don't think we're going anywhere. I think it's King George coming to get us, Father. Surely, he and his men can get past these horrible Soviet guards," added Anastasia as she patted her dog Jimmy to keep him calm.

Oh my little Substitute, how wrong you are and in so many ways, Alexandra mused silently.

The room was empty but for two chairs. Alexandra settled Alexei in one of them as Nicholas listened to their daughters' romantic notions. Once their son was comfortable, she took a moment to look upon her family and then their loyal carers. All four of them were under voluntary confinement in order to serve the once Imperial Family. What was running through their minds? Had they realised that their decision to remain loyal to the throne would not reap them reward but instead leave their children at home, orphans? While not appearing overly concerned, the encroaching smell of sweat told Alexandra otherwise. All were scared.

"Tatiana, come sit with Alexei," she asked of her daughter as she herself stood and went to try the door handle. It wouldn't move, and that fact made her skin prickle once again. They were locked in. She stood still, but her mind was racing, as were her emotions. Still facing the doors, the slowly forming tear was sheltered from view. She inhaled and exhaled slowly.

Breathe.

Please, God, don't let me cry for it will alert them all to our fate, she thought to herself, blinking quickly to stem any tears. Her eyes had witnessed so much: beauty, happiness, hardship, and sadness. Visions of life.

Breathe.

This moment had been foretold.

Breathe.

Her eyes were unfocused from the threatening tears, but she could see what was in front of her with amazing clarity. Imminent and brutal death.

Breathe.

No one was coming to save them.

She moved to stand beside Nicholas and took his hand. Whispering a silent prayer, a sense of calm washed over her. Her consciousness had finally stopped its internal struggle. She knew without question that God would bless and protect the one child not with her in this underground den of despair. The world would mourn her and her family, but not for long. Three hundred years of rule had prepared the Romanovs for the perils of such a privileged life. The Red Army might rejoice, but she and Nikky would ultimately wear the final smiles on their heavenly faces when the Bolsheviks' murderous regime came to an end. The Romanovs would have their revenge, even beyond this life.

As if sensing her thoughts, Nicholas turned to her and whispered, "She will find her way home via a path of diamonds, my love."

His words bought a warmth to her heart, but before she could acknowledge him, the double doors reopened and ten or so guards entered the room.

She willed God to end things quickly. Then she braced herself. She smiled. She had led her family through a darkening atmosphere of terror and uncertainty for so long that she would not, during this final degradation, allow their enemies to see her fear.

"Where are you taking us, Yurovsky?" Nicholas demanded.

"Somewhere – well – altogether heavenly, actually. Nikolai Alexandrovich, in view of the fact that your relatives are continuing their attack on Soviet Russia, the Ural Executive Committee has decided to execute you."

"Wh-what?" Nicholas stuttered in disbelief as gasps resonated around the small room. "What?"

Yurovsky sighed with impatience. "I repeat, Nikolai Alexandrovich, in view of the fact that your relatives and your supporters, the so-called White Army, continue their attack on Soviet Russia, the Ural Executive Committee has decided that you will be executed. *Now.*"

The guards had waited for the word, and no sooner had it been spoken than a hail of gunfire ripped through the cellar.

Alexandra's hand was torn from Nicholas' as his chest exploded in a bloody mess from multiple direct hits. She fell to the ground after him, draping her body over what was left of the once most powerful man in all of Russia. She went to stand just as quickly, instinctively looking to do anything to protect her children, but slipped in the sticky Romanov blood that now seeped slowly across the floor from under her husband's body.

She felt a hand help her to her feet as the gunfire ceased, but she couldn't tell who her helper was due to the smoke in the room. Was anyone else hurt? Were the screams piercing her brain screams of fear, pain or both? Where exactly were her children?

"I'd feel bad to shoot a woman on her knees. Even you, German," said a familiar voice.

She still couldn't see, but stood as upright and defiantly as she could, her coat smothered in the remains of her beloved husband. Her last thought, as a bullet exploded from the guard's gun aimed to render her not of this world, was of the small, beautiful baby she'd so reluctantly given up all those years ago to ensure the downfall of what she now knew was called communism.

Be brave, bold and always beautiful, our Anastasia, she thought. *Follow the Path of Diamonds, for it will bring you home.*

Breathe.

The bullet pierced her skull.

Breathe.

A moment of excruciating pain.

Breathe. No more.

Chapter 5

COPENHAGEN, DENMARK, 1925

"I will not meet with her under any circumstances."

Maria knew her voice sounded harsh and that she should perhaps confide in her daughter the reasons why she continued to refuse, but there were already too many who knew: her sister, the Auxiliary, herself, all of whom were still in potential danger.

She picked up a silver photo frame from the mantlepiece that housed a picture of herself with her children. Every time she gazed upon it, her heart seemed to stop momentarily. She had outlived all four of her sons, which was the cruellest thing a parent could endure.

Sighing, she put the frame back in place. There was no telling how long their enemies would continue to hunt them. Her remaining family were still high-profile targets for socialist and anarchist assassins. Maria also knew that they should not only be afraid of radical political movements but of something much more sinister as well.

"Mother, I beg you to reconsider my request," her daughter pleaded. "No bodies have been found, none, and many whom we trust believe this woman to be legitimate. They seek our help in reaching a conclusion. Please don't give up hope after so many years."

Maria angrily spun to face her daughter, her emotions heightened by the secrets she wasn't prepared to share. How dare anyone, let alone her own daughter, suggest she'd given up hope! She prayed every day that things would realign as planned.

"I will not continue this conversation, Olga. It's all very well to feel sorry for the woman, and I do feel sorry for her, especially with covetous people out to take advantage of her. I know you've been sending her gifts, which is a ridiculous and unacceptable endorsement from our family. There is no need for you to travel to Berlin just as there is no need for me to do so. If I had any inclination that this woman may indeed be my granddaughter then I wouldn't be sitting here. I would already be by her side."

Olga pursed her lips, turned and left the room, knowing better than to argue with the woman who was once empress of all Russia.

Maria sat down heavily in her wicker armchair and stared out the window, feeling weary. The weather was turning, which didn't brighten her mood. Waves crashed violently onto the pebble beach, and people hurried along the street, reaching for umbrellas to keep themselves dry as sleety rain started to fall.

"Oh for your simple lives," she whispered, thinking of the many hours she'd spent in this exact spot since the Substitute had surfaced as a Romanov claimant. Far too much of her time had been spent sitting quietly, pondering the past and the future. How had things gone so wrong? What had become of the security her mother had convinced her to implement to safeguard against threats to the Russian throne? Would they find her real granddaughter? The Auxiliary Measure was meant to have ensured their legacy, but right now it all seemed so very, very fruitless.

"Berlin!" she scoffed, as frustration once again engulfed her. If it wasn't bad enough the woman had appeared, she'd done so in Berlin! *Dear Lord, how she despised the Germans.*

But in fairness, she did understand her daughter's desire to make the trip. God only knew Maria had been tempted many times herself to go to the woman who had unknowingly served the Imperial Family. A woman who for her entire life had believed she was Grand Duchess Anastasia.

From all accounts the woman had been left a pathetic and emaciated figure; lonely and in ill health, her body riddled with scars from that fateful night. But knowing the truth, Maria couldn't let any sympathy for her substitute granddaughter dominate her logic. No matter how much it pained her to know the woman was clinging to life and desperately trying to reclaim her identity, Maria could never have her positively identified. That would mean she'd have to explain the security measure rather than just bring her real granddaughter into power when the time was right. It would be an added complication she didn't need in such turbulent times. Hopefully she'd soon hear if the Auxiliary had been able to enact her idea to discredit the Substitute. An idea that put her family ahead of another. *Again.*

"I'm not a monster," she reassured herself, turning away from the window. She picked up another frame from the side table – a photo of Nicholas' family taken before their execution. "I've cried many times for you, child, but how in the Lord's name could you, not even related by blood, be the one to have survived and escaped?"

A gust of wind battered the window with sleet, making her jump. She lost her grip on the frame and it slipped from her grasp, its glass shattering as it hit the floor. "Dear Lord, you forsake me!" she exclaimed as she shook her head violently.

The creak of a door diverted her attention as a lady-in-waiting entered, carrying a tray with morning tea. She acknowledged the Dowager Empress with a nod, set the tray on the table, curtseyed, and cleaned up the broken frame before leaving. Maria smiled at the young woman and again silently acknowledged her nephew, George, for looking after her so well since assisting her escape from Russia. He'd become a fine leader, King of the British Empire and a fine young man. He reminded her so very much of both Nicholas and Michael. More so Michael.

Her Michael. The first Auxiliary Child. Michael had been an exceptional man.

As Maria sipped her tea, she thought about what an exemplary job he'd done seeking women with children who had similar characteristics to their family. The Substitute had aged to resemble the other three Grand Duchesses so well. They'd been lucky that one of the women identified by Michael had given birth to a girl. Of course, they'd all prayed the Tsar and Tsarina would be blessed with a boy, but with their country bubbling with revolutionary tendencies, they'd needed to move on the next child regardless of sex. And the next child had been Anastasia.

She was thankful Michael had agreed to undertake the task so she hadn't had to burden the Tsarina. Even though Maria had thought little of Alexandra, it was an unbearable thing to ask a mother to do, and to that she could attest. When Michael had been appointed the Auxiliary Child, she'd been accompanied by her sister to choose a substitute and make the swap. It had been incredibly challenging, arguably more so than for Nicholas and Alexandra, as Michael was already three when the security measure was enacted, prompted by yet another attempt on the Tsar's life. Not only were Michael's characteristics already forming but her bond with him was undeniable and unbreakable.

Unbreakable until his murder.

The memory brought bile to her throat. Michael, his daughter Kathryn and their faithful Auxiliary agent Adri had been savagely murdered seven years before, only weeks before Nicholas' execution. The real Anastasia had been missing ever since, and for the first time since the Auxiliary Measure had been created, the throne had lost control.

Maria hadn't had time to inform Nicholas of the murders before his death, and for that, upon reflection, she was glad. Her eldest son's shoulders had borne enough weight in his final tragic days, God bless his soul. He didn't need to know that his actions had incited ordinary people to become terrorists responsible for assassinations, and whose demands for change had precipitated the downfall of their entire family.

In the time since, life had been long and torturous, a time in which the Soviet Union had been formed. Like most Russian exiles, she'd not expected communism to last, certain that uprisings by those quickly growing discontented with Soviet centralism meant a counter-revolution was inevitable. When the moment arrived, no one could be more suited to restore the old order than her son's sole surviving child, the true Anastasia.

Even if a counter-revolution failed to materialise, the acknowledgement of Anastasia by the Dowager Empress and the courts as the daughter and heir of Nicholas II would undoubtedly lead to her being hailed as Russia's Empress in exile. Maria firmly believed this would be the case, regardless of the strict imperial laws of succession that stipulated a woman could not take the throne. Anastasia would stand as a symbol of what once was and what needed again to be. She would be a living martyr. That was still a legacy.

But as it stood today, all visible efforts of a counter-revolution had disappeared, as had Anastasia. Where was her granddaughter? *Where?* This was not how it was supposed to be! Maria had set up everything so well in the face of people calling for the end of the monarchy.

"By God, I need something stronger than tea," she exclaimed, placing her teacup forcefully back on the tray.

After the abdication, she insisted that the substitute Grand Duke Michael decline the throne handed to him by Nicholas. Instead, she urged him to defer accepting power until the people could vote through a constituent assembly on whether to continue the monarchy or establish a republic. Her reasons had been twofold. First, this avenue would show empathy for the will of the people. It would show them her family was fair, and she needed that lasting memory instilled in people's minds for when communism fell and the family would demand control once more. Second, she *couldn't* have him accept the throne – he wasn't even a Romanov! He was just like the woman in Berlin who'd somehow escaped the revolutionary massacre. A substitute. A fake. A necessary evil.

Picking up her tea again, she sipped it slowly, wishing it was brandy. It was soothing to her throat, but it didn't soothe her mind. As much as she'd tried to suppress them, the most heartbreaking of thoughts now raised their ugly heads and settled right at the front of her mind.

It was her fault they couldn't find Anastasia.

It was her fault her sons were dead.

It was her fault the revolution had overthrown the monarchy.

All. Her. Fault.

She was being punished. For orchestrating murder.

She willed herself not to look at the letter again. It had arrived not long before the abdication with a message written across the back of its envelope: *He warned your son, but he didn't listen. Consider yourself now duly warned as well.*

She had opted to disregard the warning, a decision that proved to be a fatal mistake. The Red Army were nothing but peasant filth, but even so, she had underestimated them.

Frustrated with herself, she stood and tore open the drawer of her writing desk. Holding the letter in both hands, she wanted to scream as his despicable face swam in front of her eyes.

She'd continued to renounce him as nothing but a voice of sin, a debauched, lecherous peasant who had once adopted the robes of a monk, developed self-gratifying doctrines and risen to influence due only to his healing hands. He may have been able to heal, but Rasputin was no saint, and he was no prophet.

How wrong she'd been.

Had her son believed Rasputin's threats? Was that why he'd not wanted to sanction an imperial death warrant, as her daughter-in-law had told her? Had she and the Tsarina sealed their family's fate, even though the monk had died at the hands of Auxiliary agents, not nobles? Was the orchestration as much the sin as physically ending Rasputin's life?

"I should just burn you!" she exclaimed in frustration and threw the envelope towards the fireplace. She didn't need to read it again. She would never be able to forget it – not a single word.

> *... Tsar of the land of Russia, if you hear the sound of the bell that tells you Grigori Rasputin has been killed, you must know this: if it was your relations who have wrought my death then no one in the family, that is to say, none of your children or relations, will remain alive for more than two years. They will all be killed by the Russian people. I go, and I feel in me the divine command to tell the Russian Tsar how he must live if I have disappeared. You must reflect and act prudently. Think of your safety and tell your relations that I have paid for them with my blood. I shall be killed. I am no longer among the living ...*

The man she'd ordered killed now hunted her family post-mortem via his lecherous peasant faithful. Her family's blood was on her hands, and if she didn't keep watch, her life may also be extinguished.

"Your Imperial Majesty, I beg your pardon. Is now a good time to speak?"

Maria turned to see an Auxiliary agent at the door to her parlour.

"Luka! Yes, come in and please, please, tell me you bring good news," she said hopefully, beckoning him to join her.

"I'm pleased to say I do. I found the Substitute's family and, most importantly, both her sisters," Luka said as he bowed.

"Oh, thank the Lord. Did you find anything we can use?"

"Again, I'm pleased to say I did," he said. "The eldest sister, Franziska, hadn't been seen or heard of since February of 1920 following a number of troubled years in and out of asylums due to a declaration of insanity."

"And you found her? Where? Alive or deceased?"

"Everything has been taken care of to our advantage. That is all you need to know. Rest assured, Franziska Schanzkowska will be a problem only for the Substitute. The world will believe that the woman lying in the hospital bed, claiming to be your granddaughter, is Franziska. I have already begun planting the idea, and the resemblance between the Substitute and her elder biological sister is so striking that I am confident the deception will hold."

Maria felt a wave of calm wash over her. If all went according to plan, the Substitute would ideally be welcomed by her true family and live out her life as a replacement for her actual older sister, who Luka had clearly removed from the picture, even if he didn't explicitly say so. Some might view such an outcome as a happy ending. If only a Romanov happy ending could also be realised.

"I appreciate your candour and your allegiance, Luka. Adri would have been proud of you." She smiled, curtseying to the young agent in an unprecedented display of gratitude and affection. "History will look upon you as fondly as I."

"Thank you, Your Imperial Majesty. Let's hope the Lord feels the same," Luka said then bowed and retreated, leaving Maria alone with her thoughts.

"Everything has been taken care of to our advantage." Luka's words swirled in her mind as she reminded herself again that everything she'd condoned served a greater purpose. Maria was certain that the Schanzkowska family would be honored at the end of their lives with the most precious rewards of Heaven.

The windows shook as a clap of thunder broke in the skies somewhere close by. The universe was unsettled, and even with Luka's news, so still was she. The resurrection of a Romanov child would be her redemption. She needed to find her real granddaughter or else go slowly insane and, quite possibly, to Hell.

Part 2

THE NOW

Chapter 6

BOSTON, USA, 2009

Alex's concentration was scattered at best, but work provided a welcome distraction from the thoughts she preferred to avoid, which constantly vied for her attention. Carefully she pulled a painting from its protective crate and placed it on an easel so she could admire it from all angles. The Elysium Art Gallery's newest collection, a broad selection of twentieth century German art, was exquisite. She could feel her focus returning as she began to think about how to best describe the piece to their patrons.

"Well, you certainly aim to manifest more than one primal emotion," she murmured as she walked around the easel admiring the artwork, a wonderful example of early German Expressionism.

She shone a small torch onto the painting, marvelling as the change in light instantly altered the ambience of the artwork and in turn her feelings towards it.

"You were born to tell multiple stories, weren't you? Dark yet slightly light. Sombre but subtly uplifting." She smiled as she noted down her initial thoughts.

She had come to love her job, something she hadn't expected when she first joined the staff. What had begun as a part-time role to provide an income while completing her PhD in literature had transformed into a fulfilling career. Over time, artists rather than authors had become her favourite storytellers. They documented history and humanity in ways that evoked individual emotions and unique narratives in the beholder. Her role was to enhance the artists' work with the written word, enticing people to the gallery to experience the pieces for themselves.

The phone lit up on her desk and she picked it up when she saw the name on the screen.

"Hi, Mum. I don't have much time. I'm on deadline for the new exhibition."

"I won't keep you long, honey. I just wanted to see if you'd be free to have dinner at ours tonight. Your dad and I would love to see you before we leave tomorrow, and I also have some things I'd like to show you."

"Sure. I should be finished up here by about six."

"Let's make it six-thirty then."

"Can I bring anything?"

"Just yourself."

As Alex ended the call, the thoughts that had desperately wanted her attention finally won. She'd been so easily able to accept her mother's invitation as there was now no need to check in with anyone about Friday night plans. There was no one to go home to anymore. Stuart had left her.

Her love. Her fiancé.

Her *ex*-fiancé.

The memory of their final conversation was so vivid that she could almost feel the warmth of the fireplace and breathe in the scent of the beautiful flowers she'd picked up on the way home from the gallery. She was positive she'd never buy roses again.

"If we put down a deposit by the end of the week, the Boston Public Library will be all ours for the first weekend in spring."

"Alex, I don't think that's going to work."

"Ah, okay. Well, the other date available is for the third weekend in July, but it will be getting really hot by then."

"Alex …"

"And if worse comes to worst, we could book for autumn, but that's pushing things out by almost another year."

"Alex. Listen to me. None of those dates are going to work."

"Why not? Surely the firm can accommodate one of them?"

"It's nothing to do with work. It's us. Me."

And with those few short words she'd known implicitly that there'd be no wedding. After having already delayed a ceremony for over two years due to Stuart's various excuses and experiencing the myriad emotions that the arguments had caused, it was all she'd needed to hear.

She hadn't asked him what he meant. Instead, quietly and calmly, she went to their bedroom, locked the door behind her, and cried herself to sleep with her faithful dog, Monte, by her side. The following morning, she slipped past him as he slept on the couch and headed to work. When she returned home that night, Stuart, along with all his belongings, was gone. It was just her, Monte, and a cheque for three months' rent.

Alex's parents had tried to convince her to join them on their trip to the Amalfi Coast, but what she really wanted was some time to reflect, relax and cry if she had to. A staycation was exactly what she needed, although she hoped she was almost over the crying. It had been nearly three months since her engagement had ended and surely there were few tears left.

"Famous last words when it comes to the heart," she muttered to herself as she sat back down at her desk.

✝

"You'll be excited, Dad," Alex teased, winking at her mum, Beth, as they sat at the dinner table.

"Why?" her father asked.

"We're looking to secure a large selection of Kandinsky pieces for our spring collection."

"I have zero interest in that ghastly, distorted, and ugly Russian art," her dad said, using air quotes to emphasise the word 'art.' "This is my cue to leave! I'll be in the office finalising our itinerary."

Alex burst out laughing, as did Beth.

"What you really mean is that you're skipping out on doing the dishes," Alex exclaimed with raised eyebrows as her dad stood and whisked himself, along with his glass of wine, to his office.

"It's lucky I like him," her mum said wryly as the two of them started to clear the table.

Alex laughed. "Yeah, he's pretty nice."

"Did Stuart leave the Kandinsky prints we brought you back from Moscow?" Beth asked softly.

Alex smiled ruefully but could feel tears threatening. "Actually, yes. I think a loathing of abstract art was the one thing he and Dad had in common."

"Come on. Let's leave the dishes and sit in the lounge. I have something to show you," Beth said, changing the subject. "Your dad can help me later once he's recovered from his Kandinsky fit."

Alex smiled and followed her mum to the living room where some papers were spread out on the coffee table.

She leaned down. "This looks more abstract than anything at the gallery."

"Well, it's not art. It's a diagnosis."

Alex stayed silent as she raised her eyes to meet her mother's.

"Dr Morgan diagnosed me with mild haemophilia. While it's not serious and can be managed with medication, it's important for you to get tested for two reasons. First, since it's genetic, testing will help determine if you carry the gene and understand how it might impact you based on its severity. Second, if you are a carrier, you should be aware that there is a possibility of passing it on to any children."

Alex sat down slowly on the couch and let the news sink in.

"Oh. Okay, I'll … I'll make an appointment to get tested while I'm on leave. Even though I don't think there'll be children for me any time soon." She paused, trying to steady her emotions at the daunting thought of being thirty-four and starting over. "I'm just relieved it's not serious for you. How did you even know to get tested for this?"

Beth sat next to her on the couch and rested a hand on Alex's knee. "You don't know what's around the corner, Alex. Someone better than Stuart may walk into your life tomorrow. Have faith."

"I know. Thanks, Mum."

"To answer your question," Beth continued, "I went into the clinic to ask some questions about my unpredictable hormones, and after a few tests, X marked the spot."

"X marked the spot?"

"The defective gene is located on the X chromosome, of which females have two and males have one. Males also possess a Y chromosome. I've learned a lot this past week."

"You certainly have."

"A female child inherits one of her mother's two X chromosomes along with the single X chromosome from her father, resulting in two X chromosomes," Beth continued. "Those who inherit the disease have one normal copy and one mutated copy of the gene.

"Okay. That makes sense."

"But there's more. The intriguing part," Beth teased.

Alex laughed. "Okay, you have me intrigued just by using the word 'intriguing'."

"I thought you would be. So, Dr Morgan still had your grandparents' medical records archived. He requested the files, and they revealed that my mum also carried the gene. It was discovered in a test she underwent not long before she died. Why she never told me I don't know."

"Old people do silly things," Alex said.

Now Beth laughed heartily. "I'd forgotten about that saying of hers. She said it a lot, mostly to excuse your grandfather's behaviour.

And speaking of Dad, his blood records were clean; he wasn't afflicted. It was definitely your grandmother who passed it on to me. Whether she got it from her mother or her father was unknown … until I spoke to Grace this morning."

Alex smiled fondly at the thought of Grace. Now in her nineties, she was the younger sister of Alex's maternal great-grandmother, Charlotte. She embodied strength and beauty, a woman rich in life experiences who served as a true inspiration to Alex. Though Alex had never met Charlotte, she felt incredibly fortunate to connect with her through Grace.

"I asked was she aware of any family history of the disorder, and she told me that her and Charlotte's father had suffered from haemophilia. He managed it well throughout his life, but he met a tragic and painful end in his early forties when a horse, spooked by a storm, kicked him in the chest. The doctors were unable to stop the bleeding, and he bled to death," Beth explained sorrowfully.

Alex gasped. "Oh, that's terrible. Why wouldn't Grace have mentioned this before?"

"I've always known how Charlotte's father died, but I never understood the reasons behind it. As for why I didn't know the details, I suppose it's because Charlotte lived in care for most of my childhood and struggled with depression. During my visits, she didn't say much, likely due to her heavy medication, and I don't recall her ever talking about her parents. Grace mentioned that the family rarely discussed their father's condition, even when he was alive. The disease was considered a social taboo back then, and they didn't want it to reflect poorly on the family."

Alex nodded and couldn't help but feel deep sorrow. It was a sad story.

"So what with X marking the spot, Grace also carries the gene?" she asked.

"That's the intriguing part," Beth teased further. "When I suggested that she get tested, she told me there was no need. About fifteen years ago, Grace had her hip reconstructed, and the doctors were concerned about the levels of bleeding during the operation. This prompted them to test for various conditions, and Grace tested negative for haemophilia. She *doesn't* carry the gene."

Alex sat quietly for a moment with her head lowered, deep in thought about what her mother had just told her. She raised it again as a realisation hit. *If Grace hadn't inherited the defective X chromosome from their father as Charlotte had done, then …*

The thought was overwhelming, and it explained why in the few photos Alex had seen of them together, Charlotte and Grace were distinctly different.

"Oh my God … Grace and Charlotte have different fathers?"

Her mum sighed. "Exactly. Our entire family tree branching back from whomever Grace's real father was is now a complete unknown."

Alex sat stunned. "Are you going to tell Grace?" she eventually asked.

Beth shook her head. "I'm torn. Grace has lived a long life, and suddenly turning everything upside down feels overwhelming. I mean, imagine discovering that everything you thought you knew about your life was only a half-truth … I don't want to dim the sparkle in Grace's eyes any faster than age will."

Alex contemplated her mother's words. She recognised the upheaval it might cause, but she felt they had a responsibility to let Grace know about their discovery. A comprehensive medical evaluation could uncover any health issues that may have been inherited from her biological father and were currently unknown.

She crossed the room and picked up a family photo taken the previous Christmas, her gaze drawn to one cousin in particular. Turning to her mother, her resolve strengthened as she held out the photo.

"Chloe's pregnant, Mum. Eight weeks. She hasn't told the entire family yet."

Beth gasped before a look of delight spread across her face.

"I hate to spoil the surprise, but what if there's an issue with the baby because of what we now know? We have a responsibility to inform Grace. If the roles were reversed and Charlotte wasn't who we thought she was, we'd want the family to tell us. Why don't I talk to Grace while you're away? I have the time."

Beth sat in silence for a moment before standing up, beckoning for Alex to follow her back to the kitchen. "Let's talk about your approach while we wash those dishes. If I wait for your father to help, they'll sit there the entire time we're on the Amalfi."

Chapter 7

BOSTON, USA

Grace had been sitting in a quiet, anxious reverie for some time, her thoughts swirling as she awaited the arrival of her beloved great-grandniece. The topic Alex wished to discuss sent shivers down her spine and a dull ache through her body. She rubbed the tops of her hands slowly, hoping to stimulate her circulation; the gentle circles mirrored the turmoil in her mind. Having sworn to take their family secret to the grave, she now found herself grappling with the unsettling question of whether to break that promise.

She shook her head in disbelief. Her sister, Charlotte, may have had more in common with the man they had both called father than she'd ever thought imaginable. There had been a time when Grace would never have questioned the commonality between them, but that was before she'd found out the secret.

Their family history was a façade, and she was the last surviving custodian of a reality that differed vastly from the narrative presented to the world.

She endeavoured to slow her breathing. Every breath these last few weeks had felt like it could be her last. The question was, what would she do with her last breaths? Was it even important anymore to keep history twisted in secrecy? Those she had promised to, those she had most loved and who had loved her like their own, were now long gone, and it wasn't even a devastatingly huge secret.

She sighed. For her, it was the principle. *She'd promised.*

A gentle breeze fluttered through the curtains and brushed against her face, pulling her out of her thoughts. She realised she was staring out the window just as both her mother and Charlotte had done in the last years of their lives, day after day, each deep in contemplation and pain.

"There but for the grace of God go I," she whispered.

She wanted the pain to stop. She wanted the truth to be told. What their mother had told them when Grace came of age had not diminished the love either she or Charlotte felt for their parents. Now, so many years later, in a world that judged things quite differently, Grace felt it was her duty to share their story. It was one of love, not a sordid tale of impropriety.

And so, she decided. The story would be told.

The relief that flowed through her having made the decision was cathartic, but then her breath caught upon itself. There was still the other secret. A secret that was in no way romantic. A secret that tore at her soul. A secret she'd always borne alone.

"Dear God, you know I thought it was the right thing to do," she whispered as she ran her hand gently over a picture of Charlotte sitting peacefully in the gardens at Meadow Oaks. "It was the right thing to do to keep you safe, sister."

It had all happened quickly, much like their mother's decline, but Charlotte's mental deterioration had been markedly different. Before their mother's eventual passing, she had endured years of silence and the physical degeneration that accompanied her senility. In contrast, Charlotte had suffered in a frenetic haze, with only medication able to keep her calm.

It still pained Grace to think about it. The decline had begun less than a year after their mother died, coinciding with the untimely passing of Charlotte's husband. In an attempt to cope with her grief, Charlotte had decided to travel abroad, which Grace had thought was a wonderful idea. An endless summer on the European continent would surely do her sister good – or so Grace had hoped.

The call had been confronting.

"There was an incident … the authorities were called. I've been tasked to chaperone your sister home to the United States, and I must inform you that she's been medicated for her own safety."

God bless Nurse Evelyn. She'd been there from the start and was there to the very end of Charlotte's battle with her inner demons.

Instead of returning home brimming with stories about sipping fine champagne along the Champs-Élysées or browsing the exquisite fashions and linens of Savile Row, Charlotte had been committed to Meadow Oaks Asylum. With the blessing of Charlotte's daughter, Elsie, Grace had signed the paperwork for her sister's treatment. She was desperate to curb Charlotte's sudden manic behaviour, which manifested in erratic, disjointed and frightening tales about things she claimed to have uncovered regarding her past.

A past before she was Grace's sister.

A past Charlotte had only unearthed by breaking her word. She had promised their mother, the memory of their father and Grace that their family story would always begin the day they set foot on American soil. Anything before that was to be kept secret to protect their reputation. Charlotte was not one to break her promises. But she had, and so had their mother.

"That damned letter," Grace whispered with such force that it surprised even herself.

"Grace, your mother's letter is nothing but the words of a confused mind. Coupled with grief, it's acted as a catalyst to speed up Charlotte's own decline," Nurse Evelyn had counselled. *"Even without the letter, it is my professional opinion that Charlotte would have succumbed to the same illness as your mother only a short time thereafter. You must be sure to watch for signs of this yourself."*

Grace hadn't shared the letter, not even with Elsie, and their family story had remained intact, just as she'd promised it would. But here she was, for all the right reasons, about to break the same promise she'd been so angry that her loved ones had broken.

She now wondered if she had made the right decision all those years ago in assuming that her mother's letter and Charlotte's stories were merely manifestations of their respective illnesses, as Nurse Evelyn had diagnosed. Could the letter have been written by a woman of sound mind rather than one whose mental state was rapidly deteriorating? Could Charlotte have been telling the truth about what she claimed to have learned while in Europe? Had Grace committed her sister to an asylum and then suppressed evidence that might have proved her sanity, all to uphold a promise that others had already deemed worth breaking?

Deep down, Grace knew the answer was 'perhaps,' and as she acknowledged this to herself, a guttural sob escaped her. Yes, the claims about their past, before they became her family, could have been true. As unsettling as that possibility was, Grace understood that Charlotte's family deserved to know the whole truth. There were two potential outcomes to sharing Charlotte's stories: a family fully informed about the extent of their mental illness or a family reborn.

She dabbed at her eyes with a tissue. The only thing she really knew for certain was that it was too late to help her sister, who had never returned home from Meadow Oaks. God bless her soul. God bless her own.

✝

For some time now, Alex and Grace had been sitting quietly, sipping tea. The only indication that something was amiss was the whisky that Alex could taste added to the camomile. Grace was understandably anxious following what she'd learned about her father. Alex desperately hoped she hadn't made a mistake by sharing the information.

"Grace, I'm—"

"The story I'm going to share with you, Alex, is one I like to think of as a love story, albeit underpinned by undeniable tragedy," Grace interrupted.

Alex swallowed her words and listened intently.

"I feel it's time to tell the truth before I no longer can," Grace continued, smiling sadly, her eyes brimming with tears. "Charlotte and my family history is a charade and one that I've helped to perpetuate. I'm so sorry dear."

It tore at Alex's heart to see Grace in such turmoil, so she reached out and took her hand, giving it a gentle squeeze. "You don't have to be sorry for anything, Grace."

"Oh, but you see I do," Grace said, slowly pulling her hand away and lowering her eyes. "The man the world knew as my father wasn't, that much you've deducted, but please forgive me when I tell you also that neither was he Charlotte's."

Grace's words caused Alex's heart to momentarily pause, and her skin prickled with anticipation. She'd been riddled with trepidation about having shared what could only be described as history-changing facts, but what Grace had just told her was far more sensational.

"You're aware we all migrated from England due to our loved ones being killed in the war that the Germans inflicted upon our homeland, but we weren't a family unit until we arrived on American soil. Oh my goodness, Alex. Where to start?"

"I'm not sure, but I think we might need another cup of tea … perhaps with extra whisky," Alex said as she reached for the teapot and refilled both their cups.

"Let's start with me. That might be easiest," Grace continued, raising her face to look into Alex's eyes, her resolve seemingly strengthening.

"So, the man I always knew as my father, Andrew Thornton, was actually my biological uncle. My biological mother was his sister, who, along with their parents – my biological grandparents –

and Andrew's wife, was killed when a bomb devastated their home during a German air raid on London in May of 1918."

Alex's hand instinctively moved to her heart in astonishment.

"At that time, my mother and I were living with my grandparents as my father had been killed in battle in France and his parents had already passed away. Andrew and my aunt had come to visit, and while he was checking on me in the nursery at the back of the house, the bomb struck without warning. Inexplicably, he and I both survived the attack while the rest of the family perished. They found the two of us unharmed; only a portion of the roof directly above us and the wall behind my crib remained intact."

"Oh, Grace. That's unbelievably sad. I'm so very sorry," Alex said, feeling the threat of tears.

"It's okay, Alex. I was just a baby, far too young to remember any of it, and God always has his reasons. My uncle became a father to me, and I loved him so much. He also bestowed upon me a beautiful new mother and sister, Josephine and Charlotte."

"And how did you all come to meet?" Alex asked.

"Thanks to a ship's infirmary!" Grace exclaimed. "While sailing from England to start a new life in America, my fath— sorry, my uncle … Perhaps I'll just refer to him as Andrew to keep it simple … He had to be cautious with his illness. Though his haemophilia was mild, he regularly had doctors examine any bruises as a precaution, especially since he had me, his orphaned young niece, to care for. I wasn't even one, and he had little experience in looking after a child. Oh, and by the way, Andrew's haemophilia was purely coincidental and unrelated to Charlotte's condition."

Grace paused to take a mouthful of tea. She seemed less anxious, and Alex could only assume that the sharing of such a long-held secret would be somewhat of a release.

"Charlotte, the poor thing, fell gravely ill with influenza shortly after boarding, so she was admitted for treatment and ongoing observation," Grace continued. "Her father, Josephine's husband, was yet another of England's fine young men taken too soon by the war. They had no other family, and like Andrew and me, America offered them a fresh start. We adopted each other as family, and the infirmary became a place of lasting friendships."

"So out of tragedy came love."

Grace shook her head. "I use the word 'friendships' very deliberately, Alex. They loved each other dearly, but Andrew and Josephine were never married and nor were they lovers. They forged a bond underpinned by their individual grief and agreed to help each other start a new life here in America. Andrew needed help to care for me, and Josephine and Charlotte needed a home. So whilst I used the word 'adopted', it wasn't ever official. People assumed our parents were married, and they didn't correct that misconception. Regardless of their intent, society at that time frowned upon an unmarried couple living together."

Alex breathed in deeply, gathering the thoughts swirling in her mind. "So why keep all this a secret, Grace?" she asked. "To your point, people's views are very different today and have been for some time. Josephine and Charlotte both lived into the 1960s, and if there was one thing that wasn't frowned upon in that decade it was free love!"

"Oh, the sixties! That truly was a wonderful time to be alive. Yes, you're right; there was a significant shift in attitudes toward marriage and relationships during that era. However, it wasn't really until the turn of the century that living together before marriage became the norm rather than the exception. That's less than a decade ago, Alex, and by then, I was the only one left. I made a promise, and I chose to keep it," Grace said.

"Until now," Alex said gently.

"Yes, until now. Even as I share the truth with you, part of me still worries if I am doing the right thing. When Josephine revealed the truth, not long after Andrew died, Charlotte and I promised each other that this story would remain between us. I swore I would never tell. We loved our makeshift family so much and didn't want anyone to speak ill of our parents or, worse, label Charlotte and me as illegitimate children, a stigma that would have severely limited our marriage prospects at the time. We collectively decided that we would always, always remain the family that everyone believed we were the day we stepped off that ship onto American soil."

Another question was niggling at Alex.

"Grace, as much as it's obviously hurting you to break your promise after all this time, it really is a beautiful story. I can't help wondering though, why was it news to Charlotte? You were a baby and too young to remember anything about England, but Charlotte wasn't. She was eleven years older than you."

Grace nodded. "Remember I mentioned that Charlotte was sick during the ship's journey? The truth is, she almost didn't make it to America. Apparently, she drifted in and out of a feverish state for weeks, and as she slowly recovered, it became clear that she remembered little about the journey and nothing of her biological father's death or her life in England. It took her some time to reconnect with Josephine, and she unknowingly accepted Andrew as her father, just as I did. Even once we were informed, her memories didn't surface until much, much later. And that's a whole other story."

Grace stood and then bent down carefully to reach underneath the coffee table. A tear escaped her eye as she manoeuvred a beautifully carved wooden box, its corner edges protected by embossed gold, onto the floor in front of Alex.

"I chose not to believe it's real gold just as I chose not to believe the authenticity of the box's contents," she whispered. "I hope you choose to forgive me if you decide otherwise, Alex."

Alex admired the box. Whatever it was that it represented, it seemed to deeply unsettle Grace. Alex reached out to offer Grace the comfort of her hand once again, which acted as a catalyst for Grace's tears to fall.

"I'm so sorry, Alex. To you, your mother, Elsie, and most of all to Charlotte."

"It's going to be okay, Grace. Would you like me to come back another time and let you rest a little?"

"No. Please stay. I need to confess," she said, her voice dropping to a whisper. "I may have had Charlotte committed to Meadow Oaks as mentally deficient when there was a possibility that she wasn't."

Alex sat silently digesting what had been disclosed and Grace looked at her forlornly before opening the box. "These were Charlotte's only remaining personal possessions when she died. I want you to have them, Alex," she said, firstly handing her what appeared to be a very old envelope. "This is a letter from Josephine to Charlotte. She wrote it as she neared the end of her life and left it with our family lawyers, who were instructed to give it to Charlotte only after Josephine had passed. I thought it riddled with stories underpinned by senility, but I could have been wrong. The contents set Charlotte on a path to uncover her life before we became sisters, and the stories she discovered convinced me to sign her admission to Meadow Oaks.

At a loss about what to say, Alex continued to watch on quietly as Grace removed another item, her hands shaking.

"And this is an astonishingly beautiful piece of replica Fabergé that Josephine left my sister. A Clover Egg. Where she got it from I have no idea."

"It's magnificent," Alex exclaimed, her voice coming back as Grace handed the delicate artwork to her. Shards of light bounced around the room, sparkling off the intricate shell. From what Alex could see, the egg's shape was formed by tiny golden threads that created a simple pattern of clover stems and leaves. All but a few of the clovers were green, the remaining selection embossed with white stones like diamonds, while in amongst the leaves curled a very thin golden ribbon paved with red stones.

"What I know for certain is that the letter unquestionably came from Josephine's hand. It references her and Charlotte's life in England. I have never doubted its authenticity," Grace continued. "As I mentioned before, what I have always questioned are its contents."

"So the mistake you think you might have made is believing the content was a manifestation of Josephine's illness rather than the truth? Is that correct?" Alex asked.

Grace nodded solemnly. "There was apparently another letter that Josephine mentioned, from her husband – Charlotte's father – but I've never seen it. That's one reason I believed what Josephine wrote was merely a fabrication of a very ill woman's mind. However, Charlotte believed it and sought to uncover more without my guidance, which ultimately led her into her own downward spiral."

"Without having read the letter, I can see how many might make that assumption."

"It would put my mind at rest to know the truth of whether I was right or wrong, Alex."

"I'm very happy to look into it. Regardless of everything else, I have a new great-great-grandfather to learn about."

"Yes, of course," Grace said wearily. "Read it when you get home. I think I do need to rest now. I can't drink whisky tea like I used to."

Alex laughed softly as she stood to leave. "I will. Thank you for trusting me with this, Grace."

"I understand that you'll want to share the story of how our family came to be with your mum, but can I trust you not to mention the letter until we know more? I would hate to upset everyone if it turns out I was right," Grace said, her voice almost pleading.

"You have my word," Alex said and thanked her lucky stars her mum had already flown halfway round the world.

Chapter 8

MASON, USA

"So much for rest and relaxation," Alex had remarked to Monte as she stepped out the front door for the nearly hour-long drive to New Hampshire. Despite the twinge of sadness at leaving Monte behind, she was excited about visiting the place where her great-grandmother had spent her final days.

So much ivy had weaved itself around the cast-iron fence that Alex almost missed the entrance sign. She couldn't miss the buildings though. Meadow Oaks was a foreboding edifice, its large heritage sandstone buildings set on acres of lush grounds that backed onto dense woodland.

Glancing at the time as she pulled into a parking spot, she realised the general office was still closed for the lunch period and didn't open again for another ten minutes. Rather than an annoyance, it allowed Alex time to collect her thoughts. So many thoughts. The most pressing being the letter from Josephine.

"I need to read you again," she said as she gently removed the worn and fragile paper from the envelope Grace had given her. Her emotions were heightened just as they'd been the day before when

Grace had revealed its existence with so much remorse and begged tearfully for forgiveness.

Hello my love.

I don't know how long it will be before you read these words, but I do know that it will be after I've left you. In fact, according to my doctors, I've already begun to leave you. Dementia. What a horrific thing it is to know that slowly I will forget everything I've ever been taught and everyone I've ever loved. I'm not sure they fully understand what's wrong with me, but I agree with them that something is most definitely not right. I am not myself. Perhaps that is because you and I have not been able to be ourselves for a very long time.

I want you to know how proud I've always been of you. You have grown into a wonderful young woman and, in particular, your love for Grace is envied by all who know us. The maturity you showed when I told you and your sister the truth about our family's past was a proud moment to behold.

Charlotte, I ask you to draw on that same strength now as I have more to tell you, and it will be difficult at first to understand. I don't tell you this from my grave because of cowardice. I do so as once I'm with God, should you choose to pursue the information I provide, I can look down on you in what I hope may offer heavenly protection. I also know that with time comes maturity and life experiences that will enable you to have empathy for my decisions.

Before I go on, I ask you to find it in your heart to forgive me, for I, like you, were but a pawn in the deception that came to be. My decisions have always been guided by what I believed to be in your best interest, even when it resulted in a double deception being imposed upon you. Charlotte, I am not your biological mother.

Breathe, my darling. I do not love you any less. I didn't know your mother, nor did I know of her, but I know with all my heart that I loved your father. Very, very much. When I accepted his love,

I accepted that you came with him, and I have always loved you as my own. It was my love for the both of you that has kept you safe from harm, and it was your father's love for you that saw him sacrifice himself to ensure you're able to read these words today. He was a soldier, Charlotte, just as I have told you, and he did die in a war, that much is true. The war, however, was not between power-hungry countries as I've always led you to believe. It was a war between good and evil.

Charlotte, God truly blessed you by taking away your memory of that time, but it may one day again serve you, and I pray that when it does, you'll remember all the love and none of the final farewell between what was once our loving family. Danger in the most serious of forms partnered our goodbye, so much so that I changed our names and birthdates for protection. Never, ever since that time have I looked back for fear of losing more of our family here or in our homeland. However, now that I can no longer protect you in person, it is up to you to decide if you wish to seek the truth.

Your father's name wasn't William, it was Edward, and our family name was Burton-Hall. Before I married your father, I was an only child to Phillip and Ingrid Scot and was known as Hannah. My parents will have assumed me dead long before I let God take my hand. I knew your father's parents as Henry and Ruby Burton-Hall, but I suspect that this too may have been an illusion. You, my beautiful girl, went by the name Victoria and had another sister, my biological child with Edward. Her name was Kathryn. She was a beautiful, charismatic girl who you were once connected to as closely as you are to Grace today. You do have some memory of Kathryn as for many years you would speak her name in your sleep.

Kathryn and Edward were both casualties of war, a war that I know little about other than what your father gave us the last night we saw him. I include his letter within.

I have read his words over and over to the point of obsession, but I have never been willing to risk your safety in order to explore further the secrets that he alludes to or retrieve the letter that still waits for you to open in the rotunda at our once home. Forgive me if that is selfish, Charlotte, but my only priority has been to keep us safe from those who took Edward and Kathryn from us.

 You have my blessing, and it is now up to you to do what I never could, should you choose. Seek the truth to why your father and sister died. Seek the truth to your past. It is what your father wanted and is the one thing in which I failed him. I beg God for forgiveness every day, and if you are reading this letter, still breathing with life, it will mean that I have been pardoned by the Lord.

I love you.

Your mother,
Hannah Burton-Hall

Even after reading the letter multiple times, Alex found the content overwhelming. It was evident that Charlotte had chosen to uncover the truth about her life as Victoria, but any discoveries she may have made remained shrouded in mystery. The words of Charlotte's real father, Edward – which Josephine, whose real name was Hannah, claimed to have included with her letter – were equally enigmatic. They were missing. Was the absence of any other written correspondence a sign that Josephine was not mentally sound, as Grace believed? Or had Edward's words simply been lost to time?

Alex didn't have time for further contemplation. The Meadow Oaks office doors were once again open for business. Hopeful that the missing letter may by some chance still be in her great-grandmother's files, she headed inside.

At the end of an elegant entrance foyer, the office was lush with decadent furnishings. It struck Alex as an overcompensation for the sadness and necessary barrenness that no doubt would be found in the wards further inside the building.

"Good morning," a nurse welcomed her as she approached the desk.

"Morning. My name's Alex Ashmore and I'm hoping I can talk to someone about my great-grandmother who was a patient here," she responded.

"Of course, Alex. I can help with that. What was your great-grandmother's name?"

"Charlotte Charles. She was a patient here quite some time ago – 1962 through to 1968. I'm hoping someone can review her records and tell me if any of her possessions, specifically letters, may have inadvertently been kept in her file instead of being passed on to her family."

"I can certainly look for you, Ms Ashmore," the nurse confirmed. "I'll first need to see some ID, then I'll have you fill in this form with your contact details. I'll also need you to confirm your great-grandmother's full name and year of birth, please."

Alex provided the details requested and waited patiently as the nurse entered the information into her computer.

"Can you please confirm those details again for me?"

"Charlotte Charles. 1906."

"Hmmm. That's what I thought you said. That being the case, I'm sorry, Ms Ashmore, I don't have good news for you. Our records indicate that Charlotte Charles had no next of kin. As such, I'm not authorised to share any information with you."

Stunned, Alex stared at the nurse in disbelief. "Well, that's impossible," she finally said.

"I'm sorry, Ms Ashmore, but that's what our records state. Charlotte Charles, born in 1906. No next of kin."

"Okay." Alex nodded as a thought came to her. "Could I trouble you to please try Thornton? Charlotte Thornton. Perhaps she was admitted under her maiden name as her husband had passed away by the time she needed care. Perhaps who you have on file is a different Charlotte Charles."

"I very much doubt we'd have two Charlotte Charles in our system, particularly with the same birth year, but yes, I can try

Thornton," said the nurse, seemingly annoyed at Alex's line of questioning. She tapped on the keyboard then shook her head. "I'm sorry, we have no record of a Charlotte Thornton, and I can also confirm no other Charlotte Charles for that matter."

"Does the file for Charlotte Charles at least state that she had a sister? Grace – Grace Myers," Alex pressed. "Grace co-signed Charlotte's admittance papers."

Slowly the nurse shook her head. "I really am sorry, Ms Ashmore, but the records list Charlotte as a widow with no other family. When she passed, her few personal belongings, as per her instruction, were distributed by her primary carer, Evelyn Forster, who was also the one to sign her admittance paperwork."

"Yes, Charlotte's sister, Grace, mentioned a Nurse Evelyn to me. That must be her file, but an error's obviously been made."

"There are rarely errors made at Meadow Oaks, Ms Ashmore," the nurse said sternly.

Alex could feel her face flush. "*Rarely* is the word I'm going to focus on then, Nurse … Jenson," she said, reading the woman's name badge. "Tell me, if I'm able to provide you with documentation that proves lineage from Charlotte to myself, would that constitute evidence of a Meadow Oaks error and enable me to access her records?"

"Yes, of course. I've noted your details on Ms Charles' file for when you're able to provide what's required. Once I review the information verifying the relationship, and if it confirms that an error has been made, I can take your case to the board. You can expect a one-month wait at best."

Sensing she wasn't going to get any further today, Alex thanked the nurse and made her way back to her car. Thoughts raced through her mind. *How could Charlotte's records not state the existence of Grace or Charlotte's own daughter, Elsie?* Alex had seen photos of both women on the grounds of the institution as well as photos of her mum as a young girl with Charlotte at Meadow Oaks.

They existed. Alex existed. None of them would without Charlotte.

She sighed. What an anticlimax the visit had been, but perhaps the fact it would take a month to get her great-grandmother's records, meant that she could relax for the rest of her week off as initially intended. As she contemplated how nice that was going to be, the box Grace had passed on to her caught Alex's attention. Sitting on the passenger seat, its gold-embossed corners sparkled in the sun.

"And this is an astonishingly beautiful piece of replica Fabergé that Josephine left my sister. A Clover Egg. Where she got it from I have no idea," Alex recalled Grace explaining.

Alex knew of Fabergé, his work having become known as a style of its own, but she'd never studied it in any depth, and she wished now that she had. But perhaps a quick call could get her up to speed. Alex knew that Elysium's curator, Jonathan, had a particular fondness for enamel pieces, a material cherished by Fabergé. Given Jonathan's expertise, he might be able to provide valuable insights to determine if the replica egg was connected to the alternate past that Josephine alluded to.

"Alex!" Jonathan exclaimed as he picked up her call. "You're meant to be on leave! Therefore, unless it's an emergency, I'm going to hang up and let you relax."

"Well, this is an emergency. An artwork emergency," Alex teased.

He laughed. "Then how can I help? Oh, and while I have you, not an emergency but Nate from the Guggenheim called and confirmed they're going to loan us the selection for the Kandinsky collection!"

Alex loved his enthusiasm. "Well, my dad for one will be thrilled about the Kandinsky coup. But I called because I'm hoping you can tell me all you know about the House of Fabergé."

"Oh, I could talk about Carl Fabergé and his sublime work all day. How long do you have?"

Alex put her phone on speaker. "I've got a one-hour drive. Go."

Chapter 9

BOSTON, USA

Evelyn answered her phone, never taking her eyes off the text blinking on the computer screen.

Two words repeatedly flashed. Auxiliary Alert.

It was the first time those words had notified her of trouble in decades and, despite her age, she felt her training override any weariness.

The voice on the other end of the phone was well known to her.

"An alert has been raised. Her file has been requested."

"Family or foe?"

"Family."

"Direct or peripheral?"

"Direct."

"Elizabeth or Alex?"

"The latter. She was enquiring about any personal letters that might still be stored in Charlotte's files. Why, I don't know."

Evelyn was stunned into silence as she took in the Patriarch's words and read the same detail on her computer. Before she could question him further, the Patriarch continued.

"After this long and with the resurrection so within reach, you cannot afford for anything to happen to her or for her enquiries to cause others to question what's been contrived. The R.A. cannot find out. Not now. They will hunt her down and sacrifice her as they did her ancestors."

Evelyn was well aware of that.

"When did this happen?" she asked.

"No more than ten minutes ago. You need to eliminate any threat and keep her safe."

"I understand."

"I certainly hope so. The Pascha meeting is still two months away and I'm going to need all that time to gather enough support. I can't move any sooner, Evelyn. Ten years' work culminating with the reveal of the child will see us once again prevail. We cannot afford our trump card becoming the downfall of the faith."

She wasn't aware they were vying to exert control or power over other religions, and the Patriarch's words disturbed her immensely.

"The Auxiliary don't consider the child a trump card, Your Holiness. Rather she's the enlightenment our mother country needs, and people of all faiths will celebrate her. She will reignite the people's faith in Christ and his ability to conquer evil regardless of one's religious affiliation. And, with all due respect, this has been ninety years in the making, not just the ten years since your predecessor commenced strategic government liaisons, God rest his soul. The fact that the Orthodox Church with you at its helm will be the hero of this 'resurrection' should be considered purely an extraordinary windfall, not a right to secure religious dominance over the Russian people."

"Fix it, Evelyn."

The phone went dead.

"What, pray God, sent you to Meadow Oaks, Alex?" Evelyn wondered. Her head spun trying to comprehend the debacle that had unfolded. *What had she missed?* She'd been so very careful, and for so many years, to ensure the safety of the family under her watch.

She had to fix this problem and do so quickly. This was her life quest – her family's life quest – and her martyrdom was dependent on finishing the task given to her when she'd come of age.

Realisation suddenly hit. *Grace. It had to be.* The Patriarch said that Alex had visited Meadow Oaks to ask about personal letters. That would only have become a possibility by Grace having shared Josephine's letter, in doing so breaking the promise she'd said she would never ever break. The promise to keep her family secret intact.

Evelyn stood up from her desk and paced the room in frustration. Where would this unexpected turn of events lead them?

"Two more months, we only had to get through two more months!" she muttered.

Despite her frustration, Alex's interest in her family history warmed Evelyn's heart. However, that warmth quickly faded as memories of Charlotte and Meadow Oaks resurfaced. The weight of having influenced Grace and Elsie to commit their loved one under the guise of mental illness was heavy to bear. While it was absolutely necessary to keep Charlotte hidden from her enemies, it meant that the Auxiliary Child spent her remaining days confined to the asylum and, ultimately, within her own mind.

Stopping to stand in front of a mirror, Evelyn studied her reflection, willing herself to calm. Each line on her face seemed more pronounced of late, but she didn't mind. She knew too well that God didn't bestow the privilege of aging on everyone, including so many of her loved ones who had also served the Auxiliary.

Loss aside, it was a privilege to serve as an agent of the Auxiliary, a belief Evelyn held with as much fervour today as when she was anointed on her thirteenth birthday. Her grandparents, Luka and Yelena, had been the original driving force behind the agency. Plucked from an orphanage, they were promised a family among those chosen to protect the Imperial Family. Their unwavering love for their country, Orthodoxy and the church's Holy Ones was profound – 'thou shalt not kill' morphed into 'thou shalt not kill except for the enemies of God'. After a car accident claimed their parents' lives, their grandparents took them in as young children, and this mantra became Evelyn's as well as her sister's guiding principle. Or so she assumed.

Evelyn had not seen her older sister, Irina, since her infiltration into the R.A., an underground political movement dedicated to Stalin. Named for the Workers' and Peasants' Red Army that had been integral in bringing Russian imperialism to its knees, many of the R.A. founders were known to have been part of the original Red Army, disbanded after the Second World War. The Auxiliary believed the R.A. responsible for the assassination of Grand Duke Michael and his daughter Kathryn in retribution for the death of Grigori Rasputin.

Evelyn involuntarily shuddered at the thought. The cruelty of the people who had become her sister's life and who Irina had been trained to mimic was unparalleled.

It was hard to imagine Irina now, aged sixty-five. They'd been teenagers the last time they'd been face to face.

Evelyn vividly remembered that day. Two sisters clinging together in a hotel room, saying goodbye to the life they'd always known. It was the last time either of them would go by the names given to them at birth. Evelyn had said goodbye to being Mila, and Irina had said hello to being Anya.

"Irina, are you excited?"

"Mila, go and help Babushka," her grandfather told her.

"But I want to hear about the R.A."

"This is Irina's mission, not yours, Mila. Your time will come."

"Please, Deda. How else will I learn?" she pleaded.

"Okay, you can stay, but please be quiet," he told her before reaching out his hand and passing Irina a photograph. "Who is this?"

"Vladimir Lenin."

"And who is this?" he asked, passing her another.

"Joseph Stalin."

"Who are they?" he said, pointing at both photos.

"Communists."

"Right, but wrong," he said, eyebrows raised and with a tilt of his head.

"Heroes. My heroes."

Their grandfather nodded. "In what year was the R.A. established and why was it formed?"

"1957, in response to Khrushchev's Secret Speech that acted as a precursor for de-Stalinisation."

"Good. Why are you angry about de-Stalinisation?"

"Because it wrongs a man who showcased iron discipline and tore down greedy religious and parliamentary bureaucrots—"

"Bureaucrats."

"Sorry, yes, bureau … crats who defied authority," Irina said.

"Try it again."

"Because it wrongs a man who showcased iron discipline and tore down greedy religious and parliamentary bureaucrats who defied authority."

"Good girl. What are your religious beliefs?"

"As a firm believer in Stalin, I am an atheist, free of any religious chains that may bind me to class oppression." Irina paused to take a sip of water. "Deda, I don't really understand what that means."

"It's okay, Irina – sorry, I should call you Anya. You'll learn more and more every day once you're amongst them. You know enough now for any fifteen-year-old with a passion. If you're too polished, this will fail. You're doing well. You remind me so much of your mother today. I'm so proud of you …"

Evelyn's attention refocused on the mirror and she smiled sadly, remembering the reference her grandfather had made. Knowing how much their grandfather missed his daughter, the compliment had been especially heartfelt.

Sitting back at her desk, she rested her head in her hands. Her mind was brimming with so many secrets, and her stomach tightened in knots as she thought of a particularly sensitive one that involved her having kept information from the Auxiliary. A secret between just Evelyn and her sister. A secret that had the potential to bring down their plans to reinstate the heir.

The Auxiliary had not had any insight into the R.A. for a long time. Irina had gone radio silent ten years ago. Just after she killed Evelyn's husband.

Their last call had been confronting. Evelyn's beloved husband, Richard, had been killed during his attempt to extract Irina from the R.A., along with evidence gathered during her infiltration of their inner sanctum. Evidence that would render the R.A. exposed and held responsible for their misdeeds. To be more specific, Irina had murdered Richard in order to maintain her cover.

Her sister hadn't told Evelyn what had happened. She hadn't needed to. The fact Irina had cried during their final conversation told Evelyn that Irina had taken Richard's life. Something had gone desperately wrong. Neither her husband or her sister had come home, and Irina had remained undercover in the R.A. as Anya.

Irina had insisted that's how it must be. She would remain undercover until the very end, and only when they had fulfilled the mission to return a Romanov to the Russian throne would she once again become Irina. She'd made Evelyn promise not to report the failed extraction to the Patriarch for fear of him sending Evelyn to extract her. She would not lose her sister. Finally, they had agreed on the story that Richard had died following a mugging in a dark and damp Russian alleyway, not far from the known headquarters of the R.A.

As much as it hurt, Evelyn had forgiven her sister for Richard's death.

In the ten years since their last conversation, Evelyn had submitted reports to the Patriarch, pretending they were from Irina. Some things between sisters needed to remain secret to ensure the best outcome for the Auxiliary's cause, which was to guarantee no further loss of Auxiliary life. The R.A. could not discover Irina was not one of them.

Wishing things were different, then asking God for his forgiveness, Evelyn ran her hand gently over the cover of a book on her desk. Whilst they hadn't spoken, she and Irina had communicated. Twice yearly and always timely. Every six months, the gift of a book arrived to confirm that Irina was still alive. Basic invisible ink and a simple code indicated the same words on each occasion, placed immediately under the author's credit: *I'm alive.* No frills. Very Irina. Anything Evelyn had to communicate she'd done by returning the book, writing on the back of the return receipt using the same invisible ink and code.

Evelyn closed her eyes and let her hand settle on the book. Her fingers shook ever so slightly.

It had now been almost eight months since the last gift.

†

Will slipped quickly into his car as Alex approached her home. He smiled, watching as she bent down to pat a dog that had come bounding outside. As Alex encouraged the animal back inside and closed the front door behind them, Will reclined back in his seat to wait and watch.

It was his fifth week of watching Alex's every move at his mother's request. She'd wanted no hiccups in the final three months leading up to the reveal. Until this morning his surveillance had mostly been done remotely, only following Alex in person if anything out of the ordinary occurred. However, after the events at Meadow Oaks earlier in the day, his mother had tasked him with following Alex around the clock. It would remain his responsibility until the Auxiliary was confident there would be no threat from the R.A.

Will considered a threat unlikely. To date, his Aunt Irina had not found any evidence connecting the R.A. to the murders at Burton-Hall Estate, and as she had told his mother, the R.A. leadership liked to brag about their achievements.

He sighed. That was one of the few things he did know. It was just like his mother, even at this late stage, to leave him in the dark due to 'necessity'. Although Will fully understood why at times she treated him as an agent and not a son, it had gotten worse since his father's death.

"Have faith, Will," he counselled himself, recalling the words his father had said to him when he'd expressed his frustration at the lack of information given to him upon his Auxiliary initiation.

Faith.

So much of his life involved faith. Just as with God, he believed in the authenticity of Alex on the word of others who held authority over him. The unequivocal belief of his parents. But unlike God, who millions believed in, there were only five people who believed in or had any knowledge of Alex and who she was. He closed his eyes momentarily as he remembered that the number was, in fact, four. His father was dead.

Still to this day, Will was unsure exactly what had occurred. He knew only what his mother had told him, which was that in order to protect his identity and ensure the safety of the family, his dad had offered himself to death. Will had no proof of that, but he believed what he'd been told, and as such it was the third big leap of faith he'd taken in his lifetime. God, the authenticity of the child and the death of his father – there was no proof regarding any of these things, but that was what faith was, the firm belief in something for which there is no proof.

The day outside was starting to fade and it wouldn't be long until it was dark. He was glad to see Alex beginning to close her curtains and blinds. If he could see inside the house then so too could anyone who might want to do her harm.

"The people are going to need proof of who you are," he whispered as she closed the last of the blinds. "Telling them to have faith will not be enough."

Yes. The Russian people would require the Auxiliary to present clear and indisputable evidence, especially given that the extended Romanov family would demand absolute proof. While these relatives had never succeeded in reinstating a new head of the Imperial Family due to ongoing governmental shifts and internal disputes over succession, they, more than anyone, would resist anything short of airtight verification.

It wasn't long now though. His adrenalin was already running high knowing it was only weeks until he would be fully briefed alongside Alex. He was excited too that he would meet his aunt for the first time. It was the sisters' life work. Will could only imagine the intensity of the moment when they would stand proudly beside each other and deliver God's plan for a country reunited behind his new representative on earth.

His phone buzzed in his pocket.

"I was just thinking about you," he said as he picked up the call from his mother.

"Nice things I hope?"

"Mostly," he teased.

"Did the Patriarch make contact at all?"

"Yes, and my suggestions were met with nothing more than a dial tone," he bemoaned.

His mother laughed softly. "I see. Not a surprise. Alright, I need you to forge pertinent hospital records under the guise that you work for Meadow Oaks to smooth this over. Let me know once it's been done."

Before Will spoke again, he breathed in deeply. He needed to curb his frustration and consider his next comments carefully. "Let me speak with Alex. Let me tell her the truth. We need to educate her – prepare her – and you need to prepare me as there's still so much I don't know. We're all sure this is the generation to resurrect. The fourth generation."

"I lost your father to the cause. I will not lose you too. The less you know until absolutely necessary the better."

"Dad was not lost to the cause. The R.A. who killed him are not the cause. The R.A. are the enemy. The throne is our only cause!"

"Yes, alright, Will. Semantics aside, the R.A. are the enemy, you're correct."

They both fell silent until Will spoke again.

"Please let me speak with Alex … and please speak to me. I still don't know the entire story as it's never yet been 'absolutely necessary'. I'll bring her to you and you can brief both of us about everything—"

"Will. Our mission is clear and has been since before you were born. Many, including your father, have made extreme sacrifices to ensure its completion. Please respect them by adhering to the plan. Many families have a destiny and this is ours – it's what we were born to do."

"And I'm here to support you," Will said with sincerity. "We only have each other now. It's time. If not Alex, then tell me. I'm flying on faith right now, as I've always done, and with all due respect to His Holiness, I think I deserve more. Let me shoulder some of the weight."

His mother said nothing, and in that silence Will wondered if he'd crossed a line. He hadn't wanted to upset her. Not at all.

"Any sign of anything untoward there?" she finally asked, breaking the awkward silence.

"No. Nothing."

"Alright. If things stay that way until morning, come and see me at home at ten. I have some things to talk to you about."

"Of course. Is everything alright?"

"Yes. I just thought you'd like to know what it is I'll need your help with over the coming few weeks."

Will sat bolt upright in the car seat. "You're going to brief me?"

"Tomorrow. Yes. See you then," his mother said before hanging up.

Probably before she changed her mind, he thought. His excitement was palpable. He'd been worried he might not stay awake to keep a watch overnight, but the adrenalin rush that just ran through him would be enough to keep him alert for days.

Chapter 10

MOSCOW, RUSSIA

"Anya, the report is in, and you'll be pleased!"

She turned from the book she was reading to face her husband. Her 'spiritual husband'. Their marriage had never been blessed by the church, such were their atheist beliefs. *His* atheist beliefs. Viktor had been a husband of convenience at one point in time, but now, after so many years, he was a man she'd come to adore. He was her long-standing love and support, yet he had absolutely no idea who she really was.

He handed her the document he was holding. "I can't say I'm not pleased with these numbers! We're at a size now that we can be confident to go public and have our voice heard. A huge proportion of the people are ready to support us. I think this deserves a celebration!" he said before heading to the kitchen.

"Viktor, this is amazing!" Anya exclaimed loudly, feigning excitement. In contrast, her insides sank with disappointment as she contemplated the heading on the page: *R.A.- Led Campaign Nears Climax: Communism Rebirth Imminent.*

"Yes, indeed. I raise a toast to Stalin, the Man of Steel," said her husband as he returned to the dining room with two vodkas on ice.

Anya read aloud from the report:

> *It is evident beyond doubt that the condition of the current government is alienating both elderly Russians, who are nostalgic for the Stalin era, and disgruntled younger Russians, who are incensed with the continued downfall of the economy. The people's voice is loud and clear: We want, we need, a leader like Stalin.*

"Twenty-five per cent of all Russians, to be exact. About thirty-five and a half million people want a leader like Stalin!" Viktor nodded with a large smile on his face. "Thirty-five and a half million people who only need a sign to revolt against their fellow countrymen and our lame government. The 1917 revolution that gave rise to the birth of communism started in the same way. We, the R.A., will give them that sign, my love!"

Anya smiled, and it took every bit of her resolve not to frown as she continued reading.

> *Regardless of age, the presiding opinion is that with Stalin the country became a superpower, feared by allies and enemies alike. Russia was stronger than steel in the time of Stalin, yet today we bow to the West.*

"This will make that traitor Khrushchev turn in his grave." Viktor laughed with malice.

"Yes, I'm sure he'd be most offended," she offered, thinking of the man who had at one time led the Soviet Communist Party and brought her both joy and grief. Khrushchev had denounced Stalin's rule, initiating the de-Stalinisation of Soviet society, but at the same time had desecrated Russian religion due to his atheism.

"Read the bit about the call for action," said Viktor.

> *The R.A. has been integral in spreading discourse, with members from all our one hundred and forty-six cells across the twenty-one republics actively participating in the discreet use of their everyday personas to preach the need for Stalin-style doctrines*

due to ongoing instability after the break-up of the Soviet Union. The R.A. leadership calls on all members to continue the fight and stand united in protest at the upcoming Pascha festivities. Come one and all. Descend upon Moscow! The time to reveal ourselves and our allegiance is now. We will not allow the president to only display respect for the Russian Orthodox Church. We will demand his respect for the cult of Stalin as will the everyday people who our uprising will awaken. The R.A. implores you to publicly support your devotion to the Great Architect of Communism. Long live Stalin.

As she finished reading the report, Anya took a large swig of her vodka. "Well, that's certain to create the desired affect amongst the cells when it's circulated tomorrow."

"And the report, my darling, is not anywhere near the most exciting news of this evening!" Viktor exclaimed.

She smiled to hide her angst. "I'm not sure I can think of anything better than the public deliverance of a political cult dedicated to our most beloved Soviet father."

"Oh, I can. The death of another."

Anya paused to take another sip of her drink. A deliberate pause that allowed her time to think. Surely they had not found the heir? Surely not! She had worked tirelessly, taken innocent lives and lost personal contact with her sister in order to reinstate herself as a trusted member of the leadership. *Evelyn … no. No!* Could the R.A. have found out about her sister?

"The death of another?" she questioned.

"Indeed," Viktor said, giving her a sly look.

"I think we'll need to add another nip for this sensational news!" she said, handing her husband her glass in order to buy herself more time to think.

Had she slipped? Had someone else in the Auxiliary talked? Who? Had they gotten too excited with only two months until the prophecy was to be fulfilled?

She'd been wanting to contact her family for months now to check on the status of the plan, but she hadn't dared risk anything so close to the reveal. Her job was to keep abreast of R.A. activity and collate evidence about their violent and self-satisfying history. Evidence that, when put in front of the Russian people alongside her sister's evidence of a child who 'escaped' the Imperial Family massacre, would turn their country around. The Auxiliary would usurp any R.A. communistic cult uprising at the Pascha festivities, and they believed that Medvedev, their current and first openly Orthodox president, would be sure to insist on reform. The Auxiliary prayed that the president would agree to a constitutional monarchy, shared rule, when a direct descendant of His Holy Martyr returned to the people.

As Viktor re-entered the room, she called on her training to compose herself. Coming to stand in front of her, he passed the refilled glass and then held his own drink up to the ceiling.

"Let's raise our glasses to the death of the leaders of the Russian Federation."

Anya gasped. "What? That would be international suicide!" she responded to his toast.

Her husband just smiled at her before taking a sip of his vodka.

"You're telling me that the R.A. leadership is going to endorse the assassination of the Russian president and prime minister at the upcoming Pascha ceremony? What? In order to take advantage of the ensuing chaos and reinstate itself as Russia's governing body?"

Viktor's smile broadened.

"Dispose of both Medvedev and Putin?" she pressed.

Viktor raised his glass once again in acknowledgement.

"The R.A. needs to recruit and sway the state to our will, Viktor!" she continued passionately. "There may well be twenty-five per cent of the country that will support an R.A. uprising, but they will take time themselves to revolt, not to mention that there is still the other seventy-five per cent of the country that may not support a return to communism!"

A disbelieving laugh escaped her as she shook her head in astonishment. "Our kind may be the more driven, but we're still a minority. We need to wait until we have majority seats in the Duma, and, my darling, we are so very, very close. By the elections at the end of the year, we'll have the upper hand. So why? Why play a card, and such a dramatic one, before then?"

Swirling the ice in his glass, Viktor replied, "Because it's a trump card, my darling. Not even the cells will expect it. And this will be the shock we need in order to get revolt momentum started. It's not a coup, Anya, that would very much hurt our international dealings in the future. Think of it more as the catalyst required to push forward a considered and constitutional seizure of power by the R.A. It will be put to a vote in tomorrow morning's leadership forum."

She watched Viktor happily down his drink. This was bad. Extremely bad. She knew the people in the R.A. leadership. She was one of them. A few would question the decision at a vote, but none of them would want to miss the opportunity to recreate, in some sense, the original people's revolution, risk or not.

"Well," she said as she set down her empty glass and put her hand on her husband's shoulder, "I shall of course follow the will of the leadership majority, but for now, I'm going to get ready for bed. Don't drink too many more of those in celebration, my love!"

In the privacy of their ensuite, she slammed her fist into a pile of towels. "For the love of God!" she whispered aggressively. She was tired. Why this? Why a twist so close to completion? There were only three things she'd wanted to do between now and the heir's planned reveal: see her sister, meet her nephew and apologise to both, in person, for Richard's death. Now tonight's development sat on the top of her to-do list, and she wanted nothing to do with it.

If the R.A. were even contemplating taking the assassination of the Russian Heads of State to a vote then the Auxiliary needed to move now. If an incident of this scale were to rock the country before they could bring the heir to the people, it would mar the event with innuendo and suspicion. It could even be possible that people would denounce their claim, regardless of the Auxiliary not wanting to claim absolute power. The people would be looking for stability and a show of force, which was exactly what the R.A. offered. They may very well swing the seventy-five per cent, seeing the birth of a new communist Soviet Union.

Anya had to contact her sister tonight. She couldn't wait.

Making her way into the bedroom, she listened for any sign of Viktor. The sound of the late-night news on the TV in the living room satisfied her that she had privacy for a time, so she moved into the reading room that adjoined their master suite. From the shelves she retrieved a book. A book she'd never read but had definitely studied well.

A pensive sadness overcame her. The book she held was Richard's. Not only had she taken her brother-in-law's life but Anya had also taken his Bible. She'd done so to remember his life, not his death. Unlike other R.A. assassins who kept mementos of their kills, this was simply an inanimate object that in some small way linked her to the man who had been a much-loved part of her family.

Was she still a much-loved member after what happened over a decade ago? That was a question that haunted her. She had mishandled the extraction. Robbed her sister of a husband and her nephew of a father. Anya hoped and prayed every day that her family had forgiven her sin and that, God willing, they'd very soon accept her again as Irina and erase their memories of her time spent as Anya.

Refocusing her attention on the task at hand, she returned to the bedroom and sat on the bed. The Bible was tucked inside the dust jacket of a romance novel, a genre she was certain Viktor would never care to read. Discarding the jacket, she opened the holy book and carefully peeled back the modified inner layer of the hard front cover. Beneath it, secured with double-sided tape, lay a small mobile phone.

"Forgive me, God, for desecrating a Bible," Anya whispered.

Quickly, she grabbed a portable charger from the drawer of her bedside table, and moments later, the touchscreen flickered to life. She shielded the device with her hand to minimise the light spilling onto her clothing as she navigated to her contacts. Only one number was saved in the phone, and only the Auxiliary had the means to reach her. Both were intended for emergencies, and this was undoubtedly an emergency.

Tapping the touchpad, she navigated to a draft message she had composed nearly ten years ago following Richard's death.

Please send the book. Anya

She hadn't expected she'd need to add any more, and this realisation now only exacerbated her anxiety. Breathing in deeply, she hurriedly entered a new piece of text and pushed send before resealing the phone carefully into its hiding place.

Relieved, she returned to the reading room. As she nestled the Bible back into place, she noticed the shadow looming across the floor far too late. A strong arm encircled her neck, cutting off her breath almost instantly. She recognised the cologne and the voice all too well.

"There are no second chances, my love."

Her knees buckled involuntarily when he kicked them from behind and she fell forward heavily as he let go of his hold around her neck. Before she could stand, her head snapped back in pain, and she was forced to face the roof as he roughly grabbed and manoeuvred her by her hair. He didn't falter, not even as she made eye contact with her husband of over forty years.

✝

The blade cut through her skin effortlessly as Viktor drew a knife across his wife's throat. Blood flowed down her neck and her eyelids began to flutter as she desperately tried to hold his gaze.

"You will regret this, Viktor," Anya whispered, the exertion of her words causing blood to spew from the corner of her mouth.

Still holding her upright by her hair, Viktor leaned in and whispered in her ear, "My only regret, Anya, is that you had absolutely no idea who I really am."

As she struggled with her final breath, he lowered Anya's body onto the floor and stepped back to survey the scene. The knife had sliced easily through her carotid artery. It was a precise cut and looked like a professional job, as he'd intended. The police would not believe anyone less could get through their home's security.

The smile that would normally accompany a job completed was not forthcoming, but neither were tears. She'd been a wife of convenience whom he'd come to adore, but Anya had betrayed him and the R.A. He'd been watching her, tracking her every single move, for the last ten years. Not as her husband but as an assassin. Gently, he closed Anya's eyelids over her now lifeless eyes. "You should have been dead long before now, Anya, if that even is your name."

He'd never expected to deploy his craft on one so close and so loved. When his wife and R.A. comrades had told him about the encounter with the holy man, he'd supported her. Nothing had alluded to Anya having been unfaithful, and her R.A. history was impeccable. She'd been one of the earliest members of the current R.A. and she was one of their most loyal. She'd cried when the process of de-Stalinisation saw their leader's body removed from the Lenin Mausoleum and buried like a common peasant by the Kremlin walls. Whilst many claimed that this demise brought Stalin to where the values of socialism and Bolshevism stated he should be, not above any other class, to those in the R.A., Stalin transcended any class. Anya was R.A. through and through.

But then, so was he, and he was far from clean. Maybe that's why he'd always been so drawn to her?

When he'd found the Bible and the phone earlier that week, it had confirmed that she was as dirty as him. What he didn't know was the device passcode. After contemplating the best way to access it, he concluded that the simplest option would be for Anya to do it for him. There was no plan for the R.A. to immediately execute the president and prime minister; that had been a bluff to spark his wife into action. He'd needed her to fret and make a move. And she had.

Careful to avoid getting blood on himself, he stepped over Anya's body and removed the Bible from the bookshelf. Removing the phone from underneath the cover, he entered the passcode he'd filmed Anya using. 'Message Sent' flashed on the small screen, and the message itself sat underneath the confirmation.

Please send the book. Card to be inscribed: The Friday of Easter will fall early this year but remains steeped in a state of tradition. I implore you to prepare for the festivities and I know that until I see you, this gift will provide a story of hope, faith, love and luck. Anya

If it hadn't been for the way she'd requested it be sent, Viktor would have considered the note nothing more than a thoughtful gesture. She'd always been thoughtful. "Well, my love, I'll deliver the book personally."

Viktor returned to the bedroom and scattered some clothes over the floor and filled a small bag with some of their best jewellery from their bedside tables. He'd miss his pearl cufflinks, but they had to go. He'd throw them all in the Moskva later that night before returning home to find a robbery gone wrong. It was a very nice haul for the fake intruders.

He surveyed the room one last time. It looked good, legitimate. It was time for him to leave, but first he needed to conceal his wife's deception. He placed the Bible in the bag, and as he went to place the phone in his pocket, the screen lit up.

The words Auxiliary Alert in capital letters appeared, and underneath them it read:

File request made at Meadow Oaks by Alex Ashmore.

Viktor's breath stopped short. What was the Auxiliary? Where was Meadow Oaks? And who the fuck was Alex Ashmore?

Chapter 11

BOSTON, USA AND MOSCOW, RUSSIA

Home again after her uneventful visit to Meadow Oaks, Alex ran her hand gently over the replica of the Russian imperial Clover Egg that Grace had given her. Hinged on one side, the egg folded back on the horizontal plain to reveal a centre cavity that was filled with an exquisite surprise. Held in place by the tiniest of clips were four clover leaves, their edges bordered with white stones, the centre of each showcasing a miniature portrait of a girl. Girls she now knew to be four Grand Duchesses of Russia. The daughters of the last Tsar.

"What do you have to do with things?" she wondered.

The talent of Fabergé, jeweller to the Russian imperial court, was truly unmatched, and Alex had taken particular interest in what Jonathan had told her about the inextricable relationship that the Imperial Family had with the House of Fabergé.

The imperial Easter Eggs were Carl Fabergé's brainchild. When he'd produced in 1885 what was to all appearances an ordinary hen's egg containing a series of 'surprises' wrought in gold, platinum, precious gems and enamel for Tsar Alexander III to bequest to his Empress for Easter, the monarch had been enamoured. His Empress too had fallen in love with the egg and lovingly praised her husband who had bestowed the gift upon her. The Tsar was so pleased that he'd given the House of Fabergé a standing order for an egg every Easter.

Fabergé had certainly made a name for himself in Russia, setting himself apart by producing beautiful articles of fantasy. He didn't give a pearl necklace to a queen or a diamond to a duchess – they had them all. He'd reigned supreme because he recognised these facts. He produced items that no one else had ever perceived possible, and the work was so much more than Easter eggs. The Fabergé offering was broad, and the quality was exquisite, the makers lavishing every artifice of design, workmanship and mechanics.

"Yes, Monte, what set Carl Fabergé apart from all his contemporaries was that he was the first in Russia to make objects of elegance, taste and feeling, all of which were nationalised and ransacked by the Bolsheviks during the revolution. It was just another tragedy of the time," she said to her dog, who was busily nudging his leathery wet nose against her leg.

Distractedly, Alex gave him a treat and turned her attention to her computer. A scan of Josephine's letter was displayed full screen. She ran her mouse over the text, highlighting key passages of note.

> *… even when it resulted in a double deception being imposed upon you. Charlotte, I am not your biological mother …*
>
> *… your father's name wasn't William, it was Edward, and our family name was Burton-Hall …*
>
> *… You, my beautiful girl, went by the name Victoria and had another sister … her name was Kathryn …*
>
> *… Kathryn and Edward were both casualties of war … a war between good and evil …*
>
> *… the letter that still waits for you to open … at our once home …*

... seek the truth to why your father and sister died. Seek the truth to your past. It is what your father wanted ...

... your mother ... Hannah Burton-Hall.

Alex continued to stare at the screen, trying hard to solidify her thoughts. The way the letter was written and crafted was exquisitely beautiful, expressing both profound sorrow and deep love. It didn't come across as erratic, as one might expect from someone allegedly losing their mental faculties. Surely a mother wouldn't fabricate such a story and risk hurting the child she professed to love so dearly.

"Let's start with Burton-Hall Estate," she addressed Monte, who had finished his treat and was now curled up happily in his bed beside her desk, chewing on one of Stuart's old socks. "Good boy. Rip that to shreds," she said, smiling ruefully.

Alex typed into the search bar. Several results popped up on screen, most of them travel sites showcasing Burton-Hall Spa Retreat, a luxury boutique hotel on the grounds of Burton-Hall Estate in Kent in the southeast of England. The hotel was named for the family who had lived there for over one hundred and fifty years before the current owners purchased it as a deceased estate.

Clicking into the detail made her catch her breath. It was glorious. Centuries of history was captured in both the architecture and gardens. Plants and flowers draped over the stone buildings giving it a distinctly fairytale feel, and a magnificent boulevard of large evergreen trees shading lush flowering shrubs ran from the entrance gates to the front of the original house. The art showcased within the hotel was even more impressive, all one-off pieces representing the many years since the estate had been established in 1128. The collection was an exhibition worthy of a showing at the gallery.

"I hope this was your home, Charlotte," Alex said, wide-eyed. She glanced at the time then typed the hotel's number into her phone. If her calculations were right, it was late but not too late to call.

"Burton-Hall Estate Spa Retreat, this is Caroline."

"Caroline. Hi. My name's Alex Ashmore and I'm calling from the Elysium Art Gallery in Boston. I was hoping you could tell me who I might speak to regarding the history of the hotel and its artwork, please."

"Of course, Alex. You'll want to speak with our communications team. It's after hours here now so I doubt anyone will pick up, but I'll put you through and you can leave a message. One moment, please."

As she sat on hold, Alex continued to scroll through the hotel's image gallery until her hand went rigid on the mouse. Swirling on her office chair, she reached across to the bookshelf and grabbed a handful of photos Grace had given her of Charlotte's trip to England. The one she wanted was near the bottom of the pile. It was almost identical to the image on the website, although unlike on the site, the photo Alex held in her hand showed Charlotte standing in front of the fountain. She looked happy, the smile on her face accentuating her striking beauty.

Alex's thoughts were interrupted as a recorded voice asked her to leave a name and message for the communications team, which she did before focusing again on the picture of Charlotte. What had changed her great-grandmother from the beautiful, happy woman in this photo, a woman so obviously pleased to be enjoying the beauty of Burton-Hall Estate's formal garden? Had she found out something distressing about her real mother or father perhaps? Or her sister? Or did she perhaps discover what Josephine had meant about a war between good and evil?

Alex sat with her head in her hands. It hurt. There was a lot to take in, and her family history was nowhere near as easy to ascertain as the history of Fabergé had been. She was so engrossed, she almost didn't answer her phone when it rang.

"Ms Ashmore?" a male voice asked.

"Speaking."

"I'm glad I caught you. I'm calling from Meadow Oaks regarding some trouble you experienced with records concerning one of your family members."

"Oh. Please, call me Alex. Has anyone managed to get to the bottom of things?"

"Well, you exist, so that's good."

Alex smiled at his joke.

"The files *were* incorrect, just as you informed the desk nurse," the man continued. "The system was experiencing a glitch, which we've now fixed. I apologise for the inconvenience, but at the same time I thank you for helping to bring it to our attention. The not-so-good news is that we don't have any personal belongings of your great-grandmother's still at the facility. I'm sorry, I know you were hoping we would."

Alex's feeling of deflation caused her to sigh deeply.

"If I say sorry twice, will it make you feel any better?" he offered.

She laughed softly. "Maybe a little. Thanks so much for calling."

As she ended the call, Alex realised she now knew two things for certain. One, she had no idea what to do next. Two, she knew that even without Charlotte's father's letter, her family story was far from over.

†

Taking one last glance at the corpse of his wife, Viktor made his way to the front door and collected his phone and wallet from the hall stand. Dialling a number, he waited impatiently for his heir apparent to pick up.

"What took you so long?" he said when the call connected and before the recipient could speak.

"Seriously, Viktor? I'm entertaining. I had my hands full."

"Well, put some pants on and send her home. I need you to do something for me."

"Can't it wait?"

"No, Filip, it can't."

"Okay. Well, I'll do it pantless. Saves me getting undressed again as I'm not sending her home. What do you need?"

"I need a number traced, a recon done on a place called Meadow Oaks and a gathering of intelligence on someone called Alex Ashmore. I have no idea of gender."

"The number I can do quickly, the other stuff you're just going to have to wait until morning for. This sweet piece of ass needs taking care of."

"Filip, this is serious. Look them up. Now."

Viktor proceeded to give Filip the phone number, assuming he wouldn't be petulant enough to not take notes. Then, while waiting for answers, he hurriedly began to ransack the rest of the apartment. As he scattered his and Anya's belongings, Viktor couldn't help but think how he had once had a very similar attitude as Filip. Bravado driven by the knowledge of great power to come.

He smiled despite himself as he roughly pulled items out of cupboards and cast them aside. He hadn't had a similar attitude – he'd been exactly the same. He'd certainly given his father lip on occasion.

"Do you still need me to be a part of this thing?" he asked his father as they approached the building where he was to spend his afternoon working hidden away in the basement.

"It's not a thing, Viktor."

"Sorry. I meant no disrespect to the R.A. atheist scum you make me fraternise with," he said, his words dripping with sarcasm.

"Have a nip of vodka and calm down, son. You're acting like a spoiled teenager."

"I am a teenager."

"Well, I need you to act like the adult I've always raised you to be."

Viktor's smile disappeared. That had been the day he'd met Anya.

He'd had over thirty R.A. recommendations to help screen, all aged between fifteen and eighteen and all wanting to prove their undying allegiance to the Man of Steel. The R.A. wasn't like the Red Army for which it was named. The Red Army had let any common peasant disenfranchised with Russia join their ranks. No, the R.A.

was more select. You couldn't just believe in communism, you had to very specifically believe in Stalin.

Seemingly, he had chosen the enemy that day. Disarmed by the beautiful blonde girl, he had beckoned her to approach him with her endorsement papers. Up close, she was even more striking – undeniably beautiful, with an intriguing edge. He had sworn he would make her his, and he had succeeded.

"Jesus," he fumed. *Had the deceitful bitch been a mole from the very start, just as he'd been?*

He grimaced, noting the last half bottle of vodka in the fridge as he threw things out of it haphazardly onto the floor. He emptied the bottle in one long, desperate drink, seeking solace from his burning anger.

"No more, Viktor. You have a job to do," his father scolded him as he drank eagerly from the flask.

Viktor sighed deeply with a twinge of anger. "It's been two years now that I've had to be a part of this R.A. ruse. I'd much rather be readying myself for the role of Christ."

"Viktor, that role is not guaranteed yours, even with my status."

"You're the almighty Christ, host and leader of all the Khlysts. Surely you can and will make it happen."

His father gave him a steely look. "Helping the atheist R.A. to make decisions is a wonderful example of partaking in sin, which will help you become spiritually awakened and let God live within you. Only once that has occurred can you be considered suitable for the role of Christ."

"You've let multiple women have their way with me since the age of thirteen. Surely that's sin enough?"

"That's my sin, Viktor, not yours."

Yes, young Viktor had been just like Filip … in more ways than one.

Having had his sexuality awakened earlier than most had only exacerbated Viktor's brazen boldness. Whilst his friends were still having wet dreams, he had become well and truly experienced sexually, even though still under the age of consent. Once he'd become a member of the sect, he'd had the entire cell to choose from in order to obtain satisfaction.

Viktor remembered his first time vividly. It had coincided with the day his father had become the human portal in which His Holiness was incarnated and thus the anointed leader of the entire Khlyst community. It had been an impassioned service that ended in physical exhaustion for him and in death for his sister.

Viktor heard the doors seal shut and the silence of anticipation settle over the room. A morbid silence. Not all the members were completely comfortable with the initiation sacrifice ritual, including his mother.

As the service commenced, his father sat holding both Viktor and his sister's hands. People dressed in white sat silently on benches along the walls of the sacred room, and in the room's centre there was a tub of water, its damp contents awaiting the flesh of his sister.

The outgoing host and the current hostess sat in front of the gathering, and as the last of the members were seated, they opened the service with prayers that beseeched the Holy Spirit to descend upon the gathering. Bread and wine were offered as communion, and the effects of the alcohol hit quickly. Members began to chant, their combined voices bringing a chill to Viktor's skin, and it didn't take long for the cell to raise themselves into a frenzied state. The members pulled each other to the floor or pushed up against the walls, engaged in any number of sexual acts, and the holy chanting was slowly overridden with the animal sounds of carnal activity.

Viktor's father turned to face him. "You will keep our laws secret. Entrust them to no one, be steadfast and silent even under the lash or the flames; thus, you will enter the kingdom of Heaven and even here on earth receive the bliss of the spirit."

Viktor nodded his acknowledgement as he watched the hostess help his father take his sister to the tub of water and place her in it. The beautiful smelling golden steam that rose up around the child diverted from the horror that would shortly unfold.

"Only after a man has sinned greatly can he be truly repentant and pleasing to God. Nothing can debase such a person more than sin," the hostess addressed his father. "Prove to me your worth as the new host, our new Christ and the God of all the Khlyst ships."

His father stepped forward and placed one hand on his daughter's head. "In the name of Rasputin, I offer you my greatest sin. I offer the Lord my virginal child." Viktor then watched as his father slit his sister's throat.

"Okay," Filip's voice burst back on speaker, demanding Viktor's attention return to the present. "Whilst it looks like an international number, it redirects a number of times back to a location here in Moscow. It's a shop. Belov Books. Someone didn't want it traced as it was quite the elaborate web. That's why it took me so long."

"And here I was thinking you were taking care of your sweet piece of ass."

"Funny, Viktor. I wouldn't dare disobey our almighty Christ."

"Good. Always remember your place, Filip. And the other things?"

Viktor head Filip's deep intake of breath. The boy did not like his place.

"They're going to take a while longer," Filip continued. "Meadow Oaks is a mental health care facility just outside of Boston in the US, and there are several Alex Ashmores. There is one who's an employee at a Boston art gallery who might be your girl. Close to the facility. I don't have a lot on her at this stage other than some tagged Facebook pictures, which I might print out and put on my bathroom wall."

Viktor sighed. "Alright. Meet me at nine tomorrow at Belov Books. Send me the address. I'll have to be in and out quickly as I also have a small personal issue to deal with. I'll explain when I see you, but in the meantime, hack into the Meadow Oaks system. The Alex Ashmore we're looking for requested a file from the facility and that may give us more information."

He hung up before Filip could find a reason to argue.

Chapter 12

MOSCOW, RUSSIA

The bookstore had a nondescript frontage. The building itself was thin and there was no signage other than an old etching in the glass panel of the door that read 'Belov Books', and if he'd not been looking for it, Viktor would have walked straight past. *That is why you picked it, my darling,* he thought as he opened the door and a dull chiming welcomed him inside.

As he waited for the sound to bring someone to his service, he glanced along the first shelf. Their selection was good, an eclectic mix. Everything from rare edition Russian classics to relatively inexpensive paperbacks of contemporary writers in English and other foreign languages. He could see why Anya would have loved this store. She'd read every night before bed, and her last night on earth had been no different. Unfortunately for her, the book had not been as it seemed.

The doorbell sounded once more as a man Viktor knew well entered the store. Filip nodded at him as he locked the door and made his way in amongst the bookshelves. The second announcement of customers brought a man scurrying from somewhere at the back of the building.

"Good morning, sir. I apologise that no one was here to greet you. I'm Oleg Belov. How may I help?" he asked Viktor whilst simultaneously doing his best to clear the counter of piles of books.

"You have a lovely store," Viktor complimented the man with true belief.

"I like to think so," the man replied with a self-satisfied grin. "We've had the store in our family for a long time."

"Well, I'm sure Grandfather Belov would be very proud," he said as in the corner of his eye he saw Filip take a position close to the door. He knew that meant he had scoped the store and they were alone.

"Actually, Grandmother Belov. It was her passion."

Viktor didn't care. Not one bit.

He picked up a book on the counter and turned it over as if to examine its back cover. With nonchalance he said, "I'm here on behalf of my wife, Anya Malinovsky, whom I believe you know."

As the man began to deny this, Filip stepped quietly behind the counter and stood uncomfortably close to the suddenly perplexed owner.

"That wasn't a question," Filip said.

"No, it wasn't. My friend is right," Viktor said as he also moved into the man's personal space.

Belov stared at him blankly either in fear or shock and didn't utter a sound. Viktor nodded at Filip who from underneath his heavy coat produced a fifteen-millimetre pistol. The gun, hard, cold and menacing when placed in the small of the man's back, moved Belov's expression to terror and a cold sweat appeared on his face. Viktor smiled, making the man recoil slightly, but he was unable to take a backwards step due to Filip's gun being pushed tight against him.

"The man holding a gun to your back will execute you should you not provide me with exactly what I came here to retrieve," Viktor instructed. "Do you understand?"

The man nodded.

"Good. Grandmother Belov would be proud."

The man nodded again.

"My wife, Anya Malinovsky, who you know and who contacted you yesterday evening, is dead."

Filip gave him an astonished look and a small whimper escaped Belov.

"You were given a request to send a book on her behalf," Viktor said, looking at his watch to confirm the time. "It's now twelve minutes since you opened for business and only the three of us have entered, meaning that you are yet to send any book. Don't make it only two people to exit Grandma's store today."

Viktor nodded once more to Filip who brought the gun up to Belov's right temple. The sensation of metal on his skin caused the man's eyes to water and his chest to heave.

"He's gentle, isn't he?" Viktor taunted.

Another small whimper of acknowledgement escaped Belov. His face dripped with sweat that mingled with the mucus that was beginning to drip silently from his nose.

Viktor would have expected Anya to use a professional, not a snivelling civilian, to act on her behalf. Unfortunately for him, this man seemed nothing more than someone who happened to own a bookstore that Anya needed as a front. *Why did he help her? God, was she screwing this mouse of a man?* Viktor felt a small sympathetic moment for Belov as he too had been used by the woman.

"Now. Please may I have the book?"

"I have no idea—"

Filip brought the gun from man's temple down to the soft underside of his neck. Simultaneously, Filip reached into his pocket removing a long knife.

"Shall I have my friend remove your fingernails one by one?" Viktor asked.

The man shook his head, his voice once again lost.

"It actually causes a person more pain to have the fingernails pried away from the finger than to have the entire finger severed from the hand, my friend," he continued. "The knife runs around the edge of the nail and then it's like prying open a tin of paint. The edges lift bit by bit and then it's just one swift flick of the knife to render the finger void of nail. It's quite amazing how much blood flows to the fingers," Viktor explained.

The book man clenched his hands into fists.

"Okay. I think you get my point. Now, where is the delivery that my wife asked you to arrange?"

"I don't want any trouble."

Viktor laughed. "Filip, I'd say our friend is already in a spot of trouble, wouldn't you?"

"Yes, I tend to agree. In fact, I'd say he's well and truly fucked," Filip said as he forced open one of the man's hands and severed a finger.

Filip quickly put his hand over the man's mouth to stifle his scream, while Belov desperately clutched his injured hand to his chest. His severed finger lay on the floor, dust already caked to its bloodied end.

"Now," Viktor said as Belov's scream morphed into a whimpering sob, "tell me which book I'm after."

Unwilling to let go of his injured hand, the man pointed his elbow towards two wrapped parcels at the opposite end of the counter.

"Which one?" demanded Viktor.

"The larger one."

"Thank you, and thank you, Filip," Viktor said, and with that, his heir apparent pierced the man's heart with a bullet at point-blank range.

Viktor picked up both the parcels and spoke to Filip before unlocking the door. "Clean this up. Report in at midday. I want to know what you found out about Meadow Oaks and the Ashmore woman."

"And I'd like to know why your wife is dead," Filip replied.

Viktor nodded. "She wasn't just R.A.," he shared before stepping outside and pulling the door closed behind him. He reached into his coat pocket to retrieve his phone that was vibrating silently but steadily against his chest. "Yes," he answered. "I have the book and I'm on the way to decipher whatever coding she's likely used." Viktor took pause to glance around and ensure no one was nearby to overhear his conversation. "I've been watching Anya for close to a decade with the knowledge that she might not be who she said and I'll get to the bottom of this," he continued. "She belongs to an organisation that doesn't want to see the resurgence of communism. If it wasn't for the holy man that came to meet with her those many years ago, I may have thought her CIA. There is, however, definitely a religious undertone."

He began to walk again whilst listening to the response.

"All I know for sure right now is that she's not R.A.," he said. "I'll see you later today and we can discuss it in more detail. Hopefully I'll know more by then. Right now, I have to go shed some tears for my dead wife."

He snapped closed the cell. Women. Always breaking his balls.

As he walked towards home, his phone again came to life. He'd been waiting for this call and was well prepared. It was time to explain to the leader of the R.A. that his wife, one of their most prominent executives, had fallen prey to a violent intruder and that he would do everything in his power to bring the R.A. cells to revolution to honour her name.

Bless her lying and deceitful soul.

Bless his own.

†

Viktor paused at the front of an old building that had once been a church – a handsome church endowed with a single dome representing Jesus. Today, it was the façade for their headquarters, the perfect middle-finger gesture to an organisation they looked upon with scorn. The structure that had once housed Russian Orthodox believers dedicated to the worship of priesthood, holy books and veneration of the saints, was now home to his Khlysts. A home where the attainment of divine grace and salvation depended not on the church or its clergy but on seeking the spirit of God within oneself through the ritualistic attainment of sin.

Making sure he was unobserved, he unlocked the heavy wooden door that led to the lower floors. Secrecy was essential, not just because their rules demanded it but because state law prevented their right to worship. He made his way down the unlit staircase, hugging the innermost wall and carefully navigating each slippery step. At the bottom he entered a large crypt. Two solitary torches either side of the open altar lit the room and his eyes took a short time to adjust.

A creaking sound and a distinctive fragrance signified her entrance. She didn't acknowledge him as she approached the altar, placing one of the two candles she carried on the floor beside it and using the other to light six candles positioned on either side of the heavy stone structure. The fabric of her white linen gown offered little modesty as it clung to her svelte figure. His Mother of Christ really was the ultimate hostess.

"You can keep your clothes on," he said as she started to undress.

She turned in surprise. "You must have found something astonishing in that book if you're willing to wait."

"I've stumbled across something so perfect that it must surely be divine intervention."

Viktor joined her and they sat in front of the altar where he lay Anya's book and a selection of papers on the floor. "The book was as I thought, a communication vehicle that outlined information about the R.A.'s history, cells, plans and associated dates. The coded text was written in invisible markings within the margins of each page."

"You broke the code?" she asked as she beckoned for his scarf to wrap around her shivering body.

He smiled. It certainly wasn't normal for her to be sitting still in his presence.

"It wasn't difficult. Only took a couple of hours," he said, handing her the scarf. "She'd used something akin to the old Poet files. I don't think she ever expected the book to get intercepted as it was a lazy secondary precaution."

She turned a few pages of the book carefully. "I'm assuming the information holds more than just R.A. history or else we'd be doing something other than talking right now. You mentioned a religious undertone this morning – does the book provide information on the R.A. as well as content to serve us?"

"The content is better than anything our religion could have ever hoped for, my love."

"Nothing can be better than ensuring the atheist R.A. takes power over the post-communist state and subsequently purges and crushes the spirit of every single person who adheres to the Orthodox faith, Viktor."

"Well, how about, for your consideration, sacrificing the only surviving direct descendants of the man who caused our sect to be stunted and thrown into secrecy just as it had decided to strive for public recognition amongst the Russian people? The man who murdered one of our greatest ever leaders, Grigori Rasputin?"

"But that's impossible!" she exclaimed, looking at him in disbelief.

He smiled and ran his finger down her neck to between her breasts. "There's an heir – heirs, in fact. A mother and daughter in America. There was a message to Anya hidden in the book that described their planned deliverance at the upcoming Pascha festivities," Viktor explained. "That timing explains why Anya reacted so quickly to my assassination bluff last night. Any reinstatement of an imperial heir would require Orthodox sympathetic leaders, of which we currently have two in Medvedev and Putin. Anya needed to alert her contacts so they could move immediately."

"You're telling me that a Romanov survived the execution in 1918?"

He nodded and she laughed heartily.

"Viktor, you're starting to sound like the snivelling Orthodox who, even with positive DNA matching, refuse to believe that the bones found are those of the Imperial Family. The family are all dead and have been since 1918, thanks to the R.A.'s forefathers," she scoffed.

He ran his finger back up her neck and placed his finger in front of her mouth to quieten her.

"First, you forget, my love, that I am not only your Christ, I'm also R.A. The Orthodox are right to treat both the initial and the more current DNA findings carefully and with suspicion. Secondly—"

"Stop, Viktor," she said pushing his hand aside. "Please, one thing at a time. Why should the findings be questioned? The entire family are now accounted for, their graves were found exactly where their executioner described. That fact alone has laid to rest the rumours that a child escaped."

He nodded smugly. "Yes. The graves were found where Yurovsky described. But if the R.A. hadn't found the second grave before anyone else, whomever did find it would have absolutely found one body missing."

She gasped so loudly that it reverberated throughout the crypt. "What?"

Viktor smiled. That the Mother of Christ had so readily accepted those findings demonstrated just how easily the Russian people, who desperately sought closure and wished to pay respect to the last Tsar, could be deceived.

"Well, as you know, when the first grave was found, a new wave of imperial love and, worse still, hope engulfed the Russian people, which the R.A. did not need," he said. "Questions had to be answered, and quickly. Had Lenin lied to Stalin and the rest of the Communist Party? Did the absence of two bodies, a boy and a girl, mean that the rumours of an 'official story' being concocted were in fact true? Had one or even two children actually escaped that fateful night?"

He paused to take breath and she stared at him, barely blinking.

"To get answers, we needed to find out if a second grave existed as Yurovsky claimed and, if it did, find it before anyone else. Stalin had sworn by Lenin and Yurovsky's account of the execution, and the R.A. couldn't let his words be taken into ill repute based on the potential lies of his predecessors. The R.A. exists to rebuild and enforce Stalin's doctrines ready for a communist resurgence. His word had to remain undisputed. Does that all make sense?" he asked, running his hand over her soft yet taut stomach.

She nodded wide-eyed and remained silent.

"The R.A. found the second grave twelve years before the world believes it was found. There were only a few badly damaged bone fragments, a piece of pelvis, a fragment of skull. While the visual evidence suggested the use of acid, it was only through scientific testing that it could be conclusively determined that the bones belonged to a boy.

"For the love of God, a Grand Duchess did escape!" she exclaimed, finding her voice again.

"Seemingly yes, but hold that thought," Viktor nodded before continuing. "So we had no evidence of a girl, and we needed it. The Russian imperial fairytale had to end, and not happily ever after. Surprisingly, it wasn't difficult to source additional bones to provide the DNA proof required as the family's relatives are buried all over Europe. We can thank the Tsarina's mother for her femur. It took expert planning to infiltrate her mausoleum, but you know how talented I am."

She laughed and leaned in, pressing herself closer to him. "That I do, but what you did next I can only guess."

"The R.A. kept the bones under wraps until the time came that we thought it 'worthwhile' to have them discovered. That time was two years ago. We reburied the bones along with the new additions and let amateurs 'finally' find them. And now that the DNA tests have delivered maternal matches, the entire family is thought dead exactly when the R.A. wanted them to be. Exactly—"

"When it coincides with the R.A. uprising during the upcoming Pascha festivities, a time when the church and any surviving monarchists will once more be in mourning. Faith irrecoverable," she whispered breathlessly.

"Precisely." He grinned. "They'll be seeking comfort and strength, and that is exactly what the R.A. will offer them in their darkest moment. Of course, we will very carefully offer Stalin-style doctrines to the people, and we won't reverse Yeltsin's state religion law until we're firmly in seat, but after that … Goodbye Russian Orthodox Church and hello atheism."

"Oh my God!" she exclaimed as she took his face in her hands "It's genius. Anyone wanting to be at one with God will need to do so in secrecy, leading them straight to our religion. Oh, Viktor, Khlysty will finally be the leading religion of Russia. I'm mad at you for not telling me this before now, but regardless, I'm ecstatic! Please, let me now repay the favour," she offered breathlessly.

His body was desperate to take her up on the offer, particularly because she was now eagerly stroking him in preparation, but there was more to discuss.

"Okay, hands off a little longer. I asked you to hold a thought before about a Grand Duchess escaping."

"Mmmmm," she murmured, reluctantly pulling her hands away from him.

"Thanks to Anya, I now know why the church has always played coy with regards to the authenticity of the bones. They knew a child, Anastasia, had escaped, but not in the way you'll be thinking."

"This foreplay is excruciating, Viktor!"

"Well, get ready for the climax. It's a show of the faith I have in you that I'm going to also tell you this next secret. It's something that only the last four almighty leaders have been privy to, so that includes my father as Christ before me. My father, whom I now know to have been a liar and traitor to the Khlysts, and who paradoxically, may now be considered our greatest ever leader."

"You're going to claim that place for your father over Rasputin?" she said, astonished.

"My father's sin was breathtakingly astounding, my love," Viktor said as he stood. The adrenalin released at the thought of the depth of deceit, and the genius it represented, wouldn't allow him to sit still any longer. "The Imperial Family had a security measure in place whereby a child of the Tsar was taken to live in secrecy in England.

A substitute stood in their place. This was done so that if anything ever happened to the family, there would be a direct heir safe and ready to step in and maintain Romanov rule. We know about this from Rasputin who found out himself from the Tsarina."

Her mouth dropped open.

"Rasputin used this knowledge to try to blackmail the Tsar into having our religion recognised as the leading religion in Russia. If the Tsar was to refuse, Rasputin threatened to kill the child and her Keeper. The Tsar did refuse, and whilst he denied it until his dying day, he had Rasputin slain."

"What?" she said slowly and quietly.

"Rasputin had briefed his heir apparent that if for any reason he was killed by nobles, his successor was to deploy an assassin to England to take revenge on the ruling family. My father was that assassin, enticed by the promise of being appointed the next Khlyst heir apparent himself if he successfully completed the task. He found the child and her Keeper and killed them, leaving their bloody corpses in full sight. Supposedly he also killed the Keeper's wife and other child, disposing of their bodies deep in the woods where they would never be found. He wanted the extended family to have hope when there would be none, to have them always wonder if their loved ones were dead or alive."

His Mother of Christ remained silent and wide-eyed.

"But," Viktor continued, "if Anya's information is true, which I believe it is, we now know that the wife and one child were very much alive, and my father lied. He didn't kill the entire family, he killed only two, one of those being the wrong child. The wife and the other child, Grand Duchess Anastasia, escaped."

"This is terrible, Viktor. Your father, our beloved Christ, was as bad as Yurovsky with his fraudulent claims of success," she said after a moment of silence.

"Yes, but unlike Yurovsky, my father lying about a failed mission to avenge Rasputin is actually breathtakingly phenomenal! He said something cryptic to me on his deathbed that I now understand.

He told me that to be successful when I took his place, I had to find my ultimate sin, like he had. I'm positive that this was his ultimate sin. It was unforgivable but at the same time brilliant. The repentance that would have been required for a lie of this magnitude would have made him truly at one with God, if not God himself for ever more."

"The ultimate sin," she murmured, deep in thought.

"Yes, and tonight I'm going to finish what my father chose not to. I'm going to achieve my ultimate sin by absolving my father of his. I will hunt down and have the Romanov heirs killed in such a way that it will take revenge for Rasputin's murder and bring our religion to prominence. I'll no longer have to remain undercover in the R.A. to lead their strategy in our favour. Nor will I ever need turn on them and use my knowledge of their sins, for we both know that option would put us at risk of them turning on us later. All that being said … behold your greatest Khlyst leader of all time, my love."

She grinned with pride. "You'll take Filip, I assume?"

"Yes, but he's not to know about my father's genius until he becomes Christ himself, and that's still a while away. I'll want to enjoy being our greatest ever leader, at one with God like none ever before, for some time yet."

"And what of the substitute who actually escaped the execution?" she asked.

"Anna Anderson. Her claims were legitimate. She did in fact live as Anastasia Romanov."

Her grin faltered. "I almost feel sorry for the woman."

"Don't worry yourself with her," Viktor said, taking his Mother of Christ's hands in his. "Foreplay's over. It's time to worry yourself with me."

Chapter 13

BOSTON, USA

Evelyn asked herself one last time if she was ready. *She was.*

Now she'd decided to brief Will, she felt unexpectedly at peace. She'd shouldered a very large share of the emotional weight following Richard's death and Irina's self-imposed exile. Yes. It would be good to have support. With events unfolding as they did, Evelyn found herself with no one to confide in except her son and the newly elected Patriarch. Unfortunately, the Patriarch's main focus appeared to be on domination rather than affiliation.

Evelyn had always intended to brief Will at the same time as Alex. However, if there was even the slightest possibility that Irina's longest period without contact signalled that the R.A. had found out her real identity, then Evelyn needed to act now. Will had a part to play no matter what, but in the case of Irina's death, he would move from support to lead.

"Mum, what are these?" Will asked as she joined him in her office. He was leaning over her large wooden desk, which was covered with sheets of paper.

"This is the floor plan of a store called Belov Books in Moscow, and that is the floor plan of the Roskilde Cathedral in Denmark," she said as she passed him a cup of coffee, nodding alternately at each document. "I'll most likely need to visit both between now and when we present Alex as heir."

She watched his eyes light up.

"I'm ready to understand what we need to do, what *I* need to do, to prepare for the reveal."

"I know. I'm glad to have you by my side, Will." She took a sip of her coffee before commencing the briefing. "You'll recall that it wasn't until after the death of her sister, Queen Alexandra of the United Kingdom, and approaching death herself that the Dowager Empress brought the church into the Auxiliary in 1928. Maria had nearly given up hope that her granddaughter would ever be found – but not entirely. The little hope she had left, she entrusted to her beloved Orthodox Church."

Will nodded his acknowledgment.

"Now whilst since that time the sitting Patriarch has acted as the head of the Auxiliary, our family chose not to share everything with them. Just as your father and I wanted to protect you by limiting your knowledge, we chose to do the same for the Patriarch. So, rather than keep any evidence regarding the resurrection with the church, we chose instead to keep it dispersed in safe locations of our choosing. Belov Books was Irina's safe location."

Will's brow furrowed in concentration. "What evidence do we have exactly?"

"That's the problem. I'm not sure."

Will stayed silent, but his eyes widened in surprise.

"Well, to be clear, I have Nicholas' letter that he wrote to Anastasia when she was living as Victoria in England and which was recovered from Burton-Hall Estate by the Grand Duchess decades later when she was then known as Charlotte. The original prophecies we unfortunately don't have. No one knows where they are, and they could well have been destroyed. We only found out about them ourselves after the Dowager Empress' death when the church was put in charge of the Auxiliary. Before his death, Nicholas had confided in the Patriarch and made him swear never to reveal their existence, especially to his mother. It was an absolute tragedy Maria hadn't known. If the Dowager Empress had been aware of the prophecies, she may have gone to her death with some kind of peace."

"Is Nicholas' letter not evidence enough?" Will asked.

"It won't be, no. Your aunt has responsibility for the rest of the information we'll need, including the history of the R.A. Most importantly, though, she was meant to complete a final mission in conjunction with your father following the extraction, but after the incident of your father's death, it was only pertinent that we employed complete radio silence, and I—"

"But that was ten years ago!" exclaimed Will.

"I have only heard from her twice yearly since via a gift sent to let me know she's alive. It was too dangerous to be communicating in person. All I know is she used Belov Books as a front, so anything she had to keep private will be there, I'm sure. That's where I've sent her information about the dates and times for the reveal. It is the one and only time I've provided anything other than just returning her gift so she knew I was okay."

Evelyn paused, allowing Will a moment to absorb and reflect on what she had just shared with him.

"Well, okay. I'm sure then she'll just bring what she has when we meet for the reveal," he said optimistically.

"Your aunt hasn't been in contact for over eight months, and that's the longest time since we employed radio silence. Therefore, I don't know if she's been able to complete the mission to recover the information we need or even if she got my message about the dates … and I don't know if she's safe. I'm planning to travel to Russia in three weeks' time to collect anything stored at Belov's if we've not heard from her."

A silence settled between them. She moved to sit on the couch as Will stood staring out the window, deep in thought. He eventually turned and came to sit beside her.

"I'm sorry, Mum. I really, really hope Aunt Irina is okay, but … if you get to Russia to collect the information and it's not there and, worse still, if Irina's not there, then what next? We'll have nothing but our word. People are as likely to believe us as they did Anna Anderson, and we both know how that turned out."

Evelyn nodded. "I know at least that your aunt had the R.A. information. Her task was to collect that from day one of her cover up until the time for resurrection. Until things went sour, I'd been privy to quite a lot of the gathered data. We need the R.A. history and all the information regarding their planned uprisings in order to get the Russian government fully on side."

"Alright, but what was the information Aunt Irina and Dad were supposed to collect after the extraction?" asked Will. "Can we progress without it?"

"It was the Dowager Empress' personal confession. The two of them should have come home with proof of the Auxiliary Measure as well as proof of the R.A.'s sinister call for a new revolution. Neither came, and your father, we know for sure, never will."

Will shook his head. "This is all sounding very dangerous. I couldn't bear to lose you too. Perhaps I can go?"

"It'll be fine, Will. I plan to travel to Russia and check the hidden archive first. If Irina is in jeopardy in any way, my doing so covers three things. First, I can collect the R.A. information. Second, if it's there, I get the confession—"

"And third, if the confession is not there, you will know that we have to go to Denmark and retrieve it ourselves," finished Will.

"Correct. If Irina hasn't completed the mission alone then we must retrieve the confession from where it's been kept for the last eighty years – in the tomb of the Dowager Empress' mother, Queen Louise of Denmark. Maria thought it a fitting hiding place being her mother was the mastermind behind the ruse."

Evelyn paused to let Will take in all that she'd shared. She felt weary but at the same time excited at the thought of being back in the field. It had been a long time since she'd been Charlotte's nurse at Meadow Oaks, and she'd felt so useless when unable to assist the now infamous extraction of her sister. *She would finish this.*

"Is there no other way?" Will asked.

Evelyn took a breath. "There is one other avenue to explore. It wasn't suggested by the Dowager Empress, and we thought it prudent to seek the state's assistance only after they had thoroughly reviewed Maria's confession to their satisfaction."

Will nodded but frowned, deep in thought. "Perhaps we're overcomplicating things. Won't DNA prove Alex's identity?"

"Will, you're forgetting that DNA has been used in the not-so-distant past to prove that the entire Imperial Family has been found, including the last missing Grand Duchess. DNA is unequivocally of no assistance at all."

"Fair enough," he said with a heavy sigh.

She could tell he was trying to be positive, but he'd been so looking forward to meeting his aunt, and now she may not be alive.

"So what exactly is the other avenue to prove Alex's right to the throne?" he asked.

Before she could explain, their phones simultaneously began to vibrate on the table. Without having to speak, they both knew that the incoming text message would consist of only two words: Auxiliary Alert.

Evelyn felt a fear-filled knot form in her stomach. Will ushered her through into the next room where the secure line was kept. He dialled then handed her the earpiece. The Patriarch's voice resonated down the line.

"We have a problem. Your sister is dead."

If she'd not had Will beside her, Evelyn would have hit the floor a lot faster and a lot harder than she did.

†

"Right. Now we're finally alone, where are we going, Viktor, and why?" Filip demanded as he manoeuvred their rental car through

Boston airport traffic. "I'm assuming it has something to do with the Meadow Oaks system you had me hack into."

Filip was annoyed that Viktor had summoned him to travel on a mission at such short notice, especially after having left him to clean up the mess at Belov's. He'd dutifully done as ordered. Smoke had begun to billow and sirens could be heard as he'd walked down the street wearing the store owner's coat to protect him against the chill. The body would have been burned beyond recognition before the firefighters could extinguish the flames. He'd used it as kindling. That and a couple of rare first editions.

"Viktor?" he continued, quickly glancing sideways at his mentor, who was reading something on his phone and paying him little attention. "It's been a fairly one-way distribution of information in the last twenty-four hours. All I know is you killed Anya for being something more than R.A. Help me out here. Give me something, and please, not another lecture that patience is a virtue. Patience is a waste of time."

He turned again to look at him and saw Viktor eyeballing him, unimpressed. "We're heading to the address you recovered from the Meadow Oaks file request."

"Alex Ashmore."

"Yes," Viktor said and returned to scrolling through his phone.

Filip smiled wryly. At least the old man was using a phone. Although dedicated to his mentor, Filip did at times believe that Viktor was a little old-fashioned. For his age, Viktor was still sharp with strategy and the tongue, but his ideas of late were less than risqué. Blessedly, it shouldn't be long before Filip became the leader, the all-powerful Khlyst Christ. The thought brought a flush to his cheeks. Viktor had mentored many of their people, but only Filip had come close to taking his seat as host.

"And?" Filip nudged.

"And when we get there, you'll help me sacrifice a direct descendant of the last Tsar of Russia who the people my wife worked for are planning to reinstate at the forthcoming Pascha festivities," Viktor stated.

Filip swerved the car to the side of the road and switched off the ignition. He then undid his seatbelt and turned in his seat to give Viktor his full attention.

"What?"

"We're heading to the address you recovered from the Meadow Oaks file request, and once there, you're going to help me sacrifice a direct descendant of the man who had Rasputin murdered."

Filip sat in silence for a moment before responding. "You're telling me that Alex Ashmore, art gallery employee, is a direct descendant of Nicholas II?"

"Yes, that's what I'm telling you, Filip."

A guttural laugh escaped him. "You've lost your mind, Viktor. You're a part of the R.A. executive and you heard it directly from the mouths of those involved that the family was slain and buried in the forest. Not to mention that the DNA reports have come back confirming as such. Seriously, I'm turning this car around and taking us back to the airport."

"Before you accuse me of losing my mind," Viktor said with venom, "how about you try using yours for just a moment, Filip. Think about your limited knowledge of the R.A. and how much you don't know about their desire to return to power. The R.A. may just be a tool to help our religion achieve what we need, but you would do well to respect all they've done. I've been privy to more than you will ever imagine as an executive member of the R.A., including having to act like the atheist scum that most of them are, so you are in no position to question my mental faculties, nor, may I add, ready to take my position as Christ."

Filip swallowed his intense agitation and stayed quiet.

"Yes, Filip," Viktor continued. "I know of your desire to take my place and the Mother's advocacy for you to be my successor, but do not kid yourself that she thinks you're anywhere near ready. You've been tentatively chosen and have a long way to go before you'll move from a maybe to the appointed. That transition involves power of the mind, not just the cock."

Filip was so surprised that he laughed again.

Ignoring him, Viktor took a folder from his satchel. "This contains a summary of the information we retrieved from Belov's plus my notes on the pertinent R.A. intel. Actually, swap seats and I'll drive while you get across it all."

After resuming their drive, Filip read the intelligence. The enormity of the facts was astounding. He broke his silence only after reading all ten pages of Viktor's notes. Twice.

"Holy fuck."

"Elegant, Filip."

Filip smiled. Perhaps he wouldn't write off Viktor just yet. He did have more to learn from him.

"This is genius on both sides, but I'm giving the R.A. bonus points for creativity. Using the Tsarina's mother's bones to orchestrate the final daughter's DNA … that is absolute perfection."

"I like to think so, yes."

"So we go after Alex Ashmore and then her mother?" Filip asked.

"Correct. As Alex is being presented as the heir apparent, I can only assume the mother has decided not to rule, but best to be rid of her also. Women do like to change their minds."

Filip flipped back through the notes as they continued the drive into downtown Boston. "I'm also assuming the R.A. history Anya collected was to get the government nervous enough to think a Romanov miracle may be the way forward rather than standing alone, waiting for a mutiny of government when the R.A. came at them?" he asked Viktor.

"I agree," said Viktor. "It's very clever as the state are not obliged to recognise even a direct ancestor."

"Will you tell the R.A. about Anya?" Filip questioned.

"When the time is right, yes. For now, our focus needs to be on finding the heirs so we can use them to our advantage. Once we have them, I'll inform the R.A. about Anya. We'll then use the heirs as pawns to ensure that when the R.A. is back in power, they make our religion legitimate. We know the R.A. will decrease the power of Orthodoxy, but I want it dissolved. My wife has helped accelerate the dominance of Khlysty by light years!"

"So we'll hand them over once the R.A. acknowledge our religion as Russia's dominant faith?"

"Yes, and then they'll sacrifice the heirs just as they did their imperial ancestors. Plus, thanks also to Anya's and my involvement, I have the complete R.A. history should we need it to get what we want, but that's definitely a last resort," explained Viktor.

Filip frowned, confused. "How will the R.A. history help us?"

"For one, they won't want it known that the original massacre was flawed. That questions Stalin's word, even though he was briefed falsely by his predecessor and closest staff. Secondly, and most importantly, they won't want it known that they substituted bones to represent the last Grand Duchess and timed the reburial of the grave so that it was found when they wanted it to be found. There are some people, regardless of wanting a Stalin-esque regime reinstated, who do stay faithful to the history of imperial rule and are naïve, believing that the R.A. will uphold the current privileges the church enjoys. They give the R.A. their support only because they've seen the government fail consistently since the downfall of the Iron Curtain. They just want the country to flourish as it did under Stalin. If the substitution of the bones becomes public knowledge, the R.A. risk losing local and global support."

Filip smiled in absolute disbelief. "Viktor. My sincerest apologies. I'm afraid I may have severely underestimated you."

Chapter 14

BOSTON, USA

As Alex's eyes grew accustomed to the dim light, she realised it was still too dark to be morning. *Why was she awake?* Something wasn't right.

Her skin bristled as she swung her legs out from under the bed covers and placed her feet on the cold floorboards. Reaching for her trainers, she noticed Monte wasn't in his bed. *That's what it was, he must want to go outside.* She grabbed a sweater that was hanging across the arm of her wingback chair and pulled it over her head as she shuffled tiredly down the hallway.

She was about halfway to the back door when she heard it. She stopped, and when the sound came again, she instinctively pushed her back up against the hallway wall. *What was that?* She waited for a few moments but the sound didn't come again. Relieved, she started towards the back door but only made it two steps before Monte came running towards, then past her to the front door. He pushed his little nose up under the bottom edge, sniffing as if he'd found prey.

Front door it is then, she thought to herself and followed him. Just as she reached him the noise came again, this time louder, and now she could tell it was right in front of her. Someone was at her door.

As carefully and quietly as she could she leaned into the peephole and looked outside. It took everything in her not to scream. Someone was at her door, and he didn't look like a nice man. The noise was him using some sort of tool on her lock.

Quickly, she checked the chain was secure, then bent down and picked up Monte before making a dash back to her bedroom. Placing him on her bed, she grabbed her phone and started to call 911. She was just about to punch the second 1 when she heard the front door open. The man had gotten through her lock. She quickly glanced out her bedroom door and down the hall. The door was ajar, and the chain was preventing it from opening … but not for long. Some sort of cutters reached in and grasped the chain. She had no time. They had to get out now.

"Come, Monte, quickly!" she urged, sprinting to the back door with him close on her heels. As she unlocked and flung it open, the frigid night air struck her face. Hearing footsteps, she turned in fear and realised the front door was also wide open. The man had entered, and Monte was now racing towards him, barking wildly.

"Shut the dog up or I will."

His voice froze Alex to the spot, and she watched the man close the front door quietly behind him.

"Monte, come here to me," she said, the calm in her voice masking how terrified she felt. Monte stopped barking at her command but didn't come. Instead, he stood between her and the intruder making a deep guttural growl.

"Shut up," the man ordered as he walked towards them purposefully. When he reached Monte, who had started to bark again, he shoved him roughly through the living room doorway and pulled the door shut. Alex could hear Monte's little feet scratching at the door, desperately wanting to be let back out.

"Make a noise, sweetheart, and I kill the dog."

She had to get help. She had to get him away from Monte. She had to do both.

She turned and ran out the back door into the moonlit yard but stopped abruptly when she realised the back gate was locked. Her blood ran cold and her heart felt as if it might explode. She spun around to see if she could make it back in the house and maybe get past the intruder somehow.

"Well, even I knew the gate was locked, and I don't live here. That's why I came in the front, one less lock to worry about. You just wait out here. My friend will be with us in a moment, and he's going to want a word," the man said quietly from the back door before he closed it and left Alex outside in the cold.

Her heart was beating way too fast. She had to calm down and think. *What the hell was going on?* Who was the man and what did he want? There wasn't enough time to rely on 911. She had to get back in and get to Monte. But how?

"Think, Alex. Think!" she encouraged herself to no avail.

"Alex. Come over here."

She spun at the realisation that someone was talking to her in hushed tones. She looked around the entire courtyard but couldn't see anyone. *Was she imagining it?*

"Is someone there?" she whispered as she pressed her hands and face up against the gate panels. "I'm in trouble. I need help. Please … please help!"

"I need you to step away from the gate to the side wall. Quickly. And close your eyes."

She hadn't imagined it. She did as the voice asked, tears now running down her face. She heard a muffled bang and opened her eyes in surprise. What she saw was the gate now open and the lock on the ground in pieces.

"Come quickly. We need to get you somewhere safe."

She looked towards the voice and saw a tall man approaching her from the back laneway.

"How do you know my name? Who are you?" she said, backing away from him, even though she sensed he might be the only answer to getting out of the situation she'd found herself in.

"I'll explain later. You need to trust me and come now," he said with urgency.

"I can't. Not yet. My dog's still inside. He said he'd kill him."

"That I did, princess."

Alex swung around in fear. The intruder was standing at the back door, which was open again, and he wasn't alone. His friend had arrived.

"Alex, now," the dark-haired man said quietly but forcefully.

She knew she had no choice so let the stranger take her hand as they ran down the back laneway towards a car parked at the rear of a neighbour's house.

"Get inside. Quickly."

Alex had only half shut the door when her saviour planted his foot. As the car screeched out into the main street, some sort of projectile flew past her elbow.

"Leave the door. Put your head down."

He swerved violently, the car door slamming shut. *What was happening?* she thought, panic seizing her. As the car steadied, she scrambled upright, peering out the back window. One of the men from her house, gun still clutched in his hand, watched them flee.

Adrenalin was ripping through her body, causing her breath to quicken and her chest to heave. The man had shot at them and only narrowly missed.

"It's okay, Alex. Breathe. I'm here to help. We're going somewhere safe."

"Who are you? Who were those men? What the hell is going on?" she panted.

He reached across in front of her, which made her flinch, and opened the glove compartment.

"My name's Will and it's okay. I won't hurt you. There's a bottle of water in there. Drink. It will help."

The water soothed her throat, and slowly her breathing began to return to normal. She sat in silence for some time as they drove, watching the streetlights fade as the sun started to rise and willing the shaking in her hands to subside.

Eventually she turned to Will and stared at him intently. "I don't know if I should be glad you were milling around near my backyard in the early hours of the morning or not," she said. "Do you live nearby?"

"Recently I've spent a lot of time in your area, yes."

"Do you need directions for a police station considering we've passed two since we got in the car?"

He laughed, which surprised her, but also unexpectedly put her at ease.

"They won't be able to help us, Alex. We're going somewhere safer than that. I promise to explain everything when we get there."

"Help us? Don't you mean help me? Who are you, Will?"

"I'm someone who will do everything in my power to make sure you stay safe. We're almost there. I need you to trust me."

For some unknown reason, she did.

†

Evelyn knew that for Will to bring Alex to her home, he must have sensed an imminent and grave danger.

"I put a light sedative in her tea. Now, tell me what happened before I speak with her," she said to her son.

Will pulled out his phone and scrolled rapidly through a number of photos. "These men are what happened. One waited in the car while the other scoped the house. He chose the front door for access, which was game given it's on a main street, but no one was around, and I can only assume he's confident in his abilities. He was fast, I'll give him that. I made my way around the back to try to get in before he did and warn Alex, but I wasn't fast enough. I got her out, thankfully, but she's fairly shaken from the encounter."

"I can imagine. I would be too if I was confronted with Viktor Malinovsky."

Will gasped. "What?"

"The one who sat in the car while his crony did the work is …" She paused, swallowing slowly before continuing, "was Irina's husband – your Uncle Viktor."

"My God!" Will exclaimed. "The R.A. have been the ones hunting the child all along. This is our proof. Irina must have found out and that's why she's …"

Will paused and looked at Evelyn sadly.

"Dead, yes," she finished for him. "It's been quite the day."

"I'm sorry, Mum."

"We can mourn her later," Evelyn said whilst beckoning her son to follow her into the sitting room. "Now, come and introduce me."

Alex sat in an armchair, cradling her cup of tea with both hands as she gazed into the fireplace. She was startled when they entered, causing the tea to spill.

'Alex, this is my mum, Evelyn.'

As Alex turned to look at her, Evelyn was immediately struck by the resemblance to the Grand Duchess. She had watched her ward blossom into the stunning adult she was since birth, yet this was their first time face to face. The Romanov likeness was even more pronounced in real life.

"Hello, Alex. You look very much like someone I once knew. I wish she was still with us," she said with a smile and sat down on a chair opposite.

"Well, I wish I knew what was going on," Alex said quietly.

Evelyn nodded. "I knew your great-grandmother Charlotte. She was an extraordinary woman. I was her nurse."

"Nurse Evelyn," Alex whispered, her eyes lighting up in realisation.

"Yes, that's right. I see that Grace has confided in you. I'm most fond of her. I also knew your grandmother, Elsie, and met your mother when she was very little."

"Ah … yes. Grace and I spoke only a couple of days ago about you and, well … " Alex trailed off, seemingly unsure of what to say.

"It's okay, Alex. Please, let me explain. I was Charlotte's nurse and her protector for a very specific and serious reason. Your great-grandmother was a very important woman from a very important family who was hunted for simply being born a part of it. There are people, like the ones you met earlier tonight, who will do anything to end the line of your family, Alex, and I'm afraid that you and your mother are the current end of the line. You are both in grave danger. These people will stop at nothing to see you dead."

Alex's eyes widened, staring, and her mouth opened slightly, devoid of sound.

"Will and I work for an agency that has been the protector of your family for many, many years."

Alex stood up suddenly. "I want to call the police."

"I understand that this is difficult to comprehend," Evelyn said, also standing, "but the Devil protects his own, and he is still at hunt. The reason he hunts is that Charlotte's family – your family – were very prominent members of the Russian Empire."

"No," Alex said as she stepped around Evelyn and moved quickly into the hallway towards the front door. "This is crazy. I'm leaving. I need to get my dog."

"It's locked, Alex. We can't let you leave. It's for your own safety," Evelyn called after her. "I really need you to trust us."

Alex returned to the room. "Well, I really need one of you to unlock the front door or you risk me breaking a window."

"Please, Alex. Just listen to what my mum has to say," Will said, holding out his hand to her. "It really isn't safe out there, and when we do go back to get your dog, she's—"

"He. Monte," Alex interrupted.

Will nodded. "He, Monte, is going to want you in one piece."

Reluctantly and still with visible trepidation, Alex let Will take her hand and lead her back to the couch. Evelyn gave Will a small nod of acknowledgment.

"Thank you, Alex. I know this is a lot to take in. I'll make it as simple as I can."

Alex sat quietly with a look of defiance on her face.

"Your great-grandmother Charlotte was the daughter of very prominent Russians who were hunted and ultimately murdered by anti-imperial revolutionaries. Charlotte survived as she had been sent as an infant to safety in England. Her family knew the risks that coupled their status and allegiances," Evelyn said. "Unfortunately, the evil responsible for those murders is still in existence today. This is an age-old war in which your family has unknowingly been involved for a very long time, and my family has been your steadfast allies throughout."

Alex frowned in concentration before smiling wryly. "My great-grandmother was born at the turn of the century. Are you telling me that she was a child of the revolution? Please excuse the modern-day cliché for such an important historical event but is that what you're talking about – the Russian Revolution?"

"She was not just any child of the revolution, Alex. She was the Auxiliary Child, Grand Duchess Anastasia Romanov."

A silence descended on the room and Evelyn let it stay that way for some time so the information could sink in. Alex opened her mouth twice as if to speak, but no words passed her lips.

"It has taken the enemy a very long time to find you, but still today they are intent on revenge and murder in the name of their founding fathers," Evelyn finally added.

"Why? Why has it taken so long?"

That wasn't a question Evelyn expected, but people did and said unexpected things when in shock. She sat down again opposite Alex and took her hands.

"Your great-grandmother was lost to the world for many decades, here in America as Charlotte Thornton, then Charlotte Charles upon marriage. In that time, she lived a happy and fulfilled life. Her memory of the life she escaped in London, where she was known as Victoria Burton-Hall, had regressed after a serious illness on the journey here, which was a true blessing. The mind does amazing things to ensure the body can remain functional, Alex. Until she returned to Burton-Hall Estate in 1962, we had no idea if she was dead or alive. I was stationed at the estate, and thank God I was, so we found her again before the enemy realised they'd killed the wrong child."

"Kathryn," Alex murmured.

"Yes, Kathryn," Will confirmed. "My mum brought Charlotte back to Boston where she was cared for at Meadow Oaks."

Alex snapped her head up to look directly at Will. "Cared for? She was placed in a mental asylum!"

Before Will could respond, Alex hastily pulled her hands away from Evelyn's. "My God. I can only assume that what you've just told me are the same things my great-grandmother was accused of fabricating. And if they are in any way true, which I am having serious trouble believing, and you knew who she was and that she was telling the truth about her past … then you're responsible for imprisoning her and letting her family believe she was insane!"

Evelyn stood. "It was either that or Charlotte, your grandmother and mother were at risk of being murdered, Alex. We didn't know if the enemy also still had a watch on the estate."

"You're the insane ones! I want to leave, right now," Alex demanded, leaping to her feet and making her way to the hallway.

Before Evelyn could respond, a phone rang, causing Alex to come to a halt.

"She has a phone with her?" Evelyn turned to ask Will.

Will leaped forward and grabbed the phone that Alex had retrieved from her pocket.

"Put it on speaker," Evelyn ordered.

A dog could be heard barking incessantly in the background as a man's voice spoke.

"Hello, princess." The voice was steely and cold.

Evelyn took the phone from Will and signalled for none of them to talk. The barking continued and Alex covered her mouth with her hands, her eyes opened wide in fear.

"It's okay if you don't feel like talking. Your dog's doing enough of that for my liking."

"Please don't hurt him!" Alex begged, her voice coming back to her.

A single gunshot. Then silence.

"Fucking Romanovs and your dogs."

Alex fell to her knees, tears streaming down her face, reminiscent of the way Evelyn had mourned Irina just twenty-four hours earlier.

"Nothing else to say, princess?"

Once again, Evelyn held a finger to her mouth and shook her head.

"Fine," the voice continued. "Now your dog has been dealt with, I'm going to find you and the whore who gave birth to you, and when I do—"

Evelyn ended the call. They couldn't risk a trace.

"Destroy it," she said, handing the phone to Will.

"No! Please!" begged Alex, jumping to her feet. "I have to warn my parents and we have to call the police!"

Ignoring her objections, Will threw the phone against the wall with force, shattering its glass screen. As Alex watched on in shocked disbelief, he picked up the shattered device, removed the sim card and snapped it in two.

"We already have a watch on your parents while they're exploring the Amalfi, Alex. And regarding the police, they cannot help us," Evelyn said quietly but firmly. "What may help, though, is for me to share some things with you. I need you to start believing, Alex."

"You know my parents … you know my parents are in Europe?" Alex asked, surprised.

"Of course. As I told you earlier, we are charged with protecting Charlotte's family, and as it stands today, that includes you and your mother. Now, you two wait here. I'll be back shortly."

Evelyn hurried to her office where she quickly retrieved two documents from an airtight container in her safe: two letters she had taken from Charlotte long ago. *It was time. Finally.*

It was time to return them to their rightful owner.

Chapter 15

BOSTON, USA

My darling Hannah,

I cannot tell you everything I want to, my love, but I can allude to what you need to know as well as tell you how much I love you. God willing, my words will give some solace and the strength you'll need to continue.

Alex looked up, her face still wet from crying. "This is the missing letter from Charlotte's father?"

Evelyn nodded. "Yes. I kept it along with another letter that I'll share with you next. I only let Charlotte keep the one letter from Josephine as the absence of the others helped make her stories about her family history appear far-fetched. I know that upsets you, but I can't stress enough that it was only done to keep Charlotte safe. Please. Keep reading."

Alex paused to wipe away more tears before continuing.

My heart aches already, knowing that you are without me and that you will be reading these words in fear whilst suffering great angst. Knowing you, you will have listened then obeyed me quietly and with respect. You will have trusted me to hide yourself with our girls, and you will now, God willing, be far away from the estate.

I can only hope that as you left the hiding space, you took from its dark depths the box as I asked, and I pray to the Holy Father that you were able to successfully retrieve the written treasure that I left for Victoria in the rotunda, kept safe by the clover tile. I pray also that the decades-long war that rages between good and evil will subside following my passing.

Being blessed to have had you as my beautiful and beloved wife, I know questions will have risen to the surface of your mind. I ask you to guide Victoria through the contents of her letter and help her follow the path that it alludes to, for then you too will get the answers you seek regarding my past, which is not as you've been led to believe. I'm so deeply sorry that I deceived you.

I want you to know that what I was unable to share with you about my past will be made up for in the riches you will have bestowed upon you. Remember always that I carry, as should you, the Burton-Hall name with immense pride. I may not have been the man you thought, but the Burton-Hall family, as well as my love for you, was undeniably real.

In ending this letter, my darling, I borrow the words of someone I hold very dear to my heart and whom you will learn of once you assist Victoria in completing what she needs to. When you do, you will come to respect and love him just as much as I. Trust me and trust His Holiness above.

Trust that one day the people of the world will rejoice the sacrifices you have made both unknown and known. Your undying quest to ensure the protection of hope, faith, love and luck will be your legacy. Our legacy.

Edward.

A bolt of recognition hit.

"The box … the replica Fabergé egg … that's what he's referring to, isn't he?" Alex asked. "Grace gave it to me. Oh no. It's at my house … I didn't have time to take anything, not even Mon— they've probably destroyed it," Alex rambled as her anxiety levels began to elevate once again.

"I'm so sorry about Monte, Alex. I can tell you loved him very much," Evelyn said, handing her a tissue. "You're right. The egg is what's referred to, but it's okay if the replica's been destroyed. The real one I secured when we found Charlotte. It's safe."

"I'm sorry I couldn't get both you and Monte out," added Will, looking down at his feet.

"It's not your fault, Will," Alex said before turning her attention back to Evelyn. "The *real* one? A real Fabergé egg? I'm sorry, Evelyn, but I really don't know what to believe. Fabergé aside, nowhere in this letter does it confirm that Edward wasn't Charlotte's father, and it certainly doesn't state that she's the daughter of a tsar. This provides no proof of either of those things."

"I understand. Let me give you some context," Evelyn said.

"Context and evidence," Alex countered.

"Of course." Evelyn nodded. "Alright, to start, Edward was Charlotte's uncle, the brother of Tsar Nicholas II, born Grand Duke Michael. Just like his niece, Anastasia, he was an Auxiliary Child, hidden in secrecy in England in case the Romanov bloodline was ever at risk. When Nicholas had children, Edward became what is known as the Keeper of the new Auxiliary Child."

"That being true, who were the people everyone thought were the real Grand Duke and Duchess?" Alex asked.

"Substitutes. I'll come back to that," Evelyn said as she handed Alex a second document. It was written on much thicker paper than the first and at the top was a double-headed eagle. The Russian Empire coat of arms.

"That letter is what Charlotte retrieved from the rotunda when she resurfaced in England in 1962. Before you read it, let me explain why an Auxiliary Child was necessary and came to be."

"Please."

"The Auxiliary Measure was the idea of our last Tsar's grand-mother, Louise of Hesse-Kassel. As the Queen of Denmark and wife of King Christian IX, Louise gave birth to and raised remarkably successful children. The four eldest grew to become King Frederik VIII of Denmark, Queen Alexandra of the United Kingdom, King George I of Greece and our Empress Maria Feodorovna of Russia, the last Tsar's mother. Louise understood the power of a smart betrothal like no other, and the calibre of Louise's offspring was such that she and her King were often referred to as the 'Grandparents of Europe'. Their children held extraordinary and autonomous power."

Will opened a book on the coffee table in front of Alex. A family tree showed what Evelyn had just described.

"The dynastical success of her children had always been a main priority, but ensuring the succession of her children's issue to each of the thrones was Louise's personal obsession. She'd experienced many political and dynastic conflicts during her lifetime, and her rise to the throne had been more convoluted than most. Once she had the power, there was no letting it go," Evelyn explained.

Alex held up a hand. "Do you mean that there is some sort of Auxiliary security agency not just for Russia but also for Denmark, the United Kingdom and … was it Greece? One for each of Louise's four reigning children?"

"No. There's only us," Evelyn confirmed. "The activation of the Auxiliary Measure was born out of extreme times, not just extreme obsession. Louise came up with the idea, but it was her daughter, our beloved Maria Feodorovna, who decided to turn it into a reality."

Will joined Alex on the couch and pointed out a name on the family tree. "Maria became the Russian Empress in 1881 when her father-in-law, Tsar Alexander II, was assassinated," he explained. "At the time, Russia was simmering with unrest. The first of many secret political parties had begun to swell, each formed in reaction to what they considered to be abuses of Russian absolutism. Alexander II was seriously concerned by the spread of these groups, known broadly as nihilists, as well as the increasing number of anarchist conspiracies. For quite some time he'd hesitated between strengthening the hand of the monarchy or making concessions to the political aspirations of the nihilists. Finally, he decided in favour of compromise, and on the very day of his assassination, he signed a decree creating a number of consultative commissions."

"Well, that would have been good thing, yes?" Alex questioned.

"We never got the chance to tell," Evelyn said, also taking a seat. "His son, Alexander III, Maria's husband, had no intention of limiting or weakening the autocratic power he'd inherited from his ancestors. He was determined to adopt the exact opposite policy and immediately cancelled his father's decree before it could be published. The nihilists had made quite a mistake in killing the Tsar, for it put a new leader on the throne who was determined to exterminate them, as publicly as they'd executed his father."

"So Maria was afraid his unsympathetic hand would mean the political radicals would strike again?" Alex asked, now intrigued by what she was being told. "That's why the family instigated this Auxiliary Measure?"

"In a nutshell, yes." Evelyn smiled ruefully. "The nihilists and then the Bolsheviks, who later overshadowed them as the predominant anti-imperial political party, both plotted assassinations and revolutions to bring down the throne. However, due to the Auxiliary Measure, even if they'd succeeded in killing the family, there was an heir in waiting. A child not only hidden from the world but also hidden from themselves."

"The Auxiliary Child," Alex whispered.

"Yes. Does that all make sense?" Evelyn asked softly.

"Well, yes, it sounds … ah … I guess so. I do have a question, though. I know Tsar Nicholas II abdicated, but why? Why renounce the throne after his family had gone to so much trouble to ensure the security measure? Why not ride out the revolution, or at least try to?"

"Because it had been foretold—"

A sharp buzzing noise stopped Evelyn short.

"Are you expecting anyone?" Will asked his mum tensely.

"Certainly not at sunrise, and that's not the intercom, it's my alarm. Quickly, follow me!" Evelyn said as she jumped up from the couch. "We need to get you and Alex into the safe room. Now!"

†

Evelyn hurried them into her office.

"Get in quickly," she said as she punched a security code into a display panel and then leaned in closely for a retinal scan.

"What about you?" Alex asked breathlessly as Will hurriedly ushered her into the safe room, hidden behind a double-mirrored wall, that appeared to be constructed mainly of steel and concrete. "I have to get the egg. Now go."

Evelyn moved to her desk and released a leather insert, unveiling a hidden compartment. Inside, a safe and a digital display showcasing all her security cameras came into view. The front-door camera had been shot out. That wasn't good. It meant they'd already got through her security gate. Her skin prickled with increased awareness. She was trained not to fear, but her heart rate increased and her palms moistened as she entered the safe's code.

Reaching in to remove the egg, her attention was diverted as another of the security camera views dissolved. The downstairs inside hallway. Black-and-white static remained ghostlike on the screen and an eerie buzz accompanied the visual. Enlarging the view, she could make out indistinct movements. Her assailant had not damaged the entire lens. *Sloppy or intentional?* The presence of the faint figures had held her attention longer than if there'd been nothing but a black screen.

"Move, Evelyn," she scolded herself. They had found her much faster than she had anticipated, and now that they were inside, she needed to wipe everything. "Shut down," she grimaced through clenched teeth, repeatedly pressing the function eleven key on her computer to initiate a full-system deletion. The moisture from her sweaty hands left a visible mark on the key as she continued to hit it, hoping to expedite the process. "Delete and shut down, goddamn it."

"Mum, you need to get in here with us," Will called to her.

"Not yet, Will."

She knew he was right. They would be upon her in seconds. *The door.* She ran and locked the internal office door to give herself a small amount of extra time. As she returned to the computer, she heard the door handle turn and shake.

"Shut down, goddamn it to hell," she spat in hushed tones.

The screen flashed 'deletion complete' almost simultaneously with the door buckling under the pressure of something hard and strong.

She urgently scanned the room. Was anything else in jeopardy? Apart from her?

The floor plans! She'd had taken them out the day before to brief Will, and after the call about Irina, she'd forgotten to put them away.

"Mum, get in here!"

Real panic filled her for the first time, and as she contemplated if she had time to secure all the loose papers, a shattering noise filled the room and splinters of wood pierced her skin. The pain was negligible to the panic. She could see the door had shattered, but the damage from whatever explosive they'd used hadn't been enough. She was still secure but wouldn't be for long.

She was out of time. She had to decide: save herself or save their proof of the R.A. history and potentially also the Dowager Empress' confession?

She pulled together every bit of resolve in her.

Both.

As the double-wood door crumbled under the force of a second explosion, she frantically grabbed the plans and shoved them hastily into the box containing the egg. Turning and pushing aside the pain of the small slivers of wood that had sliced into her skin, she ran to the safe room.

"You in here, princess?" a man's voice called out moments after Evelyn reached Alex and Will. A bullet flew past her shoulder and into the rear wall as she turned and secured the lead-lined door.

As she caught her breath, she took the opportunity to assess her attackers. The double-sided and bulletproof glass was darkened so they could see out but their intruders couldn't see in. There were two of them. Both male. Both unsavoury. Viktor Malinovsky was the one in charge, and from all indications the younger man didn't like that at all. That could play in her favour.

Viktor reached down to the floor and her heart stopped. She'd dropped one of the floor plans. He walked to his colleague to show him the document, his mouth moving but his words silenced. As much as she didn't want to hear Viktor's voice, she needed to know what he was saying.

"Get down low under the glass line and stay there. I don't want them seeing you," she ordered Alex and Will before opening the audio between the rooms. "Hello, gentlemen."

They turned in unison to face her. The mirrored wall was now lit in such a way that they could see her.

"Your home security appears a little more archaic than your Russian counterpart's," stated Viktor as he approached, holding the floor plan for Belov's. "We've already burned the place to the ground, which will make it all the easier for us to access the double basement that I can see outlined on here," he added as his friend laughed heartily.

"Viktor. You've aged," Evelyn said.

He flinched slightly at her unexpected remark and took a step backwards. "I don't believe we've had the pleasure of meeting before," Viktor responded, quickly and expertly regaining his composure.

"I'm Anya's sister."

Both Viktor and his friend went quiet and observed her.

Finally, Viktor spoke. "I see." He then took pause again, taking in Evelyn's appearance. "Speaking of aging, you've aged nowhere near as well as she did. There's always an ugly sister," he said, his voice hardening.

Evelyn smiled. "Anya was beautiful, yes. Did you know her real name before she infiltrated the R.A., Viktor? I always thought Irina suited her so much more."

Scowling, Viktor approached her and pressed the round dark end of his gun against the wall that separated them. With his spare hand he used his palm to flatten the plans against the cold glass.

"Anya, your Irina, died in pain. She's no longer a threat, and soon neither will you be."

"The R.A. will not regain control, Viktor. It is not the Lord's desire."

"Oh, that they will, my dear sister-in-law. I have the book your sister prepared to send you, which is how I came to be at this address. And now, thanks to you, I also have the plans to where she kept her files. Boom!" He shot a bullet into the glass for effect.

"It's people like you," he continued, "the Orthodox who maintain such religious arrogance and claim to know what it is that the Lord desires, who will help the R.A. and its supporters gain control. Your eyes are so blinded by faith that you don't see what is right in front of you – millions and millions of unhappy countrymen. Stalin was real. Lenin was real. Real men. Who is God? A man? A woman? None of your kind knows and soon no one will care. If I were purely R.A. propaganda-driven then I wouldn't be here. Your religion is nothing! When the thirty-five million people who want to see a Stalin-style regime returned, succeed in bringing the R.A. to power, your kind will be desecrated."

Evelyn held his gaze as she frantically tried to piece together what he was saying. *Not purely R.A.? Who was he? Who and what had they found themselves up against?*

Viktor laughed. "My religion is not blinded by faith; it is based on knowing. It is based on having connected directly with God. God has lived as one inside me. The reincarnation of the Lord in man was not an isolated event as you uneducated Orthodox believe. God's resurrection is ever renewing. It can happen on earth anywhere, and at any time. The birth at Nazareth, where God became man, was only one such event. To my religion, God is thus human. There is no single representative. He can live only in those of us spiritually awakened to allow it, and when the R.A. takes power, God will be awakened in all those in Mother Russia who accept our doctrines."

There were only a few religious followings that he could be referring to, and the world had long thought them gone. Viktor wasn't just the enemy because of his R.A. involvement. *How had Irina missed something so significant?*

"I surprised you, I can see. Good, that makes me happy. But do you know what would make me absolutely ecstatic?" continued Viktor.

"Apart from doing to me what you did to my sister?"

He smiled and walked in a circle around the office, seemingly deep in thought before returning to stand in front of her.

"What would make me ecstatic is to burn this house to the ground with you suffocating slowly inside. Your panic room may or may not protect you from the heat and flames ... I'll take that risk because I'll have a head start. And let me see ... What else would make me ecstatic is that while you are slowly boiling in your little fishbowl here, I'll find the heir you protect. And once I do, I'll hand her to the R.A. and in doing so sacrifice her in the name of Rasputin. Your aim to reinstate 'God's representative' on earth will be left in ashes as will your churches."

With that statement, Viktor beckoned to his friend. "Filip, burn this whore and her home to the ground."

"With pleasure," said Filip, grinning. "I love to make a woman scream."

Viktor smiled and turned one last time to her. "My friend will go immediately to Belov's, and I will find the princess." He moved to leave the room, but as he reached what was left of the double-wood door, he paused. "The heir will die, and you'll be responsible. I can live with the possibility that you might survive today as I know that you'll carry this knowledge for the rest of your days."

Evelyn watched the two men leave the room before switching off the inter-room audio.

"Stay down."

"Mum, we have to get out. I have no doubt they'll burn the house."

"Evelyn, please, we have to get out," Alex begged with frightened urgency.

"Viktor underestimated me. This room is in no way inferior to the archive basement at Belov's. The fact that the technology isn't visibly prominent is what makes it so safe. We have an exit, but we can't risk leaving yet in case they're still here. They have to believe I'm about to be burned." She kneeled down and hugged both of them. "I'll get us out of here. Have faith."

Chapter 16

BOSTON, USA

Alex sat silently with Will in his car, parked in the underground garage of Evelyn's townhouse. Although she was relieved to be out of the safe room, she felt uneasy because Will's mum wasn't with them. Once Evelyn had considered it safe, she had helped Will and Alex into a small lift that transported them to a secure space hidden at the back of her garage, assuring them she would follow shortly.

Alex's emotions were all over the place. Her head ached and her body shivered in response to the unbelievable series of events that had occurred in the last few hours.

"I think I smell smoke," she said quietly.

Will didn't respond.

"Are we just going to sit here? Will?"

"Be quiet, Alex."

"I think we should go back and check your mum is okay. She's taking a long time."

"Alex, we have to sit here and wait. We don't move. We wait. Imagine just for a second how hard this is for me. I would do anything in this world to protect my mother, but my family comes second to yours. It always has. So we wait as she instructed."

They sat again in silence. *His family always came second to hers.* She sensed the underlying resentment and felt bad for him. She had not asked for any of this and nor, it seemed, had he.

"I'm so sorry if I caused this," Alex offered quietly.

Will turned in his seat to face her. "None of this is your fault, Alex, just as none of it is ours. My mother and I do what we do because we believe it is right, honourable and for the greater good of our country. Casualties and damage are unfortunate, very unfortunate, but they will occur in any war. I'm sorry I snapped at you."

Quiet settled over the car again, and as they waited, Alex thought over the information she'd been given, struggling to comprehend the implications.

"Do you know why your parents called you Alexandra?" Will asked, finally breaking the silence.

"I think it was contentious for my dad, but my mum had a favourite doll when she was a child. Actually, she still has it, Alexandra … oh …" She trailed off quietly and turned to him. "It was a gift from Charlotte."

"Yes. My mother bought the doll for Charlotte to give your mum one Christmas, and Charlotte helped Beth choose the name. The medication she was on meant Charlotte couldn't remember why she liked the name Alexandra, she just knew she liked it. My mum, Nurse Evelyn, suggested Beth make her doll regal by adding something very special. The doll has a little crown, doesn't it? Made of Christmas tinsel."

Alex nodded slowly as an overwhelming sense of anxiety began to engulf her. Alexandra Romanov. The Last Tsarina of Russia. Breathing in and out deeply a number of times, she tried her best to quell her consternation. Was it a sign that this was all real? Or were Will and his mother complicit in a ridiculous multi-generational swindle?

Before Alex had time to think more about it, her attention was distracted by the lift door opening in front of them. "Will!" she gasped.

"Stay here. I'll help her."

Although there was only a small amount of smoke, Alex felt her nose and throat itch as she watched Evelyn step out of the lift, enveloped in a thin haze. Will helped his mother pack a number of silver attaché cases, the box housing the allegedly authentic Fabergé egg and a suitcase into the car.

"Go. Quickly," Evelyn ordered.

Will manoeuvred them into the street and as they drove past the front of Evelyn's house, Alex gasped. Flames had blown out windows and now menacingly licked the exterior façade. Sirens could be heard in the distance and people milled around on the sidewalk opposite.

"I'm so sorry," she whispered.

"It's all a part of God's plan, Alex," Evelyn said quietly.

They drove without speaking until Will turned into a private underground parking facility.

"Bring everything and follow me," Evelyn instructed.

Alex took the egg box from Will and together they followed Evelyn through a heavy wooden door at the far end of the garage. They then began to climb several flights of old wooden stairs. The air was damp, and the slippery wood made the ascent quite challenging. As Alex stepped through the door at the top, she paused to catch her breath and realised they had arrived in a church.

"We'll be safe here. We're two floors down from the nave," said Will.

Alex took in her surroundings. Even in the dim light of the underground room, the gold used on the religious icons adorning the walls glowed as if lit from behind.

"What church is this? she asked.

"My husband's," Evelyn said as she began to light a number of candles around the room. "Whilst I was stationed at Meadow Oaks with your great-grandmother, Richard was stationed here. Next to the Auxiliary, it was his greatest passion. He longed to see a reunion of the church abroad with the values of the Orthodox in Russia. Unfortunately, he died before that occurred," she added as she handed Alex the suitcase. "There are clean clothes in there for you. We can't have you drawing attention by staying in your pyjamas all day."

Alex smiled despite herself. She'd forgotten she was still dressed in what she'd worn to bed the night before.

"The situation is more dangerous than I may have originally thought, but it's not something we can't handle," Evelyn said, turning her attention to Will.

Will's eyebrows raised, but he didn't speak.

"We didn't know everything about Viktor. You heard him. He confirmed he's R.A., but he's also something else altogether."

"What's the R.A.?" Alex asked as she sifted through the suitcase.

"The R.A. are the enemy, Alex. It stands for Red Army, a name borrowed from the revolutionaries that fought the 'good' White Army during the revolution. The White Army were the collective who fought to have the last Imperial Family of Russia bought back from exile and reinstated to power."

"Are you saying he's a sleeper in the R.A.?" Will pressed.

"Yes."

"For whom?"

"Viktor said he would kill in the name of Rasputin. Have you heard of the famous Russian monk, Alex?" Evelyn asked.

Alex nodded as she removed her pyjama bottoms, trying her best to protect her modesty with her large sweater. "My dad's been known to play the song often, and yes, I know the story. He was murdered as it was thought he had too much influence over the Imperial Family."

Will smiled and shook his head. "It's a crazy world where an obscure Russian peasant can rise to such infamy and, sixty years after his death, have a trash disco band write a song about him."

"Indeed," smiled Evelyn.

Will's smile was replaced by a frown of concentration. "Oh … I think I get it," he said, his eyes widening as he started to pace back and forth. "To the Russian communists, Rasputin had a seemingly inextricable relationship with Nicholas and his family. He embodied all that they thought corrupt in the old regime, which they overcame with the revolution, therefore ... the R.A. wouldn't kill in his name." He stopped pacing, suddenly turning to Evelyn. "Khlysts? I can't think of anything else. My God. There have always been theories that Rasputin was a Khlyst member, if not their leader!"

"Who or what are Khlysts?" Alex asked as she pulled on a pair of jeans.

"Khlysts, also known as Khlystovshchina or Bozhii Liudi, meaning 'God's people', were a mass religious movement," Will explained. "The sect formed in the seventeenth century and existed until the early twentieth century ... or so the world thought. It appears that our friends may still be active."

"Exactly," said Evelyn. "After today, it's my belief that the Khlysts are the ones responsible for the murders of Michael and Kathryn, not the R.A. Remember, Irina never found any evidence of R.A. involvement. But Viktor seems to be the common link."

Alex frowned in concentration. "So this is a religious war?"

"One of many," said Will.

"Yes, one of many," sighed Evelyn.

"In revenge for the murder of Rasputin?" Alex questioned.

"So we believe," Will said.

"According to Rasputin's daughter, her father considered Khlysty but rejected it," Evelyn said.

"But that's what we'd expect her to say. The Khlysts were a banned Christian sect whose impassioned services led to rumours that acts of sexual ecstasy were conducted in the rituals," Will explained.

"Oh," Alex whispered as she took a seat.

"Will's right regarding the rumours," said Evelyn. "Many mysterious rituals and strange beliefs were attributed to the Khlysts, and they were also thought to be the most dangerous religious sect. They were attacked in all possible ways, accused of debauchery, the ritualistic murder of children and other bloodthirstiness."

Alex gasped. "Oh my God."

"Speaking of God," said Will, "what I don't understand is why a Khlyst would infiltrate the R.A. in the first place. They have completely opposed ideologies. The R.A. wants to suppress any form of religion, just as Stalin did."

"My original thoughts too. But think about it, Will. We know from Irina's briefings that if the R.A. does take power, they'll do as Stalin did, which is to significantly decrease the power of the Orthodox Church if not fully dissolve it. This would be a blessing to a religion that the Orthodox Church suppressed and made illegal. And don't forget that our church helped to form the religious policy, coupled with repressive measures that saw them outcast," Evelyn explained. "Remember that the Khlysts' greatest strength lay in their aura of mystery. So much so that the original leaders insisted members strictly adhere to the rules of the Orthodox Church to avoid revealing the sect's existence. Without the dominance of the Orthodox Church, they will remain underground as always at the same time as having the monkey off their back."

"Of course," agreed Will. "And given Viktor has an implicit knowledge of the R.A., he may very well use it as a bargaining tool for when the time is right to … forge, let's call it, state favours for his religion."

Alex could feel her frustration building and sighed loudly.

"Alex?" Will asked.

"This is fascinating, but what do we do about all of this? How do we get help? How do we make sure my parents are safe, that we're safe? And where is the proof you told me you have to legitimise your claims that my family are – God, I feel ridiculous even saying it – that my family are Romanovs? I was in the room with you. It seems to me that the enemy already have a book full of information as well as a head start on accessing whatever those plans were for."

Evelyn came and sat beside her. "Are the clothes okay?"

The question surprised Alex. "Ah, yes. Thank you."

"Good. And you're right, Alex. They'll definitely have a head start on the Belov bookstore archive where our evidence to date should be stored. I doubt I'll be able to head them off, but I will try," Evelyn said with conviction. "As for the book, I don't know what's in that. If my sister was in trouble, it may very well be everything she had. So hoping for the best but planning for the worst, we're going to have to follow the Path of Diamonds."

"What?" Alex and Will said in unison.

Evelyn opened one of the attaché cases and pulled out the letter Alex had seen earlier. The double-headed eagles embossed in gold shone dimly in the low light.

"The Tsar's letter. The one we didn't get to read before Viktor turned up. It will guide us," said Evelyn, passing it to Alex to hold. "The Auxiliary wasn't aware of this avenue until Charlotte retrieved the letter from the Rotunda Garden at Burton-Hall Estate. It was a huge surprise to all of us and it became readily apparent that mother and son did not always share what they'd done for each other in the name of love."

"What do you mean?" Alex asked, noting Will had also raised his eyebrows.

"The Tsar's mother had Rasputin killed to protect her son and his family, unbeknownst to Nicholas. On the other hand, as history has told us long after the fact, Nicholas had his fate foretold on at least three prophetic occasions. A fate he didn't share with his mother. The Auxiliary knows from Nicholas' letter that these prophecies acted as a catalyst for him to establish a chain of evidence to reveal his daughter's lineage."

"Prophecies?" Alex questioned incredulously.

"Yes," Evelyn confirmed. "The first of the prophetic warnings Nicholas received from Monk Terakuto in 1891. The second, from Monk Abel, we are positive was delivered in 1901, six months before Anastasia was born. And the third, scribed by St Seraphim, was conveyed in 1903. It was Seraphim who provided the most detailed prophecy known."

"Well let's take the letter to whomever it is that can help us stop all this craziness!" Alex exclaimed.

"The letter itself is not what we require, Alex. It's but a cryptic reference and doesn't offer hard proof. However, for a Romanov or any person skilled in the history of the Romanovs, it does provide hope. Nicholas referred to what we believe is a puzzle called the Path of Diamonds. By solving the puzzle, by walking the path, we'll find the proof that the Tsar saw fit to resurrect his daughter to rule."

A hearty laugh escaped Alex, and once she'd started, she couldn't stop. Tears welled at her eyes. "A puzzle?"

When she realised that neither Evelyn nor Will was responding in kind, her laughter turned to tears and her tears turned into deep guttural sobs.

"I want to … to go home. I want to see what hap … happened to Monte. He could still be alive, and if he's not then … then I want to at least bury him," she cried as she hid her face in her hands, desperately willing her mind to stop imagining Monte lying dead, all alone in a pool of blood.

"I'm so sorry, Alex. It's just too dangerous to let you do that," she heard Evelyn say.

"My dog, your house …"

"Yes, it's been a tough morning, but things will be a whole lot worse for you and your family if you don't trust us."

As Alex wondered what choice she had, Evelyn surprised her with a question.

"Do you know what the meaning of the name Anastasia is, Alex?"

She raised her face to look at Evelyn and, trying her best to control her emotions, shook her head.

"Anastasia means resurrection. The Tsar believed that trials and tribulations would follow until the fourth-born would again bring the Romanovs to power. It is clearly evident from him addressing the letter and providing the puzzle's first clue to his daughter that the Tsar believed she, as his fourth child, would be the one to return to the throne. It made sense as she was the Auxiliary Child. He also referred in the letter to the one named for resurrection as the one that shall live and be victorious."

"But Anastasia was not victorious. You've spent all morning trying to have me believe that she was my great-grandmother!"

"The Tsar's words, based on the prophecies he received and the reality that came to be following his death, still ring true, Alex. Anastasia survived the revolution and was victorious not through sitting on the throne but by spawning children and keeping the direct line intact. To this day, there are four generations that have stemmed from the Grand Duchess, and, Alex, you are the fourth. Anastasia, also known as Victoria and Charlotte; her daughter, your grandmother Elsie; your mum, Beth; and then you. Four. This is why we are so very sure that you will be the one to bring the Russian Monarchy, the Romanovs, once again to power."

If she'd been asked only five minutes before if her life could get any stranger, Alex would have sworn that it couldn't have. Yet it just had. *Power? What on earth did that mean?*

"If we don't have the R.A. history and plans, won't we be at risk of not receiving the state's support regardless of any evidence we find? They don't have to reinstate the heir, sorry, reinstate Alex in any official way," Will said.

Reinstate? Alex mouthed silently.

"It certainly waters down our ability to showcase that there's a threat to the current government, which would have worked in our favour to get them on side and consider a constitutional monarchy. The state and imperial supporters combined would be a global sensation, sure to drive investment into our country. That being said, reinstatement can still be accomplished without proof of an explicit threat from a third party. Remember, Medvedev and Putin are key."

"Putin's United Party may call itself conservative, heirs to Russia's tradition of statehood, both tsarist and socialist, but is it enough?" asked Will.

Evelyn nodded in agreement, while Alex remained speechless and stunned. *Reinstate?*

"Unlike many of his predecessors, Medvedev has publicly declared his faith," Evelyn continued. "He's one of us, baptised a Russian Orthodox Christian when he was in his early twenties. And Putin … well, don't underestimate the influence that one's family can have on a man. Putin's father was a model communist and an atheist, but Putin's mother was a devoted Orthodox believer even during a time when the government persecuted the church. She even ensured that Putin was secretly christened as a baby at risk to her marriage. Putin has also spoken publicly of how he had a religious awakening following the serious car crash that involved his wife and he has also said that his faith deepened further during a life-threatening fire involving his family. Last but not least, his mother gave him a baptismal cross in his adult life, which he had blessed and has not taken from around his neck since. We have the sympathy we need."

Alex felt as though she might faint. "I want to … to go home," she whispered.

"Sorry, Alex? What did you say?" Evelyn asked her.

"I want go home," she said with more force.

Evelyn put her hand on Alex's shoulder. "No. Please don't ask again."

Chapter 17

BOSTON, USA

At least the hotel room had a minibar, Viktor thought as he looked through the selection. Most US hotels had gotten rid of them of late. He needed something hard after losing the heir today. Filip leaving Alex in the backyard, gate locked or not, was infuriating. Viktor had been glad to send him back to Russia to scout the hidden archive at Belov's so he didn't have to look at him. If Filip screwed up again there'd be consequences.

"My God. Smirnoff. Seriously?"

He hated Boston. Actually, he had always hated America. But now he hated it even more, which he hadn't thought possible. Their vodka was hideous. He settled on throwing back a whisky shot. Then another.

"Cheers to you, Anya," he toasted his wife before downing a third.

Viktor picked up one of the photo frames he had taken from the houses they had broken into, retrieving it from where he had laid them on the bed. Alex was beautiful. Her long dark hair and angular face reminded him a lot of Grand Duchess Tatiana. It would be a shame to sacrifice someone so beautiful, but such was life. As for the man who'd helped her escape, well, he definitely wasn't unattractive either, but he'd certainly end up ugly when Viktor got ahold of him.

He ran his hand over the faces in another photo. It had been hard to see her well in the panic room, but now he'd had time to properly look at the selection of photos, the sister did resemble Anya in many ways.

"Alex, William and Evelyn," he mused.

He hadn't been surprised to find Evelyn's details when he'd looked up the owners of the house they'd torched. Hiding in plain sight was a tactic he knew very well. William, on the other hand, he'd found from a numberplate check. Filip had managed to recall the plate even though he'd let them get away. There was one positive.

Evelyn Forster and William Forster. Same name, so most definitely related, he'd assumed. What he'd also found, which confirmed his assumptions, was an old newspaper article in the public records about an Orthodox church fundraiser that was accompanied by a photo of Reverend Father Richard Forster, his wife, Evelyn and son, Will. He'd bet his life on the fact that Richard was Anya's holy man. It was all in the family.

Grabbing the remote, he swiftly flipped through the TV channels. Every news station reported nothing other than firefighters having been deployed to Evelyn's home and continuing investigations. There was no news at all about loss of life, so he had no idea if Anya's sister was still alive. He also had no idea where Will and Alex might be, which was infuriating, and worse still, there would be no more hiding in plain sight after the events of that morning.

Seating himself at the hotel room's small desk, Viktor checked in on the police frequencies. Still nothing. *Had the bitch escaped?* Well, that would be a turn up for the books – but actually, respect if she had. Perhaps he'd found a worthy adversary, and perhaps, therefore, he'd have his way with her before he killed her.

"Take that, Anya. Just keeping it in the family, sweetheart. It's what we do."

He smirked to himself as he used his phone to snap close-up photos of each person in the stolen frames. He then uploaded the images to a 3D facial recognition app developed by the R.A. While the software itself wasn't new, the proprietary infiltration program that allowed them to intercept the computers of major airports worldwide was. This infiltration worm granted them access to any airport computer, anytime and anywhere. It was a hacker's dream come true, made all the more impressive by the fact that they had yet to be caught using it, twenty-two months after the program's launch. For now, Russia led the electronic war, a silent, non-confrontational battle that had far surpassed the technological threats of the Cold War. Things had come a long way since his father had hunted Grand Duchess Anastasia.

Now that he'd uploaded their photos, he had to wait patiently for a match.

He was going to need them to restock the minibar.

†

"Here you go," said Will as he appeared at the top of the wooden stairs and entered the room carrying a few small bundles. He'd been gone for a couple of hours to prepare for whatever came next, leaving Alex and Evelyn alone to talk about the Auxiliary.

As much as she resisted it, everything Alex had learned was farfetched but could also very well be true, and she wondered if she was experiencing similar emotions to what Charlotte had all those years ago.

"What is it?" she asked, catching the small zippered cloth bag Will threw to her.

"Your passport."

"You went to my house? Is Mont—"

"It's your new passport – well, actually, passports. Plural. After you visited Meadow Oaks, I took the liberty of making some fake credentials for you just in case we encountered any threat from the R.A. Even though we'd doctored the files to state Charlotte had no

166

next of kin, your asking questions could have alerted them. You can never be too careful. There are three new identities for each of us."

"Oh. Wow. Okay," she said sadly, opening the case to see what he'd created.

"And to answer your question, yes, I did go to your house. I found Monte."

She didn't think any more tears were possible, but they again flowed down her cheeks as her hands froze on the zip of the case.

"He'll be alright, Alex. He may not bark again, but his tail will definitely wag again."

"Oh my God, Will! Thank you! Thank you so much," she exclaimed loudly as she threw her arms around his neck, resting her face against his shoulder. "Where is he?" she said, stepping back.

"He's with a friend of mine who's a vet. I told him I'd been minding Monte and that my house had been burgled while I was at work. He'll need to be under observation for about a week, but all going well, we should be out of this mess by then and you can go and collect him yourself."

The news was like a shot of adrenalin.

"Thank you," she said, feeling a little embarrassed now for hugging him.

He smiled and nodded as Evelyn walked towards them carrying the Tsar's letter.

"I'm glad you're back safely," Evelyn said, touching his arm briefly. "We've been waiting for you to talk about the puzzle. But before we do, tell me, did you also manage to check on Beth?"

"Oh my goodness, yes – are she and my dad okay?"

"They're fine." Will smiled. "Seem to be loving Italy. I've transferred some additional Auxiliary funds to the private investigator who's keeping them secure. I also deployed security for Grace as an extra precaution."

"Good job, Will," Evelyn said.

Alex felt awful. She'd thought them both callous for not letting her go back home when she so desperately wanted to, but here they were, risking their lives to protect her entire family while keeping her safe.

"Thank you too, Evelyn," Alex offered with a smile.

Evelyn smiled back and beckoned Alex and Will to sit with her. "I'm going to read the letter out loud in the interest of time," she said as they sat. "Ready?"

They both nodded, so Evelyn cleared her throat and began to read.

Victoria,

We are yet to meet, but one day we will, bathed in the light of God. Although you do not know me, I intrinsically know you. We are bound together by blood, just as you are to the father you know as Edward Burton-Hall.

There is an enormity to the path that this letter will ask you to follow, for it paves the way into a past unknown to you and towards a family you have never had the chance to love. Take with you on every step ahead, the knowledge that you have always, always had our love.

In reading this letter you will no doubt have heard the recent news from Russia. You will know that three hundred years of Romanov rule came to an end … first, with the imperial abdication of the throne, followed by the assassination of many prominent Russians. I and my family are no more. Your father will be able to educate you about any questions you may have regarding this tragic event and will also be able to confirm with you another very important fact. Although you are bound to him by blood, it is not of a direct line. He is a brother to me, born as Michael, and he has served as an honourable and brave father to you. However, it is I, Victoria, who is your biological father.

You will be overwhelmed. Do not question the love Michael or I have for you. It is in no way diminished now this fact has been disclosed. We both love you unconditionally. You are where you are and have become the person you are in order for you to have a life. Your life, although not entirely your own, is founded on the unconditional love that parents have for their child. Always remember it is not just love that will conquer evil but only love.

I knew my life was in danger, which is why you were sent to safety. I lived with regret having never held your hand as you've grown, but I will rest in Heaven knowing that your hands will be held by so many people, and they will heal past wrongs in a time when I am no longer alive to do so.

Do not be afraid, my beloved daughter.

Michael will help lead you on the path to your past, which when complete, will direct you to your future. He will explain to you in person the particulars of who your family were. It is too much to expect that you receive that information in the written word. It is better to be told in person. Victoria, you will draw strength from him, as he, like you, is a child of the revolution.

Seek, my child. Let no one stall your rite of passage. Journey home via a path of diamonds. Hold onto hope and maintain a full circle of faith. Gain strength from the love that is all around you and luck will be your legacy. You are our family's last remaining symbol of life, and it is this fact that will see you reborn. You will live to be a great defender of all men.

Victoria, we will one day again be as one. Until that time, I, alongside your mother, will look down on you as angels of God and bless your way.

Your father,
Nicholas.

Evelyn put down the letter and looked at them in silence, waiting for their reactions.

Alex found she couldn't respond and instead stared intently at nothing whatsoever. For some reason she couldn't explain, the words Evelyn had delivered, written nearly a century ago, made her want to believe. But belief was only the start. How could she do what had been asked of Charlotte when the person who was meant to guide her had been so brutally deprived of his own life and so long ago?

"No wonder Charlotte was confused and upset," she eventually managed. "And we're never going to be able to move forward. Edward – sorry, Michael was killed. He was the guide."

"Not the guide, the leader, Alex. The egg is the guide," Evelyn said as she leaned down to remove the Fabergé artwork from its carved box.

Alex was still suitably confused. "What am I missing?" she asked.

"And me," Will added. "You weren't wrong when you said the letter was cryptic."

"I'll show you," Evelyn said as she carefully placed the artwork on a pew before beckoning them closer. "The Tsar refers to this egg in his letter, and to reiterate, the artwork sitting in front of us is not a replica. It's authentic, meaning that the Fabergé Clover Egg that sits in the Kremlin Museum today is either a fake or a twin."

"What must this be worth?" Alex wondered.

"Based on what it can provide us, it is priceless," Evelyn said as she once again picked up the Tsar's letter and held it out for Alex to hold. "Now, I'll draw your attention specifically to one paragraph where Nicholas refers to the Path of Diamonds. Alex, could you please reread it for us?"

"It's in English?" she exclaimed in surprise as Evelyn handed her the letter.

"Yes, Nicholas was highly proficient in both spoken and written English. He understood that it was unlikely his estranged daughter would have any knowledge of Russian," Evelyn explained. "Therefore, we can anticipate that all his communications intended for Anastasia will be delivered in English."

Alex nodded and began to read.

Seek my child. Let no one stall your rite of passage. Journey home via a path of diamonds. Hold onto hope and maintain a full circle of faith. Gain strength from the love that is all around you and luck

*will be your legacy. You are our family's remaining symbol of life,
and it is this fact that will see you reborn. You will live to be a great
defender of all men.*

Alex looked up from the letter and saw that Evelyn had opened the egg so that its expertly crafted surprise was visible to them.

"This egg is the symbol of life Nicholas refers to. It is the first piece of the puzzle. I'll give you that much as a start. Now, look for yourselves at the bases of the four leaves that house the portraits of the Grand Duchesses. What do they tell you?"

Alex and Will took turns leaning in to examine the egg closely.

"There appear to be four words engraved, one on each leaf. I can't read them. They're so small," Alex said.

"Hope, faith, love and luck," said Evelyn.

"What that tells us I'm not really sure," Alex frowned.

"Well, for what it's worth," Will chimed in, "Dad taught me about the blending of many Celtic traditions into Christianity. The importance of the clover was one of them. The first three leaves represent faith, hope and love, and the fourth leaf God's luck."

"Yes," Evelyn said. "And?"

As the idea came to her, Alex looked up at Evelyn. "You said the Path of Diamonds was a puzzle, right?"

Evelyn nodded.

"Did you mean literally?" Alex questioned as she ran her fingers gently over the leaves of the clover surprise, wondering if the egg itself could be the puzzle.

Evelyn smiled.

"Hope, faith, love, luck ... Yes, I think I know ... maybe ..."

"Know what?" asked Will, frustrated.

Alex carefully turned the egg on its side and observed underneath the small delicate portraits. They were affixed to the base from what she could tell. "I feel terrible not wearing gloves. Evelyn, can you please read again what it says about hope?"

"Hold onto hope and maintain a full circle of faith," Evelyn read.

"Will, can you try something for me, please?" Alex asked him. "Hold onto the portrait that has 'hope' engraved on it and gently push down, or perhaps sideways," she said. "Whichever makes it move."

"You think it's a mechanical puzzle?" he asked, looking at his mum who gave a nod of approval. "Okay … oh God, my hands are shaking!" Will looked up in surprise as the portrait moved slightly when he pushed it directly down.

An exhilarating surge of excitement came over Alex. The egg *was* the puzzle!

"Now twist the 'faith' portrait in a full circle from the base of the leaf or try turning the frame around the portrait itself."

"Nothing," he said.

"Hmm. Maybe you have to keep doing whatever you did to the hope leaf whilst you manipulate the faith leaf."

As Will followed her instructions, the faith portrait spun in a circle from its base. The first action had acted as a catalyst for the second! As Will spun the portrait a full circle, they heard a small click.

"Oh my goodness, that actually worked! What's next, Evelyn?" Alex asked excitedly.

"*Gain strength from the love that is all around you,*" Evelyn recited.

"Strength? Gain strength from love?" Alex mused.

Will gently pushed the portrait engraved with 'love'. It didn't move.

"Can you move the entire leaf maybe?" she asked him.

"No … but let me try …" Will's face lit up. "The faith leaf moves! I can position it diagonally to lean up hard against the third leaf. Surely that means it's gaining strength from love?"

Another small click gave them the answer.

"*And luck will be your legacy, Alex,*" Evelyn read without having to be asked.

"And luck will be my legacy," Alex whispered as she took the lead and carefully pulled on the leaf engraved 'luck', that held the final portrait. The portrait of Grand Duchess Anastasia.

They all sat in silence. The luck leaf had come fully loose from the egg's surprise and Alex now held it carefully.

"You've done this before?" Will asked his mum.

She smiled broadly. "I may have."

Alex placed the tiny, bejewelled leaf into Will's outstretched hand. It was so very small, but now free from its hiding place, they could see the clover-leaf stem, etched with elaborate markings on one side, was in fact a key. A key that looked to be made of sparkling emeralds and white diamonds.

Alex looked at Evelyn and Will expectantly.

Evelyn held out a small magnifying glass.

"Read it to us, Alex. Like the Tsar's letter to Anastasia, it is in English."

She leaned in closer, squinting to help her eyes adjust.

Shame on him who thinks this evil for she is the key to her master's lock.

Alex saw Will turn to catch his mum's eye and Evelyn nodded at him.

"You both know what that means?" Alex asked.

"Yes," Evelyn said. "It means the two of you need to get ready to fly to London. Tomorrow."

"You're not coming with us?" Will asked, surprised.

"No, I'm going to Moscow. Tonight."

Chapter 18

MOSCOW, RUSSIA

Filip had flown all night and was pissed off, to say the least. Viktor had made him take the red-eye, made worse with a one-stop layover. He'd gotten no sleep, but at least with the time difference it was almost night back in Russia. Sleep wouldn't be too far away after a few drinks and, God willing, getting laid.

He swayed slightly as he walked back to the scene of destruction he'd been responsible for only a few days before, the lack of sleep and jetlag now hitting hard. The all-day airport breakfast he'd had after making his way through Moscow customs should have perked him up, but the crappy watered-down coffee hadn't hit the mark. What a waste of time.

At the site that had been Belov's, the charred smell remained, even though the area had been partially cleared. The thin space where the bookstore had once conducted business was now secured with a temporary high metal fence, a large chain woven through the opening with a locked padlock. It was nothing Filip couldn't get past.

As he debated whether to climb the fence or break the padlock, a sudden movement caught his eye. Despite the darkness, Filip was certain he saw someone inside the fenced area rising from the ground and moving towards him, possibly carrying something. As he strained his eyes, it became clearer – yes, the figure was holding what appeared to be a backpack or a satchel.

It was clear the person had exited the basement, which meant Filip could abandon the building plans. They had likely already ransacked anything of value. That would save him time and energy. *Good. He would need all the energy he had for later when he visited the Khlyst Mother of Christ.*

Quietly, he retreated into the doorway of a building opposite so as not to be seen. It had to be one of the protectors, one of Anya's colleagues – if it were anyone official then the gate wouldn't be locked. The person in the shadows didn't want anyone to know they'd infringed on the space. Well, that was bad luck as he was about to infringe on them.

As the person ascended the fence and then began the downward climb on the other side, a voice bellowed out an order.

"Stop right there!"

The person froze momentarily at the sight of a police officer before jumping awkwardly from the fence. They fell heavily, crying out in pain as they sat on the ground clutching their knee.

Filip sighed. The dramatics. He didn't need this.

As the officer approached the culprit, Filip arrived as well, huffing and pretending to be out of breath. The person on the ground was a relatively young man.

"Officer! This man stole my bag!" Filip exclaimed.

The man sat momentarily assessing his situation then tried to run, an idea that was short-lived. His face contorted in pain and he slumped back to the cold ground as his injured knee collapsed underneath him.

The officer walked over and stood above the young man, his gun outstretched. Filip sighed. If it were him he would have used it by now. Instead, he had to play games. This was tedious.

"Officer, I can't thank you enough," Filip praised. "This man snatched my bag as I was getting out of a taxi. I tried to chase him, and if you'd not come along when you did, he would have escaped over that fence. Thank you so much."

Filip moved to take the bag but found himself facing the barrel of the officer's gun as well as a strong denial from the culprit.

"I don't know this man. Never seen him. This is not his bag!" the young man exclaimed in defiance before giving Filip a look that said he too could play this game.

The police officer sighed as he pushed the gun under Filip's chest to make him stand upright and step away from the bag.

"Now just hold up a minute, sir," the officer said. "From my perspective, all I was able to see was this man climbing on the fence. Who knows if he was climbing in or out, or why? So I'll take the bag, and if you can identify the contents, then I'll be happy to let you have it and continue on your way, while I take care of the young thief. Vice versa if the young man is able to identify the contents. Now, what's it to be?"

Filip was too tired for this.

"Here's my answer," he spat as he knocked the officer's arm roughly towards the sky.

The gun dropped to the ground, and before the officer could contemplate what had happened, he was sprawled facedown next to the young man, a single bullet to the head. Trickles of thick viscous blood seeped out underneath the dead officer's face and began to dissolve into the icy ground, staining it an ugly deep red.

"Jesus Christ! Take the damn bag," the young man yelled, trying to push himself away from the body. "It's got a sandwich in it."

Filip laughed. "A sandwich? You just saw me shoot a police officer and you're going to go with a sandwich?"

"You're frigging nuts, man. I was hungry. I live on the streets, so a sandwich is a goddamn feast. Some woman gave it to me along with some cash to hang around and yell out if I saw anyone snooping.

Seriously, I just wanted a feed," he said, pulling cash out of his pocket and throwing the notes frantically towards Filip.

Filip grabbed the bag and tore it open. Reaching in, his hand came across what was most certainly a sandwich. *Fuck!*

He pointed his gun at the young man's face. "Why had you climbed inside the fence then?"

The young man looked surprised. "I didn't. I ran into the woman in the back alley. The fence back there already had the chain and padlock cut. Once she was done, this way was a shortcut for me to go sink the cash on vodka."

Filip could feel a rage rise up inside him. Unbelievable. He'd been beaten to the archive by a woman. "I'll give you a shortcut," he spat and put a bullet in the young man's chest before running back to the fence. Nothing. There was nothing. No sign of her. This was not good.

After a sweep for security cameras, Filip walked briskly away and kept going until he reached a small park not far from the sect's quarters. He sat quietly on a park bench and watched the steam rising up from the cold damp streets. Just in case he'd been followed, he decided to stay away from the worship den for the time being. With their religious acceptance and subsequent dominance in sight, the last thing he wanted to do was draw any unwanted attention.

Viktor was going to be pissed.

"You know what? Screw you, Viktor," he spat. "Ah, speak of the devil," he added with a sneer as he stood up once more. As he answered the call, he resumed walking. He was less likely to be overheard while in motion.

"Viktor."

"Filip. What did you find?"

"Nothing we don't already have," he lied.

"Okay. Good work. Did you find Evelyn?"

The question took him aback. Who the hell was Evelyn?

"Well? I left you a message, Filip. I pinpointed her at the airport shortly before your flight. She went through customs under the name Jennifer Thomas, with longer, slightly darker hair than we saw in Boston. She was headed to *Moscow*, Filip. A different flight from yours, but also to Sheremetyevo. She would've landed not long after you."

That must be the sister. That's who'd beaten him to the archive. His underwhelming all-day breakfast had cost him more than a seemingly everlasting lethargy.

"I was already on the plane so my phone was off, but yes, I got your message when we landed. No sign of her so far," he lied again.

"Filip. Keep your goddamn phone on at all times. I need to be able to contact you twenty-four seven. It won't bring down the plane; I've been doing it for years. Thank Christ you got to the archive first."

"It's been a busy evening," he said, this time with no trace of a lie.

"Well, it's about to get busier. I need you to be on call all night in case the surveillance program detects Evelyn somewhere else in Moscow. So that means no fraternising with your ladies and ensuring you leave your phone on. Then tomorrow, if we haven't heard anything more of her by midday, you need to get on the first available flight to London. I'll explain everything when you arrive. Call me when you land and I'll let you know where to meet me."

"You're already there?"

"I just landed. It's been busy for all of us, Filip."

As he started to respond, Viktor hung up.

Filip shoved his phone into the pocket of his coat. The man infuriated him. Always ordering him around like a dog. He was the Christ-elect. He deserved more respect, and he wanted it now. His patience was wearing thin waiting to lead, and worse still, he had no idea how long the wait would be. He desperately wanted it now, but the rite of passage that had been bestowed upon him was of no set time frame. It was Viktor alone who would choose when Filip would be anointed, and the only way it would occur any sooner was if Viktor was dead.

A thought that had come to him often once again settled itself front and centre in his mind. *Surely, killing Viktor was an acceptable path?* Sin, after all, was the underlying foundation of their entire religion. It was the path to God. Taking the life of the current holy representative would surely be the greatest sin of all. It would potentially make him the greatest Khlyst leader of all time.

As if a sign from God himself, the moon peeked out from behind the clouds and Filip nodded, agreeing with his thoughts as he stood and began walking towards the sect headquarters. *Yes. He, Filip, should be the face to bring their religion to the eyes of the world, to awaken the masses as Rasputin had always intended.* And as for fraternising, Filip was well and truly about to try. He wanted to suss out the Mother of Christ's loyalties. If she would endorse him taking over from Viktor, he might not have to be rid of him.

The thought of taking her for the first time alone aroused him, and his heart rate quickened. He'd taken her in a group, but never alone … that was Viktor's hosting responsibility as the almighty Christ. That she'd agreed to meet with him at all was a start, and if she did in fact succumb to his suggestion, it would mean that she'd endorse his succession as the chosen one to take over from Viktor. Oh God, he hoped that would be the outcome, and if it was, he would arouse then take her violently to climax, and she would enjoy it.

It would be God's will that she enjoy it.

†

Evelyn's driver sped through the streets. As they crossed the river into central Moscow, the water danced with colours, reflecting the decorative lights and buildings that lined it. She undid her seatbelt and slid across the back seat, her attention drawn to the spectacle of the new Cathedral of Christ the Saviour where Nicholas and his family had been canonised as saints in 2000. It took her breath away.

She'd only seen photos of the original that, after standing proud for over forty years, had been demolished in 1931 at the order of

Stalin. The drawings of Stalin's vision for the site were definitely something to behold, complete with a statue of Lenin crowning the over four-hundred-metre-tall monstrosity. The communist leader had wanted to make way for a new palace dedicated to the Soviets, but the new palace never saw the light of day due to the outbreak of the Second World War and a lack of funds.

There was nothing monstrous about the new cathedral. It was magnificent in every sense of the word, a grand symbol of the people reclaiming religion. Its stone and white marble façade topped with five golden domes was lit up beautifully.

Evelyn opened the window to allow an uninterrupted view, cold air whipping against her face. The air was sour, as were her thoughts. It was bittersweet to have finally returned to her grandparents' birth country after so long then have to leave again so soon … and with empty hands.

"Damn it," she murmured. The search of the basement had been fruitless. Her initial elation that no one had compromised the location was soon deflated when she realised that Irina had either moved everything or everything she'd had was in the book Viktor now possessed.

She still had no idea if her sister had retrieved the Dowager Empress' Auxiliary confession. Was that in the book? Was that how Viktor had known about Alex? Or had the Khlysts known that Charlotte had resurfaced at Burton-Hall Estate and the Meadow Oaks file request had alerted them to a potential descendant? She shook her head. Surely if they'd known about Charlotte then they'd have come to finish her off – or had her being committed with all evidence of her descendants hidden been enough to keep them at bay, simply waiting for her to die a sad, incarcerated death?

Evelyn had absolutely no idea.

At least if the confession was in the book it would be a copy, that much she knew. The original Richard and Irina were to leave in Louise's tomb for the state to officially retrieve when the Auxiliary had them on side. So now she'd have to try to get a copy herself and do so without asking the Patriarch for help, even though his endorsement would make it much easier. He would already be unimpressed with the cost of her allowing Will and Alex the added security of a private jet, and he'd be livid if he knew why. No, she'd fix this. Irina deserved not to be remembered in any way a failure.

She closed the window as they drove alongside the grounds of the Kremlin. The inner-city fortress was also amazingly beautiful, and as they passed the Grand Kremlin Palace, Evelyn could just make out the domes of Saint Basil's Cathedral in Red Square, lit up like a beacon to God in the night sky. She would be so proud to bring both Will and Alex here and introduce them to their heritage. It was her hope that when the state accepted Alex, they would finally remove the remaining red stars atop the Kremlin and once again showcase double-headed eagles.

They passed the State Duma buildings and continued by Theatre Square, where Evelyn's breath caught in her throat.

"It's okay, Mila. We'll find ways to see each other all the time," her sister's fifteen-year-old voice ran though her mind as the Hotel Metropol, where they'd last embraced, came into view.

"Don't go, Irina."

"I have to, Mila. We were born for this."

Her sister had also died for this.

Evelyn silently made the sign of the cross and prayed that all her family had been accepted into Heaven and were watching over her, bestowing angelic strength to help her finish the Auxiliary's mission. Her hands were shaking, so she clasped them together. She'd not yet had time to properly mourn Irina, and the memories hit hard. She hadn't expected the sight of the hotel to affect her quite so much, but whilst the city had seen huge refurbishment and modernisation, the Metropol looked eerily the same.

She couldn't take her eyes off the building. They'd been so young when Irina was put undercover that it could be considered unfair, and Evelyn had often asked herself if things would have been the same if her parents hadn't been killed. Would she and Irina have enjoyed a normal childhood?

She knew the answer all too well, and as usual, when her thoughts ventured down this path, she scolded herself. Her grandparents had started young, not yet in their teens when Adri chose them for training as Auxiliary agents. Under his guidance, they mastered the art of warfare and became part of a misfit family, initially united by allegiance but eventually bonded by love.

It was her grandparents who, alongside Adri, had rid the world of Rasputin, cleaning up the botched attempt by the Tsar's nephew and his friends on the notorious monk. They were also the ones Adri selected to accompany him to England after the Tsar's abdication, providing extra security for the Auxiliary Child and her Keeper.

Evelyn closed her eyes. She needed to focus on what to do next, and right now she really had only one option. Denmark.

She felt her handbag vibrate before she heard the ring and signalled for the driver to close the dark glass partition between them before answering.

"Will?"

"Mum. I'm so glad you answered. I've been worried."

"You don't need to worry about me."

"I know, but I do, no matter how many times you tell me not to, and don't expect me to ever stop. Did you find what we needed or are Alex and I flying to London tonight?"

"No." She sighed. "Unfortunately, whilst I appeared to have arrived before Filip, Irina didn't have anything stored at Belov's, meaning Viktor most likely has everything already. So I'm going to have to go to Denmark to try to retrieve our copy of the Dowager Empress' confession. I'm on the way back to the airport now but won't be able to fly out tonight due to curfew. The next direct flight is around lunchtime tomorrow. Not ideal, but it will give me time to decide the best way to tackle things. I'll let you know which hotel I end up in when I know myself."

"Damn it. London it is."

"How are you both doing?"

"Well, Alex is a little claustrophobic, as am I, to be honest. I've never spent this much time in a room with no windows. It's a little disconcerting, I'll admit. It did help that we got some sleep overnight."

"At least you got some rest, and the lack of external stimulation hopefully meant you could both focus on matters at hand. Is she taking it all okay?"

"Yes. Still extremely sceptical, as you can imagine. There's still a lot of detail to explain to her."

"Do your best to keep educating her. The intricacies of European royalty are interesting at least. And her state of mind?"

"Good, all things considered."

"Alright, I know it's hard to talk with her there, but things sound promising. Our faith in her has not been misplaced. You're doing a great job as you'll continue to do when you arrive in the UK. I've heard back from the management and you're booked in – as Professor Lloyd – to meet with a guide, Brendan, at nine. They're very excited by your dissertation on behalf of the Russian Orthodox Church."

"I bet the Patriarch won't be!"

"I've spoken to him. It was time to bring him into the fold. Not about everything since your father's death, but certainly the ramifications of Irina's death, Viktor's involvement and him having the R.A. evidence."

"I don't envy you that conversation."

"No. Let's not talk about it."

"Okay, Mum. Well, I'll call you as soon as we've finished our appointment and let you know what we find."

"Thank you."

"And, Mum?"

"Yes?"

"Please be careful."

"Always."

Chapter 19

LONDON AND WINDSOR, UK

"We'll be starting our descent soon, so please make your way back to your seats and fasten your seatbelts. And, sir, I'll need you to shut down your laptop as well, please. Thank you."

Alex glanced at Will, who was sitting at a desk on the other side of the lounge. He hadn't acknowledged the attendant and kept working feverishly on his computer. He'd be sure to get another reminder soon, although maybe there was more leeway for those who could afford a private jet. The Auxiliary certainly seemed to be flush with cash.

She wasn't used to such unbridled luxury. Alex could never have imagined she'd get the chance to experience a plane like this. Able to carry ten people, it had a master and guest bedroom suite, an office, a lounge and a bar. Its luxurious gold and lacquered-wood accents made it feel like a five-star apartment. An apartment that could fly.

The experience had helped take her mind off her parents and Monte for some of the time, at least, and for what it was worth, when they did enter her thoughts, she'd said a quick prayer asking for their safety. She didn't know what good it would do, as whilst baptised a Christian, she'd not been to church for a very long time.

She made her way back to her seat, which was more like a leather wingback chair, and after belting up, she raised her blind to look at the view. Beautiful fluffy white clouds were lit by the late afternoon sun and the diamond wedding band she now wore on her left hand caught the sun's rays sending light bouncing around the cabin. It was quite the sparkler. A loan from Evelyn.

"Your husband didn't join you?" asked the attendant as she passed.

Alex smiled. There would be no special treatment for her 'husband' after all.

"You may want to tell him again. Men never listen to their wives," she joked, and the attendant left to fetch Will in order to prepare for landing.

Talking about Will in this way felt strange, but if they were going to pull things off, she'd have to start fully embracing their new identities. Flying out of the US under a false name was one thing, but she'd need to be even more convincing to get past UK customs.

Feeling anxious about the lie, Alex opened her passport: her face looked up at her but her name did not. Closing it again, she breathed in and out slowly. Based on everything she'd uncovered and been told in the last few days, it seemed her family had a way with changing names.

During the first few hours of the flight, she'd researched all she could find about the revolution and downfall of Russian imperialism. It truly was a tragic history. To think that the entire Imperial Family had been led into a small cellar under the guise of being moved for their safety and then massacred alongside their loyal servants and dogs was … A tear escaped her eye, which she hastily wiped away. Had those people who had suffered such a tragic demise really been her family?

What had Viktor said on the phone?

"Fucking Romanovs and your dogs," she mouthed silently.

Could it be? Could she really be a descendant of the Romanov ruling family? There were certainly a number of people who thought so, and thankfully she was with the ones who didn't want her dead because of it. For now, they seemed her best chance at returning life to some sort of normalcy. She bristled at the thought of the woman who had unknowingly served the Imperial Family as the Substitute. Her life had been anything but normal. Anna Anderson or unnamed child Schanzkowska, as Alex now understood the woman to have been born, had been ridiculed by so many when she resurfaced after the Imperial Family was massacred and made claim to be Grand Duchess Anastasia. It was heartbreaking.

She looked up, her thoughts interrupted as Will returned to his seat.

"Get in trouble, dear?"

He smiled at her. "Yes, honey. I did."

Alex tried her best not to laugh as an announcement over the loudspeaker from the pilot let them know they'd begun their descent into Heathrow.

"You okay?" Will asked once the pilot had finished speaking.

She nodded.

"You're clear on what we need to do and say?"

Again, she nodded.

"You seem a little tense."

She was. Lying her way through an international customs port wasn't exactly everyday business. It made her skin prickle.

"What happens if we don't pull this off?" she asked him.

Will looked at her intently before speaking. "Well, you'll finally get to speak to the police."

She glared at him, and he gave her a wink and laughed quietly. She didn't tell him that she'd seriously considered running straight to the police when they'd arrived at Boston International. Something had held her back, and she'd realised that whilst she might not believe everything Evelyn and Will had told her, she did trust them.

"Alex, everything will be fine. We'll go up together. I'll do the talking if you're still happy with that. Just play along. Once we're through customs, we'll make our way straight to our rental car. The drive will only take about half an hour with traffic."

She nodded and focused on calming her breathing once again as she looked out the window. They'd descended through the clouds, and the urban spawl of London appeared below them. She'd never been here before, and the expansive view of the city enthralled her.

"There are only a handful of airports around the world where you fly in directly over the city. It's a pretty clear day. We might be lucky to see a few of the famous sights," Will said.

Despite her niggling anxiety, she smiled at him like an excited child before putting her face close to the window. She might have been mistaken, but she thought she could see Buckingham Palace, one of the official residences of the British monarch. She'd love to visit there, but not today. If they managed to get through customs they'd be driving instead to the Queen's home in the English countryside. Windsor Castle awaited them.

†

A small knot of excitement balled in Alex's stomach as they walked from the car to meet their guide. There was something enthralling about the architecture of old; this was a residence built for protection yet grandeur. It was stunning.

"It's a beautiful castle," Will said, noticing her enchantment. "Still an official residence of Queen Elizabeth II, which I'm fairly sure makes it the largest occupied castle in the world. In my opinion, St George's Chapel is one of the most exquisite spiritual buildings in England."

"It's magnificent," she agreed.

Will smiled. "The chapel houses the tombs of over ten monarchs and, as you now know, is where the Order of the Garter, whose members are chosen by the Queen, meet and worship. The Garter is considered the pinnacle of the British honours system and is like a knighthood of sorts. The first part of the etching on the Clover Egg key is almost word for word the English translation of the Order's motto, which is written in Old French: *Honi soit qui mal y pense.*"

"*Shame on him who thinks this evil,*" Alex said, recalling the briefing Evelyn had given them before they'd gone their separate ways.

"Exactly," Will confirmed.

As they continued their walk to the meeting point, Alex hoped with everything in her that they'd deciphered the clues correctly. Evelyn believed that the Tsar was referring to a very distinct area inside St George's Chapel. If she was right, Alex might finally know if what had been presented to her over the last few days was fact, fiction or something in between.

Seek my child. Let no one stall your rite of passage. Journey home via a path of diamonds, she recited in her head. *Shame on him who thinks this evil for she is the key to her master's lock.*

"Are you convinced we're going to find something?" she asked tentatively.

Will stopped walking and looked at her. "I don't doubt my mum's interpretation of the Clover Egg clue. It's without doubt referring to the Order. Nicholas and his father, Alexander III, were both members, as were the Tsar's uncle and aunt, King Edward VII and Queen Alexandra of the United Kingdom, amongst many other members of the Imperial Family." Looking at his watch, he motioned for them to start walking again. "The Tsar's letter, on the other hand, mentioned to let no one stall your rite of passage. This is what my mother believes is a reference to the stalls of the chapel. After their appointment to the Order, members are each assigned what's called a quire stall, and above it, members openly display their heraldry, which are things such as crowns, banners and swords."

"And you're sure that *she is the key to her master's lock* refers specifically to Queen Alexandra?" Alex asked him.

"Yes. She's the key to understanding who guards the lock we're looking for. It makes sense. Alexandra was the Dowager Empress's sister and the Tsar's aunt so was one of only a few who had knowledge of the Auxiliary Measure. Plus, the timing's right.

Alexandra was honoured with a membership to the Order by her husband, the first woman to be given that honour in some four hundred years. So she was the only Lady of the Garter because of her 'master's' membership at the time the letter was written. We just have to find her master's lock."

"Which you think is in the stall?" Alex asked.

"More than likely it will be on King Edward's stall plate, which, unlike the other heraldic items that are removed upon a member's death, are kept in the stall. There is a stall plate for almost every member from throughout history still affixed on the chapel's walls. It really is a sight to behold and an amazing historical record," Will said. "Okay. We're almost there, and Brendan should be here soon. Are you clear on your 'husband's' research subjects?"

"I certainly hope so or we're going to end up arrested," she whispered as they reached the entrance and walked through huge stone gates, flanked either side by what appeared to be small castle turrets.

Alex paused and looked around in awe. They were in the inner sanctum of the castle, and the chapel itself stood directly in front of them across the yard. For some reason she'd always considered a chapel to be small and intimate as opposed to a church, which she assumed would be much larger. She'd thought wrong. This chapel was majestic and enormous. It stood tall and proud, the intricate yet at the same time simple architecture framed against the sky. It looked to be made of sandstone, and the contrast of its creamy beige exterior against the blue sky was breathtaking.

"Professor and Mrs Lloyd!" a voice called, breaking her out of her reverie. "I'm Brendan and I've been assigned to take you through our beautiful chapel this morning. You couldn't have picked a better day. We aren't known for our blue sky and sunshine at this time of the year, but God must be shining upon you as this truly is the best way to experience St George. The leadlight radiances will be just brilliant!"

After checking identification, Brendan led them along a beautifully paved path that crossed the courtyard diagonally to the chapel's side entrance.

"It's an honour to have such an esteemed guest with us, Professor Lloyd, and I simply must tell you how pleased the dean was that the Russian Patriarch himself recommend you visit with us. He applauds that it might signify that Russia may, someday, be more open-minded to the ways of the constitutional monarchy as opposed to the autocratic ways of the past. It's a shame you won't have time on this visit to meet with him or tour the college … But where are my manners … Let me explain the buildings you see here in the lower ward."

"If you don't mind, Brendan, being that we're on such a tight schedule, it would be best for us to complete our tour of the chapel first and leave any other sightseeing until the end if we have time," said Will.

Brendan bowed his head in agreement and stood aside to let them experience their first view of the chapel's interior. "To your left is the nave and to your right is the entrance to the quire."

In every direction was opulent beauty and elegance. The gothic magnificence of the architecture was lit in brilliantly coloured light that radiated from the exquisite glasswork displayed in the chapel's windows. It was too much to take in all at once, and Alex's eyes remained mesmerised by the huge main window at the end of the nave.

"I see that, like most first-time visitors, the leadlights have captured your heart." Brendan smiled, directing his words to her. "They are quite breathtaking even after many, many visits, I can attest. We can look at them more if you have time after we see the quire. Please follow me through here underneath the organ loft and past the Rutland and Bray chantries … and here we have the quire."

The room they'd entered was constructed from stone and intricately carved woodwork. Black-and-white tiles adorned the floor, and at the rear, another prominent window of leadlight cast rays that bounced around the many gold items that filled the room. The space was an eclectic display of finery.

"Here on the right of the quire entrance is the Sovereign's stall," Brendan informed them. "You can see at the centre the Sovereign's coat of arms encircled with laurel and crowned with the royal diadem. This is then surrounded with flower-de-luce and the star of the Order. The Sovereign's banner is made of rich velvet and is much larger than those of the Knights Companions. The mantling is also of gold brocade, which sets it apart from the other stalls and even from the Prince's stall here on the left of the entrance."

The Prince's stall was only set apart from the remaining stalls by a piece of velvet curtain matching that used in the Sovereign's stall, which genuinely surprised Alex.

"I would have thought the Prince's stall would have been somewhat more embellished?" she enquired.

"A common mistake," Will jumped in. "The Prince's stall is not distinguished from those of the other Knights Companions as according to the statutes of the Order's institution, every Knight bestowed entry by the Sovereign holds equal honour and power."

Brendan nodded fervently. "The professor is correct, Mrs Lloyd."

Alex brought her focus back to the task at hand as she saw Will's hand gesturing for her to hurry things along.

"Yes, my husband is almost always correct! Let's see if he can show us where our royals of interest, King Edward VII and Queen Alexandra, would have once sat so we can examine Edward's stall plate."

Will smiled at them. "My lovely wife will not catch me out on this one. Young Prince Edward would have initially sat in the Prince's stall, whereas once he became King, he and his consort, Alexandra, would have sat within the Sovereign's stall. Being that Edward first sat amongst the princes, this is where his stall plate will reside. Am I mistaken, Brendan?"

"Oh no, you're correct again! Please see right here the stall plate of the then Prince Edward."

The plate was like most of the others that adorned the wall, but both Will and Alex knew it housed a secret. A secret they could not uncover until they were alone.

After admiring the plate, Alex took Brendan by the arm.

"Come, let's leave the professor here to marvel on his being right and you can show me that amazing bay window at the other end of the room. Also, my husband didn't tell me that there was an observatory, for lack of a better word, in the quire," Alex said, pointing ahead of them.

"You refer to the Oriel Window, Mrs Lloyd, and the observatory is a vantage point that King Henry VIII had created so that his wife, Catherine of Aragon, could view services held in the quire. First wife of six. One of the few who managed to keep her head."

Chapter 20

LONDON AND WINDSOR, UK

"Officer, I think there's an addict passed out in one of the cubicles in the men's bathroom. Is it you I inform or are there airport security people I can talk to? I'd hate them to choke on their own vomit."

"Yes, of course, I can take a look at that. Which bathroom, sir?" said the officer, looking as if he'd rather do anything else.

Viktor led the officer around the back of the baggage carousel area to a bathroom where he'd earlier placed an 'out of order' sign on the door. He didn't need witnesses.

"It says the bathroom is out of order," the officer said.

"Yes, I was so desperate to go … I hate using the bathroom on the plane and I just didn't notice the sign, but what I did notice as I was using the urinal was the stench, and then I saw someone lying on the floor in the disabled cubicle."

"Alright, I'll take a look. Wait here, please."

Viktor had no intention of waiting. As the door was closing behind the officer, he slipped in behind, and sensing this, the officer turned in surprise and reached for his holster.

"I asked you to wait out—"

Viktor stepped forward and delivered a powerful strike with the hard base of his palm, targeting the officer's throat and compressing his windpipe. The man stumbled, dropped his baton to the floor and clutched at his neck, gasping for air. Viktor quickly moved behind him, and as with Anya, he left the officer unable to stand due to a forceful kick to the back of the knees. Unlike with Anya, Viktor didn't now use a knife. Instead, he grasped the man's head with both hands and twisted sharply, sideways and upwards, breaking his neck. Job done and the officer's uniform remained clean.

Viktor undressed the man and dragged his body into the disabled cubicle, sitting him upright on the toilet seat and securing him to a handrail with handcuffs. He then fitted his trainers onto the officer's feet. Not bad. With the door closed, no one would know it wasn't someone going about their business.

Placing his own clothes into his carry-on bag, Viktor put on the uniform. It was a little snug, and the shoes were a little big, but it would have to do. Securing the baton into the holster now fastened around his hips, he made his way back out into the terminal and towards the hire-car desks. It was as good a place to start as any.

He counted the number of desks as he approached. Five.

He got a hit at the third.

"Yes, officer. The Lloyds picked up a car about, oh, an hour and a half ago maybe," the attendant told him as she accessed the computer system. "Ah yes, here we go … The car is due back tomorrow afternoon at five-thirty."

"Here at Heathrow?"

"Yes, that's right."

Good intel, he thought to himself. Even if he couldn't work out where Alex and Will were headed, he could at least wait for them to return. But oh dear God, he hated lurking at airports. He'd rather have dinner with an Orthodox.

"Of course, they always have the option to extend the hire if we have enough vehicles available," the woman added.

Not so good.

"May I ask what the problem is, officer? The couple were extremely pleasant. Am I to assume that our vehicle may be at risk?"

Viktor smiled and shook his head. "No, not at all. No need to raise any alarm bells just yet."

"That's a relief," the attendant said. "As I said, they seemed a lovely couple. Just headed to Windsor to visit the castle."

Bullseye, Viktor thought. He thanked the woman for her help and made his way towards the other end of the terminal to find a place to get changed and another rental desk. As he walked, he reached into the front pocket of his bag to retrieve his phone. He'd a missed call from a number he knew well.

"Viktor."

"You called?"

"Filip was here. He wanted to garner my support for his succeeding you as Christ."

"In what way?"

"As you might imagine."

Viktor could feel the blood rising to his face and his breathing increase as anger manifested through his body.

"He did what?" he hissed.

"No need to worry, Viktor. I'm loyal to you."

"Did he touch you?" he asked quietly.

"He may have questionable motives but he's not stupid, Viktor. To touch me without my consent in a one-on-one environment would have sealed his fate to never, ever lead. That is one of the very few sins that we don't accept. No, he wanted to know if he had my support for him as our next leader and was hoping also to get a timeframe on your retirement. There's no harm done. I just wanted to call to let you know as I feel there's something underhanded about the way he's going about things."

"Okay. I'll take care of it."

"I know you *can* take care of it, but I actually think it would be best not to say anything. He'll expect me to tell you and will therefore expect you'll retaliate. I'd counsel staying quiet; be wary of his motives and keep an extra close eye on him. That's exactly the reason I met with him tonight. I need, as do you, to be sure he is the one to lead our people."

"I said I'd take care of it," Viktor said and hung up.

Now he had another thing to do. His face was still hot with anger, and he gave himself a moment to get his breathing under control. *How dare Filip approach the Mother of Christ without informing him. He was out of line. So out of line!* Viktor couldn't let it go, not if the Mother of Christ was beginning to question Filip's heir-apparent status. He was not having anyone else continue his legacy.

He sighed. The Romanovs, the Auxiliary and his own family had a lot in common: secret relatives all over the place.

No one knew Filip was his son. Not even Filip. That fact would only be known if and when Filip became Christ, and if he did, that would be quite the legacy. Three successive father and son almighty Christs of the Khlyst faith. At least with Anya dead he wouldn't have to hurt her by disclosing the secret. *For the love of God, what was he thinking! Jesus. Screw Anya! He owed her nothing.*

But telling himself that did nothing to stem his rage. Anya was still under his skin even in death. He'd loved her dearly, and the fact he'd discovered her to be a traitor hadn't yet eradicated those feelings. He felt his emotions swing as he realised that she'd probably never fallen pregnant, not because she couldn't, but because she didn't want to. He'd always wanted an heir, but they'd never conceived, no matter how hard they'd tried. Now he perhaps understood why.

"You probably tied your tubes," he seethed.

No. Filip wasn't Anya's. His mother was a dirty peasant who he'd deliberately and consistently screwed until she was with child before setting her up for life with an apartment and allowance. She'd died when Filip was twenty-one, having kept her word not to reveal who his father was. She'd liked her lifestyle and the never-ending flow of alcohol way too much to break her word. Filip had inherited the apartment after she passed.

Viktor laughed softly. The way his kind indulged in mass ceremonial orgies, it was likely he'd fathered multiple children. He knew Filip, at least, was his, and as hard as he was on the boy, he did love him. One day soon he'd tell him.

He picked up his pace, desperate to find somewhere to get changed and dispose of the dead cop's uniform. It was definitely too tight, not to mention it stank.

†

Will didn't have much time.

He ran his hands across the plate. It was beautifully made from gold and ceramic, and if his mother was right, Nicholas would have had Fabergé craft it. There were many, many things of great worth in the chapel, but this could be one of the finest. It had to be a replica or replacement as the Tsar wouldn't have enacted his Path of Diamonds before a then Prince Edward was assigned the stall.

He could hear Alex keeping Brendan busy, the conversation between them continuing as they stood in the middle of the quire. Their host was explaining the significance of the floor ledger stone that marked the burial place of King Henry VIII and King Charles I.

"Jane Seymour, the third wife of King Henry VIII, is also buried here," he heard Brendan remark.

"Focus, Will," he scolded himself as he took note of the security camera placement and then carefully positioned himself so his body shielded the plate from view. He ran his hands again over the plate's surface, then again. *Yes. He had indeed felt two very small adornments. Hinges. Clever.* Nicholas had designed a cavity within the plate itself so that it didn't need to be removed from the chapel wall.

He observed the plate closely as Alex and Brendan's voices started to get closer. Carefully, Will wedged a small metal file under the cavity's cover and pried it open. Beneath the hinged door was a small keyhole with a clover engraved above it. Reaching inside his shirt,

Will pulled out the clover key secured on a chain around his neck, praying that it would unlock whatever lay beneath. To his relief, as he turned the key in the lock, the small door concealing the hidden compartment gently swung open.

Alex's voice was quite loud now and, turning, Will saw she was returning with Brendan. Almost out of time, he reached his thumb and forefinger inside the small cavity and retrieved what appeared to be a folded silk cloth. Just as quickly, he relocked the compartment and placed the plate back in its original position. He tucked the key back inside his shirt and placed the silk bundle into his jacket pocket just as Alex and Brendan rejoined him. He hoped they didn't notice the line of sweat making its way slowly down the side of his neck.

"If you're happy with having seen the stall plates, Brendan can take us to view Edward and Alexandra's gravesite," Alex said, giving him an expectant look.

Will looked at his watch. "Brendan, you've been so helpful but I'm afraid we need to get on the road. It's been truly wonderful to see the place where the Order of the Garter bestows honour on both the monarchy and the exceptional commoner. We'll be back."

"Absolutely, professor," Brendan said as he guided them back towards the nave. "Oh! One last intriguing fact for you, in case you didn't know it already. The nave was where the current Prince Charles held his blessing of marriage to his long-term mistress, Camilla Parker Bowles, in 2005. She certainly got one up on her great-grandmother that day!"

"What do you mean?" asked Alex.

"Well, Ms Parker Bowles' great-grandmother was Alice Keppel – King Edward's final and favourite mistress. I suppose I should say 'companion,' out of respect for Queen Alexandra. Alice remained by the King's side for some twenty years until his death, but she never had the chance to marry the man she loved. Camilla, on the other hand, certainly did – and now, as the Duchess of Cornwall, she awaits her time as Queen."

Will hadn't known that. "Well, it seems that extramarital dalliances continue to remain a blessing of the male royal even under a constitutional monarchy. That's certainly one for my dissertation," he exclaimed, taking Alex's hand and leading them towards the exit. The bundle of silk was burning a hole in his pocket.

Brendan laughed heartily. "Please don't quote me as I will deny us ever meeting!"

Once in their car, Will carefully unwrapped the silk cloth and placed what had been folded within it on the centre console: a small box made from lightweight card and wrapped in sheaths of shredded cotton. Inside was a handwritten card and a round metal ring.

"What on earth is this?" Alex asked, picking up the ring and examining it closely. It fit snugly on the tip of her little finger. "The outer surface is smooth, but the inside is slightly buckled … and there are fine ridges engraved along one side as well."

Will didn't have an answer so instead read what was written on the card:

Spread your wings and raise your head with pride. Now is not your swan song. I ask you to base your faith on these words. Words I believe as surely as the day I was born.

Alex looked at him with disappointment. "Not my swan song. So we have more to find."

"It would have been optimistic to expect that the first find would be our last. That would have been far too easy."

"I know," Alex sighed. "I'm just really worried about my parents and, to be honest, worried for you and your mum as well. We still have no idea where Viktor is, and that scares me."

"I can't take that fear away from you, Alex. I'm sorry," he said, reaching out to take her hand in his. "But I can do my best to work through this puzzle with you."

"Yeah. Thank you." Alex smiled at him sadly and handed him the metal ring.

Examining it closely with a magnifying glass, he could make out writing. He read:

My child, seek the next symbol of life and with this key you will proceed.

Alex, who had been staring dejectedly out the car window, spun to look at him.

"What?"

"Those fine ridges you observed are in fact text on the outer side of the ring. This is the next key – we're looking for another Fabergé egg!"

"My God! Which one and where?" Alex exclaimed, a mix of excitement and panic in her voice. "Even with my limited knowledge I know not all the eggs made it out of Russia after the revolution, and of those that did, only some have been recovered. What happens if what we need to find has been destroyed or hidden?"

Will watched as the earlier look of disappointment resettled on her face.

"You're right about the dissemination and, in some instances, desecration of the eggs, but the situation isn't as dire as once thought. I pray to God that the odds are with us. My mother and I believe in the words of St Seraphim, and he stipulated that you'll be successful in this quest. That being the case, we must also believe that your path will, for the most part, be uninhibited. Please have faith. You've trusted us until now."

Alex gave him a slight smile and nodded. "How many eggs are there in total?" she asked.

"Of the fifty Faberge eggs crafted for the Imperial Family, forty-three have survived to this day."

"Well, ruling out the Clover Egg, that leaves us forty-two possibilities."

"Actually, I'm fairly certain that we can rule out all but one," he said slowly as he conducted a quick search on his phone. "If I'm right, we're going to Switzerland."

Chapter 21

MOSCOW, RUSSIA AND WINDSOR, UK

Evelyn was trying her best to look like a normal passenger, walking briskly to catch her flight, but what she needed right now was a place to hide. She had to get back to her hotel and she had to speak to Will.

Her heart rate elevated as she doubled back across the airport, away from security and towards the hotel precinct. It was a busy morning, and whilst the bustling crowds slowed her down somewhat, they also provided cover. That was exactly the reason she'd thought this would be a relatively safe place. She'd been very wrong.

With relief, Evelyn reached her destination a few minutes later and nodded to the doorman at the Radisson entrance. "Dobro pozhalovat," he said, as he returned the gesture. His words brought back memories of her grandfather, who had taught her Russian as a young girl. He'd always used the same phrase when he'd welcomed visitors at their home, acting as catalyst for many a conversation about the translation of English words to Russian.

Now, inside the lobby, she quickly observed her surroundings. It was past normal check-out time, so it was relatively quiet. Quickly she made her way towards the lift and slipped inside as the door was closing. It was just her. A win. But only once she was back in her room with the door locked behind her did she allow herself a moment to close her eyes and calm her breathing.

She shouldn't have gone any earlier than her flight required, but having been claustrophobic in her hotel room, she'd thought having lunch and a taking a walk around the airport might help her think more freely about how best to tackle things in Denmark. She'd slept well the night before, but she'd done so without firstly establishing a solid solution to accessing the tomb. And after a morning of additional deliberation, she still hadn't been entirely sure of her plan.

"Evelyn, you're off your game," she scolded as she dropped down heavily onto the bed.

To give some credit, the odds had been low. There were five international airports in Moscow, and although this was the main one, coming across Viktor's friend Filip one might assume was simply bad luck. But was it? Based on what Evelyn had heard, it seemed they'd known exactly what airport she'd arrived at the afternoon prior, and the odds were in their favour that she'd fly out of the same location.

Evelyn had seen Filip just as she'd started to read the lunch menu. He'd been seated only two tables across from her. Unlike herself, he had no disguise. He also had no need to be quiet on the phone as he was the hunter, not the hunted. She'd heard most of what he was saying, and he'd confirmed that if he didn't receive confirmation of Anya's sister 'Jennifer' entering a Moscow airport in the next hour, he'd be on a two o'clock flight to London to help secure the heir.

A cold fear had settled inside her when Filip referenced her alias and made it clear they knew she'd been in Moscow. It turned to ice when she realised that they also knew Alex was in London. How had they determined their new identities? *How?* Before she could properly contemplate the possibilities, Evelyn had left her menu at the table along with a tip and made a beeline for the hotel.

Her mind was in overdrive. *They'd all used false names to travel from Boston, so they had to have been seen, but by whom? Or by what?* She was confident they hadn't been observed at the church safe room, so the only other possibility was that Viktor and Filip had somehow infiltrated airport computers or had help from airport staff … *No, it had to be via the computers.* It would be impossible to place enough conspirators to monitor every airport. They had to have some sort of facial recognition program. That was the only way Viktor could have so quickly pinpointed Will and Alex, and the only way Filip would know if she'd arrived at Sheremetyevo or any other Moscow airport.

Carefully she reached up and began pulling out the pins that were holding her wig in place. Thank God she hadn't booked her flight or gone through security. What had been a bad lapse in judgement in heading out of her room before it was necessary had at least resulted in obtaining an important piece of intelligence.

She removed the wig then rifled through the false bottom of her case, looking for her other passport. As she did, her phone rang. She took a deep breath before answering.

"Will. You're both okay?"

"Absolutely. In fact, we're great. We have the next clue."

"No sign of Viktor?"

"Viktor? No. I'm fairly confident no one could have known we left the US."

"Well, Viktor did, and he's somewhere in London. I think they're using a facial recognition program of some description at the airports. I don't know what, and I guess it doesn't matter. All that matters is that we must change our identities immediately and keep our heads down. If you can disguise yourself in any way, please do the best you can."

"Fuck. Okay."

"Language, Will."

"Shit, sorry … I mean … sorry."

She smiled despite herself. His father used to swear like a trooper despite his collar.

"I'm assuming you're somewhere you can talk. Tell me about the new clue," she said.

"Yes, we're in the car on the way back to Heathrow and then we'll be heading to Switzerland."

"Why Switzerland?"

"We need to examine the Swan Egg."

"The second of four symbols of life," she said softly.

"Yes. The clue reads … Hang on, I'm going to put you on speaker … Alex, can you please read out the clue?"

"Hi, Evelyn. Yes, of course."

Spread your wings and raise your head with pride. Now is not your swan song. I ask you to base your faith on these words. Words I believe as surely as the day I was born.

Will was right. The first sentence was an implicit reference to the Swan Egg's surprise.

"I've been researching the egg," Alex continued. "It's very different to the Clover Egg, but just as beautiful. I can't tell from the photos if it's a dusty mauve or perhaps a light blue?"

"It's mauve. My sister and I always loved its surface, the trellis of twisted ribbons and bows formed with beautiful small diamonds. Have you seen the surprise that gives the egg its name?"

"Yes, it's breathtakingly beautiful also!"

"Beauty aside, we need some way to actually observe it," Will interrupted.

"From memory, it's currently owned by the Edouard and Maurice Sandoz Foundation," Evelyn offered.

"Yes, that's right," Will confirmed. "In Lausanne."

"From what I've read," Alex added, "the Swan Egg has only been seen twice in Swiss exhibitions since the 1970s. It's going to be extremely difficult to get anywhere near it."

"That's a fair assumption, Alex," Evelyn agreed. "However, even though many of the eggs have left Russia, the owners of most are sensitive to the requests of the Russian Orthodox Church, to whom the Tsar was considered God's representative on earth. They know that if not for the blood that ran through the streets of Russia, the eggs would never, ever have left the Imperial Family. Most owners appreciate that in principle, the Imperial Family are still the true owners of the art," she explained.

"I see. Yes, that does makes sense," said Alex.

"Would you agree it's likely that the egg will be locked in a vault at one of the Swiss banks?" Will asked. "Alex and I were only just discussing that original artworks are rarely left in public and that replicas are often used at exhibitions as well."

"I'd say so," Evelyn agreed, while thinking how best to tackle the situation. "Okay. I'm going to arrange a donation. Yes, a large donation to the foundation with the caveat that I'm allowed to examine and photograph their collection. I'll pose as an academic writing a book on behalf of the Orthodox Church outlining the material assets that represent the life of the Holy Martyr Tsar Nicholas II. The Fabergé eggs are a part of such assets."

"But I thought you had to go to Denmark?" Will asked.

"I do, but I'll come and meet you first."

"Why not just set up a meeting for Alex and me as you did at Windsor? We can manage."

"I know you can, but in order to get access to the amount of donation money I'll need, I'm going to have to visit a Swiss bank myself. As you know, Will, it's been a long time since the church or the Auxiliary have felt safe leaving our wealth in Russia."

"How much money are we talking about?" Alex asked.

"I think one-and-a-half million should get us what we need," Evelyn confirmed to audible gasps from both Alex and Will. "The Dowager Empress left substantial funding for our cause, and apart from our allowances, the rest has sat dormant for decades," she explained. "There are sufficient funds."

"Understood," said Will. "Should we plan to meet today or tomorrow?"

"Tonight. We need to get out of our current locations undetected immediately. Have your pilot fly you into Lausanne. That will ensure we're not all together at a single airport. And do your best to alter your appearances. I'll fly into Geneva and either drive or ferry to meet you after securing the money."

"You have twenty-four-hour access?" Will asked.

"I do, so all going well, I should be with you well before midnight. Call me once you've found a secure location to bunker down, and please make sure you don't check in with the same credentials you use for flying, just to be safe. I'll meet you as soon as possible thereafter."

"Perhaps you should consider taking a private plane too, if the funds allow," Alex suggested.

"I'll be fine," Evelyn said. "I'd like to leave you some of your inheritance."

†

Viktor dragged the guide's body into the rearmost corner of the chapel to the side of the altar. From what he could gather, they were still just out of frame of security cameras, which was a pity as he'd done quite the job on the man.

Not being able to bring any sort of weapon through security, he'd had to improvise, but the sharp garden stake had worked a treat. One brutal shove inward and upwards to the nose followed by a forceful slamming of the man's face into the floor had pierced the guide's brain.

"You must have had excellent metabolism as your blood is really warm, my friend," Viktor whispered before pausing to listen for any signs he might have company. He knew there was only half an hour between each guided tour, and he estimated he'd already taken up most of that. He'd had to wait for all the other tour participants to leave, and then he'd needed time to insert enough splinters under the guide's nails and around the edge of his eyes to extract as much information as possible before being rid of him. But apart from confirming that Will and Alex had been to the chapel earlier that same morning, the guide hadn't been able to offer anything else.

Viktor took a moment to look around and breathe in the disgusting opulence of the church. "I'm sure you'll all forgive me for wronging you as such is what you preach," he whispered before standing quicky.

Now he had company.

After taking one last look at his handiwork, he made his way towards the door that led to one of the chapel's souvenir shops. As expected, tourists filled the small space, jostling to purchase evidence of their visit. Viktor carefully manoeuvred amongst them to the outside patio where he found the exit. He was well clear when he heard the scream.

"The tour was pretty boring otherwise," he muttered to himself as he stopped to look around and feign surprise. Viktor saw a guard holding a hand to his ear, most likely receiving a message through an earpiece. A look of disbelief passed across the guard's face and he hurriedly secured the exit to prevent anyone leaving, making apologies to a number of people who had just been about to make their way out. Relieved he'd made his departure in time, Viktor picked up his pace, continuing to put distance between himself and the castle.

He checked his phone as he walked: eleven-thirty am. That would make it two-thirty pm at home in Moscow and meant that unless he'd had news of Evelyn, Filip should be on a plane to meet him. Checking his voicemail confirmed that Filip had no news. Evelyn's whereabouts were still unknown.

Viktor stopped to text him. "He better have his goddamn phone on," he muttered.

He got a notification almost instantly. The boy had learned!

Or maybe he hadn't. Viktor realised it wasn't a message from Filip. The notification was from the R.A. surveillance app, which he clicked into eagerly. His enthusiasm diminished somewhat when he saw that the match was only eighty-four per cent. The match he'd received previously had been almost one hundred per cent. She'd either done better with her disguise this time or it wasn't Evelyn.

He zoomed in on the photo. The woman was blonde with mid-length hair and a heavy side fringe draped over one eye. She was also wearing lush lipstick, making her lips look extremely plump, and it was possible she also had cheek fillers and contacts in. He laughed out loud. The disguise made Evelyn look just like Anya, whereas her everyday likeness was nowhere near as pronounced. "Bad choice, Evelyn, or should I say … Barbara Browning," he murmured as he continued walking.

She'd been located at Sheremetyevo, which was infuriating. Filip had flown out of there only half an hour before. Hopefully the system wouldn't take too long to conduct a search of all airlines looking for Evelyn's alias.

As Viktor reached the car, his phone beeped again. This time it was Filip. *Good.* But before accessing the message, he started the car and manoeuvred into traffic, heading as fast as he could away from the castle. He wanted maximum distance between himself and the murder scene.

Only once he was well out of Windsor did he pull over to check Filip's text, as well as a new message that had come through from the R.A. surveillance app. Filip was mid-flight on his way to London, and Evelyn would be boarding a flight to Geneva in the next ten minutes. Viktor ran the calculations in his head. It was roughly a four-hour flight to Geneva from Moscow, so with the time difference, if he could get on a flight to Geneva before two-thirty pm UK time, he'd land before her. *Excellent.*

Quickly he messaged Filip back.

As soon as you land, take the next available flight to Geneva. I'll meet you there. Will explain when you arrive.

This time the response was immediate.

WTAF?

Viktor laughed and put his foot down. He had a welcome party to plan.

Chapter 22

LAUSANNE, SWITZERLAND

Maybe it was because Alex was tired, but Will had caught her staring at him a number of times as he worked. Or had she caught him looking at her?

She still felt embarrassed about hugging Will in a moment of desperate relief after he explained how he had helped Monte. Now, as they waited together for Evelyn – herself lounging on one of the hotel beds – she certainly didn't want him to get the wrong idea.

As she did her best to find anything else to look at in the confined space, she realised that the thought of Will getting the wrong idea didn't actually seem that, well, wrong. He was an amazingly intelligent and handsome man who seemed to have a deep respect for her and her family. Of course, Alex now knew that the Auxiliary was being paid to care, but she'd become convinced that it was more than a job for both Will and Evelyn. They admired her not just for her apparent blood line but also for what she could contribute, even though her knowledge was in its infancy.

She rose from the bed, blushing at her thoughts, and made her way into the small but opulent bathroom. "What are you even thinking?" she said to herself in the marble-edged mirror. It would be crazy to believe that she could be attracted to someone who she'd met only days earlier and whose job it was to make her feel secure.

Shaking her head at her idiocy, she studied her reflection. Whilst it had been slightly more confronting earlier that day when Will had cut off her ponytail in the hire car, the bob cut was growing on her. New identity, new hair. She twirled a strand around her finger. It made her look somewhat more distinguished, as though she'd finally matured enough to be rid of her long girly tresses. Yes, it was growing on her, just as Will was.

"Oh my God!" she heard Will cry.

Alex rushed back to the main room where Will was standing with a hand clasped over his mouth, staring at the television. He slumped down heavily onto the end of one of the beds.

"What's wrong?" she asked.

He pointed at the screen. A news bulletin was on, and the anchor was reporting on a murder that had occurred at Windsor Castle.

"Oh no," she whispered.

Will flicked through the multiple news channels.

"Murder on Royal Grounds" screamed one.

"Chapel Crucifixion" offered another.

Regardless of the different sensational alerts, the core news story was the same on every channel. Their St George's guide, Brendan, had been found dead.

Alex's stomach lurched. The police were looking to speak with all parties who attended the ten-thirty am tour that Brendan would have only just finished conducting prior to his murder. They believed, based on the estimated time of death, that only minutes passed between that tour ending and his killer having struck.

"That would have been the first public tour he led after our private viewing, meaning that Viktor narrowly missed us," Will said quietly.

Alex only just managed to make it back to the bathroom before vomiting violently. When she had nothing left to bring up, she washed her mouth out and wet her face before resting her hands on either side of the basin and looking at herself in the mirror again.

Brendan was dead because of her.

She picked up the bar of soap she had used to scrub away the heavy makeup worn for the flight and threw it as hard as she could at the mirror. It bounced off the glass and landed behind her on the tiled floor. As she turned to pick it up, Will appeared in the doorway.

"Are you okay?"

"This is my fault," she said as tears began to run down her face. "This alleged legacy is hurting innocent people, Will. We should just stop. Go to the police as I wanted. He was an innocent man and now he's dead, Will. Dead!"

Will stepped forward and wrapped her in his arms. "None of this is your fault, Alex," he said.

She tried to wriggle away from him, but his grip tightened and she gave in. She let him hold her until she had no more tears left, and when her breathing returned almost to normal, she lifted her head to look at him. As her eyes met his, she looked away quickly. Being held in his arms had unlocked something in her. Not a sensual longing but rather an intense need. He somehow fitted her, completed her, and although wracked with guilt, in this very moment she had never felt so alive.

"Come with me," he said, pulling away and leading her by the hand back into the main room where she curled up on one of the beds.

"You're stronger than you know, Alex. It's in your blood. I need you to call on that strength. Okay?"

"I don't know if I can, Will," she whispered. "That poor, poor man."

"You can and you will. Don't let the fear take hold of you. We need you to be strong … I need you to be strong," he said, sitting on the edge of the bed and resting his hand on top of hers. "Why don't you try to get some sleep? Mum won't be here for a couple of hours yet. It will do you good."

Her head was so clouded with guilt, grief and uncertainty that all she could do was nod and close her eyes. Visions of Brendan ran through her head. *What would his family be experiencing as she lay in a hotel perched upon the northern shore of Lake Geneva and on the precipice of an imperial resurrection?* Tears welled behind her eyelids again. There would be no resurrection for Brendan.

Breathing in deeply, she tried to harness her distress. If everything she'd been told and had begun to accept was to come to fruition, then her way to make amends would be to serve justice on Viktor and Filip. That was all she could do. Though how she would serve it was undetermined. As she finally started to drift off to sleep, she felt Will lay down gently beside her and take her hand in his.

It absolutely felt right.

†

Alex struggled to open her eyes. When they finally focused and she saw Evelyn, she realised she'd slept for at least a few hours. Will was in deep conversation with his mother in hushed tones and neither of them had noticed she'd woken.

"It sounds farcical but I could sense him the moment I walked off the plane," Evelyn said quietly.

"We all altered our appearances and identification again. Do you think he registered Alex and me leaving London, you leaving Moscow or both?" Will whispered.

"Given he was waiting at the commercial terminal and at my exact gate, I would strongly suggest he was tracking me. It was no random run-in."

"Good point."

"Whether he also knows that you and Alex are here I have no idea."

"Why didn't he just grab you at the airport?"

"Well, for one, the substantial security. But he wants Alex most of all, not you or me. Today, Viktor was hoping I'd lead him to Alex. It was difficult for me to pretend I hadn't seen him. My best option was to just keep moving and do everything I could to get to the bank."

Alex could feel her distress returning. So many people were at risk because of her.

"Viktor's here?"

Both Evelyn and Will turned to face her.

"I'm so sorry, Alex, we didn't mean to wake you," Evelyn said, coming to sit at the side of the bed.

"Did he hurt you? How did you manage to get away from him?" she asked in quick succession.

"I'm fine. I managed to evade him with the help of the bank. One might say the church's money is well invested. The Orthodox account comes with anytime access as well as a premium security service. Their no-questions-asked concierge drove me here."

"But did Viktor follow you?"

"No. According to the bank manager, it was over an hour before our friend tried to obtain entry, asking after me and soon thereafter realising I was most likely gone. The concierge exits from a private underground entrance at the rear of the bank. My hire car is still parked out front. Once I got to Lausanne, I stayed overnight at a hotel nearby to make absolutely sure he hadn't managed to locate me and then came here once I felt it was safe to meet you both."

"Overnight? My God, what time is it? And … he didn't hurt anyone else, did he?

"He's good, but not good enough to infiltrate Swiss financial security at a whim," Evelyn said.

"And it's six am," added Will, smiling at her.

"You let me sleep all night?" she squealed, jumping up off the bed.

"It will have done you good," Evelyn said. "We need you to be alert today when you examine the Swan Egg."

"Me? Why me? I thought you were meeting with the foundation?" she exclaimed.

"Well, a Barbara Browning is meeting with them, but seeing they have no idea what Barbara Browning looks like, you're going to be her instead of me," confirmed Evelyn.

"I don't understand."

"Viktor knows I'm travelling under the name Barbara Browning. My disguise obviously didn't fool whatever software they're using. Even if I was able to speak to the foundation at the last minute and arrange a different academic to attend, there will still be an electronic record of Barbara Browning. Viktor's digital techniques are advanced, and I have no doubt at all that he's already commenced hunting down the name, especially in places with connection to Russia, the Orthodox Church or the Imperial Family. I'll be nearby as a decoy while you review the eggs."

Will shook his head. "But then we'll be putting you *and* Alex at immense risk. Regardless of the prophecy stating she'll be successful, I don't like it. Send me instead."

"It's okay, Will. I'll be fine," Alex said. The sleep had done her good and her resolve had returned. "I've worked in museums for a long time. I know my way around art and those who own it."

"I'm not letting you go alone. We'll go in together. Can that be arranged?" Will asked Evelyn.

"I don't see why not," said Evelyn. "You can act as the photographer. I'll be on watch outside ready to lure Viktor away if he appears. Remember, all we know for sure is that Viktor's aware of me being in Switzerland, so therefore we can be confident that he'll be looking for me as the first point of call."

Moving to the window, Alex carefully peeked through the curtains. She took in the magnificent early-morning lake view as she pondered Evelyn's recommendation. Alex immensely disliked the thought of Evelyn putting herself in front of Viktor as bait. Being responsible for another death was something she wasn't sure she would be able to recover from. Conversely, if it meant that a trained agent could lead Viktor away from the staff at the foundation, then as much as Alex hated to admit it, it was preferable.

"Alright, let's solidify our plan," she said.

Evelyn nodded and they gathered around a small round table by the window where she brought their attention to an aerial image on her computer. It showed a road along the edge of a lake.

"Lake Geneva, I assume," said Will.

"Yes. This is our hotel here, and this building on the water's edge is the foundation," Evelyn explained, pointing at and then zooming in on the building that they were to visit in a few hours' time. "To minimise any risk to Alex, I suggest the two of you access the site by water taxi while I drive and situate myself out the front near the main entrance. All going well, you can come out and meet me at the car once you're done. Our appointment is before opening time, just like Windsor, so we'll need to be ready to leave in a little over an hour. Here's the cheque," she said, handing Alex the donation.

"Thank you," Alex said. "What do I need to know about the foundation?"

"Just the basics to hold a conversation if need be. It was established in the early eighties with the aim to encourage and support young artists or institutions, primarily through funding or awards that carry prize money. Whilst fantastic for the local artistic community, what we care about is that they manage the collections of their two namesakes, Edouard-Marcel and Maurice Sandoz. Within the collection are two Fabergé eggs, one of which is our Swan," said Evelyn.

"Speaking of the egg, Alex and I have been thinking about what the clue might refer to, but I'd like to hear your thoughts," Will said to his mother. "We also retrieved this metal ring with the clue. The engraving suggests that we need to use it as some sort of key when we examine the Swan Egg."

Evelyn took some time to study the ring before speaking again. "I think the metal ring is to be used on the base diamond. It's about the same size, from all accounts, and the clue does refer to 'basing our faith'. I'd suggest that perhaps, knowing what we do now about the craft of Fabergé, we have some kind of combination lock to contend with."

"I was thinking the same, and that perhaps the metal ring is used similarly to how a safe's lock works, first turning the diamond in one direction and then in the other," Alex added.

"I agree with Alex. I really can't think of anything else," said Will.

Evelyn nodded. "The numbers are easy. They'll be the Tsar's birthday."

"So using the Julian calendar, that's the sixth of May, 1868," Will said.

"The Julian calendar?" Alex questioned.

"It was the old style used in Russia at the time of Nicholas' birth," Evelyn confirmed. "Back then, the calendar used in the East was twelve days behind the Gregorian calendar used in the West. You'll most often see the Tsar's birthday listed as the eighteenth of May in modern literature."

Alex nodded. "Okay, so five for the month, then six for the day, then one, eight, six and eight for the year."

"Almost," Will smiled. "In Russia they write the date as day, month, year."

A quiet settled over the room as they each contemplated the task at hand.

"Well," Alex said finally, "I for one need a shower. Any advice from the crowd about what Barbara Browning might wear?"

"Whatever you want, Alex. And by the way," said Evelyn, "I really like the short hair."

Alex reached up and touched her bob. "I didn't get much of a choice," she said as she walked towards the bathroom, placing her hand on Will's shoulder as she passed him. "But I like it too. He did a good job."

She couldn't be sure, but as she turned to close the bathroom door, Alex thought Will might have been blushing.

Chapter 23

LAUSANNE, SWITZERLAND

The only thing making Filip feel better about having to run around after Viktor was that the man had spectacularly screwed up last night, allowing Anya's sister to give him the slip in Geneva. *Good. The almighty Christ wasn't infallible after all. And who was cleaning up the mess? He was. Filip to the rescue, as always. The Christ-elect was running this show.*

He'd deliberately not done what Viktor asked of him after arriving in Geneva. The man had been more forceful and arrogant than usual, which had made Filip want to help him even less. In the last three days Viktor had made him fly from Moscow to the US, back to Moscow, then to London, where he'd hung out in transit for all of an hour and a half before heading to Geneva. He'd wanted, no, he'd deserved a night to have a few drinks and think about the best way to be done with Viktor.

Filip smiled at having conducted such blatant disobedience. It felt good. Sinful, a Khlyst might say. A greater power was growing within him, he could feel it. And the closer it came for him to take on the role of Christ, the more it was leading his decisions. It was time for the world to know and worship the ways of the Khlysts. No more waiting. Just like Viktor and Viktor's father before him, he would be anointed not only their cell's Christ but also the ultimate leader of all the Khlyst congregations.

As he continued to type in code and waited for the pain killers to help his hangover, Filip's thoughts again returned to Moscow. Why the Mother of Christ couldn't see reason beggared belief. He still felt the sting of her rejection, even if it was rejection 'just for now'. Her endorsement of his succession was conditional upon Viktor personally naming Filip as his heir. Her stance was unfortunate as that meant Viktor would have to die.

Before that could happen, though, Filip had to get his hands on the book that held all the proof of the R.A.'s plans and secure the Romanov heir. Without the book, he'd have to wait until he and Viktor completed the current mission. Filip definitely preferred plan number one for its expediency. It also meant that *he* would receive all the praise for ridding the world of the heirs and bribing the R.A. to legitimise the Khlysts.

His smile broadened at the thought, which turned into a satisfied grin as he got a hit.

Rolling off the edge of the bed, he stood and made his way to the door to the adjoining room. He unlocked it and gave it a solid whack with the palm of his hand.

"Viktor. I have something."

He heard the lock turn on the other side, and the door opened as he sat back down at his computer.

"Could you at least have put some pants on?" Viktor asked.

"Jocks are pants."

Viktor sighed. "What do you have?"

"A Barbara Browning is confirmed for an appointment at the Edouard and Maurice Sandoz Foundation in Lausanne at eight. It's seven-thirty now," Filip confirmed, looking at the time.

"And what, pray tell, is this foundation?"

"Hang on, I'm looking that up."

Viktor paced back and forth as Filip searched.

"Okay. It's an art foundation that just happens to also own two Fabergé eggs. That's a Russian connection at least. Perhaps a safe house?"

"She wouldn't need an appointment for a safe house, Filip. Anyway, it doesn't matter, we need to go. How long from here?"

"Approximately forty-seven minutes."

"Any news on the other two?"

"No, nothing yet."

"Alright. Put some pants on and meet me at the car in five."

"Wait," he said as Viktor made his way back to the other room.

"What, Filip? We don't have a lot of time."

"Seriously, Viktor? Relax. It's not my fault you lost Evelyn last night. Give me a fucking break," he snapped back.

"What do you want?" Viktor responded deadpan.

Filip stood and grabbed the jeans he'd flung on the floor the night before and started to pull them on. "I was hoping you'd let me read the book Anya prepared. It's always easier to understand a mission when fully briefed."

"No."

"Why not?"

"There's no need."

"I really think—"

"No. What we really need, Filip, is for you to focus on the task at hand. Once we have the heir, I'll brief you on next steps. Now, for God's sake, get dressed and meet me downstairs," Viktor snarled and slammed the door between their rooms shut.

Humiliation and anger flared up inside Filip. If only he could blow off Viktor's face right now. There would be no time to shower seeing as Viktor wanted him downstairs immediately. He deliberately didn't deodorise. The man could gag on the stink for all he cared.

When he got to the car, Viktor was already in the passenger seat and handed Filip the keys through the window.

"Guess I'll be driving then," Filip snarled as he snatched the keys and got into the driver's seat. Just what he needed with a hangover.

They drove in silence for some time before Viktor broke the tension.

"You were right. I was angry about losing Evelyn yesterday and took my frustration out on you. I'm sorry."

Filip wasn't sure how to deal with the apology. He'd never had one from Viktor before. He decided to ignore it, turn up the music and focus instead on weaving his way through the peak-hour traffic as fast as he could without attracting too much attention.

The road hugged the edge of Lake Geneva, and it was quite a beautiful drive. As the highway veered inland, he turned the volume down and turned to look at Viktor.

"There's something I've been thinking about."

"God forbid. Do I really want to know?" Viktor replied.

"You said that once we capture the heirs, you want to use them as pawns to ensure that when the R.A. is back in power, they make Khlysty legitimate and that you'll only use the R.A. history if need be."

"Yes."

"I don't understand why you have to give up the heirs. If the R.A. is going to be so adamant that their sordid history can't be known, why not just bribe them with that? That way, we can sacrifice the heirs ourselves and take revenge for the death of Rasputin. It's a win-win situation."

"I have my reasons."

"Oh, come on! Would you please brief me properly?" Filip exclaimed while taking out his frustration on the accelerator.

"Slow down or you'll have every cop in Switzerland on our tail!"

Filip begrudgingly decelerated and turned the music back up.

Viktor reached out to the centre console and turned off the radio. "It's because I'm one of them, Filip. As much as I'm a Khlyst, I'm also R.A. I'd rather entice them with something they want than bribe them with something they don't. And to be really honest with you, I believe we can work in harmony. Using their history is a last resort as there would be no way in hell of keeping them onside if we use that as our silver bullet."

Filip sighed. It made some sense, but Viktor was the almighty Khlyst Christ – he should want revenge for Rasputin's murder above everything else!

"Why not give them one of the heirs and we get to keep the other one and not tell them? Imagine the jubilation of our faithful should we sacrifice an heir at one of our services! Now that's definitely a win-win you can accept," Filip said defiantly.

"No, it's not," Viktor said, shaking his head at the idea. "Once they have one heir, there's too much risk that they'd find out about the other one and, again, we'd be seen as untrustworthy. We must have them on side, Filip. It's for the greater good and the longevity of our religion as the prominent faith of Russia."

Filip shook his head forcefully in disagreement and replanted his foot.

"We're going to have to agree to disagree," Viktor said, turning the radio back on.

Filip smiled. *Well, wasn't that the story of his fucking life.*

†

"I've arranged for the eggs to be set up here in our viewing area and a guard will remain with you. I'm sure you'll understand why we must have at least one person with you in the room at all times, Ms Browning," said the custodian of the foundation's headquarters.

"I don't count?" joked Will, giving the custodian a wink.

"I'm afraid not," she smiled. "I do want to reiterate, though, how much we appreciate your donation, and I wish I could leave you to conduct your work in private, but the rules are the rules."

Alex could see that custodian was genuinely humbled by the numbers on the cheque.

"That's completely understandable. It's not my money, so I'll try not to take it too personally!" Alex laughed, trying her best to play her role with aplomb.

Their conversation was interrupted when the door opened, and a guard entered wheeling a trolley carrying two secure cases. He carefully lifted both eggs out of their storage and placed them gently onto the viewing table before moving to the back of the room.

"And here they are," the custodian said as she handed both Alex and Will white cotton gloves.

"It's beautiful. So beautiful," Alex murmured as she leaned in close to the Swan Egg.

"Oh yes, she is! She's truly beautiful. As is her sister, the Peacock Egg."

"You consider the eggs female?" Alex asked the custodian.

"Aren't all who carry life female?"

Alex smiled and nodded. *She should have thought of that herself.*

"I know I'm not supposed to have favourites, but the Swan Egg is my pick of the two," the custodian continued as she looked longingly at the artwork. "The Peacock Egg is most other people's choice."

Alex leaned in to look more closely at the Peacock Egg. It too was absolutely stunning.

"We've always been respectful to the original owners and their affiliation with the Russian Orthodox Church, and we've also been extremely happy to see that post the fall of the Soviet Union, many of the Fabergé artifacts have been returned to Russia. Regretfully, my bosses aren't ready to part with these two beauties yet, but I was directed to ask if there'd be an exhibition to coincide with the book launch? These two eggs haven't often shared the spotlight with their sisters, but for the Russian Orthodox Church, who the Tsar believed in so very much, they would be happy to consider an exhibition loan."

"Oh, that's marvellous," said Alex. "I'll convey your very generous gesture back to the church. Thank you so much. There will be much rejoicing if we're able to get every known egg home to Russia for the book launch."

"What are your thoughts regarding timings, Barbara?"

She paused to think before Will jumped in.

"It's actually really exciting. All going well, the aim is to coincide the book launch and exhibition with what would have been the four hundredth anniversary of Romanov rule in 2013."

"Amazing. What a beautiful way to celebrate such a momentous occasion. The Fabergé Tercentenary Egg is also one of my favourites, such a masterpiece of history," the custodian gushed. "Carl Fabergé was a storyteller like no other. Each and every egg showcases a very poignant time in the Romanovs' lives."

"Indeed." Alex smiled and nodded her thanks to Will for the save.

"The Tercentenary Egg is also a very sad representation of a dynasty that fell into irretrievable collapse only four years later," the custodian continued. "Historians thought that the amazing celebrations during the tercentenary indicated that Russia had recovered after the upheavals of 1905, and it did seem at the time that the Romanovs would reign for centuries. With hindsight, however …" she trailed off.

Alex needed to move things along. Viktor could be nearby.

"Well, I can't wait to get started on these beautiful eggs of yours."

"Of course. I'll leave you to it. When you're finished, just let the guard know and he'll show you back out to reception. He is also fluent in English, so feel free to ask him for anything you might need. And again, thank you so much for your donation," the custodian said as she left the room.

Alex exchanged glances with Will, and he moved in close to the table, taking various shots of the eggs.

"If you can start by taking images of the Peacock Egg, I'll examine the Swan Egg. Then we can swap places," she said, doing her best to keep her back to the guard.

Carefully she picked up the small and delicate egg, which was no more than four inches high, and examined it closely before placing it back down on the table. From her bag of tools, Alex then removed a magnifying glass and the small metal ring they'd retrieved from Windsor Castle. To her immense relief, it could be positioned around the base diamond but … it wouldn't move it. She tried in both directions but nothing. Her hands started to sweat inside the gloves as she tried to think what to do next. She had to hurry.

She tried again, this time applying a downward movement. She'd not wanted to force it, but now time was forcing her. This time she felt a loosening, and a click indicated that just as with the Clover Egg, she had unlocked some kind of mechanism.

Quickly she tried to turn the diamond. Clockwise gave her no success, but when she reversed the movement, the diamond turned in place. She rotated it to the left six full rotations, followed by five rotations to the right and then once again to the left and then … *no! What year was it?* Her mind had drawn a complete blank.

"Was it in 1868 that the last Tsar was born?" Will asked her as he snapped away. "I always get the date wrong."

Thank you, she mouthed at him silently, then said out loud, "Yes, that's right."

"Shit," he exclaimed.

"Sorry?" she said, startled.

"Is everything okay?" the guard asked in stilted English.

"Sorry. Yeah, don't mind me," Will said, turning to the guard. "Just my camera playing up." He then turned to Alex and tapped his ear, giving her the sign that Evelyn had seen something. They needed to hurry.

"Got some great shots already, though. I'm almost done. You?" he asked, looking at her intensely.

"Almost," she said as she focused with fierce concentration on rotating the diamond as quickly as possible eight, six and, finally, eight times … and then watched as the diamond simply lifted off the base.

To make sure it wouldn't be seen by any cameras, Alex reached her hands into her tool bag and rolled the beautiful stone around in the palm of one hand. It's under surface was cut flat, which was unusual, and it was set onto what looked like a platinum disc, which could be folded out like a tiny concertina to reveal four panels with engravings. It had to be the next clue, but she couldn't make out the words with the naked eye. She reached for her magnifying glass but stopped and looked up when she heard it – Viktor's voice. He was in the building.

She looked at Will who shook his head. He trusted his mum.

"Any last shots you'd like?" he asked her.

"Yes, just here. An extreme close-up, please," she said, bringing her hand out of the bag and holding the tiny panels out in front of her.

Poised to capture the perfect image, Will was about to press the shutter when a shrill beep announced the camera's battery failure. With their phones locked up at reception, they were utterly stranded; there was no backup.

"How about you make your final notes while I go out to the car and get my spare battery?" Will suggested.

Alex knew he was trying to protect her and would do whatever he had to do. It was a big ask, but they really had no other choice. They needed more time.

"Good idea," she said quietly, and he left the room before either of them could change their mind.

Quickly Alex placed the diamond under the magnifying glass. With difficulty, due to her gloves, she noted down the engraved text before securing the diamond back in the base of the egg. As she hurriedly packed up their things, her heart sank once more when she heard the door reopen. *Had Viktor found her?*

She spun around quickly and breathed a sigh of relief to see Will.

He looked somewhat startled. "No spare, I'm afraid. Perhaps we can book another time to come back?"

"Ah no, I don't think that will be necessary. I'm confident I have everything I need," she said.

Will nodded and turned to the guard. "We're finished now, thank you."

The guard escorted them from the room, locking it behind him, and chaperoned them to reception. It wasn't until they were out the front of the foundation that Will spoke again.

"We're safe for now. Mum walked into the main office through a side door like a goddamn kamikaze. Viktor went after her and didn't see me coming down the hallway. I can only assume she made it to the car as it's not in the car park," he said. He pulled out his phone. "We'll have to get a taxi back."

"Maybe she'll head back to the bank?"

"She won't be able to pull that off twice, and this time Viktor has help. Filip was here as well."

Alex wasn't sure what else to say.

As Will organised their ride, Alex checked the panicked notes she'd made inside the viewing room. When finished, she passed him the notebook and looked at him expectantly.

Before you enter the islands of child, be sure to halt and enjoy the view. Do so in the veil of night and the eleventh hour will light your way bright.

He smiled ruefully. "I believe I'll be accompanying you on your first visit to Russia."

Chapter 24

MONTREUX AND GENEVA, SWITZERLAND

The fuel gauge was getting low. If Evelyn couldn't lose them very soon, she'd have to ditch the car and run.

"Come on, car," she muttered. She really didn't like her chances with the outrunning scenario. She'd only just got into the car at the foundation when Filip had caught up, grabbed the door handle roughly and started to pull the door open before she could lock it. She'd managed to knock him off balance by planting her foot on the accelerator, but as she'd driven away, she saw him jump in a car alongside Viktor and they'd followed after her at pace.

She made a quick move into the left lane to pass a slower car and then accelerated back to the right. As had occurred for the last twenty minutes, Viktor did the same. It was imperative she get off the motorway and lose them.

Quickly, she checked the GPS and saw perhaps her only opportunity to out manoeuvre them: an off-ramp to Montreux. If she could exit at the last possible moment, she might be able to lose them.

A car up ahead moved across into her lane and she quickly recalculated her plan. She smiled. This one was better, but the timing would need to be perfect. Without hesitation, she planted her foot and veered right into the exit lane leading to the off-ramp. She then swerved back onto the motorway so close to an unsuspecting driver that she nearly clipped the front of their car. To the sound of an angry horn, she maneuvered the car across one more lane to the far left and prayed.

As Evelyn saw Viktor replicate her move, she applied the brakes and swerved back across the two lanes to the off-ramp with only a few yards to spare. With quiet jubilation, she exited the motorway and slowed down to negotiate the quieter road.

Glancing in the rear-view mirror as she navigated through a number of roundabouts, there was no sign of Viktor, which let her breathe a little more easily. The side roads certainly weren't ones she could speed on, but she definitely now had an advantage. Viktor would either have to somehow reverse back to follow her or find another exit to Montreux.

As fast as she could, Evelyn drove towards the resort town, a place she'd love to come back and visit under different circumstances. Locating the Grand Rue, she followed it into the centre of town, driving slowly to avoid the tourists meandering along the road's edge. It was a breathtaking location and she longed to take a moment to appreciate it. However, her immediate priority was to find a place to dispose of the car and arrange alternative transport.

A flashing sign on top of a building up ahead caught her attention. Evelyn sighed with relief. A casino was perfect.

"Thank you," she whispered to the heavens as she found a secluded place to park at the rear of the casino's underground parking facility. As she turned off the ignition, she scoped her surroundings. Everything seemed calm and no other cars had entered the car park since she had, so after taking a few deep breaths, she grabbed her bag, jumped out of the car, and headed towards the casino entrance.

"Damn it," she mumbled under her breath when she saw a security guard at the door scanning IDs. The last thing she needed was for her ID to pinpoint her location for Viktor. Turning quickly, she deviated to make her way back up the car park entry ramp on foot.

Stopping momentarily to pull up the hood of her jacket and tighten it under her chin, Evelyn looked around to get her bearings. Seeing signs pointing out the direction to the lake, she walked closely behind a group making their way to the esplanade.

Even in the cold, the area was bustling with activity. Tourists wandered along the edge of the lake, snapping photos and enjoying the performances of street artists. Sitting on a bench overlooking the water, Evelyn used her phone to check for a nearby train station. *Yes!* It would be best for her to double back the way she had come and cut through the town instead of taking the esplanade as that route was definitely the shortest. She hated to leave this beautiful place so quickly, but she had little choice.

Keeping her head down, she made her way swiftly past the casino and ventured into the centre of town. Doubts crept in – *had she made a mistake?* Perhaps she should have walked along the lake as here there were much fewer people around; the block she now found herself on was completely deserted. Acutely aware of the danger this presented, she quickened her pace.

Her heart surged when she finally sighted the train station in the distance. It stopped when she also saw Viktor and Filip. Their car was coming directly towards her and was close enough for her to make out their faces. She stepped into a doorway, keeping her head down as their car passed. After a few moments, she stepped back out into the street. She managed to take only a few steps before she felt someone grab her arm from behind. Without hesitation, she grabbed the person's hand with her free arm and bent the fingers back upon themselves.

She heard a man's voice let out a profanity and the grip on her released. Turning, she saw Filip leaning forward holding his hand,

and over his shoulder she could see Viktor getting out of their car. As Filip stood upright to come at her again with a gun raised, she kicked out violently with her foot and caught him under his chin, causing him to tumble backwards. Then she ran.

"Go after her, but don't kill her! I'll bring the car," she heard Viktor order as she raced towards the train station. Reaching the entrance, she glanced back over her shoulder and could see Filip hot on her tail, his gun away for now. He'd know a clean shot was impossible with the number of people awaiting trains and that security cameras would be capturing the station's goings-on.

Evelyn couldn't afford the time to stop and get a ticket. She needed another solution. Looking around as she walked through the morning commuters, she saw a security guard standing by an emergency exit.

"Sir, do you speak English?" she asked as she approached him.

He nodded and smiled. "Yes."

She turned and pointed out Filip, who, seeing her approach the guard, fell back and stood nonchalantly alongside people milling about near the ticket counter. By the time the guard had turned his attention back to her, Evelyn had slipped past him and opened the exit. An alarm sounded as she slipped outside and ran towards an oncoming taxi, waving it down. "Geneva," she ordered as she jumped in and slammed the door before slumping down as low in the seat as she could. "Please," she added.

"Madam, it will be much less expensive for you to catch a train and, if I'm honest, probably faster. The trains run like clockwork here," the driver said, turning to look at her over his shoulder.

"I'll double your fare if you just drive as fast as you can."

He turned back around, and in the rear-view mirror she saw his eyebrows raised in astonishment. Evelyn maintained eye contact, and when he realised she was serious, he gave her a broad smile.

"Well, as you wish. Geneva it is."

✝

With nothing to go on after losing Evelyn in Montreux, Viktor had returned with Filip to Geneva to wait until she raised her head again. How the woman had managed to evade him three times in less than twenty-four hours was, quite frankly, humiliating. Worse still, he couldn't be mad at Filip as he'd been there each time himself.

"She's good," Filip said without looking away from his computer.

"What?" Viktor snapped.

"She's good. She's worked out it's the airports. She's booked six different flights using the same alias. All from different locations. She's basically telling us to go fuck ourselves," Filip said, shaking his head and smiling. "I like her."

Viktor glared at him and downed his drink. "Anything yet on her son and the Romanov?"

"Not since they entered the UK. And now Evelyn's onto us, it may be hard to find them again," Filip confirmed, looking up from his laptop.

Increasingly frustrated, Viktor poured himself another vodka. He drank it slowly, looking out the window over the lake towards the boats moored on the opposite side of the city. It was a cold day, as one would expect in late March, but the sun reflecting off the water gave the illusion of warmth. Yet all Viktor felt was cold hatred. He poured another drink.

"Alright," he said, turning to eyeball Filip. "We need to put an alert on all customs points in case she tries to cross a border by car. I have someone at the R.A. who can help me with that."

"Why don't I just hack the daily logs?" Filip asked. "Wouldn't that be better than trying to explain to the R.A. why you're tracking border crossings?"

For once the kid had something useful to say.

"Yes. Good. Do hourly tracking."

"Jesus. I'm sorry I offered now," Filip lamented. "Okay, but you better hope she's located before it's time to sleep or, mark my words Viktor, you're along for the ride. I'll set my alarm every hour on the hour."

"Sorry to disappoint you but I'm flying back to Moscow tonight."

"What? You mean *we're* flying back to Moscow, right?"

"No, I meant exactly what I said, Filip. I have to fly back to attend Anya's funeral. You, on the other hand, need to stay here in case we get a hit on Evelyn, in which case you'll follow that up. I'll rejoin you as soon as I can, wherever she may take you."

"Great," Filip said, slamming shut his laptop and making his way to the minibar. "How did your wife die, anyway?" he asked as he rummaged through what was left of the alcohol selection.

"Elegantly," was all Viktor gave him.

"So you did her in yourself is what you're saying. I knew that much already," Filip snarled.

Viktor couldn't help but smile at the retort. "It doesn't matter how."

"Oh, come on, Viktor. Poison? Gunshot?"

"It doesn't matter."

"Sex gone wrong?"

"Oh, for the love of God. I cut her throat."

Filip's hand froze momentarily on the small bottle of gin he'd been about to open. His reaction was exactly why Viktor hadn't wanted to say how he'd killed Anya. Slowly and deliberately, Filip opened the bottle and threw it back in one shot.

"I'm sorry, Filip. I know that probably brings back terrible memories of your mother."

Filip threw the empty bottle into the bin and stared out the window, deep in thought. Viktor stayed quiet. He didn't want to risk further triggering him.

"I've had the apartment refurbished multiple times and still I see blood every time I walk in that room … I still see her lying there. Whoever killed her didn't even have the decency to close her eyes," Filip shared.

"Your mother didn't deserve to die like that. From what I could tell, she seemed a good woman."

Filip spun to look at him. "A good woman? Far from it. She got herself knocked up and supposedly didn't even know by who. Add to that being drunk for most of my childhood … Jesus, what am I saying – she was drunk until the day she died. If there was any blessing at all derived from her alcoholism it's that she was more than likely drunkenly oblivious to the threat that ended her life. Her being passed out when it happened would have been a godsend."

Viktor flinched. He was the cause of two of those three things. The baby and the booze. The knife to her throat had been thanks to a junkie who'd broken in looking for cash.

"She looked after you, though, even with all her faults. We all have faults, including you, Filip."

"Yeah. I was so faulty my father never bothered to meet me."

Viktor flinched again. That comment was concerning.

"What do you mean?"

"Add liar to the list of my mother's faults," Filip said over his shoulder as he walked into the bathroom, leaving Viktor alone to ponder what it was his son knew. Filip wasn't the type to shy away from a confrontation, so surely he couldn't have any idea that his father was right here, right now, in the same hotel room.

At the sound of running water, Viktor silently reassured himself. *Of course Filip didn't know!* All the same, an uncharacteristic wave of anxiety came over him. He really did need to tell Filip sometime soon, but just the thought of it sent a chill through him. Until now, Viktor had always used Anya as the reason not to. Now she was no longer a consideration, he had no idea at all how to best tackle it. Viktor had put the love of his wife ahead of his child, meaning he'd never had the chance to properly know Filip, let alone openly love him.

Surely, his best strategy was to adhere to his mantra: 'Entice them with something they want rather than bribe them with something they don't'. This approach had been his guiding principle when explaining his theory on using the Romanov heirs to improve Khlysts relations with the R.A. It was more effective to say, 'Please accept that I'm your father, and I'll appoint you my successor,' rather than, 'Promise not to get mad, and I'll reveal who your father is … me.'

His thoughts were broken when Filip came out of the bathroom and sat down on the couch. He looked a little emotionally fragile and had obviously washed his face. The subject affected Filip deeply.

"So get a load of this," Filip said after they'd both sat in silence for a few minutes. "She swore up until the day she died that she had no idea who my father was, but that was a complete lie. She was accepting money from him every month. Every month! It was hand-delivered in an envelope. Cash."

Viktor felt his blood run cold. He'd counted that cash himself.

"That could have been money for anything. Perhaps she had a job you weren't aware of?" he suggested.

"No. It was for me, or I should say for her to look after me. She was a drunk. Drunks lose track of their tongue and forget what they've said. She told me once that she was too 'tipsy' to take me shopping but to use the money from my father to go buy myself something nice for my birthday. I was eight and she wasn't tipsy, she was blind fucking drunk."

Viktor didn't know what to say.

"If I managed to get to the envelope first, I syphoned off a wad of cash each month for myself. She didn't even notice. Good woman indeed, Viktor."

Oh, but she did notice, Viktor thought. He'd sacked courier after courier when Filip's mother had continually complained about the short amounts.

"The money stopped after she died, so I guess she was more important to him than I ever was. But anyway, enough of that. It's ridiculously lame for a grown man to be worrying about this. She was a whore and a liar, and as for my father, he was a coward."

A coward? A level of guilt Viktor had never imagined possible rose up inside him. A coward? That was a word he would never, ever use to describe himself. He had to set this straight. Was now as good a time as any to officially confirm Filip as his successor and tell him that he, Viktor, was his father?

"A coward," Filip repeated. "End of story."

No. Not now. He couldn't. Viktor needed this mission competed first and had to have Filip on side.

"I'm sorry you feel that way. I'm sure your father must have had a reason for doing the things he did," Viktor offered.

"Sorry if I don't take advice from a man who's never been a father," Filip said sarcastically as he headed back to the minibar. "As I said, end of story. What flight are you on?"

"The six-fifteen."

Filip looked at his watch. "Heaps of time. How about you finally show me that book of Anya's?"

Viktor could give his son that much. The book was definitely the lesser of two evils.

Chapter 25

PUSHKIN, RUSSIA

The lack of light made the night seem all the more devoid of warmth, and it brought with it a fear of what may be ahead, behind or around them. They'd been walking for a long time through snow-clad gardens, and even though it was a fine evening, frost usually reserved for early mornings cracked under their feet, making their way slippery and onerous.

"We're almost there," Will said, interrupting Alex's thoughts. "Sorry your first visit to a place so monumentally special to your family has been cloaked in almost complete darkness," he said, as if sensing her foreboding.

"It's okay. I read about this place on the plane while you slept," she said, following closely behind him as he lit their way with a small torch. She was glad Will had gotten some rest as he'd been working tirelessly to keep her and her family safe. He'd slept soundly for most of the flight, but only after Evelyn had called to reassure them that she was on her way to Geneva, after which she'd make her way back to London by car to avoid airport detection.

What Alex had learned was fascinating. No one could write the kinds of stories that history authored, and certainly no one could have written the exceptional last week that had been her life. She'd quite literally become the leading lady in a new chapter of one of the most spectacular stories in human history, and the story of Tsarskoye Selo, which she now knew meant 'Tsar's Village', was also significant. The site, now a part of the town of Pushkin, was once the residence of the Russian Imperial Family. Her alleged family. She shook her head. That part was still very surreal and hard to comprehend.

The main buildings of the residence had been lit up like beautiful beacons, but rather than gravitate to them, they'd slipped quickly into the darkness of a large park named for Catherine the Great, who had been the first Russian leader to own the area. Numerous members of the Russian Monarchy had lived in Tsarskoye Selo throughout its existence, but the town gained greater official stature after 1905 when Tsar Nicholas II made it his permanent residence. It was here that he was arrested by the provisional government during the February Revolution of 1917, and it was from here that he was exiled with his family to await what the world now knew was a brutal death. She shuddered at the thought.

"We're here," Will said, stopping ahead of her at the steps that led to their destination, the Marble Bridge. Enveloped in the shadows of night, it looked menacing, a far cry from the romantic stone and marble roofed architecture Alex had researched and been so enamoured with.

"Is it just the dark and extreme cold that makes my hair stand on end or is this place somehow ... well ...?"

"Haunted?" Will asked.

"Maybe?" she offered meekly through chattering teeth as she joined him on the steps.

"I'm pretty sure it's just the dark," he said as he moved behind her and rubbed his hands quickly up and down her arms to help warm her. It was the first time he'd touched her since holding her hand when he thought she'd been sleeping. It still felt right. So right. *He's paid to look after you*, she reminded herself, doing her best to push her deepening feelings for him aside.

"There are others that would beg to differ," he added, stepping away from her and checking his watch. "Right before his death, there were suspicions that Rasputin and the Tsarina, who many Russians never saw as more than a hated German, were secretly plotting to defeat Russia. Some of the Russian nobility, as well as a selection of the wider population, came to believe that Rasputin and Alexandra were destroying their country. It was these same people who also believed Rasputin poisoned the earth of Tsarskoye Selo."

"Physically or spiritually?" she asked.

"Rasputin was originally secretly buried here on the grounds."

Her skin crawling at the thought, Alex pulled her coat up around her face. "Well, that's something I didn't read on the plane. What do you mean he was originally buried here? Where is he now?" she asked.

"His corpse was exhumed and burned by a mob during the February Revolution," Will said, sighing as he also pulled up his coat collar to protect against the frigid air. "I'm sorry. I feel a little as if I'm constantly giving you a history lesson."

"I really don't mind." She smiled at him as he once again looked at his watch.

"Okay, only a few more minutes to see if we have this right. We timed it perfectly."

"Can you please explain to me again why you think this is the right spot?"

"Of course. The clue you retrieved from the Swan Egg said to halt and enjoy the view before entering the 'islands of child'. The islands on the other side of this bridge are called the Swan Islands. Given we retrieved the clue from the Swan Egg and that the islands are where the imperial children played, I'm confident we're in the right place. This bridge is the only entrance to the islands, so I'm also confident that this is where we must halt."

Alex carefully walked up the small flight of stairs onto the main bridge crossing then turned back to face Will. "And you believe that at eleven o'clock we'll find what we need?"

"I certainly hope so," he said as he joined her, beginning to walk the length of the bridge. "I think it's here!" he called out with enthusiasm.

Alex rushed over to him, excited to see what it was that Will thought he'd found.

"See those small lights out there that look like buoys at sea?" Will said, pointing towards the water.

She squinted to make out the dim lights in the distance. "I can see the lights but not what they're meant to be lighting up."

"The view, Alex! It is between these two colonnades that you get the best view of the Chesme Column. This has to be where, at eleven, the light should indicate something of worth. Thank God for only a scattering of clouds tonight."

"It's dark, Will. There is no view!"

"Well, yes, it's dark, but those lights out there are the corners of the column's base, which rises up out of the water. I know it's a bit hard to see now, but this is definitely the best place to see the column. Here, look at this," he said and showed her a daytime image of the column on his phone.

"Your confident it's the view the clue refers to?"

"Well, there's a magnificent garden all around us, but the Chesme Column is what you'd definitely grab your camera for when standing in this spot. On its top there's a bronze eagle representing Russia, and for any Russian, that's a patriotic view," he explained while keeping his eyes glued to his watch.

Suddenly he looked up at her and beckoned for her to kneel down with him next to the bridge wall. "Look!"

At first Alex couldn't make out anything except ghostly shadows created by the moonlight, but once Will pointed it out to her, she couldn't unsee it. A small, coloured pinpoint of light was beaming onto the bridge wall between the two colonnades that offered the best view of the Chesme Column. Looking up, she could see that the light radiated through a hole in the roof of the bridge.

"Look at this!" Will exclaimed as he pointed at an engraving not far below where the beam of light shone on the wall.

"A clover," she whispered.

Will ran his Maglite over the shape. "I know what to do. This is the same size as the keyhole on King Edward's stall plate at St George's."

Alex waited with bated breath as Will reached inside his jacket and pulled the Clover Egg key from underneath his shirt. When the key met its matching lock, a hidden door in the stone wall opened, revealing something familiar. Inside the silk wrapping and the box within it was a small card and a metal ring protected by shredded cotton.

"Well, at least this time we know what to do with it," Alex said, trying to keep positive while at the same time wondering where they'd have to venture next. The Tsar would never have thought the eggs would leave Russia, so the path should have been a lot easier than what it had been and was likely still to be.

"Time is something we are very much running out of," Will sighed. "Okay, let's see what it says on the card."

You will be all IV the temple of love. Time will unwind and set you on your new life's path. You will be a column of strength IV years to come.

"Any ideas?" Alex asked quietly, wishing she could be of more help.

Will smiled knowingly. "Well, there are only four imperial eggs that have clocks in them, and I'm thinking the Colonnade Egg might be the one we're after, but I'd like a second opinion," he said as he did a search on his phone and then handed it to Alex to see the results. "It's definitely the Colonnade Egg. It's often referred to as 'The Temple of Love'."

Looking at the egg brought a smile to Alex's face. Once again, Fabergé had created a masterpiece. Everything about it unequivocally resonated love. Two doves in the centre of the piece represented Nicholas and Alexandra. The four Grand Duchesses were represented as silver-gilt cherubs, gracefully seated around the base of the colonnades, each holding exquisite garlands of roses. Alexei, the Tsar's only son, adorned the very top of the suspended egg. A single golden cupid.

The egg commemorated the birth of the long-awaited heir to the Russian throne, and although Alexei was born in 1904, the egg itself wasn't presented until six years later.

Will nodded solemnly as he listened to Alex read. "It's devastating that it was presented at a time when its joy would have been marred by the haemophilia that afflicted little Alexei. His illness would have been readily apparent to his immediate family by then."

"I agree," she said with a sigh. "Its design was based on such love, but from the day it was presented it's been reflective of intrinsic sadness. It looks like it's made from gold with pink enamel … and the columns … I'm not sure what—"

"I know what I'm sure about," Will interrupted her.

"What's that?" she asked, still reading intently.

"We need to get back to the car and somewhere warm before we freeze."

In her excitement about the new egg, she'd momentarily forgotten the cold, but now that he'd mentioned it, she felt it bite at her bones. Bracing against the icy headwind, they started back through the park.

"I know I said it earlier," Will said as they walked, "but I'm really sorry that your first time on Russian soil has been completely under the cloak of night. It hasn't been much of a homecoming." He smiled at her sadly. "I promise we'll do it better when we come back."

She smiled. His thoughtfulness warmed her heart. "Will, until a few days ago I had no idea that my family had anywhere other than Boston to consider home, so it's okay, really. I'm sure I'll get the chance to see more. You said 'come back'. Are we leaving already?"

Will nodded, focusing intently on the ground ahead to avoid slipping on the ice. "Back to London. It works out well as we can regroup with Mum."

"So another egg in London."

"Yes. It's one of three owned by Queen Elizabeth II and kept at The Queen's Gallery at Buckingham Palace."

"Oh, I've heard that gallery is amazing!" Alex exclaimed, turning to look at him in excitement. As she did, she lost her balance, awkwardly falling to the ground and landing heavily on the icy path.

"Alex!"

Embarrassed, she tried to stand but slipped again and fell back to the same cold, damp spot.

"I'm fine," she reassured him. "Sitting in a bit of a wet patch, but apart from that, totally fine."

He laughed loudly. "I'm just going to leave that comment alone."

Bending down, Will put his arm around her waist to help her upright. As she fully straightened, she could feel her heart beating faster and faster, not from the fall but from the deep arousal that was flowing through her. The intensity she felt at this moment was overwhelming. Her mind was empty of questions seeking answers on motive and full of nothing but unbridled desire.

As Will pulled her in close to warm her, Alex instinctively leaned her head back and looked up at him, letting her eyes convey her longing. They drew him to her, beckoning his desire to merge with hers, and he kissed her, first gently, then with a raging intensity that made her knees weak. Leaning in more closely to his heaving chest, her hood fell backwards and his hands explored her hair, his grip tightening in passionate clutches each time his tongue touched hers.

Then as quickly as it had begun, he clasped her face in his hands and gently pushed her away from him. His breathed in and out heavily and lowered his head.

"I'm sorry," he said looking up again, his eyes begging for forgiveness.

She placed her hands on top of his and lowered them gently. "Let's get back to the car."

He nodded and they walked in silence for a few moments before she turned carefully to avoid another fall.

"Will?"

"Yeah?"

She reached for his hand and held it tight. "That felt like the perfect homecoming to me."

Chapter 26

LONDON, UK

"What the hell is she doing now?" he murmured.

Filip could see Evelyn quite clearly from his safe vantage point across and down the road, even though the winter light was dim. London was dark, dreary and one shade of grey. He smiled. It was just like winter at home. Perfect conditions to do his best work.

"What?" a voice said in his ear.

"She's loitering. Nothing much else," he replied, having momentarily forgotten Viktor was on the other end of the phone.

"Well, at least you have her location again. Good work tracking her through French customs to London. Let's hope she's waiting for the heir. Alex is all we care about. Nothing else."

"Not even the son?"

"Not even the son."

"Then you won't care that he just arrived and is talking to your sister-in-law?"

He heard Viktor sigh in annoyance before asking, "And the girl?"

"Nothing yet, but even a dirty Romanov can stay undetected if the wind blows just right. They're heading inside. I'll call you back once I'm in," Filip said and hung up.

Casually crossing the street, he made his way alongside the palace to the gallery. It was relatively small and the stone columns that formed the entrance looked almost Grecian. Not at all what he was expecting for a gallery named for a Queen and an English one at that. Stepping inside, a concierge greeted him with a sorrowful look on her face.

"Hello, sir. I'm afraid the gallery is now closed for admittance. We're open every day, so we'd be pleased to welcome you back another time."

"That won't work for me," Filip said as he scanned the hallway behind her. He couldn't see anyone manning the ticket counter or the security scanners. "I'm only in town today." He stood his ground and locked his eyes with hers.

"Ah, well, okay. Perhaps I can make an exception just this once." She smiled somewhat nervously and gestured for him to enter. "The gallery will be closing in twenty minutes, so it will be a bit of a whirlwind for you. Do you already have a ticket?"

"Thank you and no," he said, pulling a wad of cash out of his jeans pocket and handing it to her.

"Oh! I won't need that much," she said, taking a few notes and handing back the rest along with a brochure. "Now I'll just get you to follow me and I'll pass you through security. Everything out of your pockets, please, and then you'll be good to go."

"You're a bit of a one-woman show. Can't get good help?" he asked her as she slipped behind the security station to check him in.

"Well, as I said, we're closed now for admittance." She x-rayed his personal items. "Great, thank you. Here are your things. Enjoy the gallery."

Filip put his watch back on and refilled his pockets before venturing through the grand entrance foyer. He didn't attempt to hide or disguise himself and walked with purpose. He wanted Evelyn and Will to see him coming and feel fear. Evelyn had slipped through his hands twice in Switzerland and he wasn't going to allow her to be lucky a third time.

"I'm in," he remarked as Viktor answered his call.

"What are they doing?"

"Not sure yet. Jesus, this place feels more like a church than a gallery," he said, taking in his surroundings.

"That would be because it was once a chapel. It was refurbished into what it is today after suffering bomb damage in the Second World War."

Filip laughed sarcastically as his eyes moved around the room, observing the remaining visitors. "How do you know all this crap, Viktor?"

"Filip. Regardless of my feelings or lack thereof regarding the monarchy and religions not our own, they have helped shape our history, and it is a history rich in interesting facts."

"The only fact I like is that it got bombed in the first place," Filip retaliated as he made his way into the Nash Gallery. The walls were a dark red that commanded regal recognition. Strong and bold, the room screamed wealth. Display cabinets were filled with jewels and adorning the walls were gold-framed paintings that were likely world-famous. To Filip they looked like something he'd burn at the first chance. They really were boring. Even the ones with naked women.

In the adjoining room, he could see striking rich-green walls and what looked like arms and armour … and Evelyn and Will, shaking hands and speaking with a young man.

"Found them. I'll call you back when I'm done," Filip said, abruptly ending the call.

Keeping them in sight, he paused by a display cabinet and reached into his inside jacket pocket. Given he'd been unable to bring any kind of weapon through security, the prescription pill bottle had been one of his only options. It didn't contain the medicine the label stated but small capsules of poison. He removed a couple and put them in the pocket of his jeans, before crossing to the other side of the room, silently observing what was unfolding. From this angle he could see the young man was armed. A guard. As he wondered why Evelyn and Will were playing friendly with security, bells sounded, alerting everyone that it was time to start making their way out of the gallery.

A throng of people made their way towards the exit, but Filip held firm, admiring some bilious piece of art. As the room finally cleared, he moved quietly into the green room where he could see Evelyn and Will being ushered into an area signed for authorised people only. Filip smirked to himself. He had zero concerns about getting himself authorised immediately. It would be as simple as knocking on the door.

He knocked, and as the door opened towards him, he slammed it back, throwing the guard on the other side onto the floor. Quickly, Filip stepped inside the inner corridor and secured the door. Noting no one else around, he helped the guard to his feet before pushing him roughly up against the wall. Using his elbow and forearm pressed tight across his throat, Filip kept the man still as he quickly retrieved a pill from his pocket and broke open the liquid capsule.

As the guard gasped in pain, Filip squeezed the capsule's viscous yellow contents into the man's mouth. It took only seconds for the man's body to go limp, and as his eyes rolled backwards in their sockets, Filip lowered him to the floor before taking the guard's gun from its holster. With force he then smashed the digital security panel by the door, short-circuiting the system.

"Excellent," he whispered, before pausing to listen intently. He heard the faint sound of voices so stepped over the guard's body and moved quietly along the corridor. Not too far up ahead he saw them.

Evelyn and Will appeared to be in some sort of viewing room. The room's walls were glass from waist height to the ceiling, no doubt to allow security to watch over the items being viewed, and the room contained two rows of tables covered with black velvet. As he crouched down low and made his way towards them, he could make out one camera on the ceiling in the far back corner of the room.

"I don't like Alex being alone," he heard Will say through the still open door to the hall.

"I know, but she needed time to connect with her parents, talk to them in person and make sure they're okay. She's with church faithful who I trust so she'll be fine, and I also trust she'll keep her word not to tell her parents anything," Evelyn reassured him. "She promised you she wouldn't."

"I know, but still."

"I think we can take her at her word. It's readily apparent she's come to trust you."

Filip took a stealthy look around the doorframe and saw the son was blushing. *Ha! He'd bet any money that he was banging the princess. Actually, he had no doubt. Respect.* Filip would have her himself as soon as he could.

"I hope we've interpreted his words correctly," Will said.

"I'm confident we have," Evelyn said. *"Time will unwind and set you on your new life's path* can only allude to the clock band, and the Roman numerals used to reference the word 'for' will refer to the numeral four, as in four o'clock. I also have no doubt that in order for Victoria to have started a new life path, the clue will be referring to her birthdate."

"Are you sure?"

"For the love of God I hope so," Evelyn said. "By 1901, the Julian calendar had changed to be thirteen days behind the West, not twelve. So for Victoria to have led the life she was actually born into, she'd have needed to rewind time to the fifth of Jun—"

Filip quickly retreated away from the door as the conversation suddenly stopped, but not before seeing a door at the other side of the viewing room open and a woman and guard enter.

"I'm sorry for the delay, Sophia," he heard the woman apologise as he crept closer again to the door, "but I found the staff door unmanned and for some reason also locked from the inside, so I had to come the long way. I'll be having a serious talk with our head of security, let me tell you. Kids these days … they don't stay a minute after their shift is up. Unbelievable."

Filip could hear a slight edge to her voice indicating that the woman was unnerved by the occurrence.

"Oh dear! Well, we don't want to keep you longer than necessary, especially when it comes to matters of security, so may I suggest that we take some of our key photography today and then return tomorrow to conduct the evaluations on the eggs?" he heard Evelyn suggest.

Taking another quick look into the room, Filip could see the woman from the gallery pondering the idea as the guard was setting up what looked like Fabergé eggs on the viewing table.

"I think that might be best," the woman said, giving a weary smile. "Why don't you and Oscar get started whilst I go and check on the situation? I don't want to upset your Patriarch, who I know consulted with Her Majesty personally with regards to the viewing, so please pass on my sincerest apologies," she said and left the room.

It was time for Filip to move. Quickly.

Backing away from the viewing room, he retreated down the corridor towards the lifeless guard whose corpse was now frothing blood-infused bubbles from his mouth and nose. It was ugly. Filip looked away in disgust, slipping into a room off the corridor and leaving the door slightly ajar to wait.

†

"We need to be quick," Evelyn said as she wrote *Guard leaving post – bad* in her notebook for Will to see.

He nodded, leaning in to take photographs and obscure any view of his mum as she slipped the metal ring that he and Alex had found at the Marble Bridge, around the diamond-encrusted number four on the egg. He watched intently as Evelyn successfully turned the face one rotation to the left and then … nothing. It wouldn't move the other way. A wave of anxiety overcame him. *Had they got it wrong?*

He could see his mum breathe in deeply, calming herself, so he continued taking photos while she concentrated on what they might try next. He ran over the clue again in his head, and as he zoomed in on the clockface, an idea came to him. *Time had to unwind …* Maybe Nicholas meant literally, on the egg itself. If you wound a traditional clock counterclockwise, the time on the clockface went backwards. On the egg, the clock numbers ran in a horizontal band, so maybe …

He quickly reached in as if to reposition the egg for a photo and pushed down on the pink ceramic dome. Carefully, he rotated the top section of the egg. As it began to move, he suppressed a sigh of relief. Evelyn looked up at him with a small smile and took over.

She rotated the dome six times before returning her focus to the number four dial. Alternatively, she turned each until she'd entered all the numbers that made up Anastasia's birthday, and as she finished the final single rotation for 1901, the number four came loose from the bejewelled clock band. Attached to its base was a cream-coloured ribbon, and Will watched as his mum gently pulled. It was the next clue, written in ink in beautiful script along the length of satin. He leaned in to photograph the outstretched ribbon and the words that adorned it just as a muffled scream pierced the air.

The guard, without thinking of his wards, ran from the room, leaving them alone with three of the most precious artefacts of Russian history.

"We have to go now," Evelyn said in a forceful whisper. "Did you get a photo?"

"Just one."

"That's not enough," she said, and Will watched in astonishment as she tugged the ribbon loose from the back of the number four dial. Passing it to him, Evelyn then reset the dial into the clock face just as the curator returned … with a gun to her head.

"Hello, friends," Filip sneered as he roughly manoeuvred the curator into the room. He held her hair with one hand and with his other pressed the weapon forcefully up under her ear.

A grim realisation struck: their escape window had slammed shut. Filip's possession of a weapon confirmed the brutal cost: a guard was likely dead.

"I'm happy to kill this one too if you like?" Filip taunted them as he stood back and kicked hard behind the curator's legs. She lurched forward and fell heavily, her knees taking the full impact of the fall. The sound as she hit the floor told Will that she wouldn't walk again soon. One or both of her kneecaps had definitely shattered upon impact with the hard tiles.

"That won't be necessary, Filip," Evelyn said calmly as the curator remained kneeled on the floor in shock.

Filip responded with a mischievous grin, gently trailing the gun along the curator's neck. "But it would be fun," he replied. "And I have to say, this moment, with you cowering before me, is its own kind of entertainment!"

Will frantically scoped the room for any way out. He knew Filip needed information about Alex's whereabouts, so he wouldn't risk killing both him and his mum. However, reaching the other door before a bullet found them seemed impossible. All that was readily at hand was a pair of jewellery pliers on the viewing table that his mum had been using to examine the egg.

"You didn't come here for fun. You came here for me," Evelyn said, walking slowly towards Filip, in doing so giving Will just enough cover to quickly grab the pliers off the worktable.

"Don't take a step further …"

"Evelyn. My name is Evelyn. You didn't give me the chance to tell you my name the last time we met. You remember? At the time you were too busy ransacking and burning down my house with me inside."

"I know what your name is, Orthodox scum. Stand back to back and hold hands with your son while I take care of this bitch," Filip spat at them.

Will gasped as Filip put a bullet into the back of the curator's skull. It exited almost perfectly centred from the woman's forehead and she fell forward, the bones in her face making a sickening cracking noise as she slammed face first onto the floor tiles.

"You didn't use a silencer, Filip," he said in astonishment and relief. "More guards will be coming."

"Shut your mouth, *Will*. Yeah, I know your name as well, and I've got it covered. While you and your mother were examining pretty things, I took out the guards and the security system. No one is coming to help you. So turn around, put your back to the whore that gave birth to you and hold hands."

Will felt his mum take his hands, giving him the perfect opportunity to press the pliers into her palm. They both knew they'd get only once chance, and his mum was the more highly trained.

"Now. Which one of you is going to take me to the princess?" Filip asked as he positioned himself over the body of the dead curator, his gun aimed, ready to act.

Will felt his mum squeeze his hand. Slowly, he put his hands in the air in a sign of surrender.

"I will," he said.

As Filip glanced at him, it allowed enough of a diversion for his mum to strike.

Evelyn lunged at Filip, driving the pliers into the soft flesh of his neck. The cry that escaped Filip's lips was first from shock, then excruciating pain. He dropped his gun and grabbed at the pliers, which had pierced him just above his collarbone, causing copious amounts of blood to gush over his hands.

"Will!" she shouted as she saw him move to pick up the gun at the same time Filip's foot stamped on top of it possessively. "Leave it. We have to go now." At her order and without hesitation they both ran, leaving Filip struggling to remove the improvised weapon. As they fled down the corridor, it was immediately evident that Filip hadn't exaggerated his story of slaying security. Two bodies lay crumpled on the floor in pools of thick red blood.

As they navigated around the second body, Will heard the crack of a gun and instinctively dropped to the floor.

"How's that feel?" he heard Filip say.

Looking over at his mum, he saw she'd fallen as though she'd taken a bullet. He looked up and saw Filip coming at them from the far end of the hall, one hand still holding his wound. They had seconds at best.

"My ankle, I'll be too slow. Get Alex and finish this!" Evelyn ordered as she ripped off her scarf and began to wrap it tightly around the gunshot wound. Blood quickly seeped through the woollen fabric.

"I'm not leaving you."

As Filip continued to make his way purposefully towards them, Will wedged his arms under Evelyn's, pushed open a side door with his shoulder and dragged her inside. He locked the door, a simple mechanism that could be blown open with a single bullet. Then, he propped a nearby chair against the door handle to secure it as best he could. Quickly he surveyed the whole room. There wasn't a single window.

"There's roof access," Evelyn whispered, grimacing towards the ceiling.

Will should have been elated but was far from it. *He* might be able to get to it, but there was little likelihood he'd be able to get his mum into the access point with her injury. And even if he could, the extra time it would take to help her would mean they'd most likely both get caught – or worse, killed.

"Drag the bookshelf underneath it," Evelyn ordered.

He shook the bookshelf. It was heavy enough to hold his weight. The realisation both thrilled and devastated him. He was going to be leaving alone. There was no other way.

As he maneuvered the bookshelf, the sound of shattering wood and metal reverberated through the room. The door lock had exploded, leaving a twisted wreckage on the floor. The chair trembled violently as Filip struggled to dislodge it, its wooden legs resembling matchsticks on the verge of splintering.

"Out, Will! Now. Once you're up there, read me the clue. You need to find a way out and go finish this," Evelyn breathed heavily. "Don't worry about me. He'll need me to get to Alex. I'll be fine," she said as she tightened the scarf around her ankle.

Will had no choice. He kissed her on the forehead and scrambled to the top of the bookshelf where he crouched and forced open the roof hatch. It was a tight squeeze, but he managed to leverage himself up inside the roof.

"The clue, Will – quickly!" Evelyn exclaimed, looking up at him, as the sound of breaking wood could be heard.

He pulled the ribbon from his pocket, his hands shaking, and read:

Isn't love grand? It can melt even the coldest of hearts, and to some, love is as heavenly as the Ascension of Christ. You too will be paired one day, floored by Cupid's arrow.

Will noticed his mum frown in deep thought before her face brightened with a broad smile. However, before she could explain the reason, Filip burst into the room, kicking the now-broken chair aside.

Evelyn turned to Will again. "The Winter Palace. Go! I'll meet you in Russia. I promise you—"

"No, my friend. We'll see you on the other side." Filip smirked as he raised his arm and fired, missing Will by an inch at best. The exertion of lifting the gun above his head had very obviously hurt him. Furious, Filip lowered his arm and held the gun to Evelyn's forehead instead.

Will froze.

"It seems your son has chosen to desert you. So if you lead me to the Romanov filth, I may just prevent myself from slaughtering him once he comes crawling back. Literally. Good luck finding a way out. Go on. Get crawling," Filip yelled up at Will before returning his attention to Evelyn. "Now, let's start with what alias the girl is going by."

"Try Anna Anderson," his mum spat in Filip's face. "You're as likely to find success under that name as the poor woman did herself."

Filip's face burned red hot, and he hit her hard across the back of her neck with the gun.

"If I didn't need you I'd knock the life right out of you."

With tears in his eyes, Will watched as his mum slowly raised her head and locked her dazed eyes with his. He knew what he had to do.

As Filip once again took an unsuccessful shot at him, he crawled as fast as he could.

Chapter 27

LONDON, UK

"We timed it perfectly! There's Evelyn, waiting beside the car that just pulled up out front. Thank you so much." Alex smiled as she exited her transport and scanned the street for the best place to cross to the gallery. "Evelyn!" she called, waving.

But her efforts went unnoticed, and Alex watched as Evelyn climbed into the back seat. Just as Evelyn disappeared from view, Alex noticed a figure emerging behind her, causing her to stifle a panicked scream. She froze as Filip leaned down and appeared to shove Evelyn roughly across the seat before climbing in beside her.

As the car sped away, Alex broke into a sprint. Horns blared, and a van screeched to a halt just inches from her, but she kept running. *Oh my God, what was happening?* Her heart pounded and her head spun as she reached the spot where the car had been parked. There was a blood trail on the ground. Evelyn, or Filip, or both, were hurt.

Her breath came in laboured bursts and a guttural fear began to engulf her. She looked around frantically, wondering what to do. As she heard sirens, her breathing stopped, but her adrenalin didn't. Desperate to get help, she ran to the gallery entrance. It was locked.

She pounded on the heavy doors multiple times to no avail. No one came. In frustration, she leaned her head and her hands against the door, tears streaming down her face. How could this have happened? Where was Filip taking Evelyn? And where was Will? This was all her fault. *All her fault.* Her head and her heart felt as if they were going to explode.

"Ma'am?"

Alex beat her fists against the doors again.

"Ma'am! I'll need you to please stop doing that."

Alex fell to the ground sobbing. Too emotional to be embarrassed, she removed her scarf and used it to wipe her eyes.

"Okay. It's okay, you're okay. Can you stand up?" she heard the voice ask as the approaching sirens reached a deafening crescendo.

Nodding slowly, she tentatively stood back up and saw that she'd been joined by a police officer. Whilst he was the only one talking to her, there were many more who had arrived on the scene. Something very serious must have happened to warrant the number of first responders that now crawled all over the gallery forecourt.

"Okay, good. I'm going to get you to come with me. Here, take my hand," the officer said as he moved to usher her towards a grassed area opposite the entrance. "Were you inside the gallery just now?"

"No," she said, leaning forward as she walked, willing herself not to vomit. "But friends of mine were, and one of them … one of them came out and the other one …"

"Alright then. You just sit here for a moment. I'll be back in just a min—"

Their attention was diverted at the gallery entrance doors opening. A guard was ushering out a distraught Will. Alex made to run towards them, but the officer swiftly grabbed her by the coat and held her back.

"Ma'am, there are potentially as many as six people injured inside the gallery. I need you to stay right here."

Alex gasped as she watched Will being led away while officers began to rope off the entrance with police tape.

"By injured do you mean dead?" she asked the officer.

"That I'm not at liberty to say. Just please wait here. Don't make me handcuff you," he said and began to walk away. "Oh and by the way, what are your friends' names?" he asked, turning back to her.

Her head went into a frenzied spin. *Which aliases had they used?*

The stress caused her to vomit all over the grass.

"One's over there," she said quietly and pointed to Will, who was now standing at the rear of a police van.

The officer gave her a nod. "Don't go anywhere."

Where would she go? Alex thought as she wiped her mouth, watching the officer join his colleagues who were speaking with Will. She didn't want to go anywhere. The person she most wanted to be with was right here.

She pulled out a tissue from her bag and did the best she could to clean herself up. Will was speaking intently with the officers. He looked calm, which could be a good or bad thing. The officer who'd helped her interrupted the conversation, causing Will to look over and give her a nod, coupled with a sad smile. He then turned his attention back to the group.

What was he saying? What was he thinking? Alex thought, frantic with worry. *Would he blame her for whatever had happened?*

Breathing in deeply, she willed her thoughts to calm and reassured herself that he would not. Neither she nor Will had asked for this to be their lives. No one could choose their family.

†

Will was hurting. Badly.

What had happened at The Queen's Gallery had shaken them both to the core, but for Will it seemed to have broken something inside him. Since they'd arrived at the hotel, he'd been sombre and detached. He'd given her the basic facts and had kept everything they'd discussed void of emotion. The intense connection between them that had spawned from the intimate moment they'd shared at the Marble Bridge seemed to have faded away to nothing.

Alex watched him sitting on the hotel couch, scanning his computer for any news of his mother having been seen or found. The authorities were working under the assumption that Will had been responsible for saving the priceless Fabergé artifacts he'd been viewing at the gallery. They also believed that he had no idea what had happened to his colleague or the six dead bodies they'd found scattered along what was thought to have been the perpetrator's exit route.

Will had been asked to make himself readily accessible for any additional questioning, which meant not leaving the United Kingdom, so they were each simply going to swap to their one remaining alias and fly to Russia the following day. With any luck, the UK police would never find the photographer Oscar Harlowe again.

At a loss for what to do or say if he wouldn't open up to her, Alex lay back on the bed and willed herself to sleep. She wanted to be at her best the next morning when they would follow the Colonnade Egg's clue back to Russia.

After a few minutes she opened her eyes, exasperated. Sleep was not forthcoming. Their emotional day had left her mind in overdrive. She took in some deep, slow breaths, and just as she let her eyes close again, Will spoke. They'd been sitting quietly for so long it made her jump.

"I'm not sure if I could forgive myself if they kill her."

He was ready to talk. Finally. Alex sat up and propped herself against the pillows.

"Filip needs her," she said. "He needs her to get to me. I can't guarantee that he'll be nice about it, but he won't kill her. You must believe that."

"I shouldn't have left … I should have fought him somehow. I just …"

She waited.

"… left her."

As the words came tumbling out, so finally did tears. Moving to sit on the couch next to him, Alex placed her hand gently on his thigh.

"Your mother trusts you – as do I, Will. This is what she needed you to do, so you need to trust in her guidance. If you'd both stayed and you hadn't been able to fight off Filip, then one of you would be dead right now. No question."

Will closed his eyes and nodded slowly, breathing in deeply as he did and placing his hand on top of hers. Slowly their fingers entwined, and they sat silently.

"You need to believe that everything is happening for a very real reason," Alex said, breaking their considered silence.

He turned to look at her and gave her a small, sad smile.

"I know you've lost members of your family to these people, and I can't begin to understand what that feels like," she said, "but I can be here for you, and you can be here for me. That way, we'll be in the best position to do whatever is necessary for your mother, or on her behalf. I believe this and please, Will, I ask you to believe it too. You asked me to have faith in you when we met, and now I ask you to have faith in fate."

"Alex—"

She didn't let him finish. They were both emotionally fragile and longing for loved ones. They needed a release, and she needed him. Wanted him. She cupped his face in her hands, and as their lips brushed together, she realised it didn't matter what her past entailed or what her future held as long as she was with Will.

She pulled away before their kiss could develop and looked at him tentatively. "I'm sorry. That wasn't exactly what I meant by being here for you—"

This time it was Will who didn't let her finish.

Her whole body seemed to melt into his as Will's lips gently pressed against hers, and his touch exuded a passion that left her longing for the feel of his skin. His whole being seemed to be open to her as their tongues found each other amidst the emotion. The tip of his tantalisingly circled hers and her heart pounded with longing.

Will pulled away and kissed her neck before cupping her face gently in his hands and resting his forehead against hers. She wanted him to touch her, run his hands across her skin and stroke her body that was burning hungrily for him, but instead they sat that way for a long time, neither sure how to proceed.

"My destiny is not to love you, Alex. It's to save you," Will said eventually as he sat up straight and dropped his hands from her face.

She nodded. "For now, yes." She didn't want to rush him. "But promise me … promise me we'll talk about this when we get to the end of the path."

They sat quietly for a moment longer before she reached out and took both his hand in hers.

"I want you to do something … well, think about something really important to me."

Will smiled. "Of course. Anything."

"Promise me that you'll consider that perhaps part of saving me *is* to love me."

He ran his hand down one side of her face, and her skin tingled with his touch.

"I will, Alex. I promise."

Chapter 28

ST PETERSBURG, RUSSIA

Much like her first visit, they had arrived in Russia shrouded in darkness. Yet now, after a restless and brief night's sleep, she could marvel at the stunning sights of Saint Petersburg, brought to life by the morning light. Alex had seen photos, but nothing could have prepared her for the extravagance of where the Colonnade Egg clue had led them.

"It's … spectacular," she whispered as they approached the Winter Palace. The grandeur of the ornate façade, with its intricate carvings and majestic columns, left her in awe. Shimmering snowflakes floated in the air, adding a magical touch to the already breathtaking view. As her eyes wandered over the vast expanse of the palace, she felt both humbled and inspired by the history and beauty before her.

Will squeezed her hand as they made their way across Palace Square towards the entrance. "It is. But while it exudes opulent beauty, much of its history is undeniably ugly and brought with it a lot of pain."

Alex turned to look at him. Will's voice had softened at the end of the sentence when he mentioned pain. She knew his mother was never far from his thoughts. He was intent on them finding the next clue as quickly as possible so they could commit some time to understanding what might have befallen Evelyn. It was almost two days since the incident at The Queen's Gallery and the 'no news is good news' mantra they'd both decided to adopt was wearing thin.

"I suppose Nicholas and Alexandra's marriage in the Grand Church was more pleasure than pain," she said, returning his hand squeeze.

"Debatable. Like most weddings," he replied with a small smile. "The Dowager Empress wasn't a fan of the Tsar's choice of Tsarina. However, Maria did love this palace, as did Nicholas and Alexandra. It was the official residence of the House of Romanov from the early eighteenth century, and the last Tsar and his family resided here until it was stormed by the Bolsheviks in 1917—"

"A moment that represented the beginning of the October Revolution and the downfall of imperialism," she finished for him.

"Yeah," he said solemnly.

"Yeah," Alex repeated before falling quiet.

It was still so hard to believe that such a monumental event in history had happened to those whom she was starting to accept were her family. The more she learned and the more that was presented to her, the deeper the level of sorrow that overcame her. But so too did her resolve to see where the path would deliver them and if it would provide her with the evidence she would need to unequivocally believe.

"Thanks for taking care of the research last night," Will said, turning to face her as they joined the end of a small queue waiting to enter the palace. It was one of many buildings that made up the Hermitage Museum and it was magnificent. The palace's architecture was an overt expression of Russian imperialism's authoritarian power.

"It wasn't so much research as me fawning over the museum," she enthused. "Its artwork and collections are rivalled only by the Louvre in Paris and possibly the Prado in Madrid."

"I really wish we had the time to enjoy it, but—"

"Today we focus on the task at hand. The Grand Church," she asserted.

Will nodded as they inched closer to the front of the queue. They'd timed their visit with opening, hoping to miss the majority of the crowds. Whilst the church now serving as a public gallery made access relatively easy, it also meant there may not be a lot of privacy.

"Isn't love grand? It can melt even the coldest of hearts, and to some, love is as heavenly as the Ascension of Christ. You too will be paired one day, floored by Cupid's arrow," Alex recited quietly.

Will squeezed her hand again. "Mum might have known that the Ascension of Christ reference was directing us to the Winter Palace, where a fresco by the same name is painted, but your research will guide us inside, Alex."

She sighed. "I really hope so."

If her research was on point, they would need to visit the Grand Church at the palace, where Nicholas declared his love to Alexandra on their wedding day. In the church, they would search for a clover engraving and a hidden lock at the base of a pair of colonnades. A golden cherub, one of many adorning the walls and ceiling, would gesture toward the correct pair.

†

"There!" she exclaimed in an excited but hushed tone.

Will looked up to where Alex was pointing, high above the decorative arch that joined two groupings of four colonnades on each side of the church. The arch helped to subdivide the once consecrated space into distinct areas, in keeping with Orthodox tradition.

"Do you see it?" she said.

"I see a lot of gold and a whole lot of cherubs, but none that look like Cupid with an arrow." Will shook his head in frustration, yet couldn't help but admire the magnificent domed roof visible beyond the archway.

Alex leaned in close to him so the direction of her arm and pointed finger aligned with his gaze. Her closeness made his skin prickle with longing and anguish. *Could he ever openly love her?* It was certainly a conflict of interest at present and might still prove to be down the track, regardless of her request for him to consider it.

"Will," Alex said, nudging him with an urgency that refocused his attention. "Look at those three cherubs right in the centre of the arch. See the golden shards behind them that look kind of like … rays of God's light, for lack of a better description? The cherub on the right has a shard behind him that has a pointed end. It's an arrow. Pointing down at the floor."

"To the left," he murmured, now seeing what she was referring to.

"To the left," she said with a broad grin. "Cupid's arrow pointing to one of the three possible pairings of those four colonnades."

Will watched Alex move towards the colonnades and release her grip on her bag. It provided a good excuse for why she might be on the floor. As she examined the bases of the ornate columns and picked up her belongings, he could make out voices approaching. Until now they'd had the church to themselves, but it seemed they would soon have company.

"I can't find anything," she said as she continued to run her hands over the base of each of the group of colonnades. "Why couldn't he have been clearer about which pair it is?" She grimaced. "Left, middle or right?"

He quickly joined her and examined the floor, which was adorned with an intricately decorated octagonal pattern.

"I don't think … I don't think it's the base of a colonnade he was referring to," Will said as he noticed something unusual about a portion of the floor.

"Really?"

"Look here at these two octagons in front of the group of colonnades, more specifically in front of the pair to the left," he said. "The edging around the circular centre decoration of each has a fine black marking like a shadow. I don't see that on any of the others. I think these are the 'pair' that Nicholas wanted us to find."

"But what do we do?" Alex asked. "Apart from the faint shadow markings, I don't see anything to help us."

As the voices he'd heard got louder, Will bent down and pretended to tie his shoelace. Before standing again, he quickly ran his hands along the floor where the pair of octagons met. He couldn't feel anything of note so applied pressure, pushing down hard. Still nothing.

Frustrated, they both stood up and Alex stomped her foot in frustration. It gave him an idea.

"Do that again," Will urged.

"Stamp my foot?" she asked incredulously.

"No, just place your foot on the circle in the centre of the octagon and apply some pressure. I'm going to do the same on this one."

"Nothing … or it may have moved just slightly?" Alex frowned. "Probably wishful thinking."

"Okay. You push down first, then I'll do this one," he suggested.

As she did as he asked, he felt hope for the first time in days. Where he was applying pressure began to loosen and depress into the floor.

"I wasn't imagining it. He took a leaf from Fabergé's book!" Alex exclaimed with a look of pure joy on her face. "Well done, Will!"

Bending down, he examined the indentation in the floor. The centre circle had lowered significantly, and in the now-visible cavity was what they'd hoped to find: a clover engraving with a keyhole. Quickly he retrieved the clover key and opened the lock. Inside was a small parcel wrapped in silk that he passed to Alex.

"How do we close it again?" she asked him before quickly standing at the sound of other people entering the church.

He followed suit. "All I can think of is to push on it again and hope it releases and resets," he said before using the ball of his foot to further depress the circular patterned centre.

"Well, haven't you overachieved today," Alex grinned as the indentation raised and the floor once again looked pristine. "Come. Let's go and see what we need to do next."

Will ushered Alex out of the church, past other tourists eagerly engrossed in audio tours and back to Palace Square where they stopped to take stock by Alexander Column.

"Okay. Here we go," Alex said as she reached into her coat pocket, retrieved the bundle of silk and handed it to him.

Carefully he unwrapped the contents and, as on each previous occasion, they found themselves in the possession of a small box full of shredded cotton, a small card and a metal ring.

Your role in life will not be a cameo performance. It will be great. Do not blush. It is your destiny, as it was hers, albeit not by bloodless force.

He frowned at the sombre satisfaction he was feeling.

"Why are you frowning? Does it refer to one of the missing eggs?" Alex asked him with a look of fear on her face.

"No. Not at all. I'm supremely confident the clue refers to the Catherine the Great Egg that is also sometimes referred to as the Pink Cameo Egg. It's just, well, this will be the fourth egg in the puzzle, and being Nicholas referred to four symbols of life then it's likely the last."

Alex nodded. "Yes, it may very well be."

Will felt quite a rush of emotion. If this was the final egg in the puzzle, it was actually very poignant. Catherine was one of the most famous rulers of all Russia and, more relevant to the clue, she'd also been the last female to rule.

After her reign, her son ascended to the throne and altered Russian law to require that only a direct male descendant could become Tsar. If there was no male descendant or if the male was unable to take the throne for any reason, then the next closest senior male relative was granted the honour of rulership. If Alex was the one to reinstate the throne then she would once again bring a woman to power.

Grabbing Alex's hand, he started to lead them back towards their hotel. "We should be able to fly tonight before curfew," he told her.

"Where to?" she asked as they picked up their pace.

"Somewhere much closer to home. Washington DC."

Chapter 29

WASHINGTON DC, USA

Will pulled into the car park of the twenty-five-acre Hillwood Estate Museum and Gardens and turned off the ignition. If only he could as easily turn off his distressed thoughts.

He wished more than anything that his mum could be here with them. Hillwood held one of the most comprehensive collections of eighteenth- and nineteenth-century Russian imperial art outside of Russia, including the diamond crown Alexandra wore at her marriage to Nicholas.

The last three days had been torturous, not knowing what fate had befallen his mother. Alex had been a great support, but that wasn't how it was meant to be. He was meant to be protecting and supporting her. Not only was he worried about his mum's welfare but he was also deeply concerned about whether he could carry this mission through to its end without her wisdom, knowledge and experience.

Unbuckling his seatbelt, he turned to face Alex, who, like him, had remained silent during the drive. "This is the first clue that we haven't had my mum's help," he sighed. "Shall we go in and do her proud?"

Alex nodded sadly, and Will noticed she was close to tears. Taken aback that he'd been so wrapped up in his own melancholy to notice her mood, he reached out and put his hand on her thigh.

"Are you okay?"

"I wish my great-grandmother could be here," she said quietly. "Even if not to walk the Path of Diamonds, at least to see it fulfilled. Her father created it and went to so much effort … for her… not for me."

"Yes, but the prophecy and reality are aligning, all leading to you, Alex."

"I just hope I make them all proud."

"You will. Mum and I have never doubted it," he reassured her. "Why don't we go in now? Let's make her and your great-grandmother proud."

"Alright." She sighed wearily. "Before we do, are you absolutely certain that, *It is your destiny, as it was hers, albeit not by bloodless force,* refers to the date that Catherine took the throne?"

"I can't think of anything else," he said. "Catherine was married to Tsar Peter III when a plot was contrived to overthrow him because he'd made serious enemies within the government, military and church. Those involved in the plot wanted to name Catherine as a temporary ruler until the Tsarevich, then only seven, was old enough to rule. However, Catherine didn't want a caretaker position; she wanted to reign supreme. As such, she had her lover help her to rally the troops of St Petersburg to support her and declared herself the sole ruler of Russia. As self-proclaimed Catherine II, she then had her husband, the Tsar, arrested and demanded he give up his throne. Shortly after his arrest and abdication he died, but there was never any evidence found to suggest Catherine had him killed. So, 'bloodless force'."

"It does seem to make sense," she agreed. "I'm sorry to have asked, but as you said, this is the first clue where we haven't had your mum's help, and I just want to make sure we've both thought it through thoroughly."

"I get that," he said, giving her leg a gentle pat. "And don't forget it could be one of two dates from 1762: either the date when Catherine had her husband arrested and forced him to sign his abdication, or the date of her coronation."

"I won't forget," Alex said before adding, "actually I might, so step in if I do."

"I've got you covered. Let's go."

The curator was waiting for them when they arrived at reception and ushered them straight into a viewing room.

"Thank you both for your kind donation. The museum was very happy to accept it, and we're thrilled to provide you with this viewing so that our exquisite eggs will feature in your book for the four hundredth anniversary."

At least someone was happy with the donation, Will thought. The Patriarch was going to be seriously infuriated when he found out Will had hacked into the church bank accounts to wire the money needed.

"You're more than welcome," Alex told the curator before focusing her attention on the egg.

"Stunning, isn't it?" the curator asked them.

"It is. It's the first egg I've examined that exudes the very essence of Russian imperialism. I mean, just look at its surface! The heavily embossed gold is almost identical to the walls and décor of the Winter Palace," Alex said, obviously enamoured.

"It was an Easter gift for Tsarina Maria Feodorovna from her son, Tsar Nicholas II, in 1914," the curator explained. "The colours are similar to that of a traditional cameo brooch, which is one of the reasons it got its nickname. The other reason being the primary decoration is made up of eight enamel paintings that present as cameos."

"The Pink Cameo Egg," Will stated as he started to take photos.

"Yes, that's right. And our other egg is equally exquisite. Some say the most beautiful of all. Our Twelve Monograms Egg, or the Alexander III Egg as it's also known, was another gift from

Nicholas to his mother, but presented in 1896, many years before the Pink Cameo was. Unfortunately, the surprises from both eggs are long lost."

"That's such a tragedy," Alex said, shaking her head.

"That it is," the curator nodded. "Well, if there are no other questions, I'll leave you to conduct your viewing. Thanks once again for your very kind donation," she said and left them alone.

"Well, security is a little less full-on here compared to in Europe," Alex whispered to Will.

"I transferred *a lot* of money," he whispered back.

She smiled and immediately got to work. Will watched her place the metal ring from the Winter Palace over a small cameo near the base of the egg. When she was unable to move it, she tried again with the cameo on the opposite side. This time it shifted, and she worked quickly to enter the two possible dates that the Tsar could have referenced for when Catherine the Great rose to power.

"It's the coronation date, not the coup," Alex whispered after first trying the earlier date unsuccessfully.

As she turned the cameo in the combination reflecting the date Catherine was crowned, Will watched with delight as Alex carefully lifted the beautiful cameo from the egg's surface.

"Please pass me the pencil so I can make some notes," she asked, never taking her eyes off the inscription that had been revealed on the underside of the cameo. As Alex carefully wrote down the text, he snapped a few pictures and magnified them on the camera's digital display. This allowed him to clearly read the Tsar's words.

Walk along the Holy Ditch, the fourth and last dower on your path. Like the transfiguration of the Lord, such will be yours. Seek the one who bears your name and she will provide you with such that your life will never be the same again. N

N for Nicholas. This was the final clue.

Will couldn't help but smile. The sense of closure was palpable. They were quite possibly only one step away from completing the path, and when they did, Alex and the Auxiliary would be the ones responsible for enlightening his mother country. God would be reborn in the people's eyes regardless of their chosen faith, and Russia would be reborn in the light of the Lord. His dad and aunt would be considered angels of the resurrection of Russian Orthodoxy. It would be a fitting tribute to his loved ones, who had given their lives for the cause. His smile disappeared as he wondered if his mother had also given hers.

Pushing the disturbing thought from his mind, he watched Alex complete her notes and then reset the cameo back into its setting. She then spent some time looking over the other egg before nodding to him and also signalling for the curator.

"We just need to take a couple more photographs with me out of frame and then we'll be on our way."

"Of course. Let me help you get set up on this other table here. The dark background is the best for showing the eggs in the most flattering manner," the curator explained.

Will waited for the eggs to be positioned then took a number of superfluous images of both eggs. After then exchanging further pleasantries with the curator, they returned to their car.

As Alex buckled her belt, Will reached over and touched her hand.

"Thank you."

"For what?" she asked.

"For keeping me sane while we wait to hear anything about Mum."

"You don't have to thank me, Will."

"I do. I couldn't have gotten through the last few days without you."

"Nor me without you."

Will smiled at her kind words and they sat quietly.

"I'm just glad that after how much you've done for me, I've been of some help to you," Alex eventually said, taking his hand in hers.

"And I have an idea about what else might help," she added. "All this mutual admiration is making me hungry. How about we order a late breakfast to the hotel room and eat while we decipher the new clue?"

"As enticing as that sounds, we'll need to use plane service instead of room service."

"What?" she asked, genuinely surprised.

"We're flying back to Russia."

"You already know what the clue means?"

"The clue refers to a location that is named for the saint who gave the most detailed prophecy to Nicholas regarding the downfall of the Russian Empire. The man who seventy years after his death spoke to our last Tsar from the grave and forewarned him of his deadly fate."

He watched her eyes widen in astonishment as she realised who he was talking about.

"St Seraphim?"

"Of Sarov. Correct."

Chapter 30

MOSCOW, RUSSIA

The air was damp as Evelyn felt her way along the cold, uneven wall. Her eyes were blindfolded, but her other senses were on full alert. As she cautiously moved forward, she concentrated on regulating her breathing to prevent the claustrophobic feelings from over-whelming her.

The wall's rough surface felt like stone, but she didn't have time to stop and ponder the fact as Viktor and Filip made their way behind her, guiding her more carefully than she may have expected down slippery stairs. They'd been making a downward journey for about five or so minutes since the first step, and she calculated that they must have descended some two to three floors via the damp spiralling path. Finally, they stopped.

"Wait here," Viktor ordered, his voice echoing in a way that indicated they were in some kind of cavernous room.

Gradually the amount of light penetrating the blindfold began to increase, and her sense of smell told her that something had been lit. *Candles or … or a fire?* She'd been rendered sightless since Filip had bundled her from the plane into Viktor's car, and now as Filip ripped the cotton covering from her face, her eyes remained unfocused.

Soon they began to adjust, allowing her to see that the room was circular and the roof, if you could call it that, was quite astounding. It appeared to reach up endlessly into darkness.

It was only once her vision fully corrected that she realised where she was. There was no place they could be other than the Khlyst den where Viktor and Filip worshipped.

"We'll wait here until we make contact with the heir and your son," Viktor said to her after ordering Filip to secure the heavy wooden door at the bottom of the stairs.

Evelyn had remained silent since her capture, but now that she found herself back in Russia, and with Viktor once again leading the charge, it was time to engage in conversation with the enemy.

"My son's name is Will, and he's also your nephew," she stated.

"Well! The Romanov angel speaks!" he exclaimed, turning to meet her gaze.

"This dark and damp den is what I may have expected for your kind and your satanic rituals, Viktor."

"If you think me the Devil then you best watch your filthy mouth."

As he berated her, she took the opportunity to sit on a pew that lined the curved wall of the room.

"The state does not deny you the right to worship for no reason, Viktor. Call my words filth if you will but I think them apt."

She was pushing it. Viktor's cheeks burned red. Filip, on the other hand, sniggered at her take-down of his leader.

"Enough, Filip," Viktor snarled before turning back to face her. "I liked it better when you said nothing, woman. If we didn't need you I'd slice your tongue out and offer it to God as an entrée to sacrifice. Once he tastes the sourness of the Orthodox, perhaps then he will assist me, as the R.A. will, in ridding the world of you religious 'first-ranks' once and for all. The time of the Khlysts is here. We will be publicly honoured, and you will eat your words even without a tongue."

She reflected on Viktor's statement. The best time to get someone to reveal information was when their emotions were heightened. Viktor's definitely were.

"So that's why you support the R.A. Just as I thought," she said, using a pitiful tone. "Do you honestly believe that if the R.A. rises to power your faith will be given legitimacy? Viktor, you murder people, sacrifice people, all under the guise of the sin being a pathway to enlightenment. What makes you think that the atheist R.A., the ones responsible for the desecration of so much that the Russian Orthodox believed in and created for its followers, will allow an extreme religious cult to be supported?"

"Do not preach to me about sin, woman. Your priests molest children and I hear enjoy it, so don't think for a minute that anyone considers your faith a glowing role model of enlightenment," he sneered.

Evelyn sighed loudly. "There are sinners everywhere, Viktor. Yes, even in Orthodoxy, but for their sins those people are punished. The sin itself doesn't make them worthy to be one of God's disciples, which is where your religion gets it so very confused. All people – regardless of sex, age or race – are born a child of God, but once they have sinned they are only worthy of the Lord's forgiveness if they truly understand that what they did was wrong and they strive for salvation."

"Don't talk to me like you're my mother. Save that for your son, should he live."

Evelyn laughed and shook her head. "God forbid that I gave birth to someone as disillusioned as you, Viktor. The R.A. will not rise. It's been my personal life mission, as it was my sister's, to protect the direct descendants of the last Tsar, and it's time they are brought to the people. Alex will be the enlightenment that so many people from so many faiths, both in our country and abroad, need in order to return to the light of the Lord. Can you not see that?"

"Many faiths except for ours, you mean?" snarled Filip as he moved to stand beside Viktor.

It was only then, in that moment, looking upon the two men burning with rage, that Evelyn saw the striking resemblance. *Viktor and Filip had to be father and son. How had she not realised it before?* The greatest strength of any secret organisation was drawn from its mystery. It should have dawned on her that the Khlysts would likely pass the responsibility for leadership through family, just as the Auxiliary had done. Family always looks after their own, goes over and above for their own, keeps secrets for their own, which makes the organisation all the stronger.

"Well?" Filip demanded.

"Perhaps, Filip, if your kind could find it in themselves to not disobey the Ten Commandments then yes, even your religion could be considered worthy. We must always respect the individual differences of all God's loyal subjects, but we do so only if they're able to express that individuality within select boundaries," she offered.

Filip scowled and paced the floor angrily as Viktor approached and leaned down close to her face.

"In our religion … in *my* religion, I am God. The power of God is in me, meaning that I, and only I, will say what will happen moving forward."

Evelyn smiled at the irony. "But Viktor, it was you who only a few days ago claimed on behalf of your religion that the reincarnation of God in man was not an isolated event. You preached that God's resurrection is ever-renewing, happening anywhere, anytime. As such, there is no single representative."

He slapped her so hard across her face that her head snapped sideways. Her eyes winced and she slowly turned again to face him, the heat of his hand burning her cheek.

"You don't seem an ignorant man, Viktor," she said softly. "You told me that God can live in us all if spiritually awakened. Am I so unenlightened that I confused your laws as spoken by the almighty Khlyst Christ himself?"

He glared at her. "I am God, and I will tell my people what the way forward will be. They may have God in them at times, but not always as I do. I make the decisions on behalf of the almighty Lord, and you, like my members, will do best to understand that and quickly."

She caught a look of unbridled scorn cross Filip's face.

"You may lead, Viktor, but you are certainly not God, not even in the eyes of your people – or, dare I say, your son by the look on his face."

†

Evelyn's words cut Filip like a knife, and he felt the pain of decades without the love of a father slice into his very soul. He would have ignored her but for the fact Viktor had flinched at her words and immediately turned to look at him. *Viktor was his father? No. No ... No!* He felt something inside him crack. His innermost rage exploded and seemed to engulf every space in the room.

He turned and raised his gun to Viktor's face. "Is what she said true?"

Viktor lowered his head for a moment before looking up slowly. "Yes."

It was as though he had been punched in the chest and couldn't breathe.

"You fucking coward!" he screamed.

"Filip, I—"

Before Viktor managed to say anything else, Filip lowered his aim and put a bullet into his father's thigh. Viktor fell to the floor clasping his leg, blood seeping between his fingers.

"Filip—"

"Don't speak. You've had my entire life to speak to me rather than at me. Now is most certainly not the time. Now it's time for you to hand over the reins to the blessed fruit of your loins."

"Filip."

Turning, Filip saw that Evelyn was approaching them. "Sit back down," he said, pointing the gun at her.

She moved back slowly. "He's going to bleed out," she said as she sat back down.

"Don't you think I thought of that!" he screamed. "I want the pain to be prolonged, to last as long as possible to reflect how he's made me wait all my life for what's my birthright."

"You are the Christ-elect, Filip. Your time will come when it's supposed to," Viktor said quietly.

"I'm not talking about succession. I'm taking about my true identity," he spat as he stamped his foot down on the hand his father was using to hold his wounded thigh.

Viktor let out an anguished cry of pain, which further emboldened Filip. He put a second bullet into Viktor's shoulder, the shock of which stunned Viktor mute.

"Identity is important, Filip, yes. But family is everything. You will regret this," Evelyn said quietly as Viktor writhed on the floor in pain.

Filip laughed and turned to face her. "He killed your sister and you're advocating for me to show pity?"

"That's right," she said, slowly standing again. "If my sister taught me anything it's that others may forgive you for taking the life of a family member, but you'll never forgive yourself, no matter what your reason for doing it."

"Sit down!" he screamed and put a bullet into the wall above her head.

"Alright," she said calmly, never diverting her eyes from his.

The bitch was seemingly unflappable.

"Good," Filip said as she sat. "Stay seated. You're about to behold a very spiritual and poignant moment in the history of Khlysty and of the Lord. The attainment of divine grace and salvation depends not on the church, as your kind maintain, but on seeking the spirit of God within the individual."

Filip stood over Viktor, watching as the blood seeped from his father's body, staining the stone floor. "You look at me defiantly, Viktor, but all I see from here is an old and defeated man. A man of earth. Not a man with God within."

Viktor slowly raised his head off the floor. "I've always looked out for you," he said breathlessly.

"Looking out for someone is not the same as giving love, Viktor."

"I loved you the best way I knew. I let you garner strength from pain and become your own person without the restrictions of being the son of the almighty Christ."

"Only after a man has sinned greatly can he be truly repentant and pleasing to God, Viktor," Filip began to recite. "Nothing can debase such a person more than sin."

"If you kill me, you kill God, Filip. I am His Holiness' human form, his human representative. You cannot take control without the proper rituals—"

"No, Viktor! It is *I* who will not only be God's human representative on earth but also the God of the new world. A world where our kind is not secret. Not recessed. We will command respect and we will be the dominant faith as God intended. I have the R.A. history, I have one of the heir's protectors and soon I'll also have the heir. The sect no longer needs you. I no longer need you."

"Filip …"

"I will now take your soul then drink your blood. God will live inside me and we will be as one. Behold my ultimate sin!" Filip roared as he lifted his foot and slammed it with all his force onto Viktor's throat.

The ferocity of the movement crushed Viktor's windpipe, causing blood to spew from his mouth and run down his face. The self-proclaimed God had been rendered speechless. With a bullet to his heart, Filip rendered his father lifeless.

Filip bent over and ran his finger down the side of Viktor's face before placing it in his mouth to suck it clean. In doing so, he drank the blood of Christ. Turning to face Evelyn, he smiled triumphantly.

"I am now at one with the Lord. The time has come for me to lead my followers into a new age."

Evelyn shook her head slowly and stared at him.

"Don't defy me, woman. It's time for you to lead me to the heir."

"Do you really think that if you offer Alex to the R.A., at a time when all other religions are being annihilated, that they'll be thankful enough to let a self-proclaimed God on earth demand that his radical faction be exempt? They are atheists, Filip. "You have a better chance of gaining public acceptance by trying your utmost to adhere to 'thou shalt not kill nor commit adultery' than by having the R.A. take power!" she exclaimed passionately.

Filip glared at Evelyn as he strode around the room. "Thanks to your sister's life quest, I have in my possession full details of the R.A. history and their plans for a new revolution. That is my trump card," he taunted. "Their sordid history is what will make them agree to let us become the dominant faith. I don't even need to tell them about Alex or her mother, which is something Viktor and I disagreed on. Violently you might say," he said, looking down at Viktor's corpse.

He approached and stood directly in front of her before continuing. "You know, I actually feel a small amount of pity for those poor Chechnyan rebels who keep getting blamed for the recent rise in terrorist crimes against Russia. They're behind some of the attacks, for sure, but the evidence indicates that upward of sixty per cent can be attributed to the R.A. The R.A. has been sowing the seeds of instability, creating a nation of people who need – no, desire – the firm control of the R.A. to restore safety and prosperity, reminiscent of the era under Stalin."

He felt a great satisfaction seeing Evelyn's mouth drop open ever so slightly.

"Clever on their behalf. They've been desecrating their country and countrymen in order to cause panic and rebellion against the state, all with the aim of looking like saviours when they come to power. Terrorist action will drop by over half within months of them taking control of the government, as they'll call off their own 'terrorists'," Filip laughed.

"They're not saviours," Evelyn retorted. "They're cold-blooded killers. Many of your faithful will have been killed, Filip, and the R.A. will kill you as soon as you threaten them. Blackmail won't work."

He smiled. "They won't kill me. You see, I decide what my members will do, and they'll assist me in spreading any word I need. That was the one mistake our great founding leader, Rasputin, and our other Khlyst leaders have always made. It is why we have been subjected to ridicule and latency for so long. They didn't trust enough in their people. They are disciples, and they must carry my word, as I demand. They will carry my words and carry them very publicly. I am only one man, but I am a man whom the entire Khlyst faith will now follow. That is many voices, Evelyn. Many threatening voices. The R.A. will not kill me for fear of my people talking, and it's time for us to be heard."

"So you have your own style of revolution planned, is that what you're saying?"

"If need be, yes. A revolution utilising digital means that didn't exist in times of revolutions past. I can spread my word quickly and effectively. But the R.A. won't say no. It's a minuscule thing for them to let my people be who they are and what they want to be. A small sacrifice that will allow the R.A. to achieve the greatest political coup in the last fifty years."

"Perhaps, Filip. Perhaps. They're ruthless. I trust you know this?"

"No 'perhaps', woman. I'm the Devil, remember? Your words to describe the almighty Khlyst Christ. Part of the R.A. information I have, thanks to your dear sister and her recently deceased husband, are of the details outlining the failed Romanov execution led by Lenin. They will not want that leaked."

"Filip, the R.A. are fostering a renewed cult of Stalin, and Stalin denounced everything to do with Lenin once he took power. Therefore, proof of an historical Lenin failure, already well documented in theory, won't hurt the new regime," she said, shaking her head.

"Oh, but that's where you are wrong," he said, smiling smugly. "It's not that Stalin supported the stories of the Romanov execution being handled seamlessly without issues. No, it's what Stalin's protégés did *after* his death, to ensure his word stayed true, that is the beautifully malicious thing."

She continued to keep eye contact as he paused and smiled.

"The fact that the R.A. found the final Romanov grave containing only one set of male remains and planted female bones to convince the world that Stalin's word should not be questioned is huge! But even bigger than that is the fact that the R.A. kept the grave hidden until the exact moment they wanted it to be found. Which was right now, before the next uprising. The imperial fairytale is dead, and what better time for the people of Russia to look for a new form of leadership? You can now see why your Alex must stay an unknown."

Evelyn was unable to hide her astonishment and subsequent contempt.

"Ah, I see that at least some of that was unknown to you," he scoffed.

"If you're not going to tell the R.A. about Alex then what are your intentions?" she demanded.

"You seriously haven't worked that out yet? It's for the murder of Rasputin that I personally seek to extinguish the life of your cherished Alex and, in due course, also her mother."

"You plan to kill them to take revenge?"

"Oh, I most certainly do, and it will be so ridiculously sweet. They will be used as the sacrifice to his most Holy Spirit at my official anointment as leader. Their blood will mark the new era of our kind, and the blood will not rest on my hands. No, it will forever stain the hands of the last Tsar, for it was he who refused what our leader asked of him to save his child, and it was he who murdered Rasputin. It's time to call your son and set up a time to meet."

Evelyn took the phone he handed her and took a few deep breaths, seemingly contemplating whether to obey him or not.

He raised the gun to her head. "Call him. Now!"

She steadily held his gaze. "Who I am to refuse 'God'?"

Chapter 31

MOSCOW, RUSSIA

Will and Alex sat on the bed in front of a large, ornate window, gazing out at the wintry streets and enjoying panoramic views of the Kremlin, Red Square, and the city skyline. Alex loved how comfortable they'd become in each other's silences. She sensed Will was doing better, but she also knew his emotions were still very much on edge.

"I propose a toast," he said, turning to her and passing a glass of water. "Albeit non-alcoholic. But a toast for having found the final clue, a toast to your first time in Moscow and also … a toast to my mum, who I know will meet us in Russia as she promised, even if she's a … a little late," he sighed.

Alex smiled and raised her glass. "I have faith we'll see her soon. To Evelyn," she said before returning her attention outside, where the sun was rapidly being encroached upon by dark clouds.

Despite the moody sky, the coloured domes of St Basil's Cathedral still dazzled. Its architecture was so eclectic and the complexity of patterns used astonishing. She sighed too. It hurt to think she was experiencing the homeland of her great-grandmother when Charlotte hadn't been able to herself. What history had inflicted on her, whilst absolutely done with positive intent, was truly heartbreaking.

"What are you thinking about?" Will asked.

"I was wondering if either of the two Anastasias, my great-grandmother by nature and Anna Anderson by nurture, would ever have been able to forgive what imperialism enforced upon them."

Will nodded. "I like to believe that both women would have. The Auxiliary Measure was, after all, formed on a premise of love and of protecting one's own. And soon it will revolutionise and bring hope to millions of Russians."

That thought was particularly overwhelming to her.

"Will, from everything you've been able to tell me so far about my family's past and the role I'd be expected to play in the future, should legitimacy be proved, it concerns me greatly that I'm of no particular religious affiliation."

"Are you opposed to being open to the Lord?"

"No, not at all. I've always classed myself as agnostic, but I'm starting to think that … well … those who believe in God might say that my great-grandmother is now reunited with her family, who have watched over her ever since the Romanov massacre, an event she alone survived. And that's a nice thought."

"Yes. She's also likely with those that loved her like their own, Hannah, Kathryn and Michael."

Alex smiled. "It does help me to understand why people would gravitate to such a notion, be it real or simply a mechanism to cope with the premise of death."

"It can also help you cope with the reality of life," Will said quietly.

She breathed in deeply, watching the clouds engulf the last of the stars. The weather was turning, and she stood and closed the curtains, not wanting the oncoming storm to dampen her mood.

"As the son of a priest, did you even get a choice about what it was you'd believe?" she asked, as she sat back down beside him.

"Apart from in extreme circumstances, everyone has choice, Alex. That's something God would never take away, nor would my parents. I've always believed, but if I'm honest, at times I have questioned our church and its decisions throughout history that have led to where it finds itself today."

"What do you mean?"

"Let's just say that communism acted as a catalyst for its most serious decline, but its own inner fissures are what caused Orthodoxy to split and lose its way."

"And you expect a return of a direct descendant of the last Tsar will bring everyone back together? It sounds a mammoth task. And what do you mean when you say that it split?"

"I learned at an early age that Orthodoxy had fallen from dominance in correlation with the downfall of Russian imperialism," Will said. "Our country's enemies had known full well that Russia's greatest unifying factors before the revolution were the people's love of God and their love for their leader, the visible human symbol of the Orthodox Empire, the Tsar. By cutting off the head, they hoped to render the body powerless through fragmentation, thereby making it malleable to their evil intents. The enemy succeeded in not only fragmenting the marriage of church and state but, further still, the church itself."

She nodded, frowning. "Okay, but how?"

"The split was between our supporters in Russia versus those outside Russia. When our Orthodox leaders accepted the new post-imperial government as legitimate, countrymen abroad struggled to understand why they would endorse the communist state. It was a tumultuous time. For the first time in history, the new regime withdrew official state support from the church. It proclaimed freedom of religious expression for everyone, including atheists. This pivotal shift led to a notable decline in the power and influence of the Orthodox Church. I too was horrified when I first heard about it."

"Must you have been an atheist to be a communist?" she asked him.

"No, but the majority of communists were. Their official policy was one of religious toleration, though in practice, organised religion was discouraged, particularly through disregard for religious buildings. New churches were rarely built, and existing structures were often converted for other state-driven purposes. There was nothing in unison between church and state with the creation of the Soviet Union."

"The Orthodox leaders must have had good reason to provide their endorsement though, right?"

"Yes, and it was only after I'd lost my dad and been briefed about the Auxiliary that I was both mature and educated enough to fully understand. What they did was stand by what every religion proposes to believe in. They showed strength of faith. Faith in the belief that good will conquer evil. It was Nicholas himself who proclaimed that it was not just love that would conquer evil but only love. Retaliation would have been in direct disregard of his claim."

Alex smiled and recalled the words Nicholas had scribed in his letter. "As romantic and powerful as the Tsar's words were, do you believe that evil can ever truly be abolished?"

"Well, like the prodigal son, the state did eventually return somewhat to God," Will said. "I can clearly remember the elation back in 1988 when major government-supported celebrations took place in Moscow and other cities to recognise a significant Orthodox milestone. Many churches and monasteries were reopened, and for the first time in the history of the Soviet Union, people could see live transmissions of church services on TV. Then, in 2007, the Russian and exiled branches of the church formally reunited, ending over eight decades of bitter estrangement."

Alex looked at him intently and he reached out and cupped her cheek with his hand. "Change has been happening ever since," he continued. "All going well, it will culminate in the return of Tsar Nicholas II's bloodline."

It was so much to take in, and this being the first time they'd had to stop and relax in almost a week allowed her the chance to comprehend it all. She wasn't completely there yet, but she knew they had to finish the path before anything could come to fruition.

"Alright. Let's not get ahead of ourselves. We need to talk about the last clue. You immediately knew it referred to Russia, and here we are, but we haven't delved into the details yet."

"Of course. Sorry, I should have taken you through it on the plane, but that late breakfast lulled me into a much-needed sleep." He smiled sheepishly. "Why don't you read it again and I'll explain what I think?"

Alex retrieved the clue from her bag and read as she sat back down on the bed.

Walk along the Holy Ditch, the fourth and last dower on your path. Like the transfiguration of the Lord, such will be yours. Seek the one who bears your name and she will provide you with such that your life will never be the same again.

"Given that this will be the end of the path," Alex remarked, looking at Will, "the location named for St Seraphim must hold some special significance."

"It is special, but so too was every place we've been. St George's Chapel at Windsor was where Nicholas spent time as a member of the Order of the Garter, and of course where his aunt, Queen Alexandra, the woman who helped to keep the Auxiliary Children in seclusion, was also a member. The Marble Bridge was at Tsarskoye Selo, the Tsar's favourite family retreat, a place where he could escape the everyday of being the leader of all Russia. And the Winter Palace—"

"Was where he was floored by Cupid's arrow," smiled Alex. "Nicholas had quite a beautiful way with words."

"Yes. The chapel at the Winter Palace was where Nicholas married his Empress Alexandra. He's been taking you on a journey so you can experience places that were important to him and your family."

"So where next and why?" she asked. "You've told me previously that St Seraphim died decades before his words reached the Tsar."

"Correct. Seraphim died before Nicholas was born, but despite that, their lives were quite intricately entwined," Will explained. "You see, Seraphim is one of the most renowned Russian monks and mystics in the Orthodox religion. It was Nicholas who made him a saint, and by glorifying him, the Tsar unknowingly made himself the recipient of Seraphim's prophecy. The saint's words had been scribed not long before his death and were kept unopened until presented to Nicholas by one of Seraphim's disciples at the canonisation ceremony in 1903. The envelope was said to have been addressed *To the Tsar, in whose reign I shall be glorified*."

"Said to have been addressed?"

"Seraphim's words are long lost, Alex, as are the words of Monk Abel, the other prophet my mum told you about."

She thought for a moment before speaking. "So it could have all been different if Nicholas hadn't been the one to suggest Seraphim to sainthood?"

"That would never have happened," Will said, shaking his head. "Nicholas was destined to canonise Seraphim and was always going to be the Holy Martyr. Monk Abel also spoke to Nicholas from beyond the grave via a letter that he wrote and left with the emperor of the time, Tsar Paul I, Catherine the Great's son. Paul sealed the letter with the imperial seal and it was addressed *To be opened by our successor on the one hundredth anniversary of my death*. The letter remained unopened, stored in one of the imperial palaces, and no Tsar dared to open it before the appointed time. Nicholas was on the throne in 1901 when the time finally came for it to be opened. We also know that the Japanese monk Terakuto personally spoke with Nicholas about his future demise, even before either of these events occurred."

"Wow. Okay," Alex said and then paused for a moment to reflect once again on how difficult it must have been to know in advance that your entire family were going to die. "So where exactly are we headed?"

"Diveyevo Monastery."

"I still can't work out how you got that from the clue."

"The simplest way to explain it is that the convent was built where it is because the Mother of God designated it as a sacred place for worship and godliness. One of the cathedrals at the convent is called the Cathedral of Transfiguration."

Like the transfiguration of the Lord, Alex said softly.

Will nodded. "Sometime in the mid to late eighteenth century, the Mother of God appeared in the dreams of a nun named Alexandra and claimed Diveyevo to be her favourite place. She requested Alexandra build a monastery of 'unprecedented kind' on her behalf and which the Mother of God referred to as 'the fourth and last dower on the earth'."

"Ah, I see. And Alexandra? The clue says I'm supposed to seek the one that bears my name. Do you think it's something to do with this nun? A grave or monument maybe?"

Will stood up and gestured for her to follow him to the desk. He opened his laptop, searched for a photo of the monastery, and displayed it in full-screen mode. "That I'm not clear about just yet," he said. "This is the monastery, though."

The image showed multiple gold and silver-domed buildings, all in different pastel colours, spread out beautifully over a huge landscaped area.

"Although it was founded decades before St Seraphim became its spiritual father, it flourished physically and spiritually under his guidance," Will explained.

"What's this just inside the fence line?" she asked, pointing at the image.

"That's the Holy Ditch, which is also explicitly referred to in the clue. It was commissioned by Seraphim himself, as it's said that one day he saw the Mother of God walking around the boundaries of the monastery, which he took to mean that she was giving the faithful her protection. Seraphim believed the path she'd walked would be a blessing for those who followed in her steps. The ditch encircles the entire perimeter of the monastery and is believed to serve as a barrier against the Antichrist. However, it proved ineffective against the Soviet regime, which shut it down in the 1920s. The monastery only reopened in the early nineties after the fall of the Iron Curtain."

Alex shook her head and sighed.

"What's wrong?"

"Oh, Will, I just … it's just all so foreign to me. God, as we discussed, is not someone or something I've ever worshipped, and as for the Antichrist? I mean …"

"You're willing to listen though, Alex, which is a start."

She nodded and cast her eyes downward. "I still have so many questions. This knowledge we bear brings with it an immense responsibility," she said, looking back up and locking eyes with him.

Before he could respond, the sound of his phone ringing stopped them both cold. Will answered the call and put the phone on speaker. Neither of them spoke, waiting.

"Will, don't talk, just listen to me."

It was Evelyn. The look of relief that crossed Will's face was palpable. Alex put her hand on his arm and smiled encouragement.

"Viktor's dead. Filip is now in charge," Evelyn said.

"You'll be pleased to know that I'm taking good care of your mother, but that can change very quickly. This will all be over very soon, so long as you do as I say. Do you understand?"

Filip. Alex flinched at the sound of his voice.

"Yes," said Will.

"Good. We need to make an exchange. Your mother for the heir."

Will took a sharp intake of breath.

"Well?" Filip continued.

"I'm not doing an exchange, Filip. We need another option," Will responded calmly.

"There isn't another option, and that being the case, I'll have to dispose of your mother as she's no longer useful to me."

"No, you will not!" Alex interjected.

"Ah, the princess! How are you, spawn?"

Will put his hand on Alex's shoulder, but the fear she'd felt when Filip first spoke had dissolved. If it was her destiny to lead then she was ready to do so.

"We will meet, and we will meet on my terms," she said coldly. "If you even so much as lay your sour breath on Evelyn before I next see her in person, you son of a bitch, then I will personally ensure that you never see the light of day again. Do you understand, Filip?"

Will's eyes opened wide in astonishment.

"I'm going to openly admit that I just got aroused by the sound of your domineering demands, princess," Filip responded. "Tell me, what are your terms and what is your time frame? You best make it soon or I will kill her."

"Before I give you anything, I want to speak with Evelyn."

There was a moment of silence. Alex hoped she hadn't pushed things too far and looked to Will for a reaction. He remained focused on the phone, not glancing at her. He was angry.

"Alex."

"Evelyn, are you okay? Has he hurt you in any way?"

"Alex. You and Will are *not* to come. You must finish the path without me. If it's my destiny to survive then I will. I was commissioned by your family and his Holy Master to keep you safe. Bringing you to Filip is not safe. I am simply a consequence."

"Give me the phone. What the fuck are you talking about?" they heard Filip saying.

"No, Filip. Leave Evelyn on the line," Alex ordered slowly and calmly. Filip seemed to comply as Evelyn continued speaking.

"Alex. Listen to me. I meant what I said. You and Will must finish the path without me."

Alex shook her head forcefully. "With all due respect, Evelyn, I don't care. I need you to do as I say, and I know you can't refuse. You must obey me. Such is your duty, and your duty comes as a part of your destiny."

"Alex—"

"Evelyn, there is nothing more to discuss. As for the place and time to meet, I'll have Will decide. Now, please, put Filip back on."

"Are you ready now?" Filip asked, his voice edged with frustration.

"Yes, we're ready," said Will, his voice as unemotional as Alex had ever heard it. "We'll meet you at Seraphim-Diveyevo Monastery. Six o'clock tomorrow morning at the entrance to the front of the belltower. Does that give you enough time to get there?"

"Yes."

"Good. Six o'clock at Seraphim-Diveyevo Monastery," Will confirmed.

"Six o'clock. You've made a deal with the Devil, your mother might say," Filip said and ended the call.

Will spun to look at Alex.

"What were you thinking?" he raged. "I would never have promised an exchange. What she said is true. Taking you to Filip is *not* safe!" Shaking his head forcefully, he moved to the window, threw open the curtains and stood angrily, watching the rain drum against the glass.

"We have no other choice," Alex said quietly.

"There is almost always another choice, Alex."

"*Apart from in extreme circumstances.* Your words, Will. Use me as bait to try and save your mum."

He turned from the window and stared at her.

"Will. If you truly believe what's been foretold then I'll be fine. I've followed you all over the world this past week, driven by blind faith, as I've been asked to believe in a prophecy that none of us have seen or found any proof of its accuracy. A prophecy that you and your mother have lived your lives by, evidence or not. So, if you now forbid me to bait Filip, it tells me that you don't really believe in the prophecy. And if that is case, I ask you to take me home immediately."

Will huffed angrily. Just as Evelyn couldn't defy her, she knew he couldn't either. He knew it as well. Alex waited in silence as Will stared outside. She had nothing more to say. After a few minutes, he turned around to face her.

"Do you remember what Nicholas' letter to Victoria said about her – you – being the family's last remaining symbol of life? A fact that would see you reborn? It also stated that you would live to be a great defender of all men."

Alex nodded.

"Your name has the same meaning. Alexandra means 'the defender of men'. Anastasia means 'resurrection'. Your great-grand-mother, the real Anastasia, was the one to survive and give birth to a family that would be resurrected to the throne. And you, Alex, you will be the one to bring our countrymen a newfound existence, to defend them against corruption and the threat of the return of communism."

She stared at him, her mouth slightly agape.

"And guess what else?" he asked as he sat again on the bed. "William means 'protector', and that is damn well what I'm here to do. It's my destiny, just as much as yours is to one day rule. You can't rule if Filip kills you! Alex, I'm not putting you in front of him. No. You will not go near him. I forbid it."

"You forget who you're talking to," Alex said with a sad smile. "Please support this. You can still protect me."

After a brief moment of silent reflection, he wrapped his arms around her and gazed into her eyes. "If anything happens to you, I won't be able to love you the way you deserve. I won't get that chance."

Chapter 32

DIVEYEVO, RUSSIA

Sunrise was still over half an hour away.

Will stole a quick glance at Alex in the passenger seat. She gazed out the window, deep in thought, looking upon the sprinkling of stars trying to pry their way out from behind clusters of fierce storm clouds. He'd brought her to Russia on three occasions and all but once their visits had been masked by night. That was something he desperately wanted to rectify, but not before they completed what the Tsar had set in place for her.

"We're almost there," he told her. When she didn't acknowledge him, he asked, "And you're clear that when we get to the monastery, you'll stay in the car? I'm not risking Filip pulling any kind of trick on us. I'll signal you once I've spoken to him and worked out how to play this to our advantage," he added.

"Yes," she finally said.

"You've been quiet. Is everything okay?"

"Of course. I'm absolutely fine. I was just … it doesn't matter. It's silly," she said.

"What is it? You can tell me."

"I was thinking about my great-grandmother and sending her a silent message, hoping it would be carried to her on the stars. Wishing upon a star, as they say. I wanted her to know that I found her family and that I'll complete what history has in store for me … and that she can now rest in peace. See? Silly."

"That's not silly," he said. "You forget who you're talking to," he teased, echoing her words of the day before. "You wish upon stars. I pray. We're a good pair."

She smiled at him with exasperated amusement.

"It's a lovely sentiment, Alex," he added as he peered through the dusting of ice and snow landing on the windscreen. "Is anything else on your mind?"

"Actually, yes. I've been thinking a lot about the Tsar's letter to his brother, what he said about God bestowing the number four upon him and those that he loved." She turned excitedly in her seat to face him. "It's underpinned everything! Michael was the fourth-born son, Anastasia the fourth-born daughter and I'm the fourth generation of she who was named for resurrection."

"Yes, but we knew all that already."

"I know, but there's more. Nicholas chose a four-leaf clover as his symbol of hope. He also had us find four eggs and travel to four places of significance, the fourth, the Diveyevo Monastery, also being the fourth and last dower on earth."

"Okay, yes, that's right."

"Each egg was also presented to the Imperial Family four years apart. The Clover Egg in 1902, the Swan Egg in 1906, the Colonnade Egg in 1910 and the Catherine the Great Egg in 1914. Those eggs had to have been chosen because of the prophecy. There was no chance of us being led on a path to find a Fabergé egg destroyed in the revolution as the eggs were destined to be kept safe!"

Will nodded, his brow furrowed in concentration.

"Why are you frowning? Did I get something wrong?" Alex asked.

"No, you're absolutely right. I was just thinking about something quite amazing," he said, smiling broadly. "Four years after the last egg or symbol of life that Nicholas sent us to find was the year 1918. The year of the massacre. God did indeed have a plan, Alex."

"Can we definitely rule out coincidence?" she said quietly.

"Alex, coincidences are just God's way of staying anonymous."

The enormity of the puzzle coming together left them in silent wonder.

"He'd be proud of you, Alex," Will said after a few minutes.

When she didn't respond, he turned to look at her. She returned his gaze, her eyes glistening with tears.

"What's wrong?" he said, pulling over to the side of the road so he could give her his full attention. Despite the storm thrashing against the car windows and the tears that threatened to fall, Will sensed a newfound calm had settled over her.

Alex breathed deeply and wiped her eyes before speaking. "The prophecy could really be true, Will. And if so, it means I have a purpose, and that purpose has been paved by a power greater than myself."

He reached out and took her hand.

"I've been listening and following until now and … and now … I'm prepared to learn," she said. "We've been provided some sort of proof, Will! Something tangible to indicate that your faith may not have been misplaced."

He was overwhelmed by a surge of profound emotions. "I know, Alex. I've lived my whole life by the prophecy, as has my family. But I won't lie to you and say that I've never questioned it, questioned the fact that I've never been provided any proof to support my faith, even if the definition of faith is to believe in something without proof."

She squeezed his hand tightly.

"What you've worked out could absolutely be proof, and that is so much more powerful than faith alone. Having you also feel more ready to believe makes all the years of sacrifice worth every single moment."

She nodded and wiped her eyes again. "Coincidence or not, let's finish this."

They travelled in silence for the next few minutes, each marvelling at how all the pieces had come together. Yet, something lingered on his mind, and when he finally realised what it was, it felt like an epiphany.

"Alex?"

"Yeah?"

"Do you remember what's due to occur in 2013?"

She thought for a moment. "The Romanov quadricentenary," she whispered.

"Exactly! In 1913, the Romanovs celebrated three hundred years of Romanov rule, and four years after that celebration, the Romanov dynasty fell into irretrievable collapse with the abdication of the Tsar in 1917," he said, turning to look at her quickly to ensure she was following his logic.

"More evidence of the number four," she said, nodding.

"And, with your blessing, we plan to present you to the Russian people this year. And in four more years it's twenty thirteen, and that year, as you said, will be four hundred years since the Romanovs took power."

She gasped. "I won't just be acknowledged … I won't just be a silent symbol of hope …"

Will nodded, his smile increasing. "You'll rule."

As he spoke, the storm began to calm, and a brilliant star emerged from behind the clouds. Perhaps it was his imagination but it appeared to be shaped just like a diamond.

†

The streets were deserted.

Wind swirled forcefully overhead, thunder rumbled intermittently, and rain had been threatening for some time but was yet to eventuate. For that, Alex felt grateful; she silently thanked her great-grandmother and sought her strength. She felt relatively calm, but that changed the moment the darkness was pierced by approaching car headlights. Filip was on time.

Will turned to her and cupped his hands gently around her face. She placed her hands on top his and leaned forward, their foreheads touching.

"Stay here until I signal for you. If anything goes wrong, just drive," he said before quickly getting out of the car.

There had been no preamble. The time had come, which was why she had no intention of staying in the car.

Alex quietly opened the door and slipped out. Thankfully, the car was parked at an angle that obscured her from view. Crouching, she listened intently but couldn't hear anything. She would have to risk moving to see over the bonnet of the car. Slowly she raised her head.

Evelyn! She was alive but was clearly in distress, limping as she and Filip approached Will. In the dim light, Alex couldn't be certain, but it seemed that Evelyn's face was bruised and swollen.

"Well, I hope the princess isn't far away. If you came by yourself then we're going to have a really big problem," she heard Filip say.

"I want my mother—"

Alex missed the last of what Will said as a bolt of lightning cracked above them, causing her to duck back down behind the car for fear of being seen. Her heart beat rapidly.

"It really is devastatingly simple," she heard Filip say. "You give me the girl and then you can have your mother. Just like in the movies."

She heard Will laugh. "And I'm sure you've seen in those same movies exactly how that works out. I give you the girl and you kill my mother anyway ... and perhaps even me."

It was frustrating not being able to see what was happening, so Alex cautiously looked around the front of the car. She could see Filip smirking as Evelyn stood silently beside him, her eyes alert.

"Maybe I've seen that happen, but what I want more than anything is for you both to live. Live and spend the rest of your lives knowing that after trying so very hard to maintain checks on the R.A. and then running from the Khlysts, that you were the ones responsible for the final desecration of the Orthodox Church."

Alex maneuvered back behind the car, closed her eyes, and took a deep breath. If what Filip said were to actually happen, it would be the ultimate soul-crushing blow for Evelyn and Will, given their lifelong dedication to the Auxiliary. For the enemy to succeed in putting the communistic-intended R.A. in power with the only supported religion one that was so disillusioned it actually thought it was enlightened … *no, no!* That couldn't happen. It was more than she could bear.

"Alex is here," she heard Will say.

She took another peek.

"She's not afraid of you and knows that if you really are one with God, as you suppose, then you won't hurt her. Such is not the way of the Lord. She will come when I give the word, but first you must show me a sign of faith."

"Faith? You have to be kidding. That's probably the one thing we'll never agree on," scoffed Filip.

"Call it what you will then, but what I ask is that you remove your arm from around my mother and point your gun away from her."

Filip slowly removed his arm from around Evelyn, and the gun that had been pushed into her side he pointed directly at Will.

"Done. Now before we go on, please don't underestimate me or the revenge my kind desires for the murder of our most famous leader, for which Alex's family were responsible."

This time Evelyn spoke. "No, Filip. In fact, it was my grandparents who were responsible for the death of Rasputin. You place your blame and direct your anger at the wrong family."

Alex gasped. *What was Evelyn doing?!* That was sure to enrage Filip, one of the last things they needed, as was the rain that had started to fall heavily.

Filip swung around to face Evelyn, keeping his gun aimed at Will. "If that is in any way true, woman, then you shall die. What do you think about that?" he growled, grabbing her and kicking hard behind her knees, forcing her to fall roughly to the ground.

Alex knew she had to intervene. She couldn't wait any longer for Will's signal. Hidden from view yet still some distance away, she needed to get closer to assess the situation. Rising slowly, she began to walk toward them with a sense of urgency.

Filip, noticing her movement, smirked and called out, "Looks like the princess is coming to save you, Will."

"No, Alex!" Will shouted.

"Yes, Will," she replied, moving to stand alongside him.

"Oh, how sweet. She already bosses you around. How fortunate for you that I'll relieve you of that burden," spat Filip, his gun now pointed directly at Alex.

"I said no, Alex!" Will shouted, his tone a blend of distress and anger as he pulled a gun from inside his coat and aimed it at Filip. With his other hand, he restrained Alex, holding her back.

Standing beside Will as the rain and wind increased in ferocity, Alex suddenly recalled his words from the night before. *"Alexandra means 'the defender of men' ... And you, Alex, you will be the one to bring our countrymen a newfound existence, to defend them against corruption and the threat of the return of communism."*

She looked at Filip and Will, guns drawn, and at Evelyn slumped on the ground.

There were four of them. Four.

"Coincidences are just God's way of staying anonymous ..."

As thunder rumbled above, she pushed Will's hand aside. This was no coincidence; this was God's will. It was time to make the ultimate leap of faith. She had never been more certain of anything in her entire life. Filip wouldn't be allowed to hurt her.

She began to step towards Filip with her arms outstretched in a peaceful gesture. "I'm happy to let God dictate our future, Fil—"

Evelyn moved with such speed that it took them all by surprise. She lunged at Filip's legs, throwing him off balance and knocking him to the ground.

"Can you get a shot?" Alex screamed at Will through the now ferocious wind.

"Not a clean one," he yelled back, his gun aimed and ready as he watched Filip and Evelyn struggle to get to their feet.

As Evelyn finally managed to stand, Filip lunged at her, causing her to crash heavily onto her back. He positioned her as a shield, making it impossible for Will to fire without risking hitting her. Without hesitation Filip leaned in close and fired a bullet at point-blank range into Evelyn's shoulder. Then, he stood up, his gun aimed at both Alex and Will.

"I've changed my mind," he spat, directing his anger at Will.

Neither Alex nor Will moved. Filip held all the power in this moment and nothing good would come if either of them intervened. Evelyn was still alive, but blood was seeping underneath her, mixing with the rain on the muddy ground.

"There's a Khlyst saying that only after a man has sinned greatly can he be truly repentant and pleasing to God. Nothing can debase a person more than sin," Filip shouted as he grabbed Evelyn by her coat and dragged her backwards into the monastery grounds.

Over Filip's shoulder, something caught Alex's attention. Sunrise was approaching, and in the pale light, she was sure she saw movement. *Yes, there was someone there* – two nuns had emerged from the church but stopped abruptly at the sight of the altercation. They stood huddled together, silently watching the events unfold

Will stepped forward, cautiously following Filip and his mother. "Filip, I hear what you're saying, and I'm willing to listen. It seems my mother has sinned by doing what she just did to you. If you truly believe your words, then have mercy on her and allow her to repent to God. Let her come to me, and Alex will accompany you. Look, I'm putting my gun down," Will said as he slowly leaned down.

"Oh, it's too late for that, my friend, and you would do best not to patronise me. If your family of protectors really did have anything to do with the death of Rasputin then your mother deserves to rot in Hell. And you? You I'll let live. You'll bear the burden of knowing you were responsible for the desecration of the Orthodox Church and the death of your mother on the grounds of one of your most cherished places of worship."

Filip looked straight into Alex's eyes as he directed his gun at Evelyn. "In the name of Rasputin and the Holy Lord, I offer you one of life's greatest sins."

Instinctively, Alex turned away to avoid the murderous scene, and as she did, all the people who had died as she'd followed the Tsar's path flashed before her eyes. *No. No! She needed to be better. She would not hide from this.* Anger built up inside her, and as she opened her eyes and turned back to Filip, he pulled the trigger.

"No!" she screamed as Will lunged for his gun, but her scream and the gunshot were drowned out by a clap of thunder and a flash of lightning so intense, that it surely must have been right above them.

She covered her head with her arms, but it felt as if her eyes had been scorched by the light. Falling to her knees, her eyes shut tight, she let out an anguished howl. The realisation that they hadn't been able to save Evelyn had broken her.

"Alex," she heard Will say. "Alex! Alex, help me. Quickly!" Will yelled as she hesitantly opened her eyes.

She stood shakily, ran to him, and collapsed to the ground beside him, where he knelt next to both Evelyn and Filip.

"Evelyn!" she gasped, feeling as though her chest was about to explode. Evelyn was still alive! What had been tears of grief transformed into tears of happiness. As she sobbed, looking around frantically and wondering what had actually happened, the nuns she'd seen outside the church hurried to join them. The women assisted in helping everyone to their feet. All except Filip.

He lay motionless.

"I don't understand," Alex whispered.

"Come," said one of the nuns in heavily accented English, holding her hand out to Alex.

"Did Will shoot him?" she asked as the nun ushered her away from Filip's body.

"No, my child. Your friend was not responsible. The aggressor was struck down by other means."

Alex turned to look back. "His gun misfired?"

"No, it was an intervention from a higher power. He was struck by lightning and it was an astonishing sight, if God will permit me that admission. It was as if the Lord himself sent a bolt to disarm the man of his weapon. It's miraculous that he was the only one hit; the gun seemed to act like a magnet for the strike," the sister explained as they followed Will and the other nun, who were both assisting Evelyn. "Now he's in the hands of his Creator, and based on the violence I witnessed him enact, I'd suggest his soul has been whisked away by winged demons to the place from which he came."

Chapter 33

DIVEYEVO, RUSSIA

They sat on the floor with their backs against the wall, Evelyn in the centre with Will and Alex either side of her. Will held one of her hands and Alex the other.

"You were very lucky, Evelyn," said the nun who'd helped her inside and was now dressing her wound. "The gunshot clipped the top of your shoulder. And as for the lightning strike that saved your life, it truly was divine intervention. The Holy Kanavka did as our blessed Seraphim always intended. Its walls reached to the heavens and served as a shield to protect you and all of us on site against the Antichrist."

"Kanavka?" Alex asked.

"You know it as the Holy Ditch," Will smiled.

Evelyn felt her heart swell with pride as she looked to Will. Her son had taken on so very much in her absence and had done so, it appeared, extremely well.

"Well, that should keep your injury clean until we can get you proper medical help. Oh, and here come clothes and blankets! I'll leave you now to change. May His Holiness continue to protect you all."

Evelyn smiled at the nun and blessed her in Russian. "Thanks to you and your fellow sister for speaking in English. I haven't the energy to translate."

The other nun who'd come to their aid rejoined them, her arms laden with bags of clothes and blankets. "I've sent for the abbess who'll be here shortly. In the meantime, should you wish, please remove your wet clothes. I've collected some old garments that hopefully may fit, and you can use these blankets to warm yourselves. Would you also like anything to eat or drink?"

"We're fine. Thank you," Evelyn said at the same time as squeezing both Will and Alex's hands. She smiled at both of them in turn, and they grinned back.

"Evelyn, are you really, okay?" Alex asked once the three of them were left alone.

"I am. I'm not quite as nimble as I once was, but my training served me well," she said as Alex gently helped her remove her wet clothes and wrap her in a warm blanket. "Now stop worrying about me and get out of your own sodden clothes."

Slowly her shivering began to subside as Evelyn realised she was safe. As her body calmed, her mind began to accelerate. Looking around, she ascertained that this wasn't just any building. It was one commissioned by Seraphim himself. She'd never made the pilgrimage to Diveyevo before, but from readings she had no doubt whatsoever that they found themselves in the Church of the Nativity of Christ.

"The Path of Diamonds has led us here, but what did Nicholas want us to do at Diveyevo?" Evelyn asked Will and Alex as they joined her in the church's nave, where she'd made her way to admire the frescos and iconography.

"The last clue said that I must *seek the one who bears my name*," said Alex. "Do you think it's possible that I'm looking for a real person? Or perhaps a statue, or a grave?"

"I believe you seek me."

Evelyn turned to face the person who had spoken. A nun had entered from the narthex, and when she came to stand in front of Alex, she fell to her knees, her head bowed.

"Forgive me, please, for I could not divulge my knowledge in front of another sister, such was that behest upon me," said the nun, raising her head to look into Alex's eyes. As she did, Evelyn recognised her as the same nun who had helped Alex into the church and provided them with clothes and blankets.

"Is your name Alexandra?" Alex asked the nun in a whisper.

The woman nodded while gently placing her hands over her heart. "My parents named me Agafia, but in monasticism, yes, I bear the name Alexandra. I know I'm who you seek, and by the power of God in me, I know you come forth to cleanse our country. You are the chosen one who will awaken us all."

The nun again bowed her head and they all remained silent, each of them breathing in the enormity of the words just spoken. Alex eventually attempted to speak, but when no words came, Evelyn spoke instead.

"Will, can you please help Sister Alexandra to her feet?"

Putting out his hand, Will helped the young woman stand.

"Please, sister, tell us what you've been tasked to bear and by whom."

Agafia began to speak but kept her head bowed. "I protect a prophecy, and I do so with my life, just as every sister before me who was entrusted with this task and bore the same sacred name of God as I do." Agafia paused to look up at each of them, seemingly wanting to ensure their understanding.

Evelyn nodded and encouraged her to continue.

"Some protected it from within the monastery, aided by the Holy Kanavka of the Mother of God. Others protected it as they sat idly on the outside during the seventy horrific years that the convent sat as a silent witness to the ways of the communists."

"A truly terrible time," Evelyn agreed.

"Yes. Those years were the toughest for my fellow sisters to keep faith. The Devil had crossed the boundary built to prevent him entry because the Mother of God, our protector, had walked away hand in hand with her son, deactivating the Holy Kanavka. It was a devastating time of abandonment for the faithful, but every sister who protected the prophecy knew that our people had been deserted in order to find salvation."

Evelyn stepped forward and took the nun's hands in hers. "You carry the words of St Seraphim?"

"I do," she said quietly.

"How did you know we were the ones who would ask for you?" Evelyn asked, her hands trembling, giving away the immense emotion she was feeling.

Agafia bowed her head once more. "Your arrival has been long anticipated. The convent has prepared for this moment since just before Seraphim's death in 1833, and since then, we have been aware of the aggressor. It was prophesied that the chosen one would come hand in hand with protectors, and that the Antichrist, in the form of a man, would confront them."

Evelyn nodded silently as did Alex and Will.

"Please, you must forgive me for not coming immediately to your aid," Agafia begged them. "I know you saw me halt outside the church, but I had no doubt you'd be safe. Seraphim's words told me that upon seeing you, the Mother of God would return to Diveyevo and in a radiance of light she would prevent evil by reinstating the protective barrier of the Holy Kanavka."

"The lightning," whispered Will. "The lightning marked her return."

"And the end," added Evelyn.

"The end of Filip and the end of the path," Alex agreed.

"Yes, but also the end of God's abandonment," Evelyn said smiling. "First the Soviet reign was disbanded, and now, thanks to your homecoming, we have truly been forgiven our sins. There is a belief among many in Orthodoxy that the Antichrist would not be an atheist tyrant like Stalin but a religious figure who would persuade rather than compel people to accept him. Filip persuaded with violence and murder. He turned away from being a child of the Lord in order to segment the faithful. And that, in the eyes of the Lord, is an act of the Devil."

Agafia bent down and picked up a cloth bag she'd been carrying. Inside was a book that she handed to Alex. "This is for you. It was on the aggressor. Perhaps it may provide some additional information about him."

Alex took the book and leafed through several pages before handing it to Evelyn.

"Actually, being it's all in Russian, I think it's more likely for you." As Evelyn read the first page, a tear rolled down her cheek, followed by another as she turned more pages. Laid out in black and white was the history of Irina's infiltration of the R.A. It detailed all the despicable acts they had orchestrated, including information about the call to uprise and the planned assassination of Putin and his president. This evidence was enough to bury the R.A. forever.

"Thank you, Agafia," Evelyn said as she composed herself. "This book belonged to my sister, and although it brought upon her death, it is representative of her life. Like you, she was given a great responsibility to carry important information to those who needed it."

Agafia nodded, remaining silent for a few moments to allow for reflection before speaking again.

"I carry something else destined for this moment," she said as she pulled an object from beneath the neck of her gown. "I carry the Jewel of the Tsar."

†

Agafia had taken them to the lower levels of the church where an intimate underground place of worship was named for the Mother of God. Candles illuminated the small elaborately decorated space

311

that had either escaped Soviet destruction or had been meticulously restored.

Despite all the magnificence surrounding her, and after everything she'd just been privy to, the only thing Alex could focus on was that the roof was supported by four pillars.

"At the fourth dower on earth, my namesake has led me to the end of the path, a safe haven supported by pillars that, in total, number four," she marvelled.

Will smiled at her before turning to Evelyn, who looked somewhat surprised. "We'll explain later," he promised.

"Each of the four pillars represents what St Seraphim stated the prophecy protectors must believe in during the time in which the Lord left us in order to save us," Agafia said. "They represent hope, faith, love and luck."

The four words brought a smile to Alex's face and a warmth to her heart, and she could see from the look that passed between Will and Evelyn that it was the same for them.

"It is only the spiritual Daughters of Seraphim named for God as Alexandra who have been privy to this symbolic naming. It was bestowed upon us so that we knew there was hope for deliverance and so we would maintain faith that communism would not conquer the world and set up the Kingdom of the Antichrist. Most importantly, it was so we maintained our vigil for your arrival. And now you are here, please let us commence."

Once again, Agafia kneeled before Alex, a gesture she wasn't sure she'd get used to any time soon.

"Alexandra. I have prayed for you since I was handed the words of the prophecy and the Jewel of the Tsar. I prayed for heavenly intercession to guide us all on the difficult path we tread here on earth and also the path that you, as the chosen one, have walked to set our kind free. That you are here means that the Path of Diamonds served you well."

They all stood quietly in shocked silence. Agafia also knew of the path.

"It is here in the Church of the Nativity of the Mother of God that the last Tsar intended you, as his representative, to uncover the four relics and in doing so unleash immense joy," Agafia continued.

"Four relics?" asked Will in amazement. He turned to Alex and said, "There's a story amongst Orthodox faithful that Seraphim stated before his death he'd one day reappear at Diveyevo and, after preaching repentance, he'd uncover four relics then lie down in their midst and repose."

"Repose?" Alex asked.

"Pass on from the afterlife," explained Will. "In Seraphim's case, to Heaven."

"For now, he appears through me as his spiritual daughter, however as soon as you unlock the Jewel of the Tsar and use its secret to unlock the four relics, Seraphim will then appear to you in likeness and in word," Agafia explained.

"*My joy, four pillars, four relics,*" recited Evelyn slowly, shaking her head in amazement as both Will and Agafia smiled. "Oh my. The salvation of the believers has truly been orchestrated by many people, on many continents, in many eras, and it culminates here today as the Lord intended."

Will noticed Alex's confused look and took her hand. "There is still so much to teach you, and we will."

"We can start with this," Agafia said, holding up what they now knew to be the Jewel of the Tsar. The exquisite locket and its chain sparkled as though lit from within. "It is made of gold embossed with diamonds, and as with all of Fabergé's work, it is simply breathtaking." Agafia removed the jewel from around her neck and gently placed it in Alex's hand, "It's yours now to keep," she said, stepping back and bowing her head in respect.

Alex looked to both Will and Evelyn before breathing in deeply and looking at the object of beauty lying in her palm. The locket was magnificent. On its front were diamonds creating the Romanov imperial crest, and below the crest was a monogram: 'A'.

'A' for Agafia.

'A' for Alexandra.

'A' for Anastasia.

'A' for Auxiliary.

Alex gently turned over the locket. On its back was an engraving of a clover, with a keyhole at its centre awaiting its key. She showed it to Will, who smiled as he handed her the Clover Egg key from around his neck. The key had served them well at every stage of their journey along the Path of Diamonds, and it was proving its worth once again. With a single turn, the mechanism that had been locked for nearly a century unfastened.

"Open it, Alex," Evelyn encouraged.

"No, I'm not going to," she said, shaking her head vigorously. "There are people who have lived this destiny long before I was aware it was also mine. Agafia, please open your locket. Evelyn, please take whatever it holds inside and do what needs to be done."

Both women bowed their heads and moved to stand in front of her. Alex passed the jewel back to Agafia, who fell to the floor and prayed.

"Holy Martyrs of the Imperial House, pray to God for us!"

As she ended the prayer, Agafia revealed that the inside of the locket was lined with beautiful plush velvet, and sitting safely within the cavity was another key. Evelyn carefully removed it and held it out for Alex and Will to see. Engraved on its stem was 'IV'.

"Thank you for letting us be part of this moment, Alex, but it is only you who should complete the final task. It's not for me to open the four relics. This is the one thing I will ever disobey you on," Evelyn said, smiling as she handed her the precious key.

Alex nodded and took the key. "Agafia, I want you to keep the locket to thank you for everything you have done for me. For us."

"I couldn't!" Agafia said, holding it back out to her, but she was silenced when Alex took the jewel and placed it once again around the nun's neck. Her objections were replaced with a smile so broad it lit up the room. "God bless you" she said, clasping the locket to her chest.

Alex paused, gazing at the key in her hand as she took a deep, calming breath. She'd spent the last week riding a wave of faith, but the events of today had given life to something previously only able to be understood as coincidental. Now, everything in her life seemed to point to a greater power, a formidable force. Someone or something had been guiding her path for a very long time. Identifying who or what that was would be a decision she would make in due time. For now, she must reach the end of the Path of Diamonds.

"Alexandra, please follow me and I'll show you where you must use the key," Agafia said as she moved to stand by one of the columns. "This is the one named for luck," she said before bending down and pointing to the base of the pillar where a small green clover was imbedded.

Alex joined her and ran her fingers over the clover, searching for a keyhole.

"Push," suggested Agafia knowingly.

Alex did as her namesake suggested. She felt the area around the symbol shift, and with a bit more force, a well-hidden door gave way. A small cloud of dust and remnants of concrete spilled onto the floor as Alex pried it fully open. She brushed the debris aside before leaning forward and reaching into the cavity. Inside was a box identical to that which had housed the Clover Egg.

Using the key from the locket to open the box, Alex tentatively looked inside as she folded back the lid. It did indeed house four items, and she carefully removed them one by one.

The first item was an envelope labelled *The prophecies of Monk Abel and St Seraphim* which she handed to Will. "They have now been found," she said, smiling.

Next, Alex removed a small icon of St Seraphim that had a personal engraving on its rear. Being it was in Russian she held it out to Will to translate.

A greater power has spoken, and now it's time for you to forge your own path. What the Lord has asked of me has come of age. I will rest now in peace in his heavenly kingdom. God Bless, Alexandra.

"Oh my," Alex exclaimed, and handed the icon to Evelyn, who made the sign of the cross and wiped away tears, overcome with emotion.

The third item was another envelope labelled *Confession of the Last Tsar: The Auxiliary Measure.* Alex held it in her hands, taking a moment to absorb the significance of the three items. It was overwhelming.

"You have one more relic, Alex," Agafia prompted her.

"Of course," Alex said and carefully removed the last item that had been tucked behind the others. It was wrapped in luxurious folds of silk.

All four of them watched in awe as she carefully peeled back the fabric. What lay beneath was an egg, no doubt a Fabergé egg and the most breathtaking one of all.

Its outer surface was adorned with pink, ivory, and pale blue enamel. Brilliant white rose-cut diamonds segmented the egg vertically from top to bottom, and within each segment, crafted from pink diamonds, were the initials 'CD'. Alex smiled, realising that these initials represented the Roman numerals for four hundred, likely a nod to the upcoming 400th anniversary of the Romanov dynasty. *They could also symbolise 'communist defeat', adding another layer of historical significance,* she mused. Atop the egg rested the imperial crest in rose gold – a proud and glorious sight to behold. This was the Romanov Quadricentenary Egg.

Alex carefully turned the egg in her hands. They had one last secret to uncover.

Unlike the others she'd had the honour of handling, this egg didn't seem to have a hinged opening. Shaking her head, she looked wide-eyed at Will, who came to her aid. "Let us hope this is the last time I have to save you, Alexandra, because then I will finally have some freedom" – he mouthed the last three words silently just for her – *to love you.*

There was much to explain to Evelyn.

He took the egg, examined it carefully, and then smiled broadly as he handed it back. Moving to stand behind Alex, he wrapped his arms around her and gently guided her hand to push down and then turn the imperial crest atop the egg. As she did, the outer surface rotated, revealing four open spaces at even intervals around the egg. Inside was a surprise: a bejewelled and simply magnificent four-leaf clover. Each leaf, crafted from diamonds, bore the words that had come to define their lives: hope, faith, love and luck.

Slowly she turned to face Will, and as their eyes met, his words echoed in her mind: *"You will rule."*

As the thought crept into her mind, every possible scenario fought for supremacy, creating a cacophony not unlike cicadas on the brink of dusk. The endgame was clear, but the path to it remained deeply opaque. She glanced at the one she adored. Blessedly, her immediate future would be shaped by her and Will's choices, and with this realisation, the noise was abruptly silenced.

Epilogue

NEW YORK, USA

OPINION
ANNA ANDERSON:
THE FIRST CASUALTY OF WAR IS THE TRUTH
Madeline Hurst for the *New York Imperial Magazine*,
March 2010

She didn't remember a time when she'd not been sad, and it was because she couldn't remember that she cried. She was glad she was alone so that no one would see the inner turmoil that had just escaped the confines of her mind.

Even a thought of happiness seemed to act as a catalyst for her to be 'sad for being happy'. Sadness and grief resonated through her. It had done so for a very long time. Her level of despair on any particular day was what determined which version of herself she'd exude to the outside world.

Today?

Today she was forlorn.

On her deathbed, she was no closer to having the world recognise her as Anastasia Romanov.

I wrote those words in 1984.

Twenty-six years later, Anna Anderson, the most famous of several women who claimed to be Grand Duchess Anastasia of Russia, is to be posthumously recognised for her role in the preservation of the once-thought-extinct direct imperial Romanov bloodline.

Are we witnessing a fairytale ending or the conclusion of one of the most sordid tales of historical injustice ever lived? A tale with countless victims, spanning many families and generations.

Regardless of one's stance, there is an almost unequivocal agreement that people on both sides of the Anna Anderson debate have been vindicated. For Anna Anderson was, we now know, and through no fault of her own, both an imperial daughter and a fraud.

The fact that Alex Ashmore, the Romanov heir, felt it necessary to publish the entire confession of her great-great-grandfather, Nicholas II of Russia, speaks volumes about her character. Entitled *Confession of the Last Tsar: The Auxiliary Measure*, it has led to this history-clarifying event. Should the Russian Orthodox Church and state come to an agreement that imperialism will be reinstated, Ms Ashmore holds herself in good stead to lead as a fair and empathetic empress.

Much has already been written about the imperial security measure outlined in the confession, whereby a child of the Tsar was taken to live in secrecy in England while a substitute stood in their place. It was as much ingenious as it was horrifically flawed, as stated by Ms Ashmore herself.

What needs to be written now is Anna's truth, juxtaposed with the new facts that have come to light with the deliverance of the Romanov heir. However, I find myself unable to write this truth as the story is still missing facts, none more so than the fate of Anna's biological sister, Franziska Schanzkowska.

Franziska, who had been raised in an impecunious household, disappeared suddenly in February 1920. Her vanishing followed a tumultuous few years marked by tragedy. Among other misfortunes, her fiancé was killed on the Western Front, and she herself was seriously injured in an explosion at the munitions factory where she worked.

Franziska was engulfed by a state of extreme physical and mental anguish. This turmoil led to her being committed to several asylums before she disappeared, coinciding with the time a young woman was pulled from the Landwehr Canal in Berlin after a failed suicide attempt. Following an initial period of silence, this woman began claiming to be Grand Duchess Anastasia Romanov, a claim she maintained for the next sixty years.

DNA evidence appeared to suggest that Franziska was the young woman pulled from the water, but it is now known that it was her younger sister, Anna, the sister she had never known. Did the mentally unstable Franziska disappear of her own accord? Or was her demise orchestrated to discredit Anna by those who did so much to protect the imperial bloodline?

Additionally, what of Anna's birth mother, Marianna? There's been no explanation as to why or how Anna was offered by, or perhaps taken from, her mother. Being there is no record of Anna's birth, does this indicate that the latter is more likely the truth?

While questions such as this remain outstanding, Anna's story cannot be brought to completion. Do the people who protected the real Anastasia and the future generations stemming from her know more? Does Ms Ashmore know more? We may never know the complete truth. What we do know for certain is that historically, royalty, including the Russian Imperial family, informs us only of what they choose, and only when they choose to do so.

When asked if she thought Anna would have forgiven what imperialism enforced upon her and her family, Ms Ashmore said: *"It's my belief that both Anastasias, my great-grandmother by nature and Anna Anderson by nurture, would have sought to understand and support what history held in store for them."* It's a romantic notion that many will be drawn to, though some might argue it exemplifies cognitive dissonance at its finest.

It brings me great pain to think of the woman who trusted me with her final words. Words that were her truth. Words she did not deviate from for sixty years. Words that we now know were *everyone's* truth.

"*I was very humbled by and thankful for the people who believed in me. I welcome death as I will be reunited in the light of the Lord's domain with my beloved family,*" were Anna's last words to me. If that belief were to come to fruition, then God willing, Anna Anderson – the substitute Anastasia – might have found the answers that continue to elude the rest of us. Rest in peace, Anna. Your truth has almost been told.

Acknowledgements

First and foremost, I want to express my heartfelt gratitude to my family and friends. Your unwavering belief in me during my transition from a daydreaming storyteller to a published author has made this journey possible.

I would also like to extend my sincere appreciation to my editing team: Nicola, Lauren, and Simone, along with my mum. Your keen eyes and invaluable guidance transformed this manuscript from a rough draft into a polished story.

A special thank you to Helen for transforming my words into a beautifully formatted book, and to Katy for bringing my ideas to life with a stunning cover design.

Additionally, I want to acknowledge the many authors whose works have inspired me, especially those who draw from historical records. Your creativity and storytelling have fueled my passion, and I am truly grateful for the impact you have had on my writing.

Finally, to anyone holding this book in their hands: I hope it encourages you to delve deeper into history, discover its lessons, and find guidance in the stories of those who came before us.

About the Author

Karli Amber Smith discovered her passion for writing at Young Authors' Conferences. Her fascination with the written word led her to explore diverse storytelling forms, culminating in a decade-long career within the entertainment industry, including roles with Twentieth Century Fox. There, she immersed herself in a vibrant tapestry of narratives that fueled her love for storytelling.

Now part of the Leadership Team at a global software company, she continues to nurture her creative pursuits. A graduate of the University of Melbourne with honors in Psychology, Karli cherishes crafting stories alongside her family, friends, and pets. She is thrilled to introduce her debut novel, *The Auxiliary Child*, inspired by her deep interest in history and the multitude of stories that have shaped our world.